Amende Honorable:

A
JOURNEY
TO
REDEMPTION

A Novel of the Human Tradition

By Robert A. Christopher

DEDICATION & ACKNOWLEDGEMENTS

This book is dedicated in full sincerity and humility
to all of us in the human scene who have sinned, but sought
redemption through God's grace.

"Repent therefore, and turn to God so that your sins may be wiped out."
Acts 3:19

My deep thanks to:

Marty Christopher – my wife of fifty-five years. It is her
unflagging love, support, and encouragement that has helped me
through life, and this book.

Rebecca Salome – Tucson, Arizona, my erudite, stern, but ever
guiding-light editor, consultant, and friend. She worked with me
never to give up until the correct word or phrase was found.
She is the keel of my literary ship.

Patricia Drexel Slone – Cincinnati, Ohio, a true friend who
read the book chapter by chapter, always making meaningful
suggestions and valued encouragement.

Frank Zorniger – Dayton, Ohio, a friend who was a master
sergeant, and a combat veteran of the First, Seventh, and Third
Armies in WWII. He was awarded the Purple Heart, and has
verified from personal experience, the war chapter of this book.

The Rt. Rev. William E. Swing – San Francisco, Bishop of the
Episcopal Diocese of California for his charitable work on behalf
of all humanity. He is an inspirational role model for all of us.

DEDICATION & ACKNOWLEDGEMENTS

Sandra Desjardins – Scottsdale, Arizona, a creative writing professor at Scottsdale Community College. She inspired me to never be afraid to write. "Let your heart and soul flow," she advised.

James Ditzler – Scottsdale, Arizona, a Marine combat veteran in the Korean War, awarded the Purple Heart, who gave me factual military information.

Patricia Gill Ris – Lake Placid, New York, a friend, and someone who encouraged me to write at the beginning, as well as making useful suggestions.

Richard H. George – Palm Desert, California, a lifelong friend, and Korean War veteran, who supplied me with US Army terminology.

Charles "Buz" Biscay – Cincinnati, Ohio, US Army (ret.), cover design and for providing additional military information.

Stewart Scott, Carollyn Hamilton and **Laura Lenzen** – of Scott Communications, Inc., Olympia Fields, Illinois, for design of the body of the book, composition and production assistance.

Tatiana Lavelle – for pencil illustrations of main characters.

Cole Porter – Deceased – composer, for his romantic words in *Begin The Beguine*.

May God Bless each of these fine folks.

Bookstores and libraries offer shelves of books about World War II and the decades that followed. Avid readers may also choose from hundred of titles about Christian lifestyles, values and discovering deeper faith. But *Amende Honorable: A Journey to Redemption* might be one of the few books to combine stories about America's greatest generation and the depth of faith that helped shape their lives.

The characters in this book are on their own personal journeys to redemption, but God is leading them down different paths.

As a reader, you will see how Bob Christopher – author, businessman, Christian humanitarian and friend – expresses his own faith through the depth of his characters.

Whether you're a student of history, a participant in the American Dream, or a fellow seeker, your life will be enriched by having read *Amende Honorable: A Journey to Redemption.*

Stewart Scott, writer, advertising executive

CHAPTER ONE

Women like not only to conquer,
but to be conquered

William Thackeray
1811-1863

THE NEW YORK TIMES

TUESDAY, MARCH 20, 1945

Remagan bridge, Germany.

Strategic bridge taken by Allies. US forces barrel ahead into
Germany. Rear guard actions by retreating German forces inflicting
heavy casualties. Units of the US 7th Armored in thick of fray.
Despite hard fighting, Allies push on. Army Engineers build backup
pontoon bridge. More details, see "Remagan" page A-3.

Stephanie Abercrombee, nee Braxton, pored over the lead article,
which made her catch her breath. Mark, her husband, was a
lieutenant in the 7th Armored. Was he in this action? Was he still
alive? Six weeks had gone by since she last heard from him – two
years since she'd seen him. Where was he?

She knew her vision of him being safe in France was more
wishful thinking than fact. Several friends had talked about how
many soldiers were being recycled back to the front lines in an effort
to conclude the war. She dropped the paper, her heart racing, her
stomach tight.

She paced back and forth between the sofa and the desk, where
she had been working. She muttered, "When will I know where and
how he is?"

1

She picked up the paper from the floor and reread the entire article. Nothing there assured her of Mark's safety. The journalism jargon dealt only with the big picture. She hadn't wanted him to enlist, but she couldn't deter him. Grudgingly, she even admired him. He was a real standup kind of man – quiet, but effective. Her take was that the Allies were winning the battles, but losing a lot of men. Oh, why couldn't this damn war be over!

She folded the front page of the *Times*, placing it on her desk, and sat down to try and finish what she was working on. As the newly elected president of the Darien, Connecticut chapter, she was entering the final item of the agenda for the next Junior League meeting.

Mentally in a fog, her normally keen ability to concentrate absent, and fiddling with the paper, she again put the agenda aside and put her pen back in the cherry stationary caddy. There was Mark's last letter stuffed in the lower tier. She picked it up and, for the tenth time since receiving it, tried to read his precious words sensibly. The holes cut by the censor made understanding it comparable to deciphering Aramaic. It did tell her that he was alive five weeks ago on her birthday, Valentine's Day 1945, and that he was *scheduled* to be moved to France. He had sent birthday wishes and expressions of love. She sensed his deep longing in spite of the terseness of the letter, written for both her and the censor. Mark had never been overly vociferous in communicating his love for her, but she knew that whatever he said was sincere…honesty was his strongest virtue.

She had been following the news about the war daily and knew that the Allies were finally in Germany. Hopefully, Mark was behind the front lines. Maybe he was in one piece. It had been twenty months since he had been shipped to England and fifty months since they were married. Her first anniversary present was his announcement that he was enlisting. It started their most heated fight. There hadn't been many, maybe two or three minor ones as they adjusted to living together, and Stephanie was learning to do without servants. But no matter how hard she tried to see the big picture, and Mark's side, she couldn't reconcile why she had to give him up. Mark's enlistment seemed like his putting everything, maybe even losing his life, above her. Why would he? He could continue working at Braxton, a defense plant, and maybe get a deferment.

When she argued with him about waiting until he was drafted, or maybe exempted, he wouldn't hear of it. After an hour's discussion, which progressed into some loud arguing, Mark repeated his need to serve. He was caught up in the wave of patriotism that was sweeping like a tidal wave through the entire country. The surprise bombing of Pearl Harbor, the subsequent military set-backs in the South Pacific, and the declaration of war against the United States by Hitler and his Axis partners were fusing a nation into a determined force. Mark also carried the trait of humble gratitude imbued in him by his hardworking parents, who said they were blessed to live in America, a nation under God, and that they must always defend it. Mark's father had enlisted in the AEF in 1917, but due to his health was never sent overseas. He had served as a medical orderly at Camp Mills, Ohio.

Unable to move usually-agreeable Mark, Stephanie stomped her foot, beat her fists on his chest, and yelled, "You damn stubborn mule!"

In frustration, she ran out of their apartment and straight back to her parents. Mark sat dumbfounded, wondering if he was doing the right thing. He took a rare drink of scotch and brooded while pacing the floor. He wrestled with his decision; would it cost him his wife...his life?

Now, here she was reading this article about heavy casualties. Was she being paid back by fate for her uncompromising attitude with her patriotic husband?

*　　　　　*　　　　　*

Her thoughts were interrupted by the door chime. She jumped, and her heart skipped when she looked out the window. It was a khaki-colored bike with a Western Union emblem on its fender – a messenger with terrible news? Her pulse felt like it would burst through the side of her neck, its rapid pace a symptom of her anxiety. Telegrams to wives of men overseas were almost always missals of tragedy. She stood just inside the door, frozen. The messenger boy seemed to be moving in slow motion as he checked the russet sack on his side for the correct telegram. The metal pant-clips that kept his pants from being chewed in the chain and sprocket of the bike made him look elfin.

Usually a paragon of self-assurance and calm, Stephanie was actually shaking as her active imagination foresaw what might be on her gram. Twenty months of suppressed worry, lonely nights, and social gatherings with no husband at her side had worn her nerves raw. Was it all to end like this, with a pithy sheet of yellow paper with its pithy, truncated sentences? Stop!

Trauma and anxiety were feelings Stephanie had rarely, if at all, experienced in her twenty-six years. Born into fourth-generation wealth and social position, she never wanted for anything material. Her only worries were the adrenalin-producing twinges before she entered a tennis match, a horse show competition, or any confrontation with her peers.

Suddenly, the agenda or the next meeting of the Darien Junior League – that bastion of proper ladies motivated to do good works, altruistically, socially, and politically, as well as use the league as a forum to express themselves – was not important. The event was two weeks away, but as president, she always prepared well in advance. She had learned quickly that leading forty women, many of whom thought they should have been president, required her to be fully prepared. Before every meeting she researched every item to be reviewed – no "i" was left un-dotted, no "t" left uncrossed. This equipped her to quash snide questions and innuendos made by the half dozen members who were jealous of her. She was the youngest ever elected to the top job, which raised the eyebrows of some of Darien's older gentry.

The day before the election she was stopped by the unofficial leader of the anti-Stephanie group, Mrs. Ashton Burrmiller. "Stephanie, my dear, do you think you are ready for this responsibility? You're so young ...maybe in the future."

"Oh, I am ready. And, my dear Mrs. Burrmiller, with *your* support I know many good things will happen. I *can* count on you, can't I?"

Mrs. Ashton Burrmiller, never at a loss for words, momentarily stood agape. Grasping a shred of control, she muttered, "Ah...ah...yes, I have always supported worthy causes."

Despite the undercurrent of voices – older women who resented her charisma and self-containment, pointing out her age as a detriment – Stephanie won the election by a two-thirds majority. There were enough younger members who admired the way she did not bind herself to the rigid conventions of their upper-class set. She abhorred the phrases, "We always did it this way," or "We've never done it that way." Stephanie didn't deal in personalities, gossip, or petty politics; she always stressed principles. She wouldn't react to catty remarks by those envious of her looks, her brains, or her command of herself.

As president, she drew ideas from the group, moderated the group to a consensus, and helped outline the agreed-to projects. They included drives selling war bond, equipping and serving in USO canteens, volunteering hours at hospitals – now short of nurses and orderlies – and bandage-making bees. She not only helped organize these efforts, but eagerly participated in them. She helped the Junior League establish a pantry and soup kitchen in a low-income neighborhood near southwest Bridgeport. Braxton Industries funded the building because Stephanie convinced Harvey Braxton that some of the profits from government war materials contracts should be put back into the area. She argued that Mark, his son-in-law, was risking his life, while Braxton Industries was enjoying a huge surge in earnings. Her father gave her seventy-five-thousand dollars.

Stephanie was the epitome of *noblesse oblige.* She knew the financial power her family wielded, and she accepted the responsibility that went with it. Her mother had always taught her to think "outside" of herself. When young Stephanie was given an Irish setter, her mother sat with her and the dog and asked Stephanie who the dog's sponsor was. Stephanie knew how to answer that. "I am. He's my dog, isn't he?"

Her mother said, "Yes he is, dear, and I see that God has given both of you beautiful auburn hair...so soft and silky. I'm sure He smiled when He saw what beautiful creatures He had created. That's a lucky dog to have the same colored hair as his mistress."

When they walked the Braxton estate, Lillian Braxton would point out the beauty and wonder of all the plants, flowers, and bushes, helping her daughter to learn the names of them. One day, when Stephanie was twelve, they stopped to rest awhile. It was a sunny day in October. White fleecy clouds dotting the sky passed intermittingly between the sun and the garden, casting temporary shadows over grass, shrubs, and flowers. Lillian suggested they sit in the arbor for a few minutes.

"How's school this term, dear? Any favorite subjects?"

"School's pretty good...nothing bad. I like English lit and social studies. They've divided that into two parts, civics and a new part this year, something called sociology."

"I liked English literature too. What are you reading?"

"We just finished *Far from the Madding Crowd* by Thomas Hardy. Sorta old fashioned, but I got an A on the test about it. I think I'm going to like the one we started just before break, Galsworthy's *Man of Property*."

"Have you read much of it?"

"About a fourth."

"And?"

"All Soames thinks about is property...you know, owning things. Like that's more important than anything else, even his family."

"You've got a good understanding so far of what Galsworthy is satirizing...criticizing. Do you like reading?"

"Yes. It's like I can be in the same place as who I'm reading about. Do you think that's true?"

"Certainly, dear...good literature can teach us about a lot of things...people particularly. I'm sure you've seen people in real life who are like some of the characters that you've read about. And, many writers are good at describing the virtues...and the vices of people...real and fictional. We can learn from them."

"I guess so."

Lillian smiled at her daughter's enthusiasm for learning. Her face shone as she talked, as did the filtered rays of the sun that highlighted her daughter's auburn hair, giving her an almost angelic look. What a joy Stephanie had become. Of course, Lillian also loved her son, little Daniel. What mother wouldn't, after carrying him in her womb, giving birth and nursing him to self-sufficiency? But, Harvey had monopolized "his son." Lillian was twenty-three when she had Stephanie, but despite the age gap, Stephanie had become more than a daughter, almost a sister... a true companion.

As the years passed, polarization had occurred in the family – Daniel and Harvey on one side, Stephanie and Lillian on the other. The lesions of Harvey's penchant about having a son at all costs had never totally healed. Lillian carried the scar of knowing she was not first with Harvey. Now as she reflected on the trauma of her miscarriage, and his callused, faintly disguised disregard for it, she felt detached from the beauty that was around her...her daughter, the blooming asters, and the sunlit and manicured grass carpet stretching as far as she could see.

"Momma, what are you thinking...you're frowning?"

She knew that bad memories and experiences could disjoint one from the world, making one feel outside of it all. But the innocence and trusting dependency of her child could bring her back and give her a coat of joy and meaning to protect her from the cold of trauma...the frozenness of suppressed pain.

"Why...nothing especially, why do you ask?"

"Because, you seemed so far away."

"Don't worry, dear, I'm here with you," she said as she reached out and patted Stephanie on the head then brushed the back of her hand down her smooth cheek. "You're a beautiful girl, Stephanie. And, since you asked me, what's going on in that little head of yours?"

"Why does Daddy always do things with Daniel, like you do with me? You come to my tennis matches. He only came to one."

Lillian always knew that one day Stephanie would question Harvey's male fixation...his partiality to Daniel. Stephanie was bright and very perceptive. Lillian knew children were many times more alert to the emotional vibrations of adults than their age might dictate. Children detected quickly how they were viewed by their elders. Their barometers for measuring sincerity were most accurate and hypersensitive. Her answer to Stephanie had to be one that balanced many values – one that would assure her daughter that she was loved and not made to feel slighted. Lillian put a rein on her deep hurts so that her feelings didn't negatively influence Stephanie.

"I know you must think that your father favors Daniel, but it's only a superficial thing. He loves you. When you were born he told everyone how proud he was of his beautiful daughter. Right now he's caught up in the idea of a successor...someone to be in his business...someone he feels can run things like he does.

"Why? Is Daddy going somewhere?"

"No, he's not going anywhere. It's just that most men think that whatever they do, or whatever they build, should go on forever, even after they die. You know about the tremendous work that went into building the pyramids in Egypt. That's what they were all about – the pharaohs' desires for immortality. Leaving monuments, heirs, or any type of legacy makes them feel that they are still living. It's complicated. They worry about whether their lives amounted to anything, so if they have someone to carry on what they did, it makes them feel that whatever they did during their life was important. But, honey, he loves you. There's nothing he won't give you or do for you if he can."

"Do you think about stuff like that, like do you have *meaning*?"

"In a different way, dear. Bringing you into the world has made my life very worthwhile. You're my legacy…and a very intelligent and pretty one." Lillian smiled as she kissed Stephanie on the cheek.

"Maybe he could come to one of my tennis matches."

"I think he will. Shall we go? The sun's going to set in a few more minutes."

Walking toward the house they passed the horse barn. "Let's stop and see *Cheval*, Momma. I just curried him this morning. You should see how he shines."

"Of course…don't you have a competition next week?"

"At the Hunt Club, next Saturday," Stephanie answered as her mind went back to her last contest and the second-place red ribbon. She hadn't pressed her knees into *Cheval's* side at the right moment before the number six hurdle. He jumped a second late and tipped the top rail. She was determined to earn a blue one this time.

Her father had given her *Cheval*, a fifteen-hand-high, chestnut-colored thoroughbred jumper for her twelfth birthday. She had won both red and blue ribbons – two each in her first four contests. Her mother encouraged her to devote her non-academic efforts to riding and jumping. Lillian knew that the horse was perfect for her daughter. It gave her something male that she could both nurture, yet control – but only after she trained it. What a perfect primer for marriage, Lillian mused. "I wish I had a horse when I was your age, dear."

"Why, Momma?"

"Because, when I see you dressed and mounting *Cheval*, I see beauty, strength, and two of God's beings in harmony," Lillian said wistfully. She pictured Stephanie in her sharply-creased, taupe jodhpurs; chocolate-brown velvet coat, flared at the hips; ecru blouse; brown, knee-high polished riding boots; and all topped off with a billed brown, velvet-covered, reinforced jockey cap.

Stephanie picked up a handful of oats in her flat, up-turned palm and put it under *Cheval's* soft nose. The same nose she had hit several times, in a fit of anger, with her riding crop when he had not done exactly what she commanded. His large, penetrating eyes looked at her as his pink tongue tentatively licked the morsels from her hand. "Good boy. That's Stephies' little man."

That night at dinner, after Maude had served a leg-of-lamb, sweet potatoes, asparagus, and warm Parker-House rolls, Lillian asked, "Harvey, how was your day?"

"What...what was that, Lillian?"

"I said, 'how was your day'?"

"Oh, so, so. Well, not really. I had to lay off another twenty men. It's been two years since the crash...don't think things are one bit better. In fact, think they're worse. It's good that we have the chlorine business for water treatment in a lot of city water systems. Getting Braxton into the manufacture of chlorine in WW I is paying off now. Then it was used to make gas that killed Germans, today it makes drinking water safe. That's irony, all right. No matter how bad it gets, people need water. Still get a few orders from the Army for gas...goes into their weapons stockpile."

"What will those poor twenty men do? They have families, I'm sure."

"I gave them a half-week's pay, told them we'd hire them back soon as possible. That's all I can do now. Hoover's pushing some

10

more of those socialist relief programs. The government's going to be running everything."

"Is that likely to happen soon?"

"Hope not…might take a cut out of what we have. Will ya' look at that! There's a soup kitchen just north of town…never thought we'd see that in Darien."

Daniel and Stephanie, sitting on opposite sides of the twelve-foot-long dining table with Lillian and Harvey at the ends, rarely broke into these "adult" discussions, but now Stephanie blurted, "Laying off those men is what the depression is doing?"

Harvey turned to look at her as if she had just descended from another planet. "Stephie, why does a pretty girl like you worry about things like that now?"

She sat mute, as she always did when her father talked around her, acting as if she was just a little *girl*.

"What do you hear…what do you know about the way things are in the country?"

"In my social studies class at school, we talked about how things are bad and about all of the poor people that are going hungry. And also about all of the poor farmers that are having their farms taken away from them by the banks."

"Yes, the country is going through some hard times, but they can't last forever. Right now business is not good for a lot of companies, and stock prices are low. But, honey, forget it. The Braxtons will be all right. Say, how's *Cheval*?"

"He's fine. I'm riding him in a jump next Saturday. Come see me, please."

"Hmm, supposed to play golf with Earls of Minot Chemical…might be for sale…maybe get it cheap; he's been losing ground with all that's happening. What time is your meet?"

"It starts at two at the Hunt Club."

"We'll see…yes, we'll see. Ah, Maude, strawberry shortcake… bless you."

"Maybe you could see Mr. Earls another time so you can come see me and *Cheval*."

"I said we'll see. Now, how about some shortcake?"

That night, Lillian came into Stephanie's room to kiss her good-night. Stephanie asked, "Momma, remember today when you asked me what I was studying in lit class, and we talked about the man of property? Did you ever read it?"

"I did, in fact, the entire *Forsyte Saga*. Why do you ask?"

"Remember how you said that sometimes we see real people that we know in the book?"

"Yes, I did. Something make you think of that right now?"

"Maybe...I don't know, except when Daddy was talking about Minot Chemical it made me think about it. You know the way Soames Forsyte was...about everything he had...or that he wanted...funny, huh?"

"Yes, dear...funny...well, good night, dear. Sleep well." And when she was in the hall outside of Stephanie's room, she muttered, "Maybe not so funny...from the mouths of babes..."

*   *   *

Now as Stephanie unloaded her concerns to Lillian, her mother didn't really console her...just listened, the same as she had for years to Stephanie's domineering father. She said something about it being a man's world, and that *they* had to do what *they* had to do. Lillian and Stephanie still had a close relationship, except when it came to Lillian's almost endless deferral to Harvey. Two years after Stephanie's younger brother was born, her father's partiality for "his male heir" became the new family dynamic – the one that had brought mother and daughter much closer together.

Even though Stephanie had seen Daniel emerge between her and her father, she became attached to her brother. He was not overly strong; he needed constant medical help for his weak lungs during the first three years of his life. His vulnerability appealed to Stephanie, who soon became almost his governess. She liked the way he followed her and did most of the things she asked him to. He adored her and was dependant on her to tell him what to do in sports, with the pony, then later on with the horses. This relationship was not condoned by Harvey, who repeatedly told Daniel to make his own decisions…like any man would do. Daniel always said obediently, "Yes, Poppa." But, when Harvey was not around, he went back to the comfort and guidance of "his Sissy."

Harvey Braxton had met Lillian when she was the governess for the Ames family of Hartford. Arthur Ames and Harvey had attended Groton Prep together and were roommates at Yale. They were close friends, a relationship that would last throughout their lives. Lillian was the oldest daughter of a Methodist preacher, John Wesley Brothers, and had taken the job with the Ames family as a favor to her father. Ames senior was her father's largest contributor in his New Haven parish. Educated in public schools, Lillian had attended finishing school in New York after high school graduation. Her father figured that a year in Miss Haverford's school for "fashionable ladies" would groom her to be able to "marry up"…maybe into one of the more prominent families in his congregation. The first step of his design worked, when Ames senior asked him to recommend someone to fill a governess position with his family. Pastor John had subtly hinted that it would be a very Christian thing if Ames would consider his daughter.

To escape dorm life on weekends, Harvey and Arthur often took the train to the Ames estate, just north of Hartford. Harvey quickly became attracted to Lillian's clear, rosy face, her upright carriage, and her soft manner. At first, their exchanges were formal and always proper, particularly in front of the family. Harvey learned soon, however, that after the Ames children were bedded down, Lillian would walk the formal gardens and terraces of the estate. He would encounter her and make a remark about the coincidence of their walks meshing: "My, my...can you beat this? We meet again."

Actually, these serendipitous meetings occurred every night. Lillian, affecting a look of mild amazement, noted how fortunate it was that these "coincidences" occurred. They would walk for an hour. Soon they were holding hands and then sitting together in the rose-covered pergola, lit only by the moon. They would talk until Lillian insisted that she must check on the children – her declaration coming just as Harvey's hand glided upward from her knee. Harvey shared with her all that he hoped to accomplish at Braxton Industries, currently being run by his father, Daniel. Lillian was a very perceptive young woman, never aggressive but reflective, and an excellent listener. It didn't take her long to see that Harvey felt inferior to his hard-driving and successful father. His statements about what he would do were words echoed by a man with insecurities, but well-protected with the armor of bravado and the shield of wealth.

Lillian repeatedly expressed respect for his plans and how she understood his need to succeed. Her reception and sharing of his desires endeared her to him. She was the foil he needed as a man, as a would-be industrialist, and as a person who was respected. The more he talked and the more she listened, the more he craved her...the more he needed her, even though this realization was sub-conscious. It was a driving force within him, this wanting more and more, always more: more accomplishments, more salving of the tender quick of his inferiorities, more stroking of his ego, and more prestige with his peers at the Darien Country Club. He began to see Lillian in everything he did, everywhere he went. She was in all of his thoughts, even while he tried to study at Yale.

One night in the pergola, after an hour walking while holding hands, and her gentle removing of his hand from her breast, he kissed her repeatedly, nuzzling his face in the curve of her neck. He blurted out, "I love you, Lillian. I need you, please...uh, please marry me."

Lillian closed her eyes for a full minute, and said, "Yes, I will, Harvey."

When she told her father, he smiled. "Bless you, my child. All things happen in time, always in the Lord's time, I believe."

He married them a week after Harvey graduated from Yale. As he conducted the service, an inner *satisfaction* shone from his face. No pastor should ever be described as smug.

The new couple took up residence in the now unused carriage house of the Braxton estate after extensive renovation and furnishing – Harvey telling Lillian that nothing was too good for his wife and the mother of his sons-to-be. As Harvey became more comfortable in their life, he became more aggressive in business, even arguing with his father about company decisions. The underpinning of Lillian's belief in him had bolstered his self-image. He strode around the Braxton plant giving orders and never agreeing with his father. Perhaps the stress of the combative environment taxed sixty-eight-year-old Daniel. He had a fatal heart attack, and Harvey took over the total direction of Braxton Industries, now filling government contracts for war materials. As head of a defense plant, he was deferred from fighting in World War I. Harvey and Lillian moved into the main house, but not until Daniel's furniture had been replaced.

Three months after the armistice, Stephanie was born. Harvey bragged about his beautiful daughter at the Darien Country Club and to everyone that he could collar. Fathering a child bolstered his self-esteem. He was very kind to Lillian, constantly praising her for bringing such a beautiful girl into their family. One night when they were humming a lullaby to ten-month-old Stephanie, trying to get her to sleep, he put his arm around his wife and said, "Lillian, dear, now that we have a nice girl, wouldn't it be great if we had a son? You know, someone to follow me at Braxton."

"Perhaps someday," she answered meekly, as the involuntary muscles of her stomach contracted in a knot of apprehension.

Harvey was affectionate with Stephanie as a baby, but Lillian sensed his fixation with having a son. Although her husband kept his desire under the surface, Lillian's perceptions made her realize that having a son was foremost in his mind. She felt it meant more to him than Stephanie or herself. It was another major "more" for Harvey to prove he could sire in his own image.

Lillian knew that the son issue would always be with them...a wispy cloud that would swell to a dark one, bringing the rain of long-term unhappiness. She convinced herself, in female emotion and intuitive logic, that she should have a second pregnancy. Whether it was her will, or just the biological facts of life, she became pregnant. Hearing this, Harvey glowed. He was like a man who had found the pot of gold at the end of the rainbow. He told Stephanie that soon she would have a little brother to play with. Lillian miscarried after four months...another girl. Harvey was perfunctorily solicitous. He tried to console her...his disappointment overshadowing any deep and sincere care. He went through the propriety of trying to help her recover mentally, but Lillian knew his real thoughts...his real priorities. Sitting next to her bed, he told her he was sorry about what happened, but that she shouldn't worry; there was always another chance in the future. She quietly sighed as one of the doors of her soul closed.

The doctor equated the miscarriage to stress and suppressed emotional strain. "Poppycock," Harvey said. Harvey knew that the doctor had advised against Lillian becoming pregnant again, but he chose to minimize it. Doctors didn't always know everything... women had been having babies since the beginning of time.

Six months after Lillian's miscarriage, he asked the doctor what were the odds of a successful pregnancy and birth.

The doctor thought, then looked at Harvey and said, "Fifty-fifty at best."

"Hell, that's better odds than I ever had introducing a new product. We'll take it."

"We'll?" The doctor asked. Harvey ignored this.

A year later, Lillian conceived again, but not happily. The psychological scars of her miscarriage had not healed, but she submitted dutifully to Harvey's persistent drive to have a son. Fortunately, she gave birth to Daniel II. After the birth, Harvey showered her with gifts, trips abroad, and praise. Lillian was more relaxed, but held the hurt of knowing her husband valued a son more than her health. She loved little Daniel, but she also saw him as the manifestation of her husband's fixation – one that blinded him to her well being, to almost everything. She knew Harvey wasn't the first man who had tried to hide his mortality by siring reincarnations of himself. Her English history studies had covered the kings of England. It was easy to see Harvey's parallel to Henry VIII. As she was rocking two-month-old Daniel to sleep one night, she cooed, "Daniel, be glad your mother wasn't born Anne Boleyn." But she never said a word about her thoughts to her husband. Her mother, who had passed away when she was fifteen, had said to her more than once, "Lillian, you have a bottomless well for holding your hurts. Honey, for your own good, don't be afraid to share them...with me...your best friend...someone you can trust." Still Lillian had never felt it was her place to burden others with her woes. She drew strength from silence.

*   *   *

After listening to Stephanie air her frustration, Lillian asked her why she didn't believe Mark should enlist. "Don't you think that he feels he must do this for our country...for your ultimate freedom...for the preservation of our country and its values? He's not alone you know, millions of men are signing up. You should be proud of Mark. Better to have a man with conviction and courage than the opposite, dear."

"But, we've only been married for thirteen months...and he might get killed, or even worse, maybe have to spend the rest of his life in a hospital or a wheel chair. What would I do then? I couldn't stand by and see him suffer. That's why I wanted him to stay home…get a deferment."

"Honey, do you know what you're saying? Aren't you leaping too far ahead?"

"Oh, I know, somebody's got to defend us…it's just that I love him, I need him…he's so handsome. I can't bear to think of him all dirty and bloody. Oh, Momma, I feel terrible!"

"Like many wives and mothers during every war that our country has fought, you've got to learn to cope. We women have to fight our enemies too. No, we don't shoot rifles, we bide, we succor, and we make ourselves available. When the men come home from whatever conflict they have been in, we help them lick their wounds and assure them we admire their bravery. And, we *never* show our fears. How did you leave Mark when you came here?"

"Not good. I yelled at him for the first time since we've been married. Oh, Momma, what should I do?"

"Do you remember when you were seven and fell off your pony and cut your arms on the gravel?"

"Yes, I got blood on my nice jodhpurs. It made them look so messy."

"And what did you do then?"

"I got back on so I could get some clean pants."

"Falling off that pony is like this fight you and Mark have had. Are you going to sit on the ground all bloody, or are you…?"

"Get right back on, Momma. Thanks."

She knew she had to go back to him. The thought of his going into combat, with a gulf between them, would be a burden she knew she couldn't carry. She returned to their apartment and apologized.

"Mark, I was wrong. I know you are a very responsible and brave man. I just wish we didn't have to be apart. It'll be hell for me worrying about you every minute of every day."

Mark pulled her into his arms. "I'm sorry too…for a lot. I'll miss you every minute too. But I'd never be able to look in the mirror if I didn't do what all the other guys are doing. This is going to sound ridiculous, but I promise you I'll be as careful as I can. I want to come home to you, Stephanie...build a life with you... only you."

They both cried and held each other for a long time. Then an anticipatory smile crept over Stephanie's face as she stroked Mark under his chin. That had become their signal – into the bedroom they went arm-in-arm. Their love-making that night was more passionate than usual. Afterward, they worked together preparing a leisurely dinner, followed by several hours of listening to symphonic music. Talking about their future plans for after the war became the endorphin that dulled the reality of their immediate future. Finally, they went to bed at one in the morning and made love again. The next day, sleepy-eyed Mark boarded a train for Fort Dix, New Jersey. Two months later, he was in Officer's Candidate School in Fort Benning, Georgia.

Stephanie attended his graduation, pinned his second lieutenant's bars on his new uniform, and danced with him at the party. She felt the irony of that party...a celebration on the eve of a departure for possible death or, at the least, a painful eon of separation. A week later he shipped out for Europe. She didn't hear from him for six weeks. Finally a heavily censored letter arrived from England. She knew that serious combat was ahead if the Allies were to invade Europe. She had no idea when...or if...he would return.

In time, Stephanie assimilated the patriotism that was everywhere. She didn't want this momentous thing, this greatest of wars, to leave her out. It could be another venue to show what she could do. Also, she knew she could defuse her anxieties in work. She buried herself in charitable work, including USO duties, war bond sales drives, as well as giving blood every quarter. Whatever she took on, she took on with effective gusto, and was never bashful about going around or over someone in her way. Like the dowager,

Mrs. Ransford Wainscott III, who was driven to the USO canteen in a chauffeured Rolls, and walked around with, "Please, Ladies, align those doughnuts in a straighter line," or "Be sure to make the coffee extra strong. You know these servicemen all drink...the least we can do is help them be sober."

Stephanie let Mrs. Wainscott III order her around during her first three weeks at the canteen, until one night she replied to an order, "My dear Mrs. Wainscott, you may not realize this, but all of us here have graduated from college, indicating a modicum of intelligence, hence we are able to align doughnuts, dance with servicemen, pour coffee, and smile all on our own volition. So why don't you get off the podium and pitch in. You can start by drying these cups that we were able to wash all by ourselves."

Mrs. Wainscott III never appeared at the canteen again. But, her husband complained to Harvey over a gin game at the club.

Harvey, to his credit, just shrugged. "Yes, my Stephanie's a strong-willed lady, but usually right. Wish she were a man...could run Braxton one day..."

From the beginning, tennis was her favorite sport. With a court on the Braxton grounds and lessons from the time she was eight, she developed a proficiency in all phases of the game. She started with junior girls matches at the country club, but soon was playing in the age group three years her senior. This advancement came after a particular match when she was eleven. She drew a ninth-grade girl who was three inches taller and twenty pounds heavier. The whispered comments in the ladies' locker room were to the effect that now was when that precocious and aggressive Braxton girl would get her comeuppance. For three days before the match, Stephanie had asked her teacher to hit her balls that would prepare for her match with the fourteen-year-old Amazon, Melissa Smythe. He did that: soft drop shots, hard volleys, streaking serves, overheads, and heavily spun cut-shots. She did this four hours a day, non-stop. When the day of the match arrived, she ran a mile in the morning for her wind. Entering the court she saw over seventy spectators...quite a lot for a little girl's match. Picking up her racquet, she heard several voices saying, "Come on Melissa, you can knock her off six-love, six-love." They spun racquets and Melissa won, electing to serve. Melissa won the first three games, her height and age benefiting her. In a short time, the first set was over: Melissa winning six-one. The buzz through the stands was one of smug pleasure.

Stephanie toweled off, took a swig of water, and noticed that her mother had taken a seat near the net post. She ran her fingers over the gut strings of her racquet and sucked in her breath as she walked to service line. "Nice set, Melissa," she called over the net. "Treasure it." The next set lasted over an hour with long rallies, many of which were prolonged by Stephanie's determined racing from corner to corner to retrieve Melissa's perfectly placed shots. She was like a tireless dog fetching a stick no matter how many times its owner tossed it. Despite the finesse and brute power that big Melissa exhibited, the ball always came back from the dogged retriever opposite her. After four games, Melissa's pace slowed, but not Stephanie's. She won the second set seven-five. Set score: one-all.

Changing ends after the first game of the third and deciding set, Stephanie passed close to her mother, who winked and blew her a kiss. Recalling the earlier snickering and the crowd's partiality shown for Melissa, Stephanie hiked up her lace-trimmed panties and raised her game a couple of notches, taking the third set six-two. Melissa, afterward, had sagged on the ground as she futilely stabbed at Stephanie's piercing shots. She didn't come to the net for the customary handshake. Stephanie walked over to her side of the net and offered her hand.

During the third set, Stephanie's fighting back over older and stronger Melissa had swung most of the crowd in her favor. Americans, and *even* Darien denizens, loved an underdog who won against stiff odds. No hand from Melissa, so Stephanie patted her on the shoulder, and saluted her with her racquet. As she left the court, the spectators were quiet at first, as if in awe of this brash little girl, but slowly their approval echoed out in complimentary phrases and mild clapping. As Stephanie walked past the stands, an older, regal-appearing women stood and said, "Nice game, young lady. You played like a champion...and acted like one too." Lillian hugged her daughter, as she gave her a peck on the cheek. At home, Lillian drew hot water in the tub, laced it with Epsom salts and helped Stephanie put her blistered feet into the soothing solution. Stephanie sat on the commode, while her mother knelt and gently dried her feet.

Lillian said, "Stephanie, I'm proud of the way you handled your-self today. But, win or lose, it's how you deal with either of those things that's important. Always try to be a gracious looser as well as a winner." She reached up and patted her daughter's head, then kissed her on the forehead. "Come over here, dear, let's put some cream on those tender spots on your hands."

Later that night, when Stephanie told Harvey about her win, he grunted, "That's my gal. Nice going, Steph. Will you be a good girl for dad and help Daniel with his game? His game looks like it has promise – that is if someone like you could give him a few pointers."

"Sure...Dad...sure." 'His game looks like it has promise'...a phrase she had never heard from her father. True, her father treated her as "his little princess," buying her a pony at age six and a full-sized stallion at twelve. Her closets were furnished with a wardrobe that would make a fashion queen green with envy, but she knew that his real love and dreams were centered in Daniel. Her women's intuitive perceptions told her that to her father she was just a *girl*. Girls, to him, were to be married, have children, serve their husbands and children, and they were never meant to run companies or hold political office.

Usually, the family would tour Europe as well as spend time at their Canadian lakefront cottage. Stephanie remembered one summer in particular when she was eight, close to nine, and Daniel was five. Harvey had tried to teach each of them to fish for the bottom-feeding walleye pike. He spent a lot of time with Daniel, having bought him an Orvis custom-made pole to fit his size. He gave Stephanie a few pointers and then proceeded to catch ten walleyes. He said, "See, it isn't too hard if you do it right. This is a real man's sport." He worked with Daniel, actually holding the pole with him, and together they caught seven. "Daniel and I are going in...you coming?"

"No, Daddy, let me stay a little longer."

"All right, it's four-thirty. Come in by six; it'll be getting dark."

After Harvey and Daniel left, Stephanie started to fish in earnest – casting over and over – baiting her hook so many times that she pricked her fingers on the hook's barb. Her blood dripped on her pile of gray-white squiggling fish, their gills gasping, their eyes fixed. She was stacking them up on the pier in a pyramid of accomplishment. She tore a piece of her shirt tail and wrapped it around her bleeding hand, limiting its use. Using both hands, however, she was still able to cast the pole, putting the muscles of her sunburned legs into every cast. Six o'clock came and passed, but Stephanie kept fishing. Andrew, the hired man, came to the dock at six-thirty.

"Come on, Miss Stephanie, your folks wants to eat."

"Andrew, count the fish in this pile, please."

"Twenty, Miss Stephanie."

"Good. That's more than Daddy and Daniel caught together. We can go in."

When she and Andrew arrived at the cottage, her father said, "Stephanie what are we going to do with all those extra fish you caught?"

Stephanie blushed, then replied, "The same thing that you were going to do with all those fish you and Daniel caught."

"That so...I guess you did out-fish us at that," Harvey grunted respectively. Later he shared with Lillian the little vignette. "You know Lillian, that girl of ours is smart...and she knows her own mind...got courage of her convictions too. Wish she were a boy... no telling what she could do or how far she could go."

"Is it really important that she be a boy to do these big things, dear? You know there have been some great women leaders in history. With all of the education, travel, and sports involvement you've provided for her, who knows..."

"Lillian, we've been over that ground before. I need a man to succeed me at Braxton – hopefully Daniel...yes it has to be Daniel...family. Besides, if she were there and got pregnant...what then?"

"Yes, dear, you know best. Incidentally, *Madame de Remusat*, has been wonderful. Thank you for finding her. Stephanie has taken to French admirably, speaking and reading."

The Braxtons kept a French lady on premises to serve as both a tutor to Stephanie and her brother and to do secretarial work for Lillian Braxton. After four years of tutoring, Stephanie was reading two novels in the original French. This served her well, as the current rage of her set were the stories of Henri Guy de Maupassant, along with D.H Lawrence's *Sons and Lovers*, made all the more desirable by repeated obscenity charges. These novels, not accepted, at least on the surface, by the parents of Stephanie's friends, were covertly read. They were a balm to the arousing heat of young girls coming into physiological womanhood. Lillian endeared herself to Stephanie by giving her a leather-bound copy of de Maupassant, unbeknownst to Harvey.

Stephanie's favorites were the de Maupassant stories, her first literary description of the changes that were taking place in her maturing body. His tales of carnal unions among every strata of the human chain – whores to ladies, rues to princes – excited her with an urge and longing that would burn for the rest of her life.

De Maupassant's premise was that women were entitled to sexual satisfaction…an unheard of concept in his late nineteenth-century days…and still unknown to many in the twentieth century. But, not by young, highly charged Stephanie, whose pre-teen latent libido had now become an active volcano, ready to erupt – dynamite just waiting for someone to light the fuse. Never one to wait on getting what she wanted, she decided to explore de Maupassant's promised delights with the boys from her cotillion, a venue of boys eager to dance and press closely with well-endowed Stephanie.

The Friday night cotillion at the Darien Country Club was designed to assist young men and girls, fourteen to eighteen, to learn the social graces of dancing, sipping punch, engaging in meaningful conversation, and extending courtesy to each other and to the parental chaperones. In the fall of 1935, as the lines at soup kitchens across the country lengthened and displaced dust bowl victims inched their way westward in Model A Fords on bald tires, "the set," dressed in white tie and strapless formals, danced until eleven.

When the orchestra would finish *I'm in the Mood for Love*, a twenty-minute intermission was observed, during which couples would often stroll on the club's veranda, away from the watchful eyes of the chaperones. If Stephanie liked the boy she was with, she would lead him to the tree-shrouded end of the veranda. Her perfume and closeness quickly moved the boy to kiss her and tentatively put his hand on her breast. Hearing Stephanie's faint sigh, he became emboldened and cupped them both as his breathing raced. Pressing into the startled boy, she felt what, as she read in French, was *la difference*. She always stopped any further moves by saying, "We must get back before the orchestra starts again."

The boy would mutter a soulful, "Yeah, okay."

Stephanie was particularly attracted to seventeen-year-old Percy Withers, a blond-haired boy a year her senior. She would never agree to his pleas to "go steady," but he was her date ninety-percent of the time. His polished manners made him seem older, experienced and led her to trust him. She confided in her diary that she loved him. He was allowed to drive his parent's Packard touring car. They would go to a movie, a snack bar, and then a secluded parking place. In time, she let him work his exploring fingers under the damp, elastic edge of her panties. She always held the ultimate control, but loved her body's responses to these clandestine physical probes that made her breathing become rapid and her whole body tingle. These sensations were not recorded in her diary. When Percy graduated from high school, he went off to the South to college, ending her first "real love."

Her mother's generation rarely discussed "the act" with their daughters. Lillian was no exception, but also no deterrent to Stephanie satisfying her pulsating curiosities. A new form of entertainment for "the set" were sleepovers, where there was little sleep and a lot of talk and giggling. Dressed in their nighties, hair in some form of restraint, and cream on their faces, the girls shared stories, fantasies, and misconceptions about boys, sex, and how they looked. Most of Stephanie's sex education came from the novels she read, from older girls, and trial-and-error experience. As in all of her studies, she did well at this subject.

When she went away to Smith College, the first thing she packed was the leather-bound copy of de Maupassant that Lillian had given her. Beyond the sexual encounters, now not as mysterious as before, she liked the way some of de Maupassant's stories shattered the complacency and smugness of the upper class. In her fantasizing, Stephanie saw herself breaking some of the sacred icons of her father's group – particularly those chauvinistic, stuffy, martini-and-cigar cronies of her father's at the club... the self-dubbed "titans of industry and commerce" and preservers of "the proper life." Those condescending blue-bloods, who never said, "I'm glad to meet you," but always patronizingly said, "How nice to see you," as they extended a limp hand, pulling it back just before contact. After all, if they touched, the person might feel that he or she knew them or, worse yet, that they might be entitled to ask for something.

Stephanie was raised in a culture of wealth, highborn gentility, and propriety, including private schools, cotillions, travel abroad, and making her debut at the Waldorf-Astoria. But, she knew there was a superficial quality to many of these conventions. She always exhibited graciousness to everyone; she could never be called a snob. Stephanie longed to embrace all of life, not just the cloistered circle of her family's set. Her inner vibrancy urged her to mix with the entire social strata. That was why she chose Margery Eggers for a roommate at Smith.

She could have roomed with almost anyone, but she liked the down-to-earth humility, honesty, and naturalness that Margery exhibited. She was, in many ways, the antithesis of the girls Stephanie had grown up with. Margery made no apologies for being from a poor family in a West Virginia coal-mining town. She maintained a quiet pride in knowing that she had earned a full scholarship to Smith. Stephanie thought about the seven bathrooms in the Braxton house, as Margery told her that she had never gone to the toilet inside her house…only outside in the coal dust-coated privy…in the dead of winter or the humid heat of summer…in broad daylight or in the dark of night. Margery and Stephanie were inseparable during their first two years at Smith...the two years before Stephanie met Mark Abercrombie, the poor boy from south Boston.

*   *   *

The door chime bonged loudly, startling her from her day-dreaming. Still she hesitated. Where was her mother? Why wasn't she here? Lillian always knew how to calm Stephanie...how to help her see things in a bigger perspective. From the time Stephanie was five years old, her mother had shared stories with her...true stories of her family that made her feel warm and that she belonged. One of her favorites was about her great grandfather, Thomas Braxton, who migrated from Wales to America when he was twenty. He started with nothing, except what he wore when he landed in America, and was processed through the immigration center at Castle Garden. Thomas had a driving desire to succeed in his newfound land. He called America, "The Promised Land of the Bible." In later years, Thomas would quip in his droll manner, that God had denied Moses entry into Canaan, but that he, Thomas, was allowed into this "promised land." He worked two jobs, one at a chemical company in New Haven, the other as a cooper on the night shift. At age forty he had saved seventy percent of all that he had earned. With these funds he started Braxton Chemical Industries.

His one son, Daniel, carried on the company after Thomas retired at eighty. Daniel accelerated the business by obtaining lucrative government contracts for poison gas elements in World War I. A year after the armistice, granddaughter Stephanie was born. She was an energetic baby with a full head of red hair. From the moment the obstetrician spanked her dimpled rear, she never stopped expressing herself, nor did she sit passively for more than a few moments. Old Thomas said in his Welsh accent, "That one should have been a boy." Every time Lillian shared this tale with Stephanie, they both laughed and hugged each other. She couldn't remember

Thomas… he died when she was two. Stephanie never minded hearing her mother tell the same family stories over and over. But, she wished she had known her grandfather; he sounded so real, someone she could have been close to. The force of her will to be independent, and her penchant to control, shut out most of the normal relationships that people seemed to enjoy. Her mother's stories helped fill that void. Embracing, down-to-earth Margery Eggers also helped.

The second ring of the bell was followed by a loud and persistent rapping on the wooden door, making her jump. She knew that what was on the other side wasn't going to go away. Edging closer to the door, she braced herself, a myriad of negative thoughts hammering inside her head…a widow at twenty-six…he's too young…too handsome to die…what will I do…will I have to live alone? I knew he shouldn't have enlisted…it can't end like this…it just can't.

"Mrs. Abercrombie?"

"Yes."

"Cablegram, please sign here."

Her hand shook…her normally perfect penmanship turning to a childish scrawl, filling two lines instead of the designated one. She took the four-by-eight-inch yellow envelope with the isinglass addressee window into the living room. She sat, reached for a Chesterfield, her hand still trembling, and tried to spin the wheel on the Zippo lighter Mark had sent her from a PX. After four futile spins, she dropped it and threw the cigarette into the tray. Her eyes lifted from the gram, swept the room that she and Mark had worked together so closely to furnish and decorate. Her eyes lit on the picture of Mark in his new second lieutenant's uniform looking directly at her.

She knew that back at Smith, her friend Margery Eggers had had a huge crush on Mark and had dated him several times. One night as Stephanie was brushing her teeth, Margery, dressed in black dress and heels, with a small black pill box hat on her head, with every hair in place, came into their rooms softly whistling a lilting tune. "That's a catchy tune, Marge...what is it?"

"It's called *We're Off to See The Wizard*. Mark and I went to see the *Wizard of Oz*, with Judy Garland as Dorothy. It was in color...just a beautiful movie. It's the theme song."

"It must have been...since you're whistling the theme and all. Did you have a nice time with Mark?"

"Wonderful. He's such a gentleman!"

"He must be. I see your lipstick is just like it was when you left."

"Stephanie! He's not like that."

"That's a shame." Stephanie enjoyed teasing her friend.

"You've got the wrong idea. We share a lot. He's sort of like me. He comes from a poor family on the south side of Boston, but earned a full scholarship to Harvard."

"Hmm...you two make a perfect set of bookends."

"He's carrying a heavy load of subjects, plus he's a hero on the football team...scored the winning touchdown against Yale last month."

"Sounds like a great guy. Good for you, Marge. Are you going to see him again soon?"

"He's taking me to the Christmas dance at his club next week," Marge beamed, her eyes brightening like the stars of the heavens.

"Uh, oh." Stephanie looked at the clock on her desk. "Time for lights out. See you in the a.m."

Stephanie slid into bed, but couldn't sleep. Listening to Margery puttering around in the bathroom, and hearing her breathing, she knew Margery was still full of afterglow from her date. As she processed what she had heard, not only tonight, but on other nights, about Mark, she decided their relationship was based on the propinquity of likes...similar backgrounds. They were both a little uncomfortable with some of the people of different eco-socio backgrounds. There weren't any wealthy people in Mark's South Boston, and even fewer in Margery's coal-mining area of West Virginia.

Margery never bragged, or even spoke of any passion, nor did she ever convey a Mona Lisa-like reticence of hidden pleasures. Stephanie's intuition told her that the relationship had to be one of convenience. The Greek's precise definitions of the various forms of love – *agape, philos, altros and eros* – came to mind. There wasn't any apparent *eros*, at least on Mark's part – maybe some *altros,* a platonic relationship at best. She had never seen him try to come into their room after a date, nor had she ever seen them lingering in the vestibule of the duplex. Why not? This wasn't natural…all men are looking for physical closeness…and more.

The next day, Stephanie engineered a date to the Christmas dance at Mark's club. She asked Margery if she wanted to double.

"I don't think so, Steph. Mark's car's a two-seater. Where would we all sit? Maybe we'll see each other there."

"I'm sure. I'll introduce you to Tom Avery."

"That would be great…"

There was a sigh of wistfulness in Margery's answer that Stephanie definitely would have noticed.

At the dance, she cajoled Margery into introducing her to Mark. Margery did, but reluctantly. She didn't hear Stephanie hint that Mark should ask her for a dance, which he politely declined in deference to Margery.

But, Mark warmed with goose pimples whenever Stephanie would lightly brush against him. She was always close enough so that her perfume teased his nose, and her hint of cleavage quickened his pulse.

As the evening lengthened, Margery noticed that if she looked away from Mark, and then looked back quickly, she saw him looking at Stephanie as she and Tom Avery danced by their table. Her stomach grabbed each time she caught this. But she didn't see Stephanie slip a match book cover with her phone number on it into Mark's tuxedo pocket as they waited in the coat line.

That night as the girls were back in their room, very little was said. Margery tossed and turned until five a.m. before sleep came. The next day, she was in class when Mark called Stephanie and asked her for a date.

"Oh, Mark, I'd love to go with you, but do you think that's fair to Margery?"

She smiled when he told her that Margery was just a friend...nothing serious...just a couple of poor scholarship mates.

"Well, Mark, if you're sure...okay. How about I meet you at Trimble's restaurant at seven? It might be better...just this first time, okay?"

From the moment Stephanie had shaken hands with Mark at the dance, she had known that he was the man she would marry. Also, that she would have to make the moves – except, what about Margery? Stephanie didn't really want to hurt her friend, but Mark wasn't just some fling or some girl-versus-girl contest. This was truly serious. Marriage was one of the biggest events in a girl's life, and in achieving big things there was always a cost. Margery had her chance...so *c'est la vie!*

During the two weeks after the dance, Mark and Stephanie were seen together in local restaurants, coming out of the play house, and riding in his second-hand Plymouth convertible. Three weeks after the dance, and after a tear-filled, shouted indictment by Margery, where she compared Stephanie to Brutus and Judas Iscariot, Margery moved out of the rooms they had shared for nearly two years. As she was leaving, she paused at the door and stared at Stephanie in disdain saying, "I hope you're happy, but remember, stolen fruit usually turns rotten. I hope you don't gag!" They never spoke again.

*   *   *

Stephanie looked from the door back to the picture, knowing she had been a cool, calculating female in taking Mark from her trusting friend. Was having to deal with the fear of him being killed her punishment...her penance for what she had done? Had some nameless German snuffed out the love of her life, as she had snuffed out the romantic hopes of her roommate? The more that she went back into the beginning of her relationship with Mark, the farther away was the cablegram, held tightly in her hand, and now squeezed to a fourth its original size. What she and Mark shared couldn't be summed up on a puny piece of porous, yellow foolscap.

She had loved bringing Mark to her family's estate and seeing his wonderment at all that he saw. After Mark's first visit, her father had quizzed her for an hour about his background. When he learned that Mark had graduated from Boston Latin *cum laude*, and had earned a full scholarship to Harvard where he majored in chemistry, with minors in French and Spanish, he said, "Hmm...maybe, just maybe."

Stephanie saw how her father had looked at Mark...almost as if he was the reincarnation of her brother, who had died eight years earlier of double pneumonia. The more she saw Harvey warm up to Mark, the more she became embittered over the way he had dismissed her offer to help at Braxton. His thoughts about women in industry made her mad. She never doubted that in time she could manage a company, particularly Braxton Industries, as she had lived on the fringe of it all of her life. She had toured their facilities and had heard many discussions about its business. When she and Mark were married, and he worked there, he would be sure to rise. As Mark's wife, when Harvey finally retired, well, "Hmm...maybe, just maybe."

At least twice a month, Mark was a weekend guest at the Braxton estate. She remembered his look of awe the first time they drove up the circular driveway in his convertible with the top down. The dogwood and redbud trees, like their early romance, were beginning to bloom. His wonderment increased as they passed the neatly trimmed grounds, abundant with shrubs, trees, and flower beds. He had uttered a low whistle when the fourteen-room replica of an English Tudor came into view. She showed him the pool, tennis court, horse barn, and the sylvan-secluded gazebo at the back of the property. That was where, during most weekends after dark, they explored their strong physical attraction for each other. They always stopped just short of total consummation, with Mark's Protestant values about marriage being the inhibitor. Their clenched-teeth panting proved a tribute to Calvinistic morality and a pique to Stephanie. She was not used to being denied anything...but it made her concede a grudging respect for this man of principle. It also made her pave the way to the altar. A job offer from her father at Mark's Harvard graduation helped accomplish her plan.

She was happy that Mark would be working at Braxton, but it was hard to let go of the hurt she still carried over her turndown by Harvey. Before enrolling at Smith, she had offered to major in business and get an MBA and go to work for him and the firm. He had cut her deeply when he said it was a man's job to work in Braxton management. She could still hear his words, "You're an intelligent and beautiful girl, Stephanie. I love you dearly, and I know you will bring us a grandson someday to take Daniel's place...mine too...in time."

She had bit her tongue; but she would be damned if she'd be his brood hen. She would never subscribe to any of that barefoot, pregnant, and in the kitchen hogwash. From that day, her relationship with her father was cool...proper, but devoid of warmth – an absence that was filled by the heat of ambition to prove she could run anything she chose.

Harvey seemed to withdraw into himself after Daniel's untimely death. Her brother had died at fourteen, succumbing to double pneumonia. His lungs, weak from birth, couldn't shake off the lethal virus. Harvey had flown him to Johns Hopkins Hospital and gotten the best doctors available. But after three weeks in an oxygen tent, with Harvey, Lillian, and Stephanie at his bedside, Daniel died...a look of bewilderment on his childish face. When his eyes went blank, they looked last on Stephanie. To her they seemed to be saying, "Help me, Sis." How many times, since she was old enough to care for him, had he said this to her, always with those big blue eyes looking up to her in total trust? Stephanie had carried and actually relished his dependence on her. She enjoyed directing his life, and his ever present gratitude sated her need to be needed. She walked to the bed, and smoothed his blond hair, then said, "Goodbye, little brother, I love you."

Lillian observed how well Stephanie curbed her emotions in times of trauma and sorrow. As she watched Stephanie's caress of Daniel, she knew Stephanie felt deeply for him and would grieve for a long time after his passing. But, Lillian knew her daughter had the stoic manner of a Native American...an Algonquin probably. She always met crisis and challenge with a calm and pragmatic resolve, at least externally.

Once in the hospital corridor, despite her outward placidity, Stephanie had tears running down both cheeks, as if an internal wellspring had been unleashed. Lillian put her arms around her smoothing her auburn hair. Their bodies pressed together, Lillian felt each of her daughter's contractions reflecting the depth of her love for her lost brother. "Momma," she choked, "I'll miss him so...why him...why? He's so young...too young to die like this. He had his whole life in front of him...it's a terrible waste."

Harvey put his hand on Stephanie's shoulder, "You were good to him...good for him, Stephanie. I'm glad we have you. Your mother and I need you more than ever now."

Stephanie almost said, "Do you mean it?" But held her tongue, she knew how deeply her father would miss Daniel...how much he would inwardly grieve, but not show it. It was Lillian she felt the sorriest for. She wondered how much her dad would miss her if it was she who had just passed away.

Lillian and Stephanie walked slowly down the corridor a few

yards behind Harvey, the sour-sweet smell of disinfectant nipping their nostrils, symbolizing the sterility of the hospital…and of death.

"Dear, he does love you. He just doesn't know how to show it. I'm proud of your not making any remarks that would hurt him."

Harvey had secluded himself in his den. Lillian and Stephanie walked the terraced back lawns of their estate. For a long while they walked in silence, retracing the steps they had taken so often. The shrubs, flowers, and manicured lawns were still as beautiful as when they had walked them year after year. But today, hours after Daniel's burial, the entire vista took on the dull gray of their sadness. They were pressed close together – close enough for Stephanie to almost feel her mother's internal weeping.

Finally, Lillian spoke, "Remember, Stephanie, how you and I walked here so many times, ever since you were tiny? Today, I feel that little Daniel is walking with us…well not exactly right here, but just a little above us on the terraces of our Lord." Lillian seemed so calm. Suddenly, the pain that had been gnawing within her came out in a wrenching gasp and she began to sob openly. Stephanie waited. She knew her mother's strength, and she couldn't think of anything to say. Sure enough, Lillian pulled herself together like she always did.

Her face drawn, her eyes sunken with puffiness under them, she patted Stephanie's head and said, "It must be God's will."

"God's will…" How many times had Stephanie heard that, not from her father but from Lillian, and from Lillian's father, the pastor? She had had this vague mental picture of an old man seated on a throne, somewhere up in the sky, pointing with a scepter to one person or another…"willing" something to happen, or "willing" it not to happen. She never understood the basis for that will…why some people lived, why others died horrible or untimely deaths…like her brother. It was too inconsistent for her eighteen-year-old mind.

She turned to her mother, a skeptical look on her face, "God's will? If there is a God, why is it "His will" to kill harmless little boys who never did anything bad? Or whose will lets a depression starve innocent people in a land of plenty like America? *If* there is a god, he must be blind. I don't think there is one…at least I'm not sure anymore."

*   *   *

Standing near her desk, now several years later, the unopened cablegram in her hand, Stephanie's eyes misted over with tears. She was president of three organizations, had a full shelf of tennis trophies, a board of horseshow blue ribbons, and was married to the catch of the year. Yet she was afraid to open a stupid cablegram. She picked up a Chesterfield and Mark's Zippo. She got the cigarette lit, took a couple of puffs, coughed, and crushed it out in disgust. She'd tried smoking after Mark shipped out…no good…no substitute for anything…and it smelled up the apartment. All of those movies that showed suave people tapping cigarettes on silver cases, lighting them for each other, and putting on camera-ready smiles through clouds of tar-laden smoke were Hollywood staging, not reality. Dropping the cablegram, she took the pack and threw it in the garbage. But she kissed the lighter, pressed it to her breast, and put it in the desk drawer.

The phone rang. It was Lillian…just checking in.

"Oh, hi Mother." Lillian could hear the glumness, unusual for her usually upbeat daughter. She asked Stephanie how she was doing.

"So, so…well, not really…I just received a cablegram, and believe it or not, I'm afraid to read it! Could I come see you…could you be there when I open it?"

Lillian felt Stephanie's anxiety in her own heart. Of course her daughter could come over right away.

Stephanie threw on a blazer, jammed the cablegram in the side pocket, and got into her 1940 wood-sided Ford station wagon with the B gas ration sticker on the windshield. At least she got that from Braxton Industries, now a defense plant making chemicals that would end up in munitions and airplane coatings. Backing out of the drive, she flicked on the radio and caught the end of a news broadcast telling of Hitler's orders to his retreating forces to employ a "scorched earth" policy as a beaten *Wehrmacht* was being pushed back into The Fatherland. Next, she heard an Alka-Seltzer bromide commercial...fizz...fizz...timely, as fear cramped her stomach about whether Mark was on the receiving end of Hitler's scorched earth policy. Next, the melodic Martha Tilton singing, *I'll Walk Alone*. When the theme of the popular song registered, she turned it off shouting, "No...I won't walk alone!"

She drove through west Darien, watching the people pursuing their normal routines: men and women walking and window shopping, high school kids on lunch break, and delivery men double-parking their trucks in front of stores. Had any of them received cablegrams from overseas? Were they already widows, fatherless children, girls without a lover, or parents without a son? Glancing in the rear view mirror, she pushed her soft auburn hair back – remembering her mother's words about how it matched that of Toby, her Irish setter – and said to her mirrored image, "Maybe I'm still attractive enough if I have to go through it again." Then, as the lump came up in her throat, she again looked in the mirror, "I don't want to...I've got the man I want. He's got to be alive...he's just got to be...I need him!"

The gates to her parent's estate were open. She drove up to the house, chanting a mantra about Mark coming home. Suddenly she said to the mirror, "You've been a little-girl-coward about this. Whatever it says won't change, regardless of when you open it." The determined young woman who mirrored back at her was more like it. She pulled the cablegram from her pocket. She'd be with her mother in just a few minutes.

CHAPTER TWO

Courage is the price that life
extracts for granting peace

Amelia Earhart Putnam
1898-1937

"Holy shit…no…God no!" he cried. He pulled his binoculars away, rubbing his bloodshot eyes with the back of his mitt, the only one he had. The other hand was jammed into his pocket to ease the pin-prick tingling from the zero-degree temperature. His other mitt, and a lot of clothing and equipment, was strewn over the bloody route from St. Vith to Bastogne. Son-of-a-bitch! He had just placed his First Platoon three-hundred yards to the south, and here came eight Krauts with a machine gun. He put the binoculars up again. He saw the enemy, mechanical snowmen, each one wearing a painted white helmet and a white parka, moving up the grade from the road to a line of trees in the foot-deep snow. An *Oberfeldwebel* – master sergeant – was in the lead, followed by two riflemen, two men carrying the MG 42, with its Lafette 42 tripod, and three more with rifles and entrenching tools. The leader pointed to a spot just below the trees. Two men started hacking at the frozen ground, their cloudy breath adding to the eeriness of the scene. Three others went back – probably for ammunition.

Lieutenant Mark Abercrombie wiped his eyes again on his sleeve. No sleep over the last forty-eight hours, he wondered if he was seeing right. Again, he raised the binoculars. Nothing had changed. Those guys were going to set up the machine gun where they could sweep First Platoon. His stomach felt squeezed in a vise. Somehow he had to get them out. He had led them – they were like family – every step of the way from France to this hell hole. The twenty-four who didn't make it were somewhere back there. He only had half their dog tags. It was when he was reaching for Munroe's that the captain had got it. Maybe somebody would find the others and notify headquarters. He wanted to write the family of every one that was gone.

He shoved the binoculars tighter against his near-frozen face. Maybe the horror would go away. When the gun was dug in where the sergeant was pointing, his guys would be right in the line of fire. Why had he put them there...why...why?

"What's the matter, Lieutenant?"

"Take a look, Sergeant."

Maybe Pellini would see something he missed. He had learned to count on Mike, an Italian from Chicago Heights. Pellini had been with him since they landed in Europe seven weeks after D-Day. Pellini could swear better than any man Mark had ever heard, but he also said his rosary twice a day, and kissed the photo of his wife and kids at least six times a day. So far the platoon had been in reserve, but not now. They were the front line just like they had been at St. Vith, where Pellini had stuck to him, ready to carry out any order.

Abercrombie took a half step back and watched Pellini. He wanted to see the sergeant's reaction to what was out there. With a shake of his head, Pellini handed back the binoculars. "If they get that gun set up, they'll nail our guys."

Mark didn't want to hear confirmation of what he already knew. They had to get those men out pronto. How? Being company commander weighed on him. His decision would mean life or death. He wondered what Redding would have done.

When the American forces were driven from St. Vith, it was a hurried retreat up the road toward Bastogne. Mark had been alongside of First Platoon, his command. He heard the muted whistle of an incoming shell. "Duck!" he hollered. He saw the explosion a hundred yards ahead, right where Captain Redding, company

commander, was marshalling the scattered and dazed Second and Third Platoons. He ran to the spot and found Redding lying in a twisted mass, his abdominal cavity open, his intestines and blood flowing onto the snow. A piece of 88 shrapnel had torn him from sternum to groin. Mark knelt, cradled the captain's head in his arm, and tried to hold the flap of skin over the gaping hole in his body. Redding looked at Mark with deadened eyes and gasped, "Mark…Bastogne…get…"

Mostly in shock, Mark received Captain Redding's last order and his last gush of blood. He looked at the face of the man who had helped him learn his job, had promoted him to first lieutenant, and was always up in front of the company. Despite the non-stop artillery fire all around them, he was now in solitude with his captain – a communion amid the chaos and confusion – a brief reprieve from hell to bid his friend and leader goodbye. On his knees, oblivious to the men running by, he moved his chapped hand to the captain's face and closed each eye. He unbuttoned Redding's jacket and clipped his I.D. tags. He made the sign of the cross on the captain's forehead and eased his body off the road, throwing a few loose twigs over it. He grabbed a handful of snow to wipe the blood off his hands, whispering a prayer as he hobbled to the head of the decimated column. Few men were with their own units. Mark's first job was to get order and direction into the dazed remnants of Able Company. "Close ranks, and follow me!" he shouted as he moved alongside of his new command. Slowly, some one-hundred-and-fourteen men became a phalanx of bloodied, but determined American GIs who now had a leader.

A day later, they were dug in on the perimeter northeast of Bastogne. Lieutenant Abercrombie, with what was left of Able Company, was charged with defending a three-thousand-yard-wide sector on the northeast corner, which was either surrounded, bypassed, or flanked by German Panzer and SS troops in Hitler's last-ditch offensive in the Belgian Ardennes. Hitler, in desperation and in an apparent absence of reality, wanted to block the Allies from landing supplies at Antwerp. Most of Hitler's generals felt it was the desperate strategy of a delusional maniac. Worked on personally by the Fuhrer in secret for over three months, it was the plan of a man already beaten with nothing left but the continual sacrifice of life. A plan based on the Germans capturing thousands of gallons of American tank gasoline – hardly a sound idea upon which to send men to face death. But, Hitler was not to be dissuaded by experienced generals. He transferred tens-of-thousands of troops from the now unpopular, disastrous eastern front. He increased their ranks with youngsters, mostly sixteen to nineteen years-old. None of them had been trained to fight.

The "bulge" of German SS, Panzer, and *Wehrmacht* troops was a lethal aneurism in the artery walls of Allied troops fighting their way from the beaches of Normandy to the heartland of Germany. Bastogne became an indestructible nodule. At 5:30 a.m. on December 16th, a cold foggy day, the attack had started with an opening cannonade of nearly nineteen-hundred pieces of heavy German artillery that shook the Belgian forest for more than an hour. Every man and vehicle in the area was a shadowy silhouette in the flare of non-stop muzzle flashes. The barrage was followed by a raining hail of 30 cm rocket fire, and a massive line of tanks, men, and artillery. The eighty-mile-wide spearhead steadily forced the American positions to yield rearward, until most of them were surrounded. Despite the skepticism of Hitler's generals, the plan almost worked, catching the thinly stretched line of the Allies by surprise and out of position from their extended supply train. The Germans, whose plan was steeped in concealment and deception, exploited the over confidence of the Allies, who had been gaining hundreds of miles without stiff resistance…that is until the Ardennes offensive, when the roles were temporarily reversed. However, after a few days of fierce combat, it was the Germans whose supplies were overextended, if non existent – no gas, just stalled tanks and trucks. In later years, the Battle of the Bulge, and the tenacious defense of Bastogne, would be described as the "Gettysburg" of the war in Europe, a thermopylae of modern warfare. After General Patton broke through the German ring around Bastogne the day after Christmas, the Germans were in retreat until their surrender the following May.

"Lieutenant, we gotta get those guys out of there."

Pellini's words slapped him in the face. He knew they had to get them out, but the dead certainty of his subordinate's observation became a command, as if a gauntlet had been thrown at his feet. His mind raced over alternatives. He thought about waving to them…signaling them to retreat to the west. But if he did, the Germans would see their target…him and Mike as well. His men probably wouldn't understand the waving anyway. Might overre-act…stand up…get shot…give their position away.

There was only one plan. Someone had to get to First Platoon and lead them quickly and silently back toward Bastogne – away from the German machine gun pocket before they were spotted. Then again, no one was sure where the lines were. The Germans had infiltrated many of the American positions. Mark had heard Captain Redding say that Eisenhower wanted Bastogne held. That had to be the best bet...he hoped.

"Lieutenant, want me to crawl over there and tell 'em to retreat...one at a time?"

Abercrombie looked into the serious brown eyes of his master sergeant – Pellini would go with a nod. He remembered the dog-eared photo Mike had shown him so often – Maria, with dark hair, black eyes, and a full mouth, with her arms around a boy and a girl, both under seven. The picture was crinkled from Mike's constant handling. Even now Pellini had his hand over the breast pocket of his jacket where the photo was stashed, next to his heart.

"How far?"

"About a hundred yards, maybe a little less. I can make it under ten minutes on my belly."

He knew Pellini was up to the job – probably the better man for it. He also knew that he was rationalizing – trying to justify not going himself. He took some deep breaths, fighting to relax his cramping gut. He stomped his left foot. The tingling was getting stronger. The damn upper was pulling farther away from the sole of his combat boot. It would be hard to push along the ground with that foot. Maybe frostbite. He better not put himself at too high a risk. Who would command the company? Turning his head, he saw Pellini fingering his rosary in his side pocket

For a second he froze as if he were a wax replica of himself...an inanimate suspension of blood, tissue, and feelings – as inert as the surrounding amphitheater. The entire area was covered in the silent, winter blanket of snow. Everything was serene, too quiet to be the venue of the mortal combat that was certain to begin any hour, any minute. A pine cone dropping on the frozen ground was a rifle shot to frayed nerves. The atmosphere was charged with invisible, but emanated fear, hunger, fatigue, and the fading hope of these hidden men, locked in a duel of death. There was no firing yet – the leaden-gray sky hung about them like a cloak of inevitable doom but with the impersonal air of the unknown. The Americans thought they were surrounded. They weren't sure. It was just a gut feeling fed by garbled transmissions, rumors and anxious guesses. A visceral prophecy made more ominous by the empty bellies that had had nothing but one box of K-ration and less than a pint of water in the last forty-eight hours. Most of the men were eating snow in place of water. They hadn't heard about General McAuliffe's December 22nd retort: "Nuts!" to the German's demand for surrender of the 101st Airborne, sealed in Bastogne.

Mark convulsed back to the present and to the field of fire that the German MG-42 could potentially command. He looked at the Germans and he looked into his soul. Today was Christmas Eve, the eve of the birth of the Christ Child, the one who was sent to bring peace to the world. It was pretty evident to him that, here in the death-dealing forests of Belgium, someone had not gotten the Word.

Suddenly it was Christmas Eve twenty years earlier. He had just returned from midnight service at the First Presbyterian Church with his mom and dad. At home was a small tree with a handful of ornaments and a few strands of shiny tinsel hanging from the scrawny branches. But it looked huge to sleepy six-year-old Mark. He sat between his parents on the lumpy couch in their five-room flat in a blue-collar section of South Boston – an island of Protestants in a sea of Irish Catholics. They both put their arms around him and told him about Jesus' birth. About how that baby had brought salvation, eternal hope and joy into the world. "Just as you have for us, Mark," his mother had said as she kissed him on the forehead.

The throbbing pain in his foot was getting worse. The bone-penetrating cold that surrounded them was crawling with deadly purpose into his open boot. He stomped his foot again to help the circulation, and crawled back into that Christmas Eve in 1924.

"Just as you brought joy and hope into our lives, little Mark." His mother's words played over and over. Were they telling him to bring hope to his First Platoon? The tricks of his mind were luring him back to childhood. He was pedaling his two-wheeler, the one his parents scrimped for a year to buy for his ninth birthday. Riding to school helped him to get quickly through the gauntlet of parochial school kids, who shouted, "You dirty pagan," as they tried to pelt him in a hail of rocks. When he came home, his mother listened. He asked her if those kids believed in God. "Yes, Mark, they believe in God, they just don't always understand Him. I know it's hard, but pray for them." Should he pray for the Germans? The warmth of his parent's unceasing love…it was a haven away from this doorstep of death.

Then he was with Stephanie, snuggled up to her warm body…a body with everything a man would want to see, touch, smell and taste. He knew if he made it for another two weeks they'd be married four years. He saw her auburn hair and olive green eyes and heard her soft, alto voice asking how his day had gone. He touched his breast pocket where he had placed her last two letters, written a month ago. He wondered if he would ever see her again.

"I'm ready to go, okay, Lieutenant?"

"You're not going Mike, I am."

"No! Uh…uh…no sir. You need to be here for the company."

"I'm going Mike…need to. Cover me. Here's my carbine and extra clips."

"Use your rifle…keep rotating it with the carbine so it looks like there's more than one of you. I'm going."

He pulled a bed sheet around his upper body. Pellini had given it to him when they raided a Belgian manor house during their retreat. It had been at a crossroads, overlooking barren fields that had once yielded wheat and alfalfa. The house was still, apparently abandoned by the owners fleeing from the onslaught of gunfire.

Mark had pulled the company off the road for a ten-minute rest. He ordered Pellini, Adams, Cox and Rosenberg to follow him in. The huge oak front door was smashed in, riddled with bullet holes. They put their rifles at the ready as they went from room-to-room. The sinister quiet hit them. On the floor in the kitchen was a woman shot through the head and a man bayoneted several times in the chest. The bodies were rigid, contorted in the desperate attempt to escape their murderers. Their faces showed horror – they were probably husband and wife. The back door led to the barn, half blown away by an artillery shell. There they found two dead Belgian draft horses, thick chests torn open, sturdy legs and large, unshod hooves pointing stiffly to the overcast sky. No flies in the open cavities – it was too cold for flies even presented with such a feast. The first time Mark had seen Belgian drafts they were pulling the milkman's cart through his South Boston neighborhood.

In the house, they found no food, only cupboards full of white linens. They all had seen the white-painted helmets and snow parkas of the Germans. Mark told them to take the sheets for camouflage. Pellini had handed him a fine one trimmed in Brussels lace, "Here, Lieutenant, this is a good one for you."

Even now he could still see the dead couple and those prize horses. He undid the top button of his ice and grime-encrusted jacket, stained with urine, Redding's blood, and last week's food. A far cry from the new second lieutenant's uniform he'd put on proudly at Fort Benning, Georgia when he graduated from Officer's Candidate School two years before. His class of "ninety-day wonders," as wartime commissioned lieutenants were called by regular army personnel, held a graduation dance. Stephanie was there and was allowed to pin on his shiny gold bars. She performed well, as she always did, masking the bitterness she'd expressed so vehemently when he told her he was enlisting. They had danced to *Dancing in the Dark, Tonight We Love* – and others, all songs they had shared during their courtship. *Begin the Beguine* was their favorite. While they were dancing, Mark whispered some of Cole Porter's romantic words into her ear. They were a beautiful couple, happy together, suppressing their unspoken thoughts of where Mark would be in the months ahead. The exhilaration of that night faded in the grim reality of Bastogne…no bands, no soft dresses and lights…no wife to crawl in bed with later. Just blood, fear and trance-like plodding.

Aw hell, get on with it.

Discipline, instilled by his parents and the army, jolted him back to the moment. It was time to go. He reached inside his jacket and fingered one of the silver bars. He unpinned it from his right shoulder. Holding it brought back Stephanie again. He could feel her hand on his shoulder…smell her delicate perfume, feel her eyes looking into his very soul.

He knew they would send his bars home to her if he got it.

He crouched over, tapped Pellini on the shoulder. "Mike, in case I don't make it, you're the man," he muttered through clenched teeth, handing the gold bar to his first sergeant.

"You'll make it, Mark. Class always wins…I…I uh…mean, Lieutenant."

"It's okay, Mike…it's okay."

He sucked in his breath and fingered the St. Christopher medal his parents had sent him. Mrs. Kelly from the flat upstairs had given it to his mother when he enlisted. "I know St. Christopher was Catholic, Mrs. Abercrombie, but he looks out after Protestants too."

They were both kneeling below the hastily formed snow parapet around the edge of the hole. Eyeball to eyeball, they were caught for a moment in the tacit bond of men who had shared everything…every basic body function, the full spectrum of human emotions, and the congealing into a single body…a single mind…fighting to stay alive. Pellini turned his head, hanging onto his M-1, its butt in the snow, his left hand on the lower barrel, his right hand raised. He slowly made the sign of the cross in the space between them – his fixed gaze on Mark never wavering, "In the name of the Father, and of the

Son, and of the Holy Ghost." Then he added, "Lieutenant, I'll nail every fuckin' Kraut that raises his rifle in your direction."

"Thanks, Mike...thanks," Mark said, as a couple of tears wet his cold-reddened cheeks. Then as Pellini's words hit him, a grin broke on his chapped lips. Blinking, he injected a shell into the barrel of his service .45, eased the exposed hammer off, re-holstered it, and inched out of the shallow dug out. Then he was on his belly crawling over the frozen snow toward First Platoon. In the first hundred yards, no shots came from the Kraut machine gun nest. His left foot was numb one minute then hurting like hell the next...it felt like someone was driving eight-penny nails through the sole, or his toes were in some demon's pincers, tightening with each forward push...probably frost bite. Damn. Couldn't let it stop him. Maybe if he got out of this he could get a medic, or maybe it wouldn't matter. His whole body ached. He was shivering from the cold and sweating from the stress. Shivering had become as normal as breathing for all of them...Americans and Germans alike. His mind was flitting between here and his childhood. He saw his mom sitting at her treadle-operated sewing machine hemming a formal gown for some Back Bay debutante. He was nearby playing with a handful of World War I cast-iron soldiers bought at Woolworth's – a little boy playing soldier at his mother's feet.

"Ping." A Mauser rifle bullet hit close. Had they seen him? Maybe just a stray shot. He stopped, flattened himself even tighter to the ground, burying his face in the snow. The ice cut into his cheek. He saw his own blood on the snow in front of him. "Ping." Another shot just a yard away. Then he heard Pellini open up with his Garand, "Crack, crack, crack"...eight times. He saw the machine gun swivel toward his buddy, but it didn't fire. He guessed the ammo hadn't arrived yet...maybe a frozen jam...*please, God, a jam*. He could see the muzzle flashes of three rifles now firing toward where Pellini was dug in. Then he heard the whispery pfft, pfft of his carbine as Mike kept returning fire. When a German fell out of the nest, his coal-bucket shaped helmet rolling down the hill like a discus, Mark bolted up and ran the last few yards half crouched over. In an eternity of steps, he reached the trench the twenty survivors of First Platoon had wrested from the frozen ground and dove in.

If he'd been the Easter Bunny, the sunken-eyed and bearded buck-sergeant couldn't have looked more surprised. "What the hell?" he growled.

"Stay down...I mean down! Gotta get out of here! Pronto! The Germans got a heavy machine gun up above us, just below the tree line. Can't call any artillery fire on them...no walkie-talkie. Besides, we're too close. If one of those 105's fell a little short, we've had it."

"Aw shit, we just got dug in."

"You wanna die here?"

"No sir...no sir...what's the plan?"

"Come over here, Sergeant...just you and me."

"Yes, sir," Sergeant McCormack was all ears.

"Don't want the men hearing this yet...don't want any panic. We've got just a couple of minutes to do something. Thought about charging the nest...no good. Running up that hill they'd mow us down...even if a couple of us made it, we'd lose most of the platoon. Can't shoot it out with them, that 42's got us beat all to hell. Best bet is to crawl out the back of the trench, single file. If we make it back a quarter of a mile, we can zero the artillery in on the nest."

"The guys are pretty beat, but they'll do whatever you say, Lieutenant."

"We've lost too many already. We'll file back, hoping we get out of range before they know what we're doing."

"Say the word. Should I brief the guys?"

"Hold it a minute. What you got here heavier than your rifles?"

"Nothing," he said loud enough for a private who had been inching up to them to hear.

"Hey Sarge, O'Reilly's got a grenade launcher an' one, maybe two pineapples."

Mark turned to see Sutkowski, the man that had been his runner at St. Vith just before Captain Redding had been killed, pointing to the other end of the short trench. A stocky GI sat with his head bowed, lips moving silently, perhaps in prayer, and holding a rifle across his lap with the launcher affixed to the muzzle. Mark decided what he would do.

"Sergeant, can O'Reilly hit that nest from here?"

"He's good, should be able to...saw him hit a Panther tread from a hundred yards back in France."

"Good. Here's the plan." Need you to help me pull it off."

"Yes, sir...yes sir!"

Mark knelt close to McCormick, making a simple map in the snow. As he drew, McCormick, a fifteen-year career army man, stared with new respect at this "college boy" officer, the kind they turned out in a few weeks down there in Georgia.

No chicken shit stuff. Talks to me like a man.

With his hand on McCormick's shoulder, Mark pulled him close. "Sergeant, you'll lead the men out that end of the trench. Take my compass and head exactly two-hundred-seventy degrees toward Bastogne. Go single file, as low as you can. Use all the white sheets we lifted...give them to the first guys out. You're in charge...get them to town, report to the highest rank you can find. Tell them we'll regroup there, and give them these co-ordinates – but not until after thirty minutes from when you leave. They'll put some 155 or 105 shells on those Krauts if O'Reilly hasn't already knocked them out."

"Got it," McCormack said, and despite his fatigue, his mouth issued a wry smile. Cautiously, he put his gnarled and blue hand on Mark's arm, "Good luck, Lieutenant."

"Ask O'Reilly if he'll stay with me, and go for that gun when I tell him."

"Done," the sergeant said as he duck-walked to O'Reilly, whispered in his ear, and led him back to Mark.

McCormack and Mark synchronized their watches just before McCormack started out of the trench, followed every few seconds by a soldier, all bent low to the ground. Half of them were wrapped in white Belgian linen. Pellini's fire kept the Germans focused on his dugout, but now the Garrand and the carbine were matched with the steady staccato of the MG 42 at 1200 rounds a minute. As the fourteenth man crawled out of the trench, Pellini's fire ceased. Then after a couple of short bursts from the machine gun, all was quiet. Mark's face went white, as his intestines cramped. He looked toward where Pellini had been firing...his vision blurred, making it hard to see, but he blinked and kept looking. Pellini's rifle was not visible. *Oh, God, no...no.*

He ducked, then inched his head up again to the rim of the trench, hoping to see any sign of life. Nothing, just little piles of snow-mud mixture dug up with 7.92 millimeter machine gun slugs. *Ping, ping, ping*...gobs of snow kicked up a couple of yards in front of his face, then a head-rattling hit on the side of his helmet from a bullet that had ricocheted off a rock. He jerked his head down in the trench, bumping into O'Reilly. "Shit, that's too damn close." He leapt to the exit end and yelled, "Don't wait...get out now! Run up the guy's ass if he's doggin' it! Push the guys in front! Tell 'em to run. Move it! Move it!" The last six men were out in a flash.

He pushed Pellini out of his mind, but not his twisted gut. "O'Reilly, we gotta knock those bastards out. Can do?"

"They're about twenty yards too far, Lieutenant...but maybe if I lob one in I can hit 'em. Got two grenades...first one to get the arc...hit it with the second one."

"Do it! Our guys aren't out of range yet...we sure as hell aren't either."

O'Reilly stuck his head above the line, then ducked, fixed a grenade on the launcher, stood full upright and fired. *Fifteen...twenty yards short...damn.* The grenade's harmless explosion triggered the machine gun. Mark and O'Reilly split further apart as bullets tore

up the ground in front of where they had been.

"Want me to go for broke, Lieutenant?"

"Go, I'm betting on you."

Before he could say more, O'Reilly crawled over the front of the trench, ran a couple dozen yards, knelt and fired the last grenade. It whistled in the air. Mark watched, stupefied at what he was witnessing. He saw the *Oberfeldwebel* stand and point to O'Reilly. The machine gun inched to the left and ran a string of slugs like nail holes in the snow up to O'Reilly. He went down just as the grenade landed in the German's dugout. Machine gun parts, a helmet, and pieces of men flew up. A silence descended. Mark, like a man in a slow motion film…the black forests and white snow his backdrop, moved out of the trench. He crawled to O'Reilly. "Got those Hun bastards, Lieutenant," O'Reilly said, putting his hand over the gush of blood from his right thigh. Flat on his belly, next to him, Mark almost stared himself blind trying to see if any Germans were still moving…no life showing.

He took the belt out of his pants and made a crude tourniquet for O'Reilly's leg, twisting it with his knife. "Gotta get you to a medic, O'Reilly. What's your first name?"

"Timothy...don't laugh. It was me mother's father's name."

"After what you just did, Tim, there'll probably be a Saint Timothy."

O'Reilly tried to smile, but the adrenalin had stopped injecting into his blood. He went white and slack, loosing consciousness, collapsing like a rag doll. Mark put a hand under each armpit and pulled him back to the trench. He threw his white sheet over O'Reilly. He stood hesitatingly, turning slowly toward where Pellini had been. He saw nothing. *Go there, see if he's alive. Take O'Reilly toward Bastogne. Which?*

His sergeant was one man. The whole company was in or near Bastogne without a leader. What if Pellini were alive and suffering? Mark's decision would be with him for the rest of his life. He knew that if he abandoned his company, he'd never be able to face his men again. He saw the photo of Mike's family and turned toward that dugout. But he recalled the oath he had taken to protect whatever command he was given. Redding's dying order had been to take the company. "Nothing's easy," he said to a comatose O'Reilly.

He worked O'Reilly up to a standing position. The pain in O'Reilly's leg brought the wounded soldier to consciousness. "What...what...Lieut..."

"Gonna take you to a medic," he grunted as he hoisted O'Reilly's one-hundred-sixty pounds on his shoulder and started for Bastogne.

At first he staggered with the load. O'Reilly moaned as he floated in and out of consciousness. Finally, Mark found a position and a pace that allowed him to make a hundred yards...then rest, then another hundred, hard-won yards. With heavy panting and gritted teeth, he tried to play mind games to keep from buckling. He'd think back to his days at Harvard. Four years of chemistry, loved it,

straight A's: inorganic, organic, physical and the split year of bio and metallurgical. Not much chemistry here. Back there, old Professor Hines...*Ah, Mr. Abercrombie, what's the molecular weight of pain? Do you know the valence of diminishing hope, or the ph of dread: is it alkaline to corrode away the resolve of enlistment...or acidic to eat away one's guts? What is the atomic number of death? Is the temperature of frostbite expressed in Fahrenheit or Celsius? And, the big one: is fear the catalyst that completes the reversing equation of faith in an Almighty?*

"Hang on, Tim, we're gonna make it."

After ten minutes more of trudging, each step heavier than the one before, he fell with O'Reilly landing on top of him. As they hit, O'Reilly let out a shriek of pain. Mark took the Syrette of morphine from his first aid kit and put it in his mouth to thaw it from its near-frozen state. He opened the thin metal case with his thumbnail. He pushed the Syrette through O'Reilly's pants, with a quick jab into the muscle mass of his buttocks – the morphine, mercifully took effect a few moments later. *Can I get him up again?*

55

Mark looked around. He saw nothing except the disorienting white scene. *Which way? Gave the compass to McCormack.*

He tried to get his bearings, looking for the tracks he had just made. There were only a few that the wind had not covered with glittery snow crystals. With all the effort he could muster, he got O'Reilly up on his shoulder and started slogging westward. He staggered for a few more yards, before collapsing, out of breath and exhausted. *I don't think I can get him up again. Maybe we can just stay here. It's getting warmer, maybe just a little nap...just a little one.*

"Put your head in my lap, Mark," his mother said.

"Hey, Lieutenant, wake up...wake up."

He fought through filmy cobwebs. Was his mother getting him up to run that Catholic gauntlet again? No, it was a man's voice he heard. Where? Finally, his eyes opened. He saw a gaunt, unshaven face just a few inches away from his own. *Know this man...I'm sure I know him.* A light came on in his head...it was Sergeant McCormack rubbing his cheeks and hands. He was lifted onto a stretcher. On one next to him was the stocky Irishman wrapped in the white sheet he had worn on his crawl to First Platoon.

"Come on guys, let's get them to the aid station," McCormack barked at the four men who were lifting the two wounded soldiers – their heaving breaths vaporizing in the heavy damp air.

McCormack walked alongside. "Lieutenant, there wasn't any artillery to knock out that Kraut gun. The guns in Bastogne were down to two and three shells apiece, and they was savin' them for anti-tank firing if the Kraut tanks came at the town. We figured you and O'Reilly had bought it. I took a couple of guys up the path, saw you, and sent one back for the stretchers. And I sent Sutkowski up to see what happened. Said you knocked 'em to pieces."

"O'Reilly did. How is he?"

"He'll make it. He's tough. Eased off on the tourniquet... no bleeding."

"Get all the guys back?"

"Yeah...yes sir...all okay.   And, Lieutenant, we got a hot meal...beans, canned ham and peaches."

"Even Pellini...did we get him out?"

"I don't know, Lieutenant.   That's the guy that covered us from your dugout?"

"Yes." Mark's whole body felt flushed as he was back in the dugout, kneeling with his former aide and friend while he had made the sign of the cross over Mark. "No sign of him?"

"No sir."

"We have to find out...soon as we can." *Did I leave him to die for me, for the company? Dear God, please be merciful.*

"The town still in our hands?"

"Yes, sir.   Rumor is General Patton will be here any day...overheard a colonel tellin' a major."

"What time is it?"

"Eight.   Ya know Lieutenant, in four hours it'll be Christmas."

Christmas...the time of goodwill and peace to all men.   Guess the word didn't get from Jerusalem to the Ardennes.   Wise men went the wrong way.

The aid station was located in a church with a shell hole in the roof.   The 101st Airborne still held the town despite being totally surrounded by German SS and Panzer units.   The surgeon, weary from twenty-hour days of fixing wounded men, looked at Mark's foot. "Frostbite.   Might have to take a couple of toes Lieutenant...save the rest of the foot."

A corpsman put Mark out.   Two hours later he was swimming up from the deep pool of the anesthetic.   Dressed in his tuxedo, and his black high-top Keds, he was riding his bike to a Christmastime dance at Harvard.   Stephanie was there, saying, "It's good to meet you, Mark Abercrombie, Margery has told me so much about you." He looked up and wondered why there was a big hole in the roof and a lot of pews pushed against the wall.   He looked down the olive-drab blanket covering him from chin to sole. He saw his left foot sticking out from under it, bandaged in dirty white wraps. He tried to wiggle his toes but felt nothing.

He put his hand out and felt the stone floor, sticky from the offal of torn, battered and sick soldiers. His stretcher was on the ground in a row with at least twenty-five others. He smelled the sickly, sweet smell of disinfectant – vainly trying to overcome the pervasive, fetid smell of excrement, the result of wounded men who had lost control of their bowels. Bullets, shrapnel, fatigue, dysentery and fear were horrific, explosive cathartics. The odor was accompanied by the low bass mutations of moans, occasionally punctuated with the treble screams of acute suffering. Doctors and medics with blood-splattered aprons were moving between the stretchers. In the apse were two operating tables with generator-powered overhead lights. Under the surprisingly intact Rose Window, leaning against the wall, was the processional cross and a pile of bloody bandages at the base.

"You're lucky, Lieutenant. You'll walk again. A few more hours, and it might have meant an artificial foot."

"How soon, doctor?"

"Couple of days. It was the two outside piggies. Didn't have to go back into the foot."

"Would you know how the man who was brought in with me is...the one with the two slugs in his right thigh?"

"Thanks to whoever got him here, he'll be okay in a few weeks. Lost a lot of blood...without the tourniquet he'd have bled to death. The bullets missed the femur and the big nerve. Tore up the muscle ...made a graft. He'll walk too. Merry Christmas, Lieutenant."

Five years ago on Christmas he had phoned Stephanie after meeting her two days earlier at his club's dance. She had slipped a matchbook into his tuxedo pocket as she and her date left the dance...its terse directive inside, "Mark, call 653-7241 SB." Stephanie, he soon learned, was never shy about going after what she wanted. None of the matches in that paper book were ever struck, but they ignited his avid pursuit of Stephanie Elizabeth Braxton, daughter of Harvey Baynes Braxton, major shareholder and CEO of Braxton Chemicals, Inc. A year and a week later, they were married in Darien's Episcopal Church, the compromise between his Presbyterian roots and her Congregational ones. At the reception held at the Darien Country Club, there were three hundred guests, all in someone's social register or America's *Who's Who*. The Braxtons provided an array of food that sated the most blasé of palates, an extravaganza far from his blue-collar, South Boston roots. He wondered how many of the ladies' fine gowns his seamstress mother had made. It was easy to drift from his present surroundings to the comfort of his married life, couched in the luxury and social position of the Braxton realm.

He could still see the lavish Christmas decorations at Stephanie's house and grounds. But now over to his left, a private in the narthex had set up a two-foot, scraggly bush dotted with pieces of tin foil chaff, dropped by American bombers to fool German radar. The chaplain read a few Christmas prayers and gave a five-minute homily about the Christ child and His message of peace, concluding that the sacrifices of all those healing in this house of God were help-ing to bring that peace about. About half of the soldiers echoed *amen*. The general announced to all of the troops in Bastogne, that no matter how many Germans were "out there," his men would have a Christmas dinner. Thanks to the *Luftwaffe* being non-existent – their limited supply of aviation fuel having been spent in the first two days of the offensive – the skies were owned by the Americans. The C-47's droning overhead, dropped food, ammunition and sup-plies…manna from heaven for men deprived of everything, except the constant fear of being surrounded by the enemy. Everyone enjoyed a hot meal of turkey, cranberries, and some reconstituted mashed potatoes, served by smiling GIs and a few townspeople. One GI, wearing a Santa Claus hat, stood near the altar. "This is Christmas, Belgian style…ho, ho, ho," he said. Then he passed out chocolate bars and cigarettes.

Some of the wounded laughed, others let out a good-natured groan and an "oh, no." And some said silent prayers. Mark knew he was lucky to be alive. *Lucky...was Pellini unlucky? Am I here because of him...because of God's providence...why did I survive all of that out there?* He saw the altar cross, now in a corner covered with dust. Then he looked at all of the wounded. Weakly, he whispered, "Thank you, dear God."

In one of the transepts, a GI with a bandage over one eye was playing *Silent Night* on a harmonica, while a few weak, mostly off-key voices sang the words. Some of the perimeter guards, rotated off their posts, stopped in the church to see some of their buddies and said they had heard *Stille Nacht* from the enemy lines. Mark, never able to sing a note on key, hummed the tune, thinking, *I'm alive...it is a holy night, thank God.*

Later, coming out of one of his many naps, he saw the day fade outside. The only light in the church was the eerie glow cast by the generator-powered bulbs, creating dancing shadows over the stretcher-ridden wounded and the doctors bent over the operating tables. He was struck by the dedication of the doctors working hour after hour to save lives. Their tables were parallel to the altar...the table of the Lord. Both brought hope...the spiritual renewal of the altar and the life-saving work of the doctors on the wounded.

He awoke to the rumble of a heavy, mechanical clanking in the street. A corporal ran in the door shouting, "Hey, yaw'll, Patton's here! He done broke through the German lines. His whole damn army's come to save us." A cheer went up from all those able to yell. The Fourth Armored Division of General Patton's Third Army had marched and driven hundreds of miles, almost non-stop, to save the soldiers surrounded in Bastogne. They had blasted their way through the German ring around the town with tanks, howitzers, bazookas, and plenty of rifle fire from the rugged foot soldiers who slogged through snow and mud on roads and trails full of land mines, ruts, and quagmires.

He tried to wiggle the three remaining toes on his foot. They moved, and they hurt. The more he tried, the more he felt. He knew he would make it...but, what about Pellini? Was he still in the hole they had shared two days ago? Was he alive...wounded, maybe dead? *Gotta find out.* He knew he'd carry Mike's last words about nailing any Kraut that threatened him for the rest of his life. The family photo was etched in his brain. *Was it the mark of Cain?*

When the doctor stopped to check on him, all Mark wanted to know was when he might try to walk. The doctor told him the next day. The next twenty-four hours were the longest of his life. He drifted in and out of sleep, besieged by horrible dreams. He always came out of them in a sweat, sometimes with tears running down his cheeks.

Sergeant McCormack, now shaven, with some color in his cheeks, knelt by his stretcher. "How's it going, Lieutenant?"

"Pretty good, Sergeant...thanks to you."

"You saved us, Lieutenant, and all the guys know it."

"Anybody assign you to an outfit...give you a commander?"

"Not yet. Things are pretty disorganized. I hope you don't mind, I pulled the guys from First, Second, and Third Platoons together and told them about what you did."

"Yeah, I guess I lucked out getting across that strip." *Was Pellini as lucky?*

"I counted eighty heads."

"Only eighty? God, where are the rest?"

"Near as I can figure, Lieutenant, about forty between here and St. Vith, mostly there I 'spect, an' another thirty-five or so out there," he said pointing to the east. A guy in Second Platoon told me they took a direct mortar hit near those crossroads. If you hadn't come for us, we'd be out there too. Same with Third...when they saw us sneaking back, they did the same"

"Hear anything about Sergeant Pellini?"

"Not a thing."

"Where are the men?"

"In a school house on the west end of town. Got us a mobile stove and some real food...hot, too."

"Who's in command?"

"Ah...I guess I am, 'til you get back. I'm the highest rank...both lieutenants bought it at the crossroads. Talked to a Major Collins in the 101st. Told us to sit tight – said he'd get back to me soon. Supposed to stop and see you...said our outfit is on the other side of the Kraut's lines. We're in the circle with the 101st."

Mark felt he could trust this man. "Sergeant...oh hell, what's your first name?"

"Rufus, sir," he said with a grin as he looked at his feet. "But everybody calls me Buck."

"Buck, I got to get to the dugout where Pellini and I were. But, don't know if I can walk there or if the area's been cleared of Germans."

"I'll see if I can find out anything."

Just then a six-foot-tall major, with a ruddy face, easy gait and a smile approached Mark's stretcher. McCormack saluted and left. The major looked at the tag tied to Mark's jacket button. "Lieutenant, I'm Major Collins...glad to see you're making it. Heard about what you did...good stuff."

"Thank you, sir."

"I understand you were in command of a rifle company of the 7th Armored...at St. Vith, and then you were on the fringe of the encirclement. That correct?"

"Yes, sir. Captain Redding was killed on the retreat from St. Vith. His last words were for me to take the company. Some colonel from 12th Group put us on the perimeter of the town...must have been right on the edge of the spearhead. Things were pretty disorganized for a while."

"Lose a lot of men?"

"Yes, sir…at least half," Mark said slowly, as he reached into his inner pocket. "I have the captain's tags and several others from men in the company." He passed the tags to the major.

"I'll get these processed. I can't tell you today where to go. Not sure the road to 7th Armored has been cleared yet. We know the Germans have started to pull back in a couple of areas, but there's still a lot of shelling. And there's always the chance of a counter attack. It's only to the southeast that we can move out of town. Stay here and let the foot heal for a couple of days. Your sergeant has your group housed in a school…catching up on some sleep and meals. I'll check back tomorrow. Oh, by the way, you're in for a medal. You saved a lot of lives. The general wants to personally pin it on."

"You heard about Private O"Reilly's action with the Kraut machine gun?"

"Yep, he's up for a decoration too."

Decoration…how many guys deserved it more than Mark? How many bodies should have been dug up and had a star or cross pinned on them – all testimonies to the premise that some had to die so others might live?

That night when Sergeant McCormack came by, Mark got him to help him stand. He put his weight on the bandaged foot tentatively. It hurt, but he was able to stand unassisted. He managed a few steps accompanied by some ohs and ows.

"Sergeant…Buck, come back tomorrow morning and we'll see if we can get out of here. Find anything out about the area we vacated?"

"Yes, sir. It's been cleared by Third Army. General Patton stopped long enough to eat a meal, shake the general's hand and gas up. Then he said, 'There's still a lot of Germans out there to be killed or chased, and off they went."

"Will you help me check on Pellini?"

"Yes, sir."

The next morning, McCormack showed up with a cane and a bright face. The day was sunny and cloudless. Overhead, a couple dozen P-47's droned, like a flight of angry hornets, as they continually stung the retreating German forces. McCormack pointed to an idling half-track, its .50 caliber pointing benignly to the now friendly skies, the white star on its side nearly obliterated with mud. Mark looked at him quizzically.

McCormack's face broke into a wide grin as he said, "The driver's from Corbin just like me. We quit the mines together, enlisted together, but we ain't seen each other since Fort Campbell, until last night. He's gonna take us out there."

"Sergeant, you worked a miracle...thanks. Uh...has this been cleared?"

"Yep, it's been cleared. Tomlinson here got his captain six cases of good Belgian cognac."

"I see."

McCormack nodded and helped Mark into the right front seat. Corporal Tomlinson, his wide mouth tobacco-stained, his neck like that of an under-fed chicken, gave Mark a toothless grin, a silent acceptance speech of this officer that McCormack had praised.

"All set, Lieutenant?" he asked as he revved up the Chrysler engine, ground the gears and pulled into the line of tanks, trucks and half-tracks being marshaled by an arm-waving MP. They drove at five-miles-per-hour through the town, passing vacant shells of buildings in what was once a prosperous borough. Some were reduced to just one wall – a lonely sentinel for the lives and possessions buried beneath. He saw townspeople, intermingling with their olive-drab-clad 101st Airborne protectors. The road was a mire of melting snow, mud and the debris of war. The half-track groaned and crunched through it all, and finally passed the outskirts of Bastogne. Once free of the town, McCormack instinctively stood and grabbed the twin handles of the .50 caliber, swiveling it, his head and alert eyes in a wide arc. Mark directed Tomlinson to the area Able Company had covered.

"Stop here, Corporal," he suddenly said. McCormack helped

him down. He gingerly poked around with his cane as he limped in an ever-widening circle. He quit when his cane sank two feet into the snow.

"Bring the shovel," he barked.

Tomlinson lifted it from the rack on the rear of the track, came to the spot and started to shovel snow away from where Mark pointed. "Do it carefully," Mark said.

Slowly, Tomlinson skimmed layers of snow and mud from the ever-deepening hole. Mark held his breath. "Uh, oh," Tomlinson said as he stopped digging, "There's something here that ain't snow or dirt, Lieutenant."

Mark fell to his knees and started to scrape snow away from the hole like a dog digging for a place to hide a bone. He knew what he touched when he felt something soft. Something that was covered in cloth...cloth just like he was wearing. "Help me," he said. Together, they uncovered Pellini's stiff body. They saw the bullet hole in the center of his forehead. The blood around the wound was frozen. Empty .30 caliber shell casings were piled a foot deep, and empty ammo belts lay all around...Pellini's steady fire had kept the Germans from shooting at First Platoon.

Mark was transfixed, looking at his friend, his thoughts branding his conscience. At the sight of his former aide...a man who had become the friend that only shared combat can make. *Did I make him stay here to prove to myself that I could go to the others?* He was filled with remorse, the gnawing grab of sorrow, guilt and responsibility, and the humbling realization that no matter what decisions he made, they were never all right. Nothing was done without a price. His personal loss at Pellini's death overrode the logic of doing what was best for the whole, not the individual. His emotional pendulum swung between guilt and knowing that he had done what he thought was right at the time. His decision to go himself was one that came from a tortuous weighing of duty, personal loyalty and his belief that a leader should always be in front of his command...never asking anyone to do that which he would not do himself. He stared at Pellini's body, then at Sergeant McCormack who represented the surviving platoons. *Forgive me, God, but what did you feel when they crucified your Son, who died so that the rest of us might live?*

McCormack, standing close to Mark, sensed what his lieutenant was feeling, "It's a gall darn shame...Pellini was a good man...but, Lieutenant, we still got the whole company...least most of us that made it out of St. Vith."

"Yeah, Buck, the whole company...yeah." McCormack's words were a welcome balm for his hurting soul. Mark knew that no matter how much he commanded, or however objective and detached he was, he still wanted the approval of those he led. He looked straight into McCormack's dark eyes, "Thanks."

Mark clipped Pellini's tags, and retrieved his rosary, the photo, and his gold bar. Tomlinson and McCormack placed Pellini's body in the half-track. Tomlinson looked at Mark. "What's next, Lieutenant?"

"Back to town, please."

The three rode in silence, Mark began composing the letter to Pellini's wife. *What do you say to the widow of the man you left on death's doorstep?*

They saw that Pellini was buried, his grave marked with the standard white cross, just one more among thousands in the fields of Belgium. Maybe he should put Pellini in for a posthumous medal. He knew he wouldn't be here, nor many of his company if it hadn't been for Mike's distracting fire...the firing that cost him his life.

*　　　　*　　　　*

In January, Mark received an arm wound as he led his company, now back with 7th Armored, in the campaign to retake St. Vith. McCormack again helped him to an aid station.

This second injury sent him back to the States.

On a cloudy day, salted with sleet from the North Sea, he looked at Buck McCormack's weathered face, and saw some tears. McCormack shifted from foot to foot, then suddenly stepped in close to Mark and threw his arms around him, "Lieutenant, you're the best damn leader I ever had." Embarrassed, he jumped back. "I…I'm sorry."

Mark smiled, took a step toward McCormack, put a hand on each shoulder, squeezed and said, "And Buck, you're the best damn side-kick I ever had." Waving goodbye, he climbed into the waiting jeep, but kept looking back until Buck was out of sight. What he'd said to McCormack was true about Pellini, also a damn fine side-kick. He had the letter to Maria Pellini in his pocket. He'd have to post it soon…he couldn't put it off forever.

The captain of the *Leviathan* ordered the lines cast off from the Cherbourg pier, and soon had the troop ship, a converted liner, at full speed, steaming for New York. As Mark watched the trailing white water, churned by the ship's twin screws, he murmured a silent prayer of thanks. And to his right he saw a rusty old tramp steamer, the *La Mer*, holding in order for the *Leviathan* to clear the port. About twenty people were on the railing of the freighter waving to the GI's on the *Leviathan*. Mark smiled and waved.

"Seaman Jones, can you send a cablegram for me?"

"Yes, sir…just write it out."

"Thanks"

He noted the calendar over the telegraph key, March 20 – 1945. Tomorrow's the first day of spring…and his first day back in the States!

He started writing. *Hi Steph, my love Stop Landing New York tomorrow Stop*

CHAPTER THREE

*As full of spirit as the
month of May
and gorgeous as the sun
at midsummer*

William Shakespeare
Henry IV

"*Mademoiselle* Devereux, your papers seem to be in order. As a French citizen, you are permitted to return to France, but are you sure you want to go back at this time? The war is still going on."

Daphne Devereux looked over the bursar's head to the large poster-sized wall calendar, displaying a print of Delacroix's famous painting, *Revolution*, with its heroic, bare-breasted woman carrying a bayoneted-rifle and the tri-colors of the new Republic...March 7, 1945. She was moved by the spirit of the picture.

"Yes. My mother and I have been here on Martinique ever since the *Bosch* started the war. We have not heard from my father and others for five-and-one-half years. Now that the Germans have been pushed out of our homeland, it is time to return."

She smiled at the man behind the desk, "What time to board the ship?"

"At eight tomorrow morning...*La Mer* should arrive in Cherbourg on March 15th, if there are no delays. The town has been devastated, but the Americans have cleared the harbor. Be prepared for the ruins of the city...it will be rebuilt. *Bon Voyage, Mademoiselle* Devereux."

Daphne saw no need to correct her title to *Madame*, since legally she was not. She had met Pierre Sauval on her first day of art school at the Louvre. When her easel fell over, he set it upright for her and smiled over the top of it. She was immediately infatuated with his dancing blue eyes. After class, he helped her disassemble the easel, offered to carry her paint box, and told her she was the prettiest girl he had ever seen. She had feigned a scoff, but warmed every time he looked at her. They became a couple, sharing everything and ultimately Daphne's rooms. When they committed themselves to each other, he told her that with the threat of war he did not want her to be linked to him through any records. They were "married" in the eyes of God and themselves, and one never knew what an enemy would do to the families of soldiers. He said the rooms they shared on the left bank were a heaven on earth. Would a piece of paper make them any sweeter?

Maybe when she returned to France, and she and Pierre were united and married in a church, she could become *Madame* Sauval. Then and only then, would the cruel hand of loneliness, guilt, worry, and fear that had squeezed her heart these last five years be loosened. She could not exorcise the knowledge that she had lived as a married woman, but without the ceremony and blessing of the Catholic Church. Her indoctrination into church dogma had started at a very early age...it was something not easily compromised.

"*Merci.* We will board tomorrow."

Daphne returned to the waiting area of the departure lounge at the port of Fort-De-France on the western side of Martinique Island. She took her mother's hand, telling her of their scheduled departure. Often mistaken for sisters, both Dharma Devereux and Daphne were petite, dark-haired, and tanned to the color of roasted chestnuts. Arm in arm, they walked into the sunny brilliance of France's Caribbean jewel looking for a horse-pulled taxi to take them to their residence in the town of Le Robert.

There was much packing and preparation for their return to Rouen. Daphne's father had insisted, just four days before Hitler invaded Poland, they must be out of the country. Martinique was to be their safe haven for the unknown duration of the inevitable war. Raoul Devereux, a noted publisher, possessed a political astuteness

that foresaw the expansion-driven mania of Hitler and insisted that his wife and daughter be safe. His friend, Rene Marquis, in the ministry of transportation, arranged the passage on the only vessel scheduled to Martinique.

"The submarines of the *Bosch* I cannot predict, *Monsieur* Devereux, so may God go with them. As you must know, many ships have been sunk by the Nazi wolf packs."

Raoul, his face grim, reflecting the tension of both the moment and the times, said, "But I cannot have them here to be exploited or trampled by the Germans. Who knows how many bombs will be dropped?"

"*Monsieur* Devereux, you believe there will be war...soon?"

"Yes I do, Rene, I must do what I think is best for the ones I love. Yes, as you say, may God go with them."

The family's parting at the port of Cherbourg was a heart-wrenching scene of anguish, so many tears, and sighs. Dharma wailed that she would rather stay with Raoul and face anything than be torn from him. But he was adamant. A WWI veteran, he had been wounded at Verdun. That blood-drenched slaughterhouse, that became a historic monument to the blindness of both political and military leaders, had ingrained in him the horrors of war. Lucky to be alive, Raoul was determined to have his daughter and wife out of the country during the war. He knew the weapons of this war would be devastating. Many more civilians would be killed than previously. Masking his belief that his country would be occupied soon, he kept assuring his family that should things go well for the French army, they could return very soon.

He was ashamed of the inner bickering and lack of organization that existed between his country's political factions and the military. It had been written that since the Revolution of the eighteenth century, France's history had been characterized by political conflict, often settled with the guillotine. Early on, monarchists versus republicans: later, conservatives, socialists, Catholics, and anti-clerics all boiling in the crucible of human differences. Just a year before the war, some politicians had been for total disarmament as a prelude to negotiating with the Germans for a peaceful coexistence.

The leftists cited the German Naval Agreement that Chamberlain had struck in 1938 for Britain. The prime minister's words on his return from meeting with Hitler, "Peace in our times," blew for the British a bubble of short-lived and false security, soon burst by the lethal needle of the Nazi's invasion of Poland. Many battles of words, slanderous cartoons, even fistfights raged between the French leftist internationalists wanting to deal and the right-wing nationalists who wanted no part of submitting to the Nazi crowd. The current joke was, "Put two Frenchmen on an island, and shortly three political parties will emerge."

The smugness and naiveté of the "We're safe behind the Maginot Line" syndrome had ill-prepared his country for the juggernaut of Hitler's mechanized, *Blitzkrieg* war machine.

With a forced, half-smile on his face – the Greek player's on-again, off-again mask of joy – Raoul Devereux looked at the two most valuable beings in his life. "You must go. You are more precious than life itself to me. Do not fear, do not fret...we will meet when it is over...here or there," he said in compassionate firmness.

Dharma knew he would not yield to any further pleading to stay. She was familiar with Napoleon's Family Code, which entrenched into law the absolute power of the father to make all decisions concerning other members of the family. Besides, she adored him.

Wasn't it Raoul who had delivered her from poverty in her native Albania at the end of the last war? She might have starved or been killed without his help. Even though she was a fine arts graduate, there was little money to pay her to teach dancing or for her part-time appearances in the ballet. The post-World War I economy was geared more to the businesses of agriculture (corn, wheat, and tobacco) and industrial products (coal, chromium, and copper). There was little money for the arts.

Dharma called Raoul an angel of mercy, sent by the Lord Himself. It was a miracle that had brought him to Tirana, the capital of Albania, on a mission for the French Government, which was reestablishing a consulate there. When he seated himself next to her at the train station, the chemistry was instant. He later told her that her flashing black eyes would have lured the holiest of saints. Dharma loved the way he was wise and caring, never autocratic. The well-being of his wife and daughter was his highest priority.

Raoul's stoic calm lasted until the women reached the deck, just as the deep whistle sounded and the shore crew cast off the mooring lines. When Dharma and Daphne were no longer visible, he turned away, wracked with sobs he could no longer suppress. A few days later, his forecast was a reality; German Panzers, the *Wehrmacht*, and the feared SS moved into Poland on the heels of the non-stop, indiscriminate bombing of Polish border towns by scores of shrieking Stuka dive bombers. France and England immediately declared war on Germany.

Raoul knew he was too old for service. In the resignation of aged wisdom, he returned to his publishing house in Rouen wondering how long he would be able to operate the business. But he was determined to find some way he could serve France – no matter how menial or humble. Maybe Jacques Bonhomme could guide him. His friend's name denoted generic peasantry, which was a joke between them – he was anything but a peasant. He was a successful investor, property owner, and influential force in local provincial politics. He and Raoul had grown up together in Rouen.

At the *Cathedrale Notre-Dame*, on his way home, Raoul lit a candle and prayed to the Virgin Mary to look after his wife and daughter. Unbeknownst to him they were doing the same for him...in front of a small statue of the blessed Lady in their cramped quarters on board the freighter, now steaming at eighteen knots for Martinique.

His intuition about the occupation of his native France was quickly proved. Nine months after the invasion of Poland, Hitler's troops were goose-stepping through the *Arc de Triomphe*, while Mercedes command cars, swastika flags flying from both front fenders, motored smoothly down the *Champs-Elysees*. Soon, the Parisian sidewalk cafes were dotted with monocle-eyed German officers sipping French wine and making passes at French women. A few days later, the "little corporal" strutted into the railroad car at Compiegne where the Germans and the French under Marshal Foch negotiated the Armistice of November 1918, thereby ending "The Great War." That war had lasted four bloody years, but now, after only nine months of defensive resistance, the proud French were under the Nazi heel.

*   *   *

"Come, *Maman*, here is a taxi," Daphne called to her mother as the carriage stopped. Her face lit up with a bright and infectious smile, "Oh, *Maman*, we must go home and pack! Tomorrow we sail for home and Papa." She almost said Pierre, but caught herself...

she hadn't been able to share with her mother her relationship...maybe soon.

"Yes, we have much to go back to."

"And my school...it will be so grand to paint again. Oh, freedom again! *Viva la France!*" The two women chattered like magpies – French magpies as it were – during the hour-long ride to Le Robert. Dharma had quickly picked up French after marrying Raoul – she had a natural affinity for languages. Born in Rouen, Daphne knew only French, with smatterings of German and English. They planned what they would take, what they would leave, and what they would do when they found Raoul.

The small house they shared with Simone Abrail had been their home for more than five years. *Madame* Abrail was a widowed-refugee from war-torn, occupied France. Her husband, Alexandre, a captain in the French First Army, had been killed in a futile counter-attack near Cambri just a few weeks into the war. News from home was almost non-existent, but one ship had docked bringing newspapers that published casualty lists. Simone hid her grief by working ten-hour days in the one remaining sugar factory on the island. Sugar was the eighteenth-century business that boasted so many plantations. An insatiable thirst for the island's "white gold," harvested by slave labor, made Martinique a prosperous department of Mother France. In the nineteenth-century, producers on other islands developed cane fields forcing the once-lucrative plantations of Martinique to close, except for one.

Simone, a college graduate with a degree in philosophy, was now making sure that the correct number of kilos of refined *sucre* went into each bag. Daphne and her mother paid Simone one-hundred francs a week for room and board, drawn from the one-hundred-thousand francs Raoul Devereux had deposited in their name. Daphne had earned a little money sketching people in the market places and the few visitors from nearby islands. They had lived there for several weeks before Simone spoke about the death of her husband. They were the first people with whom she shared her loss.

"*La guerre…la guerre*, the futile works of men," Simone exclaimed later that night as they sipped a rare *café au lait* by candlelight. "It is only us women who know the true cost and foolishness of men's wars."

Dharma looked up, the flickering candle reflecting in her jet black eyes…the same sparkling black pearls she had passed on to Daphne. "And it seems we are to suffer one every twenty years. Will it ever cease?"

"Men run the world, what do you expect? They are always chasing their tails." Simone smiled sadly.

"*Oui*, Simone, first they chase the mammoth and mastodon with the club, then the *cheval*, and then each other with stone axes, spears, and arrows…then muskets and machine guns…and tanks and terrible bombs that kill innocent people…women, children, old men." Dharma threw her hands up. "Every year, more and more terrible things to kill…kill…kill. What next?"

Simone's eyes flashed as she began to speak with vigor. "There would be no people if it were not for us women. I ask: who gathers the crops, processes the food, succors the sick, bears and raises the children, and cleans up after men and their follies? Since the beginning, we have always been in the shadow of these fools who seem determined to kill each other…to destroy all that our nurturing has made possible."

A tear crept into the corner of her eye. "*Ah*, civilization itself was born of woman's womb and nursed by woman's toil. Wasn't our hope of salvation born of the Blessed Virgin?"

She made the sign of the cross. Then her shoulders seemed to sag under the weight of her suppressed grief. She realized she was alone in the world. She had known that Daphne and Dharma would return to France. Now she was faced with the harsh reality of their immediate departure.

Simone felt the bitter irony of being cast into solitude by another man's war. Her *joie de vivre* had been ended by a stray bullet from a nameless German. How many other lives had now been crushed by some goose-stepping, blond, blue-eyed youth who had sworn blind allegiance to a power-mad lunatic? By the late 1930's, the little World War I corporal, with the impotent moustache and chin, had mesmerized a nation of followers. The German people quickly became addicted to the rhetoric about a super race of pure Arians. The Nazi ethos, under Hitler, included the systematic genocide of a successful and cultured minority...the Jews. Hitler had created the "new religion" for the German people. Unfortunately, many intelligent and Christian people adopted this new credo...that eliminating the Jews would produce a better world and a better Germany. For good measure the *Fuhrer* threw in other *untermenschen* (sub-humans) such as gypsies, homosexuals, and Arabs.

"Is there a God who watches as we destroy each other?" Simone flicked the tear away and sighed...then sipped more coffee.

Daphne and Dharma sat in silence – they too had asked this question many times over the last year. And unspoken between them were the fear-laden doubts about Raoul's safety. But Daphne could not share her worry for Pierre, her husband-in-name-only. She had hidden her relationship with Pierre in her deepest inner being. They had heard nothing from either man since they had sailed from France.

They had repeatedly tried to get word from home and to send mail to Raoul. The postman seemed both amazed and mildly irritated. "*Madame*, do we address this letter to the German commandant of Rouen? Maybe the Gestapo *attaché*? *Mon Dieu!* It is hopeless, and who will carry the mail? We have learned the last boat with mail was torpedoed."

They left the post office fraught with frustration and sapped with powerlessness. Their hearts yearned to communicate, to let Raoul know they were safe...yet here was this old man, with a hoar-frost beard and a voice that whistled through the gaps in his teeth, telling them that nothing could be done. *"Damner...damner!"* Dharma exploded in a rare use of profanity, "How can we tell dear Raoul about us or find out how he is?"

They asked Simone if there was any way to contact their loved ones.

*"Non...*there is no oceanic cable and there is a curfew on any wireless transmission. Everywhere there is fear of spies. I wish I could help, but I can't. I hate those filthy *Bosch*!"

The next day they went to the French Governmental office, where they were told that if they addressed a letter to their husbands, and the Germans intercepted, it might be trouble. "But, *Mesdames...Mademoiselles*, whichever, this is an academic discussion...there are no ships to carry the mail if you did try to send a letter. I am sorry."

Maybe the official was right. And what if Raoul and Pierre were in *La Resistance*? In all probability they were in the occupied areas, rife with resistance saboteurs, hunted relentlessly by the Germans. Dharma bit her lip; she couldn't let Daphne see her fears, yet she couldn't stop the eruption of her fearful thoughts.

"I know my Raoul. He won't be satisfied to watch the *Bosche* absorb our country...our culture...our people. I just know he'll do something dangerous in his patriotism that is his very core. I have heard that if they are caught, the resistance fighters are tortured to reveal the names of their accomplices and then executed." Dharma shuddered as she fought to escape the mental image that forced its way into her mind. It was all too terrible to think or talk about. Her Raoul being executed...no, no, no!

Both women spent countless hours worrying about whether Raoul or Pierre were in the Resistance Movement. Daphne whispered nightly prayers for Pierre. On many nights she dreamed that he was on the end of a German bayonet or being run down by a German tank. Nightmares made her cry out and bolt upright in bed, drenched in tears and perspiration. Dharma would run to her bedside and try to comfort her. "Dear child, what is it? Tell me, please, tell me."

"Oh, *Maman*, a terrible nightmare…Pierre was being killed."

"Please, Daphne, try to forget. It is the separation…the not knowing. I understand what you suffer. Raoul is in my dreams…I worry so. We must have faith. Come to my bed…as you did when you were a little girl." In a short time, Daphne, now in her mother's arms, would go back to sleep.

Nothing they did, however, calmed the dull ache of anxiety. The life force on this beautiful island was dimmed by the hollowness of existing without their beloved mates; no matter how much they rationalized about having done the "right and safe thing," they would have rather been with Raoul and Pierre. And they knew that men felt differently – at least acted differently. Men always thought about protecting their women. In medieval times, they put their women in castle towers, while they rode off to battle. The syndrome was the same now for Dharma and Daphne, *sans* the castle.

Women dreamed about being with those they loved, regardless of the risk. Were not the columns of women camp followers with Napoleon's legions legendary? Daphne and Dharma were no exceptions; they both possessed the quiet, enduring courage women had always shown when tried. They had counted the minutes…the days…the years until they could return. Now that the Germans were pushed totally out of France, they booked passage on the first available ship, a rusty tramp steamer, scheduled to carry sugar and twenty passengers to France.

"Simone, we will miss you. You have been everything to us…a friend…like family…your home was our haven. Thank you."

With tears in her eyes, Simone reached out, "And you, Dharma…and dear Daphne, you *are* my family. I have wished to return with you, but what would I have there? Charles is gone…I have no other family. Here I am someone. *Oui*, someone…ha, a *sucre* checker. That's someone, *n'est pas?*"

"*Oui*, you are someone, Simone. You are an angel to us. You will be in our hearts forever. Who knows, maybe someday we will meet again...yes, here on beautiful Martinique. Now we must go to bed. We leave early tomorrow. Good night, our dear angel. Come Daphne."

They slept in the same bed that last night at Simone's. Daphne tossed for an hour before she got up and knelt by the bed, asking God to give them a safe trip home. "And, dear God, please protect Papa and Pierre."

As she slid back into bed, Dharma whispered, "Prayer will always help my beloved daughter. Better to sleep some, tomorrow is a big day."

*   *   *

They arrived at the dock two hours ahead of departure. Their ship, *La Mer*, its rusty side plates picking up the morning sun, gave off a golden glow. At least it looked golden to Daphne. This was her water chariot back to what she loved...her father, Pierre, her home-land, and her work at the *Louvre*...all that was in her future. When the boat was clear of the dock, she looked once more at her home and said to her mother, "I wonder if we will ever come to Martinique again?"

Dharma gazed with her. "Who knows, my child? The paths of life are like the corridors of a maze, we never know which ones we will walk. Perhaps one day, all of us will visit here, not for refuge, but for a time of joy."

It was on the second day of the voyage, as they crossed the twenty-fifth latitude, east of the Sargasso Sea, that a sleek, gray United States destroyer pulled within two-hundred yards of *La Mer*. Daphne and Dharma could not have known what the American captain signaled. A German submarine had been reported in the area. An announcement came over the address system, "This is

Captain Vergakis," he said in broken French, heavy with his Greek accent. "Everyone please take your lifeboat positions. Do not panic, do not be afraid. This is merely a precaution. The American destroyer is standing by us. Please move now!"

The davits, those curved cranes that held the lifeboats, were highest on the port side. Daphne and Dharma moved to the number three position. A seaman and twelve other passengers joined them in their lifeboat. Suddenly the sailor gasped, as he looked out from the ship. There were two bubble-churning metal "fish" headed for *La Mer. "Mon Dieu...mon Dieu...no...no*, he shrieked, folding his arms around his head. Daphne watched as one of the torpedoes hit right under where their lifeboat was. "Oh, God...Pierre...dear Jesus please...please." She cried, frozen in her seat, her eyes fixed on the torpedo. Seconds – that seemed like hours – passed, and no explosion. Daphne whispered, "God has put His hand between the torpedo and our boat."

A man in the boat said he saw the second torpedo pass a few feet to the stern. The seaman said, "Even the Germans can make duds...*merci, mon Dieu.*"

Every face in the lifeboat reflected relief...some with sighs, some with faint smiles, and others in disbelief. Daphne crossed herself. Her mother took her hand and pointed to the destroyer that was cutting hard a port. It started belching black smoke from its funnel, the wind carrying it like a protective shroud around *La Mer.* As the sooty carbon surrounded them, little black particles fell on them like rain. One passenger pointed to the stern of the destroyer. Large metal cylinders were being rolled from racks on the deck into the sea. Smaller ones were being shot over the sides into the air before descending below the surface of the gray-green Atlantic. As the smoke settled around them, they heard and felt dull booms under the surface of the water. Boom...boom....boom...twenty in all.

The smoke settled below deck level, bringing the destroyer into view again. It was circling in wide arcs. Suddenly, like an apparition, a large metal sea monster nosed up from the water. Everyone in the lifeboat gasped...was their ordeal not over? What was this new threat from the depths? The monster had a black swastika in a white circle on the side of its conning tower, and underneath: U-122. It leveled off, as the five-inch guns of the destroyer were pointed on a direct line to the submarine. The U-boat's conning tower opened and a man's head appeared, then his arm waving a white flag.

The destroyer approached the sub in a flanking movement, keeping the sub's deck gun forward of it and its torpedo tubes pointing away from the destroyer. The destroyer's captain was aware of booby traps and suicide bombs. With a powered megaphone, he told the German captain to bring all hands on deck and then put a live grenade down the barrel of his deck gun. The explosion rendered the gun inoperable. Daphne knew some German. She could hear the German captain say that he knew the war was almost over, and he didn't want to lose his men a few weeks from a cease fire. Would the American captain tow them to America? They were willing to surrender.

The American captain said he could not return them to America. He ordered the entire German crew to get into their rubber boats and come along side the destroyer's side. After all of them were imprisoned on the destroyer, three five-inch shells sank the U-boat. Captain Vergakis told all of the passengers to return to their normal quarters. The destroyer sailed parallel to *La Mer* for a hundred miles, then with a display of signal flags and three blasts of her whistle, turned westward.

Daphne, Dharma, and all aboard gathered in the dining room. They chattered nervously about the close call they had just survived. And they wondered if there would be other German U-boats. A Catholic priest who was part of the group led them in a prayer of thankfulness. In her own private prayer, Daphne asked God to spare them. "Dear Lord, we have waited so long, please let us finish this journey. I will be your servant…to do whatever you bid me to do… for the rest of my life, however long that may be. Amen."

She remembered when, at age sixteen, she had wanted to be a nun. She had been so deeply impressed with the life of Catherine of Siena, the first of only two women to receive the title of doctor in the Roman Catholic Church, that she wanted to follow in her hallowed footsteps. Catherine, one of twenty-five children, was nevertheless born of an independence that always sought the truth.

To carry out her zeal to serve her fellow man, Catherine had attached herself to a tertiary of the Dominican Order. There she tended the needs of the sick and the poor. Between 1375 and 1377, she dedicated her depleting energies to two causes dear to her: a crusade, or more of a pilgrimage to the Holy Land, and the restoration of peace in the church. She wrote almost 400 letters to encourage this, as well as the summation of her life's work in the *Dialog*, which concluded the desire of her soul: "…The more I enter you, the more I discover, and the more I discover, the more I seek you…" Like her Savior, Catherine died in her early thirties.

Pierre's entrance into Daphne's life had convinced her that she was better off not being in a convent. The love they shared erased any lingering thoughts she might have had about being a nun. She also was touched by the delicate, but convincing manner in which Raoul, and particularly Dharma, had been able to persuade her to rethink her desire. They said that her many talents and inner faith could be spread farther in a non-cloistered environment. But, they never quenched the embers of desire to help and serve that were encoded in her genes and fanned to a flame by the inspiration of Catherine of Siena.

Standing on the deck with her mother, and looking out at the vast spread of blue-gray water, Daphne said, "I wonder if I will ever want to sail again; there is only the one color to it all. The rest of nature comes from God's palette in many tones. Oh, to see our beautiful Normandy again: green shrubs and flowers, the neat rows of trees in the apple orchards, their red fruit waiting to be plucked then pressed into France's sought-after Calvados brandy. And, I want to finish my training at the *Louvre*. It was so wonderful learning about all of the world's great painters...maybe someday I will paint a little bit like one of them."

"It was good that you were able to keep practicing by doing the sketches at the hotels. My child, you can achieve whatever you set your heart on. God has blessed you with beauty and a keen mind. Yes, my dear Daphne, the angels have kissed you. You have the ability to bring to life, on the paper or the canvas, what you see. Your pictures give off the light of all that is good within you."

Daphne smiled and kissed her mother on the cheek. "Maman, you make me feel good. I pray I can serve with my life...my talents after all, they came from God."

"Oui, all comes from God," Dharma smiled too. "My Raoul certainly did. He was my earthly savior." Her face grew serious, "Oh, Daphne, we must find him...and Pierre too. Please tell me more about him...about you and him."

Daphne had shared very little about Pierre, but Dharma in her wisdom had never pried. She knew the value of letting loved ones find their own way, with maybe just an occasional nudge. Wasn't that how God handled all of us? Yet, she also sensed a dark cloud hanging somewhere over Daphne's relationship...what was it? She knew that Pierre and Daphne had met at the *Louvre*, and that they lived together, but the depth of their relationship she really did not know. Her mother's instincts told her that it was a deep relationship; it also told her that Daphne held a painful piece of that union in her inner self. A mother knows when her child is not whole...when she has sublimated something she cannot share with anyone...not even her own mother.

"Look *Maman*, see the porpoises chasing each other."

"*Oui* my dear, just like us people...always chasing after something." Then, as a shadow passed over her face, "May God be merciful when we begin our chase to find Raoul and Pierre."

"Yes, *Maman*, yes may He," Daphne said. Suddenly she was racked with sobs, tears running down her cheeks in a steady stream – the expulsion of pent-up worry suppressed for over five years.

Dharma jumped to her side and took her beloved daughter into her arms. "What...my child...what? Please tell me. What is it that makes you cry out from the depths of your soul?" As Dharma hugged her daughter, she felt her tremble with a slight convulsion.

Daphne took a step back, turning her head to see her mother. The moon bathed her face, now the full countenance of a mature woman, lined with resolution...the resolve of forthcoming honesty and confession. Dharma sensed an aura of light from the lifting of a burden, carried too long. She whispered, "Tell me, child."

"Pierre and I met at the Louvre my first day there...we were in three classes together. He is so handsome...six-feet tall, black curly hair, and eyes that are the deepest blue." She sighed, remembering. "He was studying to be a graphic designer – perhaps work for an advertising agency for a few years; then, he would start his own firm. Maman, he was always so much fun to be with. We would study the paintings in the Louvre, and after class we'd take a little wine and some bread and cheese to a hillside. We would sketch what we saw...sometimes each other. Pierre and I would lie on the grass, looking at the sky and the passing clouds, and just talk until dark. It didn't matter what we did, it was all wonderful...all close and warm."

"You were in love. What you describe are the feelings of true love...of two people made for each other. Did you and Pierre think of marriage?"

Daphne's face brightened, "Oh, yes. One night he took me to a café...candlelight, Gypsy violin music, pheasant, and a white *Bordeaux*, as light as our hearts. After dinner, he gave me a ring and asked me to marry him. He told me his life began when he met me, and he would care for me as long as he lived."

"He must be a caring man...so romantic too. And...?"

Daphne's face turned to the soft sweetness that it had always been from her early days. "I took his hand and looked into those deep blue eyes, and said, 'yes, my Pierre...*mon cherie'.*"

"Why didn't you tell me and your father? Didn't you want us at your wedding? Daphne, dear, I'm hurt, You know we would approve of whomever you love."

"*Maman*, I'm sorry, but things didn't go as you are imagining."

"Pierre left you?"

"No, no." Daphne squeezed her mother's hand, secure in knowing that she could now tell her everything...relieved that her emotional gates that had been locked for years could now be opened. "The week after he proposed, he was notified that he would have to join the army in a few months. I don't know what you were hearing in Rouen, but in Paris, the talk of the streets and cafes was that there was going to be a war with the Germans, and soon. Pierre didn't want us to have any record of a marriage...anything that could tie me to him. He was very strong on this. He had a premonition that we would be invaded and maybe occupied. If the Germans found out that he was a soldier and had a wife, he wasn't sure I would be safe."

"I'm sure he was right. That is why Raoul sent us to Martinique."

"Pierre was always concerned about me...about my safety. It's just one of the things that make me love him so." Dharma reached over and touched Daphne's arm, then smiled as she saw her daughter's face glow with an inner beauty as she told of Pierre's love.

"You are blessed, my child...such true love."

"He told me of all the cruel things the Germans were doing to the Jews in Germany. Then, something he hadn't told me before...he said he was one-eighth Jewish. His great grandmother on his mother's side was a German Jew from Alsace-Lorraine. However, Pierre said he was raised as a Protestant; his father's family could be traced back to the Huguenots. He took me by the shoulders and very seriously said that if the Nazis occupied France, and found out that I was married to a part Jew, I'd be in serious trouble."

"Oh, *mon Dieu*, my darling Daphne, that's awful. You poor dear...such a terrible threat over your head! But I admire Pierre's honesty...and his protection of you. He is honorable. So, what did you do?"

"We tried to get a priest to marry us, but he wouldn't. He said he would be violating his vows to marry a Protestant to a Catholic girl, especially without a license. He said he would be adulterating a sacrament by condoning what was in effect a pretense to hide a 'common fornication'."

Daphne paused, trying to sense how her mother felt about what she had done, hoping she approved. Her mother's supportive nod gave her courage to continue. "So we knelt together in my rooms and asked God to bless our union. We promised Him we would marry when it was safe. I know in the eyes of the church we were committing a sin and were living in sin everyday from that date. *Maman*, I have sinned, but I loved him so, and if he went in the army and didn't come back, I would be hollow forever if we hadn't pledged our love...if I hadn't totally given myself to him."

Dharma heard her daughter with her heart and with her own deep beliefs about what God truly wanted. She spoke passionately now. "The rules of the church would say that you and Pierre had sinned, but my dear child, those rules were written by men...not God. They were written in their Diets of Worms, their Councils of Trent, and other male-only councils. These were meetings of men who never marry, never bear or rear children, or pay anything to raise all of the children that they say we women must keep bearing – as if we are good for nothing else! My child, marriage is made in the heart and in the soul. From what you have shared with me, you have a better marriage than many who walk down church aisles and then keep a mistress a few months later!" Dharma's eyes were flashing as she finished.

Her mother's zeal and acceptance of all that she had shared encouraged Daphne to share more. "Oh yes, *Maman*, Pierre and I agreed on almost everything. We would work at school, then come to our rooms, fix supper together, share beautiful music...or he'd read poetry to me. It was wonderful. On Saturdays, we would go to the market and meet our friends at a coffee house. We all laughed, jested with each other, and we shared our dreams." Once again Daphne stopped her cleansing narration. She turned her face fully toward he mother, searching for her approval. Dharma gave a slight nod.

"One day, Claude, our closest friend who was a writer, said his rotation had come up and that in a few days he would be leaving for the army. We knew this was an evil omen...that there would be a war. From that day on, Pierre and I had a ghost living with us...the possibility that he would be called. This is when we had our only disagreement. I wanted a child, he said no. He said if the worst happened, he didn't want to be responsible for putting a fatherless child into a country torn up by war or ruled by barbarians."

"You agreed with him?"

Daphne turned away from her mother, her face passing out of the moonlight into the shadows, where she murmured in a barely audible hoarseness, "This is when I committed another grievous sin." She stopped as another spell of deep sobbing shook her. Dharma said nothing, letting her distraught daughter collect herself. After a moment, she reached out and stroked Daphne's ebony hair.

"Tell me, my love."

"I cheated on the after procedure. I didn't tell Pierre." Taking her mother's hand from her head, she kissed it and continued. "I conceived, but in the third month, before I showed, Pierre was called into the army. He was put on the Maginot Line. I was torn apart. For days after he left, I didn't eat. I stayed home from school. I would just sit and stare at our bed and our little collection of his favorite poems. Every time I heard the word Maginot, I saw Pierre in those deep tunnels...like a mole in the ground. What if the Germans bombed them and he was buried alive? I know I was so tense from worry that I caused something terrible to happen!"

"What terrible thing, my dear child? Why didn't you call us? We would have come immediately from Rouen." Dharma's face reflected sudden confusion. "But, where is the baby?"

"He's gone!" Daphne shrieked as she sank to her knees, clutching the ship's railing. Her whole body shook as she let go of the years of shame and sadness.

Dharma waited again, then once again reached out to her daughter. "You lost the baby...you miscarried?"

Daphne stood up, clutching the railing for support, her legs trembling, her breath in short pants. She looked at her mother with a blank face and said in a wooden monotone, "Yes, at three months...just two weeks after Pierre left. It would have been a boy." Her face suddenly grimaced with a look of fright. *"Maman*, do you think that he is in purgatory because he was born out of wedlock?"

"Jo! Ai ne Qiell" (No! He is in Heaven). Dharma's emotion was so strong at the injustice that had warped her daughter into a guilt-ridden shell of herself, she unknowingly slipped back into her native Albanian tongue. "The baby is innocent...as you and Pierre are. You have done nothing wrong in the greater moral law. Your motives and actions were pure, my poor loveable daughter. And you went through this hell alone?"

"Yes...except for my friend, Francis. She helped me, nursed me, fed me, listened to me...she was an angel. She called a doctor to our rooms. He said I was physically healed, but that before I considered another pregnancy, I should have an examination, just to be certain I would be able to conceive without risk. When we return to France I will do this. Will you go with me, *Maman*?"

"Of course, my dove. But, why...why did you keep all of this to yourself all these years? You didn't feel you could trust me to understand?"

"I was ashamed. I didn't want to make you a part of my sins."

Dharma's cheeks became flushed, her black eyes flashed; her words were like the staccato of a machine gun. "Bah! What sins? You *have not* sinned, my daughter! What is your crime…to love an honorable man…to want a child…to want to protect your mother…to obey your father? I say, bah again, to all that made you feel as you did."

Catching her breath after her short diatribe about the church, she walked a few steps from Daphne, then turned toward her. "Those are false codes. You followed the true codes of goodness, those of a loving God. Daphne, look at me…and at our misguided world straight in the face. We will find Pierre; then you can live out your dream. I curse myself for not reaching out to you and helping you to clear your soul."

She pulled Daphne to her breast, "Never…never…never say, I've sinned!" Leaning back and smiling at her daughter, she said, "Everything about you is the best, even your over-working conscience…a conscience that even a saint would find a heavy load!"

Daphne just stood looking at her mother; then a tentative smile came. "*Maman*, thank you. I'm sorry I didn't confide in you sooner. I still have so much to learn. Oh, I hope we can be with Papa and Pierre soon. I know you will love Pierre. You are so wonderful. I love you so much." She hesitated briefly. "Do you still love me after all that I have told you?"

"My child, from the moment I felt you in my womb I knew you would be a joy to your father and me and a servant of our Lord. I just felt that you would be a doer of meaningful things. I wish Leonardo Da Vinci would have painted me while I was carrying you – maybe then, I would be hanging in the *Louvre*!"

They laughed together. For Daphne it was the first truly happy laugh that she had enjoyed since she left France. "The Blessed Virgin could not have reflected any greater inner happiness than what I felt."

Dharma grew very serious. "You will bring good to whomever you touch. I feel the Holy Spirit is in you. After all that you just shared with me, I love you even more…if that's possible."

"Thank you, *Maman*."

"Come child, let's go to our cabin. We can prepare for the dinner party the captain's throwing tonight. He wants us to celebrate our arrival in Cherbourg tomorrow."

The captain's dinner party was attended by twenty passengers, the captain, and four of his top staff. It didn't take long for Dharma to establish that both she and Captain Vergakis shared an Eastern Orthodox religious upbringing. She had become a perfunctory Roman Catholic when she married Raoul, but had never accepted the infallibility of the Pope or the rule of celibacy. She had come from a small pocket of non-Islamic Albania, where Greeks had migrated. The daughter of a local storekeeper, she grew up with both Albanian and Greek children. Her village was in the north, where the Greg portion of the population lived. The Tosks were in the south. Dharma, a college graduate, could speak fluent Albanian (Greg dialect), Greek, French, and smatterings of English, as from the British Isles, not America.

As they prepared for bed that night, Daphne sat on the edge of her mother's cot. "*Maman,* thank you for making me whole again. Whatever we face from here on out, I will always be strong…you have made me that way."

"My child, it is you who have made yourself strong…and the Holy Spirit that I see residing in you. But, Daphne dear, we will need all of the strength we can muster. There are going to be severe challenges ahead. With God's blessing, we will face them together…now good night, my sweet."

The next morning, just eight hours from Cherbourg, Daphne had a spring in her step as she walked the length of the ship. Her mother teased, "Daphne, you are like a reborn child; do your feet even touch the ground as you walk?"

"Yes, yes, my dear mother. Only eight more hours," she exclaimed, and began to hum a melody, interspersing it with an occasional English word or phrase.

"What a lovely tune...where did you hear it...what does it say?"

"When I was sketching at the small hotel in *Le Carbet*, I met an American lady who was teaching English in the local school. She had brought a record and the sheet music for this song written by the American, M*onsieur* Cole Porter. It's called *Begin the Beguine*."

"*Beguine*, what is that?"

"It's a native dance that was originated on Martinique in the 1700's. I saw a dozen creoles dance it one night at the hotel in *Fort-de-France*. They were dressed in very colorful costumes! It was so exciting. She asked me to sketch her, and while I was doing it, she asked me if I liked the song. I told her that I liked it very much...it is so romantic."

Dharma smiled, happy to see her daughter so animated after all that she had suffered...after all that she had gone through in relating her long pent-up tragedies. "You liked this woman?"

"Oh, yes. She shared so much with me. Her French was very good...particularly for an American. She had met *Monsieur* Porter at his family's home in a place called Indiana. She asked me if I wanted to hear how he came to write the song."

Dharma again smiled. She hadn't heard her daughter talk so enthusiastically or so consistently since she had gone to Paris and school at the *Louvre*. She wanted to keep her talking and extend this joyful mood. "And, did the lady tell you the story of *Begin the...the, Beguine?*"

"Yes, *Maman*. Do you really want me to tell you this amazing story?"

"Yes. Anything that is as romantic as you say, and can excite you as it seems to have, will make me happy. Please tell me." Dharma knew it was good for Daphne to keep talking...to keep her mind filled with music, romance...beautiful thoughts. Hopefully, her revealing of all the sadness she had endured would make her whole again. Damn the Germans, damn the church. "I'm listening, dear."

"The lady said that *Monsieur* Porter got the idea for the song in France, not too far from our Rouen, during the Great War. Even though he was an American, he volunteered early in the war as a French army lieutenant, just like Papa. While he was in bivouac, some Zouave infantry from Algeria were doing a similar dance to the beat of a skin-covered drum. The pattern of the beat kept repeating in *Monsieur* Porter's head. The story is that he had just started to make some musical notes, hoping to catch the Zouave's beat, when a German shell exploded near him, wounding him. Many years later, as a very successful composer of musical shows, he wrote this song. He had carried the rhythm in his head for two decades! Oh *Maman*, the words are beautiful...romantic... I hope that someday Pierre and I can walk on the beach at Martinique and live the words of this song."

"I hope so. I'm glad that your heart is again light...that it sings of romance and love."

"Look, *Maman*; we're rounding the Brittany Peninsula. We're almost home!" Daphne was interrupted by the crackling of the public address system.

"Ladies and gentleman, this is Captain Vergakis. We are approaching the Cherbourg harbor. If you will go to the port rails, you will see a ship crossing in front of us. We have been asked to hold for that ship. It is a troop ship carrying American soldiers home. All of them have seen combat in freeing your native land...many are wounded. Please wave to these brave men. I will blow a whistle salute. As your captain, I bid you God speed, and I am grateful we made it to port safely."

"*Maman*, we are home! Let's go to the rail!"

The troop ship was still under control of the harbor's tug that was nudging it clear of the dock and into the channel. Daphne's eyes widened at all of the olive-drab dressed men hanging on the rails of three decks. She could see white bandages everywhere: on arms, faces, chests, legs. When the captain blew the whistle, many of the Americans waved and blew kisses. Daphne saw the ship's name come into view, *Leviathan*. She waved and saw at least a thousand of the soldiers wave back. *"Vive le GI!"* she shouted.

*   *   *

Near the stern of the third deck of the *Leviathan*, First Lieutenant Mark Abercrombie saw the rusty old freighter. He peered at the ship, saying to the man next to him, "Where did that old bucket of bolts come from? Wonder who's on it?"

About fifteen to twenty people were on the one railing of the freighter's superstructure, probably half women and half men. Seeing several of them wave and throw kisses, he did the same. *Maybe they're going to their native home, like I'm going to mine. I pray I never have to travel to theirs again with a rifle, leading men to their deaths.*

*   *   *

With very little baggage, Dharma and Daphne cleared the hastily set up and disorganized customs procedure quickly. Cherbourg had been liberated from German occupation for only a few months. Very few functions were running smoothly under the beginning pains of the French taking hold of their land again. The Germans had literally shut many things down or controlled them with an iron fist. The French were just picking up the shreds of what was once their comfortable city. Daphne and her mother stopped in the doorway of the terminal, suddenly wondering what they would do next. There was no one to meet them. Where would they go…to Rouen? Yes, but how? In their zeal to return to France, they hadn't planned the micro moves of their trip. The first five-thousand miles were behind them...but what of the next fifty...or even the next few steps?

They walked out into afternoon sun, horrified at the destroyed buildings that seemed to be in every direction. They took one another's hand.

"Daphne, we are lost...we are home...but we are lost...we are alone. Your father didn't answer the cable we sent from the ship yesterday. He isn't here! Do you see him?" As Dharma cried out in near hysteria, she felt a large knot in her stomach, causing her breathing to become labored. "I have a terrible feeling."

"*Maman*, maybe he didn't receive the cable. Where did you send it?"

"To our home...where could I send it?"

"He might have had to live somewhere else...you know, the Germans."

"We must get to Rouen as fast as we can. We still have some of the money he deposited for us. If there are no trains, we will hire a car. We must start there."

For a solid week, the women went from bureau to bureau – all were disorganized – each passing them off to some other office, as they tried to obtain permission to travel through zones now under American military control. As each frustrating day wore on, Dharma had to steel herself to keep from breaking down. She knew she had to be brave, not only for herself, but so that Daphne did not get discouraged. Despite the hopelessness that was growing within her, she pulled strength from that bottomless well of courage mothers always seem to have when their offspring are threatened.

Daphne sensed that her mother was tiring, not only physically, but emotionally as well. Stepping forward at one office, she boldly asked the French official if he thought that the Americans might be able to help them get to Rouen. His face became flushed, as he bristled at the implication, but fixed in Daphne's steady gaze, he saw the anxiety in both daughter and mother. These were countrymen...French citizens...he must help them. What matter who or how, as long as they were taken care of. He had lost his wife to a German shell four years earlier.

Compassionately suppressing his nationalistic pride, he said, "*Mademoiselle*, let me give you a note to the American colonel. Perhaps he will clear you to travel the roads that the Americans are *temporarily* controlling."

The American colonel in charge of the occupation of Cherbourg read the note dispassionately. At first, he was non-committal, listening attentively, but with no facial expression. After an hour and Daphne's impassioned plea, plus the effect of her flashing black eyes, the colonel smiled, knowing he was bending a rule. He secured a ride for them in an army six-by-six truck.

Seated on the bench seats that ran down each side of the truck, under a canvas cover, Dharma and Daphne were jostled along with seven American soldiers and their lieutenant, Stephen Parks. It was a bumpy ride, made passable by the politeness of the GI's, who shared their rations and water with them. The eight men, who hadn't held a woman in more than a year, couldn't help but stare at the two black-eyed beauties sitting with them. To their credit, there were no leers or suggestive comments. But, they sorely strained their eyes and conjured up many mental fantasies.

The soldiers, after "liberating" some local *brioche* and red wine, shared it with the women. The driver, a corporal from New York with a trace of French ancestry, drove them to the street where their home was located. The lieutenant and three of the soldiers went into the house with them. No one was there. It was a mess of strewn papers, most of which had the official German swastika or the spread-winged eagle logo on the letterhead. Many windows were broken, and there were bullet holes in some of the door jambs and window sashes. "The Krauts must have used this place as an office before we drove them out. There was some pretty intense door-to-door skirmishing in this end of town," Lieutenant Parks said. "You can't stay here. Let me see if we can get you into a hotel, at least for a few days."

They drove through Rouen until they found a small two-story hotel, the only building on the block that wasn't damaged. As in Cherbourg, there were many bombed and shelled buildings – some half-standing, some leveled to a pile of rubble spewing into the shell-pocked streets. The lieutenant talked to the inn keeper, who at first indicated that they were full, until the lieutenant pulled his forty-five and moved toward the stairway, saying he was assigned to investigate all places that might be harboring German soldiers. "*Monsieur*, do you care if I bring my men in and we search your premises for Germans – you know, kicking doors in, maybe shooting through them?"

"There are no hated Germans here...*Mon Dieu*...no *Bosche*! I have two rooms for you."

"Fine...these two women, who are special guests of the American Army, will be thankful, as I will. I will mention your coop-eration in my report," he fibbed.

"It is my pleasure to have them. The first week of their stay will be our treat."

Daphne and Dharma were grateful to the soldiers. With a smile and half of a salute, Lieutenant Parks said he would check back in a few days to see if everything was as promised and if he could be of further help. He gave them a slight bow as he departed. Dharma smiled a little to see the adoration and longing in the eyes of this tall American when he looked at Daphne.

Once in their two-room suite, they collapsed on the beds. The strain of the trip, and the greater stress about Raoul, had exhausted them. They fell asleep until morning...ten hours later. "Let us go to the publishing house," Dharma said. "There is a taxi in front...the old Citron."

Raoul's publishing business was on the *Rue Des Bon Enfants*. There were severely damaged buildings, yet a few that were intact.

Bombs and shells could be capricious in what and whom they struck. After driving up and down the street three times they could not find the building. Daphne asked if her mother had the correct address.

"Yes, yes I do. I have been here many times before the war. It was two buildings away from that one with the sign hanging from its balcony. Now there is just rubble."

The driver had been silent from when Daphne and Dharma entered his cab. Many of the town's people, who were forced to serve both the occupying Germans and their own countrymen, learned quickly to follow the rule of silence. He had developed the discipline of listening without comment. One never knew who was friend or enemy. There were collaborators, spies, Nazis, and those who would sell anything or anybody for favor with the occupiers. But, as he studied their faces in his mirror, and listened to their voices, he sensed they were true patriots. They were sincerely looking for their family. He said a quiet Hail Mary, then told them that the building they sought had been set on fire by the Nazis.

Dharma cried out, "No…no…where is my Raoul?" For a moment she could not say more. She held her hand over her mouth until she became calmer. Then, through choking sobs, she asked the driver if he knew why.

"Because, and this is only gossip, an underground paper was being printed here. It was part of *La Resistance*."

"The owner, before the war, *Monsieur* Raoul Devereux…was he a part of *La Resistance*?"

"I do not know, *Madame*. These things were never discussed…no one used names."

Dharma remembered hearing what the Nazis did with people from the resistance movement. Had her Raoul been one of them? The thought of him being tortured by the SS was too evil. She pushed the terrifying idea from her head. She reached over to Daphne. Taking her hand, she murmured, "Daphne dear, hold on to me; there is nothing here. I fear the worst…where can Raoul be?"

"*Maman,* is there anywhere he might stay…with a friend, perhaps…since our home and now his building are both gone?"

Dharma grasped at this slim ray of hope, as someone drowning tries to stay afloat in a swallowing sea. Yes, perhaps he went to his friend's house.

"Driver, take us to the *Rue des Minimes, vite!*"

"What is there, *Maman?*"

"The home of his friend, Jacques Bonhomme…perhaps he can help us."

During the ride to Bonhomme's street, Dharma kept folding and unfolding her hands. Daphne patted her mother, trying to ease the mounting tension that was building in her. Dharma was chewing her bottom lip as they arrived at *Rue des Minimes.*

"I'm not sure of the number, but I will recognize the house. There, that is the one."

The taxi stopped in front of the finest house on the street. It appeared to be in excellent condition with flowers and shrubs surrounding a lawn of green grass. It was the antithesis of their own house: no damage, no bullet holes, and no broken windows. It stood as if there had never been a war.

With a strange look, the taxi driver asked, "Are you sure you want to go into *this* house?"

"Yes, it is where *Monsieur* Bonhomme lives, *n 'est-ce pas?*"

"I do not know the owner. I know there has been much talk about why it has never been damaged."

"Talk…what kind of talk? Who is doing this talking?"

"Many French people…that is all I know. I wish you good fortune in your search for your husband. I am sorry that I cannot be of more help."

"*Merci,* here is the twenty-five francs for your service. Come Daphne."

Three raps on the brass knocker, a minute's wait…no answer.

Three more knocks, another minute's wait, still no answer. Still more knocks before the door was opened slowly. "Yes, who do you wish to see?" A maid in a gray and white uniform asked.

"*Monsieur* Bonhomme. Tell him the Devereuxs are here. Tell him it is urgent that we see him."

"Please wait here, I will tell the master."

Another five minutes passed before a portly man, red-faced, balding, and slow and labored in his speech, appeared. "Why, my dears, I am sorry that you have been kept waiting, if only I had known it was you. Please come in. It is so good to see you. Where have you been these last few years?"

"Surely, Raoul told you that he sent us to Martinique for the duration of the war?"

"Oh yes, he did...certainly a noble and protective thing."

"Jacques, where is Raoul? What can you tell us about my husband...your friend?"

"Ah yes, Raoul. I am sorry to have to tell you that he is gone."

"Gone...what do you mean, gone?" Dharma gasped as she grabbed her stomach and sank onto the silk brocade-covered settee behind her.

Daphne jumped to her mother's side, trying to comfort her. "Gone where...how, *Monsieur* Bonhomme?"

"I am sorry to be the one to bring this horrible news to you. I know you are in shock. It was a very sad thing...his, ah...his execution."

"Execution! Why...by whom?"

"The Germans, of course."

"But why...what had he done?"

"Perhaps you didn't know. Your husband, your father, Daphne, was a...let us say, a brave worker in *La Resistance*. As you know, he published children's stories, a few text books, and bound works for the government before the *Bosche*. It was discovered that when he prepared to stop his presses at night, he ran off a newspaper for the underground organizations. He secreted the papers for distribution in certain designated text book boxes. It was two years ago, the German SS came and took him to their headquarters for interrogation. The next day they burned the building to the ground."

Dharma burst into tears. More than five long and lonely years of worry, in a brief moment of disclosure, everything she loved was wiped out with a single sentence. The two women sat mute. Their eyes, misty with tears, moved around the room, highly decorated with fine pieces of art, expensive furniture, and at least two servants scurrying about in the adjoining rooms. The contrast with their house was so severe that Dharma wondered why. Why had Bonhomme's house been so dramatically spared...so meticulously preserved? So many streets and houses in Rouen had been damaged, but not this one...why? Was it luck...or was it something else? Bonhomme was Raoul's lifelong friend, and yet he sat untouched in this obviously protected luxury. She knew that this wasn't right. But, how could a man Raoul loved and trusted be anything but a loyal Frenchman? Her instinct told her to be cautious... to proceed slowly.

"Wh...where is Raoul's body? Was he buried? Did he see a priest at all?"

"I don't want to tell you. Just let it go that he is gone to the next world. He was a good Catholic, he must be in heaven."

"Tell me, Jacques. I must know."

"No...well, I can sense that you won't have peace until you know. I am sorry to have to be the one to share this with you and Daphne. Raoul must have been tortured by the SS in an effort to find the names of other *Resistance* men and women. He was only half alive when they hung him in the square from a lamp post...an example to all the others who were in *La Resistance*."

Dharma didn't like this man. His telling of her beloved husband's torture and grisly death was too matter-of-fact. When the truth of what the fat man was saying hit her, she gasped, buried her head in her hands, and sobbed. "And I was not here with him... to comfort him, to work by his side. My God, why did this happen?"

"If you were here, Dharma you would be dead too, and Daphne as well."

As she heard his unimpassioned pronouncement about their deaths, she could see the street judges who stood in front of *la guillotine* after the *Bastille* had been stormed. Her intestines cramped at the thought of the merciless deaths that the Germans handed out; at the same time, she felt her loathing intensify for this two-faced toad who proposed to be a family friend. Again, she reached deep into her resolve to not let this beast see the wounds he had inflicted on her.

"How did the Germans find out about Raoul?"

At the question, Jacques Bonhomme looked away. Dharma's sharp eye spotted the beads of perspiration on his brow and upper lip. He started to speak, caught himself, looked up, then back down at his feet, "I don't know. Does anyone know how they get their information?"

"I see," Dharma said. Something was not right here. This was all too glib...too smooth. She remembered when she had lost a school girlfriend to pneumonia, she had cried for days. With controlled emotions, she baited him, "I thought a man of your influence would hear things."

Again, in his passive monotone, Bonhomme said, "My influence? It wasn't much in the occupation."

"Mmm," Dharma hissed, as she again took in all of the finery in *Monsieur* Bonhomme's rooms. Despite her horrified grief, she mustered up the stoicism of a proud lady. She wouldn't let the callousness of this questionable friend make her appear vulnerable.

"I thank you for telling us about Raoul's fate. It is a loss that can never be filled, never be accepted. Can you tell me where we might go to find out the whereabouts of other people?"

"I am sorry. I wish I could, but I am out of touch with the emerging government. Please let me know if there is anything that

I might do for you and Daphne otherwise. Now, I must leave for a previously scheduled appointment. May I help you to return to wherever you are staying?"

Hardly waiting for Dharma's head shake, Bonhomme hurried on. "So good to see you...sorry it was under such dreadful conditions. My maid will show you out. I really must go," he said as he wiped his forehead with a linen handkerchief while backing out of the room, red-faced and attempting to make a bow.

"Thank you, Jacques. We are fine. Good day."

When they had walked a hundred meters from Bonhomme's elegant home, Dharma almost fell, again clutching her stomach. Daphne grabbed her around the waist and under one arm. She led her mother to the street, where Dharma vomited, then almost choked as she dry-wretched repeatedly. She sat down on the curb, sobbing with her head in her folded arms. A few minutes later, a *Gendarme* and two American MP's, who were patrolling the area, stopped and asked Daphne what was wrong. She told them what they had just learned. The *Gendarme* asked where they had heard this. Daphne pointed to Bonhomme's house. Under his breath, in French, he muttered, "He should know."

One of the MP's used his walkie-talkie to call for a jeep. In a moment a jeep showed up with an MP flag on one front fender and an American flag on the other. The MP sergeant asked if they wanted to go to an aid station, which they declined. They wanted to return to the hotel, to be alone with their grief. It had been the worst day of their lives.

As they were being helped into the vehicle, a drape in the Bonhomme house was being pulled aside so that the owner could see what was happening on the street. The sight of the MP's jeep and the *Gendarme* gathered around Raoul's widow and his daughter caused him to blanch. He again wiped his forehead with his handkerchief. When they drove away, he went to his desk drawer, unlocked it, and took out an envelope tucked under a nine-millimeter

Luger pistol. The letter was addressed to Dharma. Bonhomme flipped it back and forth against his open palm wondering what he should do with this missal from the last communication he had had with Raoul Devereux. At a hurried meeting, Raoul had implored his life-long friend to give the letter to his wife if anything should ever happen to him. "Certainly, Raoul, certainly. But, you jest…what could ever happen to a fine person and citizen like you?" The next day the SS came for Raoul.

Back in their room, Daphne broke into tears. She had made herself stay calm while Dharma was absorbing the devastating news of her husband. Daphne knew if Raoul was killed by the Germans, what about her Pierre? Had he been *in La Resistance* too? She wanted to be strong for her mother…hadn't her mother been so understanding and supportive when she had told her about Pierre and the lost baby? But now her mind was flooded with all the good things she and her father had shared, from as early as she could remember, until the day he had unselfishly sent them to Martinique. As she cried, Dharma again became the calm and supportive one, holding Daphne in her arms.

The next day, Dharma decided they should go to church to pray for Raoul's soul and to ask for God's guidance in finding Pierre. They hired a taxi to take them to *Cathedrale Notre-Dame*, where they had worshipped most of their lives as a family. Dharma hoped Monsignor Desmonde was still there. He had married Dharma and Raoul, baptized Daphne, and conducted her First Communion. He had also heard their confessions…he was a true friend of the Devereuxs. When they entered the hallowed, world-renowned space, they genuflected and went to an alcove that contained a small altar beneath a statue of the Virgin Mary. The votive candles, flickering in their red glasses, cast their tiny shadows in a spiritual dance with each other. Dharma and Daphne lit one, knelt, crossed themselves, and prayed silently to the Blessed Mother.

After five minutes, their eyes red-rimmed from crying, they left the alcove and walked down the long aisle of the nave in search of Monsignor Desmonde. A curate directed them to his office. As they entered, a seventy-year-old man in a scarlet cape and skull cap slowly rose from his desk. "My dear Dharma, my dear Daphne, you are like two angels that have dropped from the heavens. Come closer...my tired eyes...please."

"Yes Monsignor...no, you are a Cardinal now?"

"Yes, the badge of fifty years with Mother Church. But, that is not important. It is good to welcome you back. Raoul told me of his plan to hide you away on Martinique until the Nazi plague was purged. Oh, forgive my crassness...I know of Raoul's fate. It was wicked...a dastardly deed...a mortal sin for his life to be taken as it was. But, let me tell you, he will be with our Lord. He did all that he could in his quiet courage to help rid us of the Nazi infestation. I have said several masses in his honor."

He didn't know what he could say to comfort these women, whom he had known for so many years. He knew the words of the Gospels, and those of his missal, but somehow they were good, but abstract when applied to an immediate suffering.

"I share your grief, Dharma and Daphne, Raoul was a true believer. I respected his loyalties to you, his family, and to his country. Please believe that he is with our Lord...what better place?"

Dharma knew Father Desmonde was trying to help them. He was so human...so much deeper than the dogma of his religion. Maybe he was right...Raoul in heaven put him beyond the suffering he must have endured during their separation, and his tortuous end.

"Thank you, Father...Cardinal...?"

"Father...we are family," his face attempting a smile.

Talking about Raoul to this servant of God made Dharma feel he was with them. "Did you see Raoul...did he attend mass? Did he talk about Daphne and me?"

"Yes, until a week before his execution. He was a faithful Christian, a good Catholic. And yes, he never failed to talk about when you would be reunited and when this horrible war would be over. He always asked me to pray for you. Whenever he left me, he would light a candle. I'm sure he was asking our Blessed Lady to protect you."

Dharma could see Raoul, dressed in his double-breasted suit, white shirt, and Paisley tie, kneeling in the alcove. "Did he ask you to tell us anything?"

The old priest's eyes went blank for a moment; then he said, "...Oh yes, he did. He said he had given his friend, Jacques Bonhomme, a letter that was to be given to you if anything happened to him. Yes, that's it. You must see *Monsieur* Bonhomme."

Dharma and Daphne both gasped in disbelief. Dharma's quick mind blocked out her grief as she thought back to what she had seen at Bonhomme's house, coupled with his detached and evasive manner. She had always been slow to anger, but what she had just heard inflamed her Albanian spirit of right and wrong. She hated anyone who wore the mask of falsehood.

"Thank you, Father. We will go to see about the letter."

They took their leave of Cardinal Desmonde politely, but expeditiously. On the street they hailed a taxi.

"To the *Rue Des Minimes, plaire! Vite rapidement!*"

CHAPTER FOUR

He who receives a benefit
with gratitude repays the first
installment

Lucius Annaeus Seneca
4 B.C. – A.D. 65

Stephanie swerved into the circular driveway leading to her parent's front entrance, rushing to get to the cablegram, now burning a hole in her pocket...in her mind. What would it say? Was he all right? She jammed on the brakes; and in her haste, forgot to depress the clutch. The station wagon lurched forward as the engine stalled. "Damn," she expelled as she rubbed her stomach, poked by the steering wheel. "Slow down, idiot, before you hurt yourself."

She jumped onto the paving stones, leaving the wagon's door open as she ran to the Braxton's huge oak door. Her mother, who had been pacing the front hall, pulled the door open. "Come in, dear...come in."

Stephanie pulled the cablegram from her blazer pocket. "Momma, let's open it."

"Perhaps you should sit down. You look distraught. I can understand. Oh, I hope it's good news."

"No, here goes. I've been stupid about this." She slid her index finger under the envelope flap and pulled out the crinkled sheet. She couldn't have read it any faster if she had taken a course in speed reading. Lillian stood at her side, one hand on Stephanie's free arm, her eyes focused on her daughter's face. She sighed as she saw a smile come over Stephanie's clear-complexion.

"He's all right...he's alive...he's well?"

"Yes! Yes! Momma, he'll be home tomorrow. Here read it."

Lillian lifted her reading glasses hanging on a chord around her neck. Adjusting them on her nose, she lifted the porous, yellow sheet with its cryptic message. She scanned before reading it slowly, aloud:

Cablegram USS Leviathan to Stephanie Abercrombie
20 March 1945 - 7:10
Hi Steph my love Stop Landing Brooklyn Naval Yard
tomorrow approx. 13:00 Stop Pier 53 the Leviathan Stop
Tell Mom and Dad Stop Can't wait to hold you Stop
Make reservation Waldorf bridal suite Stop
All my love Stop
Mark

"Oh, thank God, dear, he survived!"

"More than likely his luck in dodging German bullets. Funny, after our fight over his enlisting, he said he'd be as careful as he could...guess he was."

"Mmm...how does one be *careful* in war? I think God was with him."

"Does God only direct the bullets that kill Germans?"

"We don't know how many wondrous ways the Lord works in our lives."

Her mother's association of God with any matter of life and death took her back eleven years to the hospital bed where she watched her brother struggle for his last breaths. She hadn't felt the Almighty's presence in that sterile room.

"If, as you say, *God* was with Mark, I wonder why *God* wasn't with little innocent Daniel?"

Taken aback by her daughter's apparent doubt of God, a mode she had detected ever since Daniel died, Lillian exclaimed, "Oh, Stephanie, you shouldn't feel that way! There are many things we don't know the answer to. There are reasons for everything. Maybe we cannot always see or understand what they are, but I trust that someday we will know them if we are supposed to."

"Yeah, perhaps...we'll see.   I need to call the Waldorf."
Stephanie didn't feel like carrying it any further.

"If you have any trouble getting what you want – they say most
hotels are overbooked – I think your father knows someone there in
management."

"I'll see if I can get the reservations on my own," Stephanie said
with a flounce of her auburn hair. It never failed to annoy her when
it was intimated that she needed to depend on her dad for *anything*!

She was finally able to book three days in a deluxe suite at the
Waldorf, but only after she had told the clerk about Mark's military
service. Luckily, the clerk had a cousin in the 7th Armored. Harvey
Braxton entered the library and, noticing her on the phone, waved.
When she hung up, he said that Lillian had shared the good news.

Seeing the elation in his daughter's face, Harvey gave his
daughter a rare pat on the shoulder. "Honey, that's wonderful. You
and Mark enjoy your time in New York. When you come back to
Darien, we'll throw a little party for you. Time enough after that to
talk about Mark's role at Braxton. I'm sure he'll do us proud...good
man...ought to do well. In time...who knows?"

Stephanie grimaced inwardly at her father's patronizing,
male-only air, but she put on the smile of the grateful wife and daughter.
"That's good of you, Dad. I'm sure Mark will be pleased." Mark was
smart enough and certainly had the drive of over compensation...his
poor background and his determination to rise above it. Who knew
where they would both end up...maybe there was even a place for
little old *girl* Stephanie.

"Stephanie, when you go to the Waldorf, you just tell them that
you're my daughter and they'll charge it to my account. That's the
least I can do for you and Mark...enjoy it."

Suppressing her dislike of his patronage, she said, "Thank you,
but I don't know how Mark will go for it. He's funny about taking
from others...always wants to pay his own way."

"How long do think a lieutenant's pay is going to last at the Waldorf? Tell him it's a signing bonus or a delayed anniversary present from your mother and me. You've been married more than four years, right? I'm sure you can persuade him to accept a three-day hotel stay – you did a pretty good job of getting him to the altar."

"Harvey, shame on you! Mark courted Stephanie in a proper manner before proposing," Lillian exclaimed, her cheeks reddening at her husband's implication. Yet she had to concede that her daughter was never bashful about going after what she wanted.

"Tch, tch, dear, we all know it's the woman who captures the man. Look how you roped me in," he laughed. Before the two women could come back at him with their protestations, he asked, "You going to meet his ship, Steph?"

"You're kidding, of course," she said, not sure whether he was being funny or not.

"Yes, I was, honey. I'll bet you're counting every minute until he lands. How about spending the night? I'll have Andrew drive you to the yard, then take you and Mark to the Waldorf in comfort."

On guard about whether her father was trying to extend his control to Mark at this early stage of their marriage, she answered, "No, Dad, but I thank you for your thoughtfulness. It would probably be best if I drive...in case we want to do a little roaming around the city. Also, Mark and I may want the car to drive up to Boston. I'm sure we'll go to see his parents...whatever he wants to do."

"Your devotion is admirable – a real dutiful and supportive wife."

"Yes, just like Mom." She didn't say her next thought out loud, but it must have permeated the room – she's been your doormat for thirty years – somehow her tone had been picked up by her parents.

Lillian blushed and saw Harvey's jaw tighten a trace. But, his face quickly became controlled. A successful player in the competitive field of business, Harvey Braxton had learned to never show emotion, unless it was beneficial. Smoothly he asked, "I understand your desire for you and Mark to be on your own. But, why don't you stay for dinner and then spend the night? Haven't seen much of you lately…like to catch up on what's up…what you and Mark might plan when he's discharged…if you want to share any of that with your mother and me. You can leave as early in the morning as you like."

"Okay, Dad, that's nice. I'll stay. And, I'm starved…haven't eaten all day…too tense, excited, and *worried* about Mark's cablegram."

Lillian smiled. She was glad to see this amicability between her husband and daughter…something that was not always there. "I'll tell Maude to set your place. She'll be glad to see you and hear about Mark. She might even be able to whip up some of that shortcake that you and Harvey love. It'll be great seeing you across the table again. How about we all have a little toast to Mark's safe return? There's that fine old sherry we've been saving for a special day."

*   *   *

Stephanie went into her room and called Mark's mother. Joyce Abercrombie answered, "Why Stephanie dear, it's good to hear you. You've heard from Mark?"

"That's why I'm calling. He's safe and will be landing in New York tomorrow!"

"Thank God, he's all right. Oh, Stephanie, bless you for calling! I must tell John."

Stephanie could hear Mrs. Abercrombie's muffled sobs. What a sweet woman! Stephanie had come to love this unpretentious and kind person. She knew the Abercrombies were overwhelmed with the Braxton's holdings and position. But, she had worked hard at never conveying any patronage, only respect. Mark had been raised on an economic shoestring, but with a wealth of values. Despite all that she had, Stephanie felt a twinge of envy.

"Mother Abercrombie, Mark and I are going to spend a few days in New York, but then we'll come to Boston. I know he'll call you tomorrow when he lands. Oh, isn't it wonderful? He's home; he's safe!"

"Yes, dear, thank you. You and Mark enjoy getting to know each other again."

"Oh, we will. It's been so long. I love him so. Isn't it great that we can all be together again?"

"'Tis truly wonderful, Stephanie. Please tell him we love him and how grateful we are that he's home. Come see us as soon as you can." In her relief and joy, Joyce Abercrombie hung onto every word about her son. She admired the way her daughter-in-law thought to call her as soon as she had news of Mark. Class always tells, she thought. "You know, dear, God must have been with him. His uncle Mark, who he is named for, is buried in Flanders Field. He was also a lieutenant in World War I."

Whenever she talked with Mark's mother, Stephanie always sensed the undertone of faith that was rooted in her. She had to admit that Mrs. Abercrombie never wore her beliefs on her sleeve, but they were there in a strong, but gentle aura. Stephanie mused…she wondered – maybe there was something there. She couldn't buy it, yet she had to admire this wonderful woman with such a deep faith.

Stephanie had never heard about Mark's uncle. She recoiled when she felt the parallel with *her* Mark. He could have been in Flanders field too. "Yes, we have a lot to be thankful for," Stephanie said. She was glad that she was able to be a source of good news and joy to Joyce. She felt warm as she thought of what to say next. "Mother, in his last letter, he said to tell you he still has the Saint Christopher's medal that you gave him."

Joyce touched the small silver cross around her neck, feeling the peace and strength that it brought. That medal from her neighbor, Mrs. Kelly, must have brought that same strength to her son. "Bless him…and you too, Stephanie dear. I'm going to tell John right now. Goodbye dear."

When she hung up, Joyce Abercrombie sat on the same lumpy couch that six-year-old Mark had shared with them on Christmas Eve, 1924. She bent her head and said several prayers of thanksgiving. When she finished, she rose and put on the new warm coat Mark had given her, purchased with his first Braxton Chemical paycheck. She took a quarter from her purse and went to the streetcar stop in front of their apartment building. A stiff wind was blowing onshore from the Atlantic and across Boston Harbor, stirring up the debris in the gutter. A gamin-like newsboy was hawking the *Boston Globe*, rife with the newly released photos and descriptions of the liberated Nazi death camps. Joyce shuddered when she saw the emaciated, near-skeleton people in their striped rags. "Dear God, how can people do this to others?"

She boarded the cross town streetcar for the half-hour ride to the Acme Shoe Company and slid her diminutive, five-foot-three, hundred-pound body onto the oilcloth-covered bench seat, occupying less than half of it. She smiled at all of the times Mrs. Kelly had said, "Joyce, how did such a wisp as you bear such a big, strappin' son?" Mark had gotten her and John seats by the player's ramp for his final Harvard-Yale game. When he entered the field in his football gear, he did look like a giant…a *strappin'* giant at that.

Turning to look out of the dirty window, she saw her reflection. A few strands of hair – some blond, some gray – dangled from beneath her five-year-old hat. She tucked them back, and hummed softly the song John would often sing to her when she complained of turning gray… *Silver Threads Among The Gold.*

As the electric car clanked along, she thought about how blessed she and John were to have a son like Mark. He had always been a good boy, getting summer jobs to help with expenses and earning a full scholarship to Harvard. She just knew that God had something planned for Mark. Tears started to run down her cheeks…she saw him playing at the foot of her sewing machine with his soldiers. Now he had just escaped a deadly soldiers game where the bullets were real. "Thank you, dear God, for bringing him home."

The car stopped near the docks to pick up several fishermen, who had been out all night on their trawlers. Now that their catch was on ice, they were going home or to a corner gin mill for some drinks. Mark, when he was old enough, would ride his bike to the docks and get some fresh scrod (seafood catch right off dock) wrapped in newspaper and bring it home for their supper. One of the fishermen took a liking to Mark and often gave him a half dozen fish free. She was warmed by the thought of how many people were attached to Mark.

She pushed the signal buzzer, and a block later the car's steel wheels screeched to a stop, jolting her from her happy dreams. She descended the metal steps and stood looking at the Acme Shoe Company's brick building, with its stone *Established – 1843* façade over the front door.

John had worked at Acme Shoe for thirty years running a punch press that cut ten shoe soles with each hit. It was hard and dangerous work – he had lost two fingers. Eight hours a day he would swing a stack of five leather slabs, weighing fifty pounds. When he had a stack of ten on the press bed, he would carefully place the ruled die to maximize the number of soles from each slab. With the die in place, he engaged the planetary clutch of the three-ton press, making sure his hands were clear. As soon as the press completed its down stroke, it rose and he cleared the newly cut soles. He would cut a minimum of five-hundred an hour. Cutting more than that number earned him a piece-rate bonus. Many times during the Great Depression of the thirties he would go without lunch in order to earn a few extra dimes. With a greatly reduced demand for new shoes in America's economical crisis, he often would only get two days of work per week. The few extra cents he earned by driving himself beyond his quota helped put food on the table. In 1934 and 1935, without those few blood-earned cents, he would have had to go on welfare; something he swore he'd never do.

Despite their struggling through the depression, many nights having only potatoes and gravy for dinner, she never heard John complain. And, no matter how tired he was, he was rarely cross with either her or Mark. When he would wash at the kitchen sink, and wipe his muscular arms on the roller towel, she would see, not the shoe press operator, but a gentleman of the highest order. As an eight-year-old girl in her native England, a year before her family immigrated to the States, she had once seen a baron riding from his manor house in Sudbury. Complete with tweed jacket, matching knickers, and cap – he tipped his hat to her as he rode by on his fine horse. Many times during those hard years, she had pictured her John as that baron…he certainly would have equaled or bested that man in character and honesty. She knew her son Mark had many of his father's qualities.

It was noon; John would be in the lunch room. She went up to her husband of thirty years, kissed him on the cheek, and told him the news. John sank into a chair at the lunch table and cried. "Thank God, Joyce, thank God." Joyce told him almost every word of Stephanie's call. He said, "She's got class that one. No matter how much that family has, there's some good stuff in that girl. Mark's lucky she's his wife."

"She's lucky too. I pray that they have as good a marriage as you and I have…maybe some grandchildren. Stephanie said they would drive down to see us in just a few days. Now, they need to be together. He's been gone almost three years."

"You're right. They need to rebuild what they had before he went away." And as he said this, he started to cry again.

Clarence Murphy, his foreman, saw him crying and came over. When John told him why, he said, "Glory be." He told John to take a couple of days off when Mark came to Boston. "John, I'll punch ya in for the days you're off. It's the least I can do for your son that was fightin' the Krauts for all of us."

*   *   *

Mark Abercrombie descended to the second level below deck in the *Leviathan* and slowly made his way through the maze of swinging hammocks. The area smelled of sweat, the damp, musk of drying skivvies hanging from everywhere, and every other male odor that two-hundred men can emit. As an officer, he bunked in a row of hammocks that was only two-high, as opposed to the three- and four-high tiers of the enlisted men. He had opted for the top bunk, as the fellow below him was without one of his legs below the knee. Lieutenant Harold Brenner, a First Army artillery officer, had protested at first, but Mark insisted, even lying about being able to sleep better farther from the floor.

"Getting excited about tomorrow, Harold?"

"You bet, going to see my wife and our son. He's four…born a year before I shipped out. He won't know me, but Agnes has been showing him my picture…says he can say Daddy."

"Where you going to live, Harold…what's home?"

"Brooklyn…home of 'dem bums.' Can't wait to take David, that's our boy, to Ebbets Field…sit in the bleachers…eat hot dogs and see 'em play. I used to play for Erasmus Hall…second base."

"Played first at Boston Latin…at Harvard too. I'd like to shake your boy's hand when we dock. Hope to have a couple of kids myself someday."

"You'll never be sorry. Say, who's meeting you?"

"My wife…we were married four years ago. I was just thinking, been away the biggest part of our married life. We're lucky, pal, to be here…really lucky." He caught his breath as he saw Harold's crutches and the turned-under O.D. trouser leg.

With the sensitive perception of the handicapped, Harold said,

115

"Don't sweat it, Mark. I feel just like you…lucky. The doc says I can get an artificial leg and foot. You know, from just below the knee. He said that with the peg and some good rehab, I'd be able to do almost everything. Hell, I'll be playing softball in a year. My kid can run for me."

"What did you do before the war?"

"Sales…worked for a steel supply depot. You know, cut sheets, bars, rods, beams…anything out of steel. I covered New England, Jersey, and New York. How about you?"

"I was with my wife's family's company, Braxton Chemicals. Just started in a training program a few months before enlisting…got a lot to learn."

"Braxton, huh? Some of the mills we handle steel from use their coatings…rust inhibitors…pickling fluids. That's some sweet family you married into, buddy."

"Yeah, I guess so…a long way from the neighborhood I came from in South Boston."

"South Boston, huh, my family was poor too. My dad drove a street car. But, I'm going to bust my tail to make it in steel. There's gotta be a lot of it used for cars and building beams now the war's winding down. That's if we lick the Japs. Gonna go to night school at NYU and study business."

"Good program. How about giving me your address? Like to stay in touch?"

"Sure," he yawned. "Old sandman's getting me, Mark. See ya in the morning."

Mark hoisted himself up to the top hammock, settled into the permanent sag of the canvas, and thought about seeing Stephanie in another ten hours. What would she be like? What had their long separation done to her? Had she fooled around? That strong libido of hers was always there. No, she had too much pride and control. But he knew her urges. She initiated their love making just as many times as he did…never bashful about what she wanted. His mind drifted into pretty sweet stuff, remembering Steph this way. *Man was it good! Hell, stop it you fool! You'll get off just thinking about her...no salt peter in the food for weeks now. Hold on...just a few more hours...* As he dropped off to sleep he faintly heard the ship's bells – eight bongs – four a.m.

The next morning, after helping Harold up to the top deck, they ate – honest-to-God real eggs and pancakes – shaved, and showered. A walk to the starboard side of the ship brought the Statue of Liberty in view.

"That's the most beautiful sight I've ever seen," Harold said. "All my life in Brooklyn I looked at it, but not until today, did I really see it. What a great lady."

"Yes. Like I said, we're lucky to be standing here looking at her." Mark's tone changed, the lump in his throat affecting his speech. "There's a lot of guys in my company that won't be seeing her...too many...way too many."

"Same here."

*   *   *

Stephanie was up at five a.m., grabbed a cup of coffee, kissed Lillian goodbye, and drove to her apartment. She took a long time getting ready. She was going to be super clean and sweet. Might not be time to shower at the Waldorf...she'd better be ready...almost three years. God, it had been a long time! And the more she thought about their reunion, the more excited she became...a tingling went through her entire body, then a flush of blood to her face. Before dressing, she looked at her naked body in the full-length mirror on the back of the bathroom door. "Not bad, Lieutenant Abercrombie...it's yours for anything you want."

With a little-more-than-usual perfume, and a tight-fitting, navy blue sweater under her camel's hair suit coat, she hurriedly packed. The thin, lace-trimmed negligee she had worn on their wedding night was the first thing into the leather case. She also packed a bag with Mark's suit and shirts. Pushing a loose end of her auburn hair up, she found herself whistling *My Dreams Are Getting Better all the Time*. Throwing the two bags in the wagon, she headed for New York. Gas rationing had reduced the number of cars on the streets and avenues of Manhattan, so driving to the Battery was a breeze. She crossed the Brooklyn Bridge, the bridge that Roebling had built and paid for with his life, and headed for the Navy Yard.

Thinking about being with Mark in just a couple of hours made her smile. She started singing with the radio, now playing the Andrew Sister's rendition of the calypso Lucky Strike Hit Parade leader, *Rum and Coca-Cola*, with its punch line, "Wuking for the Yonkee Dollar." She hoped Mark would be working for the "Yankee Dollar" at Braxton. If he got a good salary, they could get that salt-box colonial in east Darien. She knew it was the only way he'd go for it. They had talked about a house before he enlisted, but he always said it would have to be when he was earning enough to qualify for a mortgage. She remembered his crisp words, "Honey, I appreciate all that you and your family want to do for us financially, but I'd rather pay off the bank's mortgage than a mortgage on my soul." Stubborn as a mule...but she had to admit he was his own man.

At the gate to the navy yard, she was stopped by a blue-clad, grizzled shore patrol petty officer with hash marks on his sleeve, wrist to elbow. He saluted Stephanie, holding up his other hand, commanding her to halt. He approached her wagon. She said "darn" to herself, then smiled as she looked into his steel-blue eyes. He put his hand on the window sill, "Can't go any farther, ma'am. You need to turn around."

Feigning a sigh, she looked demurely at him; then asked how she might be able to park her car close to the dock so that she could help her wounded husband into it. She'd endured almost three years without Mark, and here she was being held up by this man wearing a white helmet, leggings, and a billy club. "Sorry, ma'am.

There's a lot of folks that would like to park close...can't let everybody in."

Seeing the extended conversation, the Officer-of-the-Day came out of the guard shack. Stephanie guessed him to be twenty-two at the most; his single gold ensign's stripe might have been two months old. "What's up Petty Officer?"

"Lady wants to drive to the dock. Says her husband's wounded...needs to get close."

"I see. I'll handle it."

"Yes, *sir*!"

"Ma'am, tell me about your husband."

Stephanie explained that Mark was in the Battle of the Bulge and lied about the extreme difficulty he would have in walking long distances. She rolled her window all the way down and placed her hand lightly on the ensign's arm. Looking into his eyes, she told him of her long separation. Perhaps her perfume teased his nose, or maybe her smile and light caress moved him. He winked, patted her hand, jumped on the running board, and said, "Go where I direct you."

She parked fifty yards from the pier. The officer saluted her, "Good luck, ma'am." She got out and thanked him, then bussed his cheek, making it turn red. He gulped, "Hope all's well with your husband...and thanks." He turned, and walked away, lightly stroking that cheek.

Stephanie worked her way through a throng of people, all clustered around the area. She adroitly maneuvered her way to the edge of the pier. There was no ship moored, but she heard someone say that one had just been picked up by a tug and was close to docking.

Then she saw the huge, gray mass of metal being shepherded by a tug into its berth. What looked like thousands of vertical bodies, all in olive drab, lined the rails. The ship was blasting its whistle. The men were waving and shouting. Multi-colored confetti streamers linked ship and shore. Behind every railing on the ship was one giant sea of elated faces, all in the euphoria of relief and thankfulness. Standing on her tip toes, she waved, yelling in uncustomary abandon. Her heart was racing, her face aglow...a truly happy woman, shed of all sophistication and vestiges of control. Stephanie, the leader, the manipulator, and the driven woman, was absent from Pier 53 on that sunny, first day of spring 1945. In her place was a pure, uncomplicated female, longing to be held by her husband, to be one with him, fulfilled in every way. In that moment, her ambitions and her plans were forgotten...she was inured in the most basic of humanity's needs...to love and be loved.

After a half-hour, the *Leviathan's* lines were secure and two gang planks were lowered. Stephanie's breath came faster. At first no one descended the planks. Soon a steady stream of stretchers appeared carried carefully by men with red crosses on their arm bands.

Stephanie gasped, "Oh, no, he'll walk down. He never said anything about being a stretcher case. I know he'll walk down."

Next, the walking wounded – hundreds of men with crutches, men with faces bandaged, led by comrades, and men with an arm missing, or an arm in a sling, slowly inched down the walkway...still no Mark. Would she recognize him? Would he be the man she had said goodbye to almost three years ago? She remembered him the night they had met – tall, crispy black hair, manly face...as he smiled at her in his tuxedo. Was *that* man somewhere up there on one of those decks? Was he whole, in body and mind?

Up on the second deck, Mark and Harold strained to see their wives. Suddenly, Mark blurted, "That's her...there! The one in the camel's hair coat, just a foot from that last capstan."

Harold looked where Mark was pointing and said softly, "Wow. Is she a movie star?"

"No, but she could be. Thank God she hasn't said she had any such thoughts." And as he said this, he saw his parent's humble five-room flat, and he saw all that Stephanie's family had. Would she really be satisfied with a guy who was going to have to earn his way up the scale? Movie star, maybe someday president of Braxton Industries...his boss? *Have to make it big on my own...have too!* "See your wife, Harold?"

"Not yet, but she'll be here...and my boy too. Hey, looks like we can start toward the plank. They want me to go first," he said with a self-depreciating smile, adding "The crutches. Mark if we get lost, it's been great, and I would like to stay in touch."

Mark put his hand out to Harold, who shifted his crutches so that he could shake. When their hands met, there was a bond far deeper than the clasping. It went back to all that they had suffered in their respective areas. Mark thought of all of the men in his company who had died on the bloody snows of Belgium. He saw Captain Redding breathe his last breath as he had cradled him in his arms. He saw Pellini trying to talk him out of going for the German gun. He knew Harold had been there too. He dropped his hand and put his arms around Harold. "God saved us. There's got to be a reason why we made it."

"Yeah, Mark...gotta be a reason. You'll stay in touch?"

"You bet...got your address. We're in the Darien phone book. Maybe I'll see you and David at a Dodgers game. Maybe someday more than that."

Finally, after all of the wounded had been evacuated from the ship, Mark's turn came to start down the gangplank. He walked slowly, savoring the jubilation that was everywhere...in the crowd, in the faces of his fellow soldiers, even in the ship's crew. Step by step he walked down to the dock looking toward where he'd seen Stephanie. Then, in a magical moment, she turned as he looked right at her. For an instant, and for both of them, the earth stood still. All noise ceased, as they were alone in the vacuum of each other. The weight of the hours in a fox hole with Pellini dropped from him, as did the grief, moans, and smell of the Bastogne church hospital. She was here...he was alive... home...in one piece. He held the key to all the doors she wanted opened.

Mark gave her a big smile, a half wave. She ran toward him. He moved to her and then she noticed it – the slight limp.

"Oh, Mark, Mark, you're limping...oh...oh," she cried as she threw her arms around him. They held each other for several minutes, saying nothing, her perfume and the pressure of her body intoxicating him. Finally, he pushed her back just a little, so that he could kiss her. And as she kissed him, she felt tears running down his cheeks. "Oh, Mark, it's okay...I'm here...we're together...you're all right!"

Wiping tears of joy brought on by his realization that he was not going to face combat anymore, he said, "The limp's nothing, Steph, unless you'd be afraid to go to bed with a guy missing two little toes on his left foot...frostbite."

Believing he might have some sensitivity about his flaw, she reached out to him and said, "I'd love you if you had no toes." And then, with her eyes shinning and one eyebrow arched, "But, that's all... *everything* else is okay?"

"All here...nothing else is wrong."

"Great." Inwardly, she sighed, I got a whole man!

"I feel great," he smiled. And then he said in a somber tone, with a wistful look toward the stretchers lined up on the pier awaiting ambulances, "I'm lucky, Steph. I'm okay...thank God." Smiling again, he said, "I'm going to be even better now that I'm with you. I'm ready to start our life together. Did you get the reservations at the Waldorf?"

"You bet I did...a deluxe suite, three days! Oh, Mark, it'll be wonderful!"

She realized they were partially blocking the gangplank – the descending soldiers having to squeeze by them. She took his arm and started toward her station wagon. When they neared it, she stopped and turned to face him. With her appraising eye she saw the same handsome man she had married. She saw too that his face, and the soul behind it, had aged more than the chronological time they had been apart; his whole being displayed underlying stress. The innocence of the twenty-two-year-old Harvard halfback she had met at a Christmas dance was gone. Here, standing before her, was a mature Mark, whose soul and mind had been annealed in the fires of hell. She also saw the face of a man who would never be a little boy again. Would she be able to live with this person recast in the mold of near-death combat? Had his normal gentleness and devotion to her been sacrificed on the altar of Ares? Only time would tell. She would have to be patient and understanding. Her challenge would be to unlock the doors that held back the trauma of his last three years...to open his mind to all that they might share and to all that she might achieve.

"Hey, Babe, where are you?"

"Here. Just looking at you," she sighed. It's sure been a long time." She put her hands on his shoulders and gently squeezed them. "Yes, you really are here. Oh, Mark, there's so much to talk about...so much to plan for...can we go?"

"Yes, sure," he said gently removing her hands, and folding them in his own. Then he lifted her chin and gazed right into her heart through those sparkling eyes. "Steph, there are a lot of ways to talk...most of which are better said in the room."

"Are you propositioning me?" Her blush reflected her delight.

"How'd you guess?"

For a few moments they were both caught in the aura of their mutual regard, the wonder of the moment, the indescribable joy of her having her man back, of his being safe in her arms...away from pain, exhaustion, and killing. And, each had their unspoken question of how things would go between them. Would the elation of the present carry forward?

On the drive to the Waldorf, she told him about calling his mother. "Mark, I just love her." She brightened to a laugh. "Why not, she raised me one hell of a lover and husband!"

"Lover...what's that?" Mark was joking, but the truth was he was slightly on tilt – he couldn't believe he had lived without her for so long.

"That's what you're going to be very shortly!"

He was elated at her playfulness. "Well, if you think so," he teased. Suddenly he put his arm around her so tightly she almost hit a parked car.

She laughed. This was going to be perfect after all. "Hold on, Romeo, just a few more blocks."

As they approached the Waldorf's registration desk, the clerk stared unashamedly at Stephanie and Mark. Appearing before him was all that he fantasized about being and having. He adjusted the thick glasses to help his myopic sight take in this returning warrior and his modern-day Aphrodite. A 4-F because of his eyes, he had to be content to raise a twelve-by-twelve victory garden in the Bronx and work two nights a week at a Manhattan USO.

The man coming toward him was in an army officer's uniform, wearing the silver bars of a first lieutenant, the Distinguished Service Cross, and a Purple Heart. There were two rows of campaign ribbons on his left breast and the golden eagle of the USA on his hat. He walked with a slight limp, probably related to the Purple Heart, but he stood erectly, at least six-feet-two. The clerk sucked in his breath as he saw the wife...maybe the girl friend...too classy to be a one-night stand. She really had it: auburn hair, a figure to match or beat anything in Hollywood, and a face that could launch a thousand ships. God, he thought, how does one guy get it all?

Finally his reverie was broken. "A reservation for Abercrombie?" The lieutenant asked.

"Uh, yes sir," he stuttered. "Yep, here it is: three days in a deluxe suite, all prepaid."

"Prepaid! Are you certain? Who?"

The clerk ran his finger across a large ledger page. "A Mr. Harvey Braxton. Here's your key, Lieutenant. Oh, I almost forgot, there's a package for you," he said as he passed a large manila envelope to Mark.

"Thank you...uh..." Mark looked at his name badge,"...Denis." Which way is the elevator?" He was annoyed but didn't want to spoil the magic that had surrounded Steph and him since that first moment at the dock.

"To your left, sir."

Mark and Stephanie started toward the elevators, unaware of the intense ogling of her legs by Denis. He whistled under his breath at the sensual image Stephanie projected. Wanting somehow to keep this couple engaged, he called after them. "Sorry, folks, I need to see you for just a moment."

Back at the desk, Mark was terse. "What is it?" The clerk hesitated, staring again at Stephanie. Mark's tone was frustrated. "We really need to get to our room...been on board a ship for eight days."

"Sorry, sir, but my cousin was in the 7th Armored like your insignia indicates. He was killed near St. Vith."

The mention of St.Vith brought a wave of mixed emotions over Mark. Here was another death in that bloody defeat. Had he seen the body of the clerk's cousin? Had he trod over it as he marshaled his fragmented company to Bastogne? His stomach tightened. In a dry voice, "That so? I know about it...I was there. I'm sorry about your cousin. It was a rough battle...maybe our only retreat. You should know how it finally came out. That retreat led to a victory later." He paused, looking down from the clerk's intense face. "Now, I need to get to our room. Is there anything wrong with the reservation?"

"Oh, no...it's all okay. I just wanted to say why I wasn't called to serve...4-F," he said pointing to his eyes. "Can you share a little about it...or about your tour, please, sir."

That door had almost closed in Mark's mind. It was the door that led to the inner sanctuary of the fraternity of those who have shared the life and death ordeal of combat. Combat veterans are a select group, always reluctant to share with those who have not been initiated. He started to turn away. But, as he looked at the clerk's diminutive frame and his thick glasses, he softened. The guy had probably wanted to serve, but had been rejected.

"I was in England, shipped to France in mid '44, fought our way out of St. Vith, was on the perimeter of Bastogne...center of the Bulge, and ended up in the recapture of St. Vith. I picked up a German machine gun slug in the arm and was shipped back to the States. I'm lucky to be here and glad that you asked me about it."

"Oh, yes sir. I wish I could have been there. I just had a Victory garden and worked at a USO, nothing that amounted to anything...nothing like what you did, sir."

"Denis?" Mark straightened up, suddenly becoming taller and seeming older, wiser. "Everything that was done, both by the people in the service *and* the folks at home, added up to the total effort. It takes everybody...here, there, everywhere."

"Thank you, sir," Denis said, as his face turned a deep red and his eyes shone, even through the thick glasses. He looked at his papers again. "You know, Lieutenant, I may have made a mistake with your reservation. You are supposed to have the three-room bridal suite. Perhaps Mr. Braxton wasn't clear when he phoned in the reservation...maybe we messed it up. It's yours...no extra charge." Then he whispered to Mark, "The champagne and roses will be there in five minutes, if you can stall your wife...and they're on the house...ssh."

It had been worth it after all, to talk to this fellow – and not just because of the perks either. "Thanks, partner," said Mark, which again brought a blush of gratitude to the clerk's face and straightened his back.

In the elevator, Mark told Stephanie what Denis had done for them.

With a wry smile, Stephanie said, "That's great, Harvey Braxton being one-upped by a near-sighted clerk from the Bronx."

Mark noted the sarcasm. What was behind that? He could only say, "Hmm...great." They could talk more about that later.

Once in their suite, they dropped everything. In each other's arms, their kisses were long and deep...expressing the wordless gratitude for an end to the separation.

Stephanie ran her hands over his chest as she helped him unbutton his coat. Their need for this moment had become the guiding force – leaving her nearly powerless to choose her next move or thought. Suddenly she stopped. "Mark, I told your mom that you'd call her. Maybe you'd better do that first...before..."

He groaned, "Yeah, I should. God, I almost hate you for asking!" Then immediately, "But I love you for thinking of her! You're such a doll...and a considerate one too!" His words tumbled out, making them both laugh.

His mother cried when she heard his voice. Mark told her repeatedly he was all right. She kept thanking God that he was back safe. It could have gone on quite awhile, but Joyce stopped it herself. It might have been her Scotch sense of economy, or it might have been a woman's sense. "Now you go be with that sweet wife of yours...she needs you. I'm so happy we've talked. I'll tell John all about it. I love you. Bye...for now."

Mark hung up the phone and turned to his wife "I love you all the more for making me do that first. Then he winked at her. "Now where were we?"

She backed off and began slowly removing her clothes, one piece at a time. Mark was overwhelmed. He had almost forgotten what a lovely and alluring woman Steph could be behind closed doors. Their first culmination was quick...a pent up, three years ...basic animal passion driven by purely physical needs. Nestled in each other's arms they talked about being together, about little nothings, until desire rose again. This time their union was slow and prolonged, the expression of sharing, mental and soulful...the rite of companionship...of reciprocal love.

An immeasurable time later, their passion momentarily abated, they lay side-by-side noticing, as if it had just appeared, the roses and the chilled champagne. Mark got up, not even bothering to cover himself, opened the champagne, and poured two glasses. He raised his, "Here's to our life together...a long and happy life, Steph. Thank you for being my wife and being here with me."

"To you, my handsome...and very naked....husband." She giggled, "And where would I be, if not here?"

"I'd be jealous of wherever that would be." It was back right away. They both felt it. That easy way they talked to each other. And it was great.

Mark walked back to the bed and picked up the manila envelope. In it, he found a book of checks on a New York bank, the stub showing a deposit of ten-thousand dollars. When Stephanie saw the contents, she let out a whistle. There was a note enclosed. She tried to read over Mark's shoulder.

March 20, 1945

Dear Son,

Welcome home. We're all glad that you are here and safe. Enjoy your time with Stephanie at the Waldorf, a small present from Lillian and me to honor your service.

Please accept the enclosed new account in your name with Chase-Manhattan. It's some of the wages you missed because you were defending all of us in the war. We want you back at Braxton, Mark, but we can talk about that after your discharge. Plenty of time, but let me say again, we want you. Enough for now.

Dad

Mark picked up the checkbook, turning it over several times in his hand. He'd never seen ten thousand dollars before. Was it a bribe...would it be something he would pay for with a piece of himself...would he be owned by its giver? His thoughts started to come very fast – and surprisingly clearly. He had to earn this. If he gave it back, he'd insult her father; and what would he support her on? Maybe if he'd agree on a job at Braxton, he could work it off. Yes, that was the best, and he'd try to not spend anymore of it than he had to. But, he'd be beholden to them until he could get on his own. What else could he do? Staying in the army for a few hundred a month wouldn't pay her clothes bill. If he got out, twenty bucks a week for fifty-two weeks...big deal! No, he better take the money and work his tail off to get on his own. Phone Harvey tonight and thank him. Needed the job, needed him.

Stephanie noticed his mood change. She stroked his hair. "What's all the deep thinking?" Then it occurred to her. "If it's about the checks, just keep them, and forget it. He made millions on the war, while you were laying your life on the line."

She knew her father wanted to bring Mark into the business and that he saw him as a possible successor...now that Daniel was gone. She also had seen for years how Harvey tried to bargain heavily for whatever he bought. The ten thousand was a good start, but she'd be damned if that was all he could buy *her* husband for. "Don't give it another thought, lover. We can use it...you deserve it."

Reaching toward her, he patted her hand, "Just thinking about what we're going to do for the next few days. And a few thoughts about how to support you in a style you deserve."

"That's not too hard, there's good old Braxton Chemicals."

There it was again...Braxton Chemicals...the Braxton family. He had heard his dad once say, "Beggars can't be choosers." Funny, how the old time-worn *clichés* always seemed to be appropriate.

"Stephanie, tell me honestly, do you think it would work out if I went with the company? Would it affect you and me? That's the most important part...what do you think?"

"I think it would be great. No, I won't let it affect us. If you're who I think you are, you'll be running the whole damn show someday."

He started to say something about wanting his own company, but thought he'd better hold up on that until he was truly supporting her on what he earned.

Feeling the Braxton issue was settled, she picked up his hand and saw the scar on his left arm for the first time. She winced, "Mark what happened? That's horrid looking!"

"Oh, it's not much. It's a scar from where a German machine gun bullet creased me. Sure did tear up the sleeves of my jacket and uniform though." He ran his hand over the white ridge of skin. "It's okay. I was lucky...doesn't hurt...all healed up. I only spent a day at a dressing station." He wanted to change the subject. "Maybe if we spend some time on a sunny beach it'll tan." He stroked her soft shoulder. "Still got that navy blue swim suit...the one that makes you look like a beauty queen?"

Even as she smiled at the compliment, she felt the scar slowly along its eight or nine inches. She started to say something about why she hadn't wanted him to enlist but caught the recrimination on the tip of her tongue. They had had that heated argument about his enlistment...the one she had to apologize for. She'd lost that battle. She didn't want to lose another one. She'd watched her mother lose too many arguments – which Lillian euphemistically called discussions – to her father. That wasn't going to be the *modus operandi* of her marriage!

She knew this moment could go either way. It depended on her to strengthen the bond they had recreated in the last few hours.

"I think, Mark, you suffered a lot more than your letters indicated. I cannot imagine what it was like. No one could who wasn't there. I won't pry into wounds or memories; but, Mark, I'm here to listen to anything you want to unload. You can trust that."

She was wonderful. "Thanks, Steph," he said. The crinkled picture of Pellini's family suddenly flashed in his brain. He saw Mike's frozen body in that fox hole east of Bastogne, the blood encrusted hole in the center of his blue-gray forehead staring at him like a Cyclops from Hell.

Stephanie saw the pained and confused expression on his silent face. "Mark, what is it? Where are you?" He couldn't answer.

She pulled his head to her and stroked his black hair. "I'm here...it's all right...you're all right." She felt his tears on her bare breast. She held him tighter.

CHAPTER FIVE

*O Deliver Me From The
Deceitful And Wicked Man*

Church of England
Prayer Book 1662

As they left the *Cathedrale de Notre-Dame*, Dharma and Daphne rode in the rusted, pre-war taxi with the coughing engine. Dharma sat very still. Her body was tensed with the indignation of one who has been duped by a supposed friend. Her eyes were glazed, her cheeks red, her mouth tight, and her breathing short and rapid. Daphne held her hand, but knew her mother's state kept her from feeling any touch.

On the *Rue des Minimmes*, Dharma said, "Stop in front of this house. Wait for us here."

They sat in the taxi as Dharma gathered herself. She planned on how to confront Jacques Bonhomme about the letter from Raoul. She knew he was hiding it; a true friend would have brought it forth at once. This man was up to something. He was somehow guilty in Raoul's death. She could feel it in every one of his glib words – their oiliness slipping off his fat tongue with practiced ease. He was too evasive...too unemotional telling her of Raoul's execution. Then there was the "coincidence" of the SS taking Raoul away the day after his last visit with Raoul.

"*Maman*, why would *Monsieur* Bonhomme keep Papa's letter from us? Wasn't he Papa's friend?"

"A friend, no he was not! Perhaps on the surface...but underneath that facade, he was only true to what he could get. I believe he is a dishonorable man, who would use anybody to further his own ends."

"How could he use Papa?"

132

"Your father did some printing for some of his businesses at a very favorable price. Then, and this is only suspicion, but I truly feel it...he may have informed on him to the SS to curry favor for himself...maybe for money."

Daphne gasped...such horrid behavior was beyond her comprehension. The next thought came immediately. What of Pierre? Had someone turned him in for favor? There were stories about Frenchmen who collaborated with the occupying Germans. Some did anything to preserve their lives and belongings. Usually, the Germans gave only a minimum compensation, often none, for what they gleaned from informants. Since the liberation, many collaborators were being routed out and either shot, hanged, or in the case of consorting women, having their heads shaved. It made her sick to think about Pierre and the apparent duplicity of her father's supposed friend. It was almost more than her tender spirit could tolerate.

"*Maman*, there is so much evil in the world. It seems that everywhere you and I turn we come across killing and deceit. What drives people to do these horrible things to each other? I cannot believe what Hitler was doing to all of the Jewish people in Europe...millions of innocent people murdered. It's almost too terrible to believe, but we see the pictures, we hear the news. Is it because they don't believe in God? Or worse yet, do they think they are God?"

Dharma pushed Bonhomme out of her mind to attend to her daughter. "Daphne, do not let the actions of some, no matter how vile, soil your bright faith in both God and most people. Yes, there are many evil people in the world; but, in spite of what we are facing, I still believe that most are not bad. Greed and survival can bring out our worst traits if we let them. You, my beloved daughter, have never shown anything but fine desires and behavior. Oh, Daphne, I wish Raoul could be here to see just how wonderful his daughter is." Her eyes started to tear as she patted the side of her daughter's head. "As I have said to you many times, I believe that God put you on earth to carry out some of his work."

"I hope I am worthy." Bolstered by her mother's confidence, Daphne said, "Let us go to this *bete noire's* door and demand Papa's letter."

Again, they were made to wait. Finally, the uniformed maid answered and told them that *Monsieur* Bonhomme was out and would not return until the morrow. "He has gone to Paris on business. Who shall I tell him called?"

"Are you certain he is not hiding from us?" Daphne asked.

"*Mademoiselle*, I beg your pardon…he is not home. Please give me your name and leave."

"It's the same as yesterday…Devereux. *Monsieur* Bonhomme knows us. He has something he was entrusted to give us. Have him contact us at the *Hotel Grand Boulevard, s'il vous plait.* "

The women exited the elegant house, not knowing that the day before, after he had seen them getting into the American jeep, Bonhomme had opened the letter given him by Raoul. He had held it in his pig-like, shaking hand. Whenever he was nervous, he reached for his placebo, a linen handkerchief. He must have felt that wiping away the heavy beads of perspiration would wipe away problems…or guilt. The letter instructed Dharma how to access the two million francs he had deposited for them in a numbered Swiss Bank account. She would know where to find the number if she remembered the hallowed place where their souls were united. Bonhomme copied this abbreviated phrase as he prepared to burn the letter. He reread the last sentence, which amazed him. It stated what a good friend and patriot Jacques had been. Despite his nervousness, he chuckled. He should have been on the stage. He reached for a lit candle and an ashtray. Lifting a corner of the letter to the flame, he paused…maybe he should keep this testimony by such a credible French patriot as Raoul. It could be a way out of any disagreeable inquiries into how he had survived the occupation so comfortably. There was also the possibility that some jealous ne'erdo-wells might wonder about the survival of his businesses in Switzerland and Austria.

Aloud, he muttered, "Everything has its price...I paid it!"

He folded the letter and placed it behind the original *Czeanne* on the wall that faced his large bed. Yes, he thought, old Raoul would never know how he helped his friend...even from the grave.

∗   ∗   ∗

Back at the *Hotel Grand Boulevard*, Daphne and Dharma stopped at the desk for their key. Daphne noticed that the clerk averted his eyes from the women and looked instead at two men sitting to the left of the desk. He nodded toward the two women, thus identifying them to the men. Daphne saw them, dressed like the apaches of the left bank night clubs. Still wondering about the interplay of the clerk and the men, she went with her mother up to the rooms. A few moments later there was a knock at the door. Stunned, at first they did nothing.

Finally, Daphne called, "Who is it?"

"We are friends of Raoul Devereux. We must see you."

Dharma bolted out of her chair. Was this some cruel hoax? Didn't they know Raoul was dead? But, her deep longing to learn anything about her husband forced her to gamble – in a rarity, logic overcame emotion.

"Yes, I will open the door as much as the chain will allow. Prove who you are...no tricks or we will both scream. There are *Gendarmes* and the American M.P.'s close by."

Peering in, the tall man said, "We know you are Devereux's wife and daughter and that you have been to the house of the collaborator, Bonhomme. Your husband was with us during the occupation. We know how, and by whom, he was betrayed. We are here to see that you are cared for as Raoul instructed us to do a month before his execution."

"Oh, *Maman*, please let them in. Maybe they know something of Pierre!"

The presence of her father's associates brought the grief and horror of his death into sharp focus, but her love for Pierre consumed her entire being. The bond of a woman and a man surpasses all others...it is the emotion that combines all the facets of love.

The word collaborator to describe Bonhomme moved Dharma to trust these men. "Yes, come in."

They took off their caps and made a slight bow as they entered. Dharma looked intensely into their faces, as if to see if they were who and what they said they were. Cautiously, she said, "Who are you really? What are your names?"

The taller one said, "I am Claude Hoche. I worked with your husband in circulating the papers and bulletins to the members of *La Resistance*."

"The work that got him killed?" Dharma hissed.

"*Madame* Devereux, your husband was a true patriot. He loved his country, as he loved you. He could do nothing else. He dreamed and prayed for the day when France would again be free. He was driven to do what he could. It is men like him that have made our country free and strong."

Sadly, Dharma knew he was right. She was well aware of Raoul's feelings for his country. He had always put others ahead of himself...Daphne and herself, his church, his God, his country, a beggar on the street. Her tears began to flow. It seemed that she saw an apparition of Raoul behind these two men. Their words brought him right into their tiny sitting room. Her beloved husband's aura would live on after him...it would always be in her heart...and any place that she might be.

Daphne knew her mother was seeing her father, if but in her memory. The tears that were wetting her mother's cheeks evidenced that. Daphne had known Pierre for such a short time, and yet she felt their separation so painfully. Her mother's loss of Raoul must be many times deeper…they had been married for twenty-seven years, had birthed Daphne, and had shared everything. Seeing her mother's anguish made her think of poor Pierre. Where was he? Was he alive, if she could only know?

"*Maman*, do you think these men might know about Pierre?"

Distraught over the retelling of Raoul's ghastly betrayal and death, Dharma just wanted the matter of Bonhomme resolved. She felt for Daphne and her lack of knowledge of Pierre, but these men were here about Raoul.

"Of course we will ask, shortly. Let them finish what they came to tell us about Raoul's betrayer."

Dharma turned back to the men, wanting to know, but afraid of the ugliness of it. Knowing more of the details would not bring Raoul back, but no one should deceive his friends and cause them harm, and even worse, death. Raoul would never be with her again on earth. But, in the hereafter…Who knew? If she saw justice brought to Bonhomme, there would at least be a closure. Perhaps she would be more at peace.

She sucked in her stomach, steeling herself. "What do you know about how Raoul was caught? Do you know who informed the SS?"

She caught her breath. "And why would someone do this? Was it a Frenchman?"

This was an unnecessary question. She already knew the answer. But her own values made it difficult for her to believe a man's supposed friend could do this. And yet, there was Jesus' supposed disciple, Judas. Was it that those to whom we are closest are often those not to trust because we are blinded by that affinity? Was Raoul blinded by Bonhomme's façade of friendship? Would these men, who said they were in *La Resistance* with Raoul, tell her it was Bonhomme, as she felt so surely that it was?

"*Madame* Devereux, near the end of the occupation we had finally worked one of our men into a clerical job at SS headquarters.

Jacques Bonhomme was seen leaving their offices the night before they came for Raoul. Bonhomme had no legitimate reason to be with the Germans for more than several hours and then get into a chauffeured car. We also learned that a few days after Raoul was hung, Bonhomme received a large order for food and wine from the German garrisons in Rouen. It was for millions of francs."

Dharma and Daphne both recoiled at this testimony that solidified all they had suspected. Bonhomme's despicable actions, recounted in such detail, came as sharp blows to both women. Dharma went white, while Daphne started to cry. For a long moment, there was no other sound in the room. The two men looked at the floor, their eyes averting from the grief and shock before them.

Finally, Daphne, now the more mature one, asked, "Can anything be done to bring this vile man to justice?"

The second man, Rene Latour, a swarthy man, whose facial skin was pocked, stepped forward. "Ladies, there will be justice…fear not…and soon. We wanted to see if you knew all of the facts. I apologize. But let me ask what this rat said to you on your visit."

Again, Daphne, newly a woman of action, tempered in the fires of tragedy, answered before her mother could speak.

"He was very evasive about my father. He finally told us of my father's execution, after Mother prodded him. When we asked him how the Nazis found out about the underground papers, he just shrugged his shoulders. I will never forget how cold and dispassionate he was about the torture and death of someone who he claimed was his lifelong friend."

As they heard this, Claude and Rene gritted their teeth, their eyes ablaze with hatred. Daphne sensed their passion and knew these men were true patriots and loyal to Raoul. She nodded her head in appreciation and continued.

"Later, Cardinal Desmonde told us that my father had given Bonhomme a letter for us. He did not give us the letter. When we went there today, we were told he was in Paris."

She sank back on a chair, wiping her face, now heated from the outpouring of her deepest emotions.

During her retelling of the past day, Dharma looked at her daughter with a new respect, seeing her as a fully matured woman. She had grown emotionally from her exposure to the rigors of separation and pain. The last six years had brought little happiness to her beautiful child. How well Daphne had coped with each shocking tragedy, exhibiting a maturity based on her deep inner faith. She wished with all of her heart that her daughter would find her man...and not only become an artist, but a mother as well.

Rene said, "Yes, Bonhomme is in Paris. We have tracked him. We also believe he has betrayed other members of our group. But, he will return to Rouen soon...then..."

"Then? Then what will happen?" Dharma asked.

"Would you like to be at his trial, *Madame* Devereux...and your daughter?"

"Trial...where is the trial to be held?"

"The courts...the courts of loyal French people," Claude Hoche smiled grimly.

"Where will that be?" Daphne asked.

Claude, in a tight-lipped tone, answered, "In his own *court* yard. Most fitting...don't you think so?"

*   *   *

His business in Paris completed, Jacques Bonhomme nervously got into his chauffeured car. Things were becoming more difficult now that the country was totally free of the German occupation – too many American checkpoints. Thankfully, he had the necessary diplomatic papers. They had cost a mere thousand francs paid to a government clerk. And for a million francs, and an original Matisse, he had procured an official Nazi directive telling him to report to Gestapo headquarters to explain his activities, implying that he was working with or had knowledge of the underground. Fortuitously, he had foreseen the Allied invasion a month before it occurred and had gone to his contact *Oberst* Max von Heiffel. He would save this trump card for any trial. Then again, maybe he should avoid all of that and move to Switzerland for a while. Yes, that was it. Many Nazi officials had taken that route. Money could buy anything there. Yes, to Switzerland where Raoul's two-million francs were on deposit in Zurich. All he had to do was decipher that cryptic message about the number. He pulled his scribbled note, "if she remembered the hallowed place where their souls were united."

Hallowed place...hallowed place, he kept repeating in his mind. The Cathedral Notre Dame! What other place was more hallowed? The Devereuxs had always worshipped there.

*   *   *

Daphne asked Claude and Rene how they planned to accomplish their "trial" of Bonhomme.

"*Mademoiselle* Devereux, it will be easy. I will not burden you with the details. Just let us know if you and *Madame* want to attend."

Daphne looked at her mother. Dharma nodded.

Rene spoke, "Fine, we will drive you there tomorrow. Be ready at five o'clock in the morning."

Daphne took Claude's sleeve, pulling him back into the room. "Before you leave, can you tell me how I might find out where my husband is? I don't know if he was with your group...I know nothing of his whereabouts. He was in the army at the start of the war... stationed in the Maginot Line. His name is Pierre Sauval. Can you help me, please?"

No matter how much she grieved for her father, and felt deeply for her mother, her longing for Pierre was with her every waking moment. Her love for this wonderful man had never ebbed despite their separation. To have him again was to become whole again.

Maybe these loyal patriots could help her.

"I didn't know you were married, *Madame*. I do not know a Pierre Sauval, but our organization is widespread. Give me few days, and I will make inquiries. You might also ask the military authorities. But, I will start today to help you."

"*Merci*, Claude. I will pray for you…that you will find him."

When Claude and Rene left, Daphne went to her mother who was shaking…her whole being consumed in waves of hate, sadness, and fear…and a new feeling for her, hopelessness. What would she do without Raoul? If Daphne found Pierre, they had their lives to live. She wouldn't be a burden to them.

"*Maman*, what is it? Tell me."

Dharma could surrender to the realization that she was like the child, and her beloved daughter was the mother. How many times as she watched her daughter grow up had she listened to her and helped her find the answer to her problem or doubt. Now, she saw the roles reversed, but that was fine. It made her feel good to know that Daphne was a mature woman who was so willing to help her mother.

"My dear, Daphne, help me through this business with your father's betrayer. Then let me help you with your search for Pierre. After that we will see what is next." She extended her arms, "I love you, Daphne, come here; let me kiss you."

As Bonhomme's car pulled up to his house, he was still trying to imagine where the Swiss bank account number might be hidden in the *Cathedral*. The more he thought, the tenser he became. No need to waste that amount of francs on a couple of women. Besides, some of that money was what he had paid Raoul for printing his forms and bulletins. As a matter of fact, he had just settled twenty-two-thousand francs on Raoul three days before he had been taken away. Perhaps the Germans had gotten that. Stepping out of the car, he thought he saw someone pull back into a clump of bushes. He must be seeing things. Too much stress today, too many American GI's, and way too many crazy, liberated French running around trying to control everything. The Germans were so much more predictable and efficient.

When he retired to the second floor, he retrieved the letter and pored over it until midnight. No new thought came to him about the hidden number. He put the letter on his night stand to study again in the morning, took a large drink of brandy, and slept. He woke up to a loud crashing on the first floor, followed by a stampede of thumping footsteps up the stairs. Before he could get his senses, men in rough garb burst into his room.

"Who are you? What is the meaning of this? Get out now…I'll call the *Gendarmes*."

"Go ahead and call them, you murdering traitor. What will they do? Stretch out what we will do quickly?" Pointing an automatic pistol at Bonhomme's head, Rene Latour commanded, "Sit in that chair…now!"

When Bonhomme was in the chair, Latour put a garrotte around Bonhomme's neck, tightening it just short of total strangulation.

"Now, dirty collaborator, tell us how you betrayed not only this lady's husband but another three of our loyal people…people who gave their lives to free France. You caused the murder of those who fought to rid us of the Nazi pests, while you slept with them."

Bonhomme saw the two Devereux women standing in the doorway. He felt the look of stern justice in their eyes more than the wire around his neck.

"I had to live," he gurgled. "I had to protect all that I had built up in my life. They would have caught them anyway…"

The wire was tightened, his eyes bulged, but he managed to grab the letter from the table and crumple it into a ball, which fell from his now-slack hand. As his head rolled to the side, he soiled his fine Belgian linen nightshirt…his final act. Within a minute his whole torso slumped over. The last cognitive thought he had was, "two-million francs…"

Daphne and Dharma shivered as they saw Raoul's betrayer die. Yes, they wanted justice…this sentence was just; but death, violent death, shocked their sensitive cores. They turned their heads away, clutching each other.

Claude, curious about why Bonhomme had made crumpling the paper his last determined act, picked it up. It was addressed to Dharma.

"*Madame* Devereux, this is for you. It would appear this piece of filth had gotten it away from you?"

"Yes, my husband, thinking that this man was his friend, gave it to him to keep for us. He did not give us the letter, as you can see."

Dharma quickly read the note. She was touched deeply by the thoughtful prudence in the amount of francs Raoul had provided for Daphne and herself. Poor Raoul must have felt his end was coming. Suddenly she was filled with opposing emotions – the fright of what she had just witnessed – and the warmth of Raoul's love. She swooned, Claude catching her before she fell to the floor.

They all stood motionless, not knowing what to do. Fortunately, in less than a minute, she came to…a confused look on her face…her eyes blank. Daphne took the paper from her hand and sat next to her. Gradually, Dharma focused on the present.

"I am sorry…it is too much." Seeing the letter in Daphne's hand, she said, "He was such a wonderful man. Even in his last days, he thought of us."

Then she looked at Bonhomme's body, "And that *keg besterd* did him in…for what?"

Daphne knew her mother was at her height of disgust and exasperation. She only resorted to Albanian profanity when she couldn't find the correct word in French.

Dharma couldn't believe Raoul's statement about Bonhomme being his trusted friend. Perhaps he said that to ensure its delivery, or maybe he still believed in his childhood friend. What a different path their two lives had taken – one honorable, the other, its antitheses – like Peter and Judas.

Rene turned to Daphne, "*Madame*…it is *Madame*?" She nodded.

"We are communicating about your husband with others in our group. Some are in other parts of France. Please be patient. We will come to you at your hotel as soon as we learn something. In the meantime, ask everyone that you can…one never knows where information comes from. Now, you and your mother should leave. We must clean up this mess. Paul will take you to your hotel. Good day. Your father's death has been avenged. We are sorry that we cannot bring him back. He was a brave man."

Daphne looked with appreciation at the group and touched Rene's arm. Their offer of help gave her some comfort. Just maybe they would find her Pierre. "*Merci*, you are good friends. We know you helped free France. God bless you."

They left the room with Paul, without looking back at Bonhomme's body. They would see it often in their dreams.

The two women stood looking out of the hotel window and at each other…seeing nothing. Their feelings were numbed; neither had ever witnessed a killing. But, Dharma sobbed every time she thought of Raoul. Her life had become a shapeless gray, amorphous blob. On Martinique, she had been without him, but there was always the thought of being reunited after the war. That hope had sustained her. Now, it was gone. Finally, she reached deep into herself and accepted that she had to help her daughter.

She sat on the edge of Daphne's bed. "It was a terrible day. We must try to forget what has happened. Now we must go forward and find Pierre."

She knew her daughter was consumed with desire to find her love, but Daphne didn't need to be floundering in a sea of anxiety and endless days of fruitless searching. She must be occupied.

"Those men from *La Resistance* seem to be sincere in their

promise to find Pierre. Dear, you have a great talent…don't you want to develop it?. You may want to finish your schooling…do you?"

For the first time in weeks, Daphne saw a glimmer on the horizon of hope…the ray of a life free of sordidness and tragedy. "If we find Pierre…yes…yes, I want to work in the field of illustration, maybe for a magazine."

"Why can't you be working at the Louvre while the search goes on? Maybe there will be some information there about Pierre."

There was truth in what her mother was suggesting. "*Maman,* you are right. I must work. I hope my talent can be trained. It would be a sin not to use what God has blessed me with. Do you remember Papa's cousin, Charles Duboise? He is a stockholder in a magazine publisher. He might help me get a position – if my work is good enough."

Dharma smiled…she had always admired her daughter's lack of self-aggrandizement about her talents and deeds. Daphne had the confidence of inner faith but had never boasted about herself. She had the humbleness of those who think about how to serve, not to be served.

"I'm sure that in time it will be, as you say, 'good enough,' probably better."

She continued, "If we can access the money dear Raoul left us, we can send you back to the *Louvre.* I am sure there will be enough for that. And, perhaps you will be selling some of your work in a year or two."

"Thank you for helping me. Do you think we can find the bank number?"

"Here is your father's letter. I'm not sure yet where he has placed the number."

"What does the letter say?'

"It says, '…the hallowed place where our souls are united.' But, there are six random letters around the margins. See, a, o, r, s, another r, and a v. I don't know what they mean."

After playing with the letters for a while, Daphne asked, "Do you think Papa was using a language other than French?"

Dharma's eyes flashed. "Maybe that's it. Let me work with these letters as if they were in Albanian." In less than five minutes she came up with *varros*, Albanian for "bury." She kept saying the word, then, "where our souls will unite."

"That's it! He put the number in our burial vaults at *Notre Dame!* That is the hallowed place where our souls will meet...for eternity."

They told Cardinal Desmonde what had happened to Bonhomme and about the number in the vault.

"My children, it is sad that we must resolve so many things with violence...guillotines...guns...garrottes...even crosses...always violence. I often wonder how God tolerates the way His sheep treat each other. We know there has been wholesale torture throughout this terrible war, and it is one thing to crack under extreme torture, but to betray for money or favor is a grievous sin. Your loss can never be understood, but we must trust in our eventual resurrection and the life hereafter, as demonstrated by our Lord. You are wonderful people. You must go forward with your lives as you know Raoul would want you to. Let us retrieve Raoul's message."

Below ground, the Cardinal led them through faintly-lit corridors. He opened the small vault with their names on it. Removing the two urns, they extracted a piece of paper with the bank number encased in a protective wrapper. In the other urn was a dried rose with a simple note, "Until we meet again. I love you, Raoul."

Turning the rose stem over in her hand, Dharma began to cry. Daphne embraced her. Cardinal Desmonde put a hand on her head, making the sign of the cross with his thumb on her forehead.

"God is with this fine man, my child. Go in peace. Someday we will all be united with Him. Always know what an honorable man our Raoul was."

*   *   *

In May, Dharma and Daphne decided to take an apartment in Paris to be close to the *Louvre*. They also thought they would be able to get more information about where Pierre might be.

With the money from the Zurich bank, Daphne reregistered at the *Louvre*. But everyday the two women relentlessly pursued the search for Pierre. They rejoiced with all of France, and much of the Western World, when the Germans finally signed an unconditional surrender. The work of rebuilding the war-ravaged countries of Europe began. Millions of lives lost, trillions of francs, pounds, marks, rubles, dollars, and other currencies of valuable materials wasted, all because of the ego-centric, maniacal whims of a lunatic committing a nation's people to conquest and genocide.

One afternoon, Dharma took Daphne to a sidewalk café on the *Champs-Elysees*, hoping she could bring a little joy into her life. She worried about her daughter's health...her obsessive pursuit of Pierre was blotting all else from her life. As they sipped a rare aperitif, they watched the joyous crowds walking, kissing, and laughing, as newsboys waved papers telling of the German surrender. They also saw crippled men in rag-tag uniforms, fighters from the Free French Army on crutches or with bandaged limbs.

Dharma turned from the crowd to Daphne "More fruits from *La Guerre!* What was gained? Are we not where it was before it all started...only without our loved ones? Damn that murderer who caused it all."

"I cannot believe that an entire nation could be convinced to kill millions of innocent people...why, *Maman*?"

"I don't know...who knows? There have always been wars...always greedy struggles for power."

"If only we could trust in God...live by His laws, not our own...then Pierre and father would be here."

"You are right, dear. Never give up that wonderful faith that you have – no matter what those around you might do. Shall we go to the army offices and make another inquiry?"

The people at the reorganized French Army offices tried to be helpful, but they claimed many records had been destroyed. There was a record of Pierre, but it was incomplete. In the hasty retreats of both French soldiers westward, and the British to Dunkirk, most information was lost. It was a chaotic melee of men running for survival before the onrushing, crushing force of German Panzers. A captain of the newly formed French forces promised Daphne he would keep trying. After a day of calls at various bureaus, the women returned to their flat exhausted and discouraged.

"*Maman*, no matter where we turn, we find nothing. I fear the worst."

"It is discouraging, but there is still hope. I will stay with you until we find Pierre." She started to say, "Or until we learn the truth," but maternal compassion stopped her tongue.

"We must continue to pray. You are starting at the *Louvre* tomorrow; ask everyone there who might have been a friend of Pierre's."

It was an early September evening when Rene Latour appeared suddenly at their door. He took off his cap and made a slight bow. "*Madame*, I must talk with you. Maybe we should go inside."

At first she was overwhelmed with joy. Maybe Rene had news of Pierre. But her joy quickly turned to anxiety; she felt the seriousness of his words…the absence of a smile, and his wanting to talk in private. Her starved soul reached out for any hope, for any good word, but she sensed how uncomfortable Rene was. She began to prepare herself for the worst.

She took his arm. "It's…it's about my Pierre? You've found him?"

"I have information. Shall we go inside?" He said looking away from her, indicating the door with his cap.

Rene made only brief eye contact with Daphne, speaking

haltingly, "I am sorry to bring you this news, *Madame* Sauval. We…ah…we have learned of your husband."

Suddenly, she knew what was coming. Her body knew…her every nerve ending tensed. She had seen Rene in action in Bonhomme's bedroom. He had been forthright and decisive. Here, he stood like little boy, afraid to tell his mother bad news.

"Please, Rene, tell me what is it?"

"*Madame*, your husband fought with our group for more than two years. He was an expert at demolition. He and his associates would blow up German supply trains and trucks moving to the west. People say he may have participated in over sixty raids on the Bosche."

Rene paused as if to gather his nerve. He shuffled his cap from hand to hand, looking at the floor.

Daphne stiffened, taking her mother's hand. Her voice was stunningly calm. "And something happened?"

"His squad planned to blow up a train at the rail junction just east of Reims. We had learned of a German train scheduled to pass a certain switch point at an exact time. The train was bringing more armament for the Atlantic Wall defense against an Allied invasion…vital things for the Germans. Everything was well organized, but an informant warned the Germans…"

He stopped again. The look on Daphne's face seemed to paralyze his speech. "Pierre was killed by a German machine pistol. Despite his wounds, he tried to detonate the charges along the tracks. He died with the detonator in his hand. We were told that he was the bravest man in that cell of fighters."

At first, she stood woodenly, as if she hadn't comprehended. Then she sagged onto the divan and into her mother's arms. Dharma pulled her head to her breast, saying nothing, but holding her tightly.

Rene had seen death and the pain of those whose loved ones were lost…he stood respectfully silent as he crossed himself.

Dharma laid Daphne's head on the divan and walked to Rene. As she showed him out, she spoke, "Rene, we are sorry that you had to be the one to bring us this news, but we thank you. You are a friend."

She also wanted to thank Rene for dealing with Bonhomme, but it was too painful – the picture of Bonhomme, his horrible gasping, flashed before her.

"I am sorry too, *Madame*...sorry for the terrible losses that your family has endured. Is there anything that I can do?"

"You have done so much...not today." Dharma sighed. She remembered her manners quickly. "If you are ever near here, please feel welcome to visit us. Now I must help my daughter."

The days that followed were all drab...no beginning, no end. Like an automaton, Daphne forced down tasteless food, but only because of her mother's urging. Her one comfort was her daily attendance at church – the only refuge she found from the constant pain of her loss. On her way to school, she would stop at church and kneel in front of the Virgin Mary, light a candle, and ask that Pierre's soul be with God. She devoted more and more time to prayer and spiritual reflection.

For days, her painting was a smear of ideas and colors...no theme, no composition...just blurry streaks. Every time she set up her easel, she saw Pierre peering over the top of it, as he had done so often when they first met. Even though she had not actually seen Pierre for more than six years, these visions of him were as real as the canvas and easel themselves.

One afternoon, after looking at her latest work, the instructor told her to stop in his office. He asked her patiently what was wrong. He was concerned.

"Has something happened to you? I see someone in whom there is so much talent and promise now doing poor work."

His first job was to teach painting techniques...color balance, composition, perspective…but he knew it was more important to awaken the soul of the artist. Even monkeys, he mused, could be taught to daub pigments onto a medium…but true art could only come from the soul…a soul awakened to share with the world what was inside. This young lady standing in front of his desk had the soul of an artist, and the skills to bring out the inner spirit that dwelled within her. He must challenge that spirit. He must pull her from whatever current trauma…or diversion…blocking the release of her talents.

"*Mademoiselle*, you are troubled. At present you are not the painter who displayed such promising talent." He waited to see if his words were registering. Seeing an upturn of her face, perhaps a slight flicker of light in her eyes, he continued. "I am your friend. In my small way I want to help you to fully develop what I have seen in you. Please tell me, what can I do?"

Daphne was touched by his concern. Other than her mother and Rene Latour's brief condolences, she had lived in emotional isolation since the news of Pierre. Could she believe again in herself? Was what the *Professeur* said true? Did he really think she had talent? She needed to go forward. This man was offering his hand to her. She asked him if he remembered Pierre. He did.

She told him about Pierre's death…how it happened, and how she had been on Martinique for the five years since their "marriage," never having seen him again before his murder. As she said this, she cried.

He looked away pensively, staring at the window behind his desk. In a few moments, he turned to her, handed her his handkerchief, and with a look of resolution said, "Can you hear me? May I ask you something?"

"Yes…please, I am listening," she murmured as she pulled herself to full attention.

In a slow cadence, he asked her if she would do several pieces depicting the heroic work and sacrifices of the men and women in

La Resistance. This work would be part of a special, war-related exhibit at the *Louvre*, as well as in other public places.

"Take a few weeks, *Madame* Sauval. These pieces must come from the soul. They must show the world, and especially future French generations, that even though our country was overrun and occupied, true Frenchman never stopped fighting for *Liberte, Egalite, Fraternite!* Will you do this? It could be a fitting memorial to your beloved Pierre."

Daphne sat blank-faced. The impact of *professeur's* words didn't register at first. Then she realized the broad scale of what he was asking. Momentarily it made her forget her grief. He was offering her a chance to commemorate her Pierre, maybe immortalize him all over France.

"Do you think I am capable of such an important work?"

"Yes...that is, if you believe in what I have said...in what you feel the people want to see and know."

They were both silent. Then he asked, "Do you believe your Pierre was a true hero who put his country ahead of his own life? Or was he just an unlucky man at the wrong place? Was his life in vain, or was it of great service to all of us who have survived. Was he one of those who died so that others might live?"

His words were a key...a key that unlocked the door for her to a whole gallery of pictures. Pictures of both Pierre and of how much the country suffered through the occupation, yet never gave up. For a moment she was back on Martinique, seeing Delacroix's painting, again in the shipping company's office. Could she be like the woman in the painting? Leading people, through her painting, to believe once more in the glory of France?

The words sank in, awakening something she knew was there – a feeling of pride, of determination – a desire to serve. Pierre was gone from the secular earth, but he could live on in her heart, and in her portrayal of him in the best of her talents – illustration.

Her eyes gleamed – tears welling to excitement. "Yes...yes,

Professuer Longuet, if you believe in me, I will do it!"

"I believe in you. I also believe…no, I know…that this vital work will reawaken the great store of talent you have. Three weeks…three illustrations." He knew he had penetrated the barrier of her grief. She was focusing on something outside of herself by an outpouring from within.

On Saturday, Daphne took a bus to Reims, arriving at dusk. She hired a cab to take her to the rail junction east of the city. She stood on a small rise of ground near the switches and interweaving of tracks. The vestiges of previous train sabotages were only in her imagination. Daphne walked, trying to picture her Pierre and his group – and the Germans hiding in ambush. At first it was unbearable – her stomach felt sick. Then, her clairvoyant vision brought Pierre in black turtle-neck and pants, black beret, his face blackened with grease paint, creeping along the track to the switch points.

The last sliver of sun sank below the horizon, its final glimmer of radiance leaving a back-lit, gray and white sky. Daphne sat down with her sketch pad. Her eyes shone with the light of love and purpose. The fire of meaningful service glowed from her perfect features with the radiance of inner beauty…and, at last… peace. She sketched the area, and from her intimate knowledge, her Pierre. As the moon lit the Southeastern sky, she wended her way back to the small room she had reserved for the weekend. Her heart was lighter than it had been for years. How could she be filled with joy…with this new desire, when all she and Dharma had felt was death's cold hand on their hearts? But, was not the world brought new joy after the shock of the crucifixion? The legacy left behind from the resurrection? Hadn't the legacy of Pierre and all of those who died for humanity's salvation also brought a joyous life that springs from death?

After a light supper of soufflé and tea, she stayed in her room and sketched scenes until the first light of day inched its way under her blinds. Exhausted, but fulfilled, she slept for several hours, waking at noon. She ate a quick *brioche* and coffee, before she had to go back to the rail junction. The loss of Pierre had become a silent memory, like an heirloom jewel in a velvet-lined box...to be taken out and savored when needed. Her conscious self had been made lighter by the *Professeur's* faith in her. Walking up the tracks, playing a form of hop-scotch on the cross ties, she suddenly came upon an older man.

"*Bon jour, Mademoiselle*...are you a railroad repairman?"

Startled, she blushed. The man must have thought she was a silly girl playing on the tracks. Seeing his kindly look, she said, "No, *Monsieur*, I am doing research for a painting."

"A painting? What a funny place to do that," he said with a teasing tone.

Daphne explained what she was trying to accomplish. The more she told, the more the man became interested. When she had outlined what she wanted to capture and why, he said, "My dear, I know of what you speak. My wife and I live just beyond that rise. We saw from our house the ambush that killed your husband. It was a terrible night, many Frenchmen were killed. No one ever knew who betrayed them." Then looking cautiously behind them, he added, "I used to hide their explosives under the floor of our small barn. When the war came, I was too old for the army. I tried three times to enlist. But always, 'You are too old.' So, in time I found a way to serve. I may have seen your husband...but, there were so many, and always at night with blackened faces. I did what I could."

He said his name was Eugene Gachet, and he was more than twice her age. Despite the difference, they warmed to each other and talked for more than an hour. He gave her many details of what Pierre's group had accomplished, and about the night of the ambush. It felt as if she was with her father again, particularly when he told her he had fought at Verdun in the Great War. She took his arm as they walked over the uneven gravel ballast and wood ties. Eugene, touched by her trust, invited her to his home. Michele, his wife, was delighted with this beautiful young woman, thinking wistfully how she wished they had had a daughter like this girl. Over a glass of wine and some local *fromage*, they chatted for several hours. Daphne was warmed by their total acceptance of her and their expressed admiration of her love for Pierre.

When he learned about Daphne and her mother spending the war on Martinique, Eugene said, "*Madame*, I too spent some time there after the first war. I was working for a sugar importer – we were setting up an arrangement with one of the plantations."

"It is a beautiful place, is it not?"

"To be sure...maybe now that this awful occupation is done, Michele and I can go there someday," he said, with a smile, "You know a second honeymoon." His suggestion brought a giggle and a blush from his cherub-faced wife.

The setting sun, nature's clock, caused Daphne to say that she must return to town and catch a bus. Eugene and Michele insisted that they drive her back to Paris. So the three of them bunched into his pre-war Peugeot and chugged off to the City of Lights. When they reached Daphne's apartment, she invited them in to meet Dharma.

"Michele and Eugene, thank you for being so kind to my daughter. Please come again...I will cook you a fine dinner."

Over the next three weeks, Daphne spent exhausting ten-and twelve-hour days at the *Louvre*. But, tiredness didn't affect her...she was on a mission...driven by a desire to immortalize her Pierre. After four hours in class, she spent the rest of the day and evening working on the three paintings. The role of Pierre, and *La Resistance* in the war became her *cause celebre*. Painting with all of the passion that was within her, she made the events of Pierre's last heroic deed come alive. She mixed bold, striking colors to convey determined heroism and soft, muted ones to depict the pathos of sacrifice. The figures seemed to speak from the canvas, telling, through Daphne's deft application of oil and pigment, of the struggle for victory...and its cost.

One painting showed Pierre, clad in his all-black outfit, pushing the plunger of a detonator. In the background, several German trucks were exploding. In the upper corner a broken swastika was half-covered with the tricolor flag of the revolution. The other two paintings showed both men and women derailing German supply trains and underground partisans commandeering German trucks.

Professeur Longuet studied them silently. Slowly, his face broke into a smile. He was pleased with the work and gratified that his assignment had brought Daphne back to reality.

"*Madame* Sauval, you have put your heart and soul on the canvas. The government will surely select the one with your husband to be made into a national poster. It will be hung all over France. Congratulations on this fine work. You reflect well on the *Louvre*."

Daphne was thrilled with his acceptance of her work. She knew she could now become an illustrator…but had this realization come at the price of Pierre's life? Would she have done as well without the internal suffering so many artists pour out onto their canvases?

"I thank you, my *Professeur*. It is you who pulled me out of my depression. Not only are you a fine instructor, but you have a kind soul. *Merci*."

As she walked down the halls of the *Louvre*, she thought how happy Raoul, Pierre, and her mother would be to know that their work, and hers, was being appreciated by the entire nation. She felt proud that her work would in some small way help to lead France into a new republic. She would never forget Delacroix's painting with the bold and proud woman, carrying a rifle in one hand, and the tri-color in the other.

She stopped in front of a painting by Millet, always her favorite painter…her idol…and whispered, "If I could just combine your skills with the dedicated services of Catherine of Siena, the woman in *Revolution*, and our Savior, maybe my life, even without Pierre, would be meaningful."

Longuet's prophesy came true. By year's end, Pierre's image was in every major city in France...in train stations, government buildings, and small museums.

In her last month at school, Daphne went again to Reims and the rail junction where Pierre was killed. After standing awhile at the switch he was trying to blow up, she walked up an embankment and sat in a small glen. The afternoon sun filtered through the branches, creating a montage of shadows and bright sun streaks. She leaned her head back against one of the trees. Soon she was dozing, until a brisk breeze blew strands of her ebony hair across her face. It roused her, and for an instant she thought she saw Pierre walking toward her. He wore the same smile he had when he first looked over her easel, ten years before. He was so real she started to call out. Later she would swear she heard a whisper. "You will be with me in paradise."

These sacred words and the vision of Pierre brought a state of ecstasy, that while brief, would be with her for the rest of her life. She blinked, and then saw what looked like a radiant, white-clothed mirage ascending upward. She was mesmerized...her heart beating furiously...she tried to speak...but no words came. Shaking her head, and rubbing her eyes, she now saw only the tracks and a few railcars on the siding. Still in a transcendental state, she looked again at the tracks hoping to see Pierre. The ethereal image was gone. She walked back to the city, as if on air. Gazing up at the blue sky, she announced to the heavens, "I know what I will do with my life. I will serve Thee in every way I can."

CHAPTER SIX

*Only when he has ceased to
need things
can a man truly be his own
master and so really exist*

Anwar al-Sadat
1918-1981

"Hello, Dad. It's Mark. I wanted to call you as soon as I could and thank you for the much appreciated gift. Steph and I are really enjoying the suite at the Waldorf. You're very generous and thoughtful."

While Mark was talking to her father, Stephanie was making faces at him across the bed. When she heard his solicitous tone, she made a sign like cutting her throat. She knew her father was wooing Mark, as he had done with so many people at the club, and especially anyone doing business with Braxton Chemical. It hurt…he had never courted her like that. True, he had always given her anything she wanted. He had even bragged to his circle about his gifted daughter, but he had never actually accepted her as an equal. She was, in his eyes, a woman. Women were pretty, had children, and served their husbands. On the other hand, if her father was satisfied with Mark's work, her husband would be the heir…the son and successor Daniel would have been. And Mark would probably go for it – South Boston to CEO of a large corporation – who could turn down that meteoric rise?

Realizing that Harvey Braxton was to be his entrée into the business world, Mark ignored her, turning his back so as to concentrate on this very important step to his future. He listened intently to every word his father-in-law said throwing in an occasional, "yes sir," or a "sounds good."

"I'll look forward to seeing you and Mom a week from today, and thanks again for the great gift."

Putting the phone down, he turned to Stephanie, who sat poker-faced with a slight hint of disbelief on her face…one eyebrow was arched, reflecting the skepticism that was a trademark of her view of other people's behavior, particularly in any relationships with her father. She had never bent to her father; now, here was her war-hero husband acting as if he were beholden to him.

"Did he cast a spell over you?"

"Funny question, what do you mean?"

"All I hope is that you never, ever become a toady to that man. Yes, he's my father, and I respect him, but I've seen him dominate my mother ever since I can remember – and anyone else that submitted."

Not to be put off from what he saw as his civilian opportunity, Mark shot back, "Wasn't it your thought that I might work for Braxton Chemical?"

She didn't like having the ball returned so quickly. She turned away for a moment.

"Yes, I thought it might help us get a house…maybe some other things. But, don't let him prevail over you. You have to be your own man."

"I see. Do it, but only on my terms…right?"

"Yes, since you put it that way."

"Things don't always work like that. More than three years in the army showed me. But, I promise you, I'll never sell my soul for a dollar. I agreed that we'd talk about a job next week and that, after my discharge in late April, I'd report for work if we agreed on a program that I could fit into." He got up and came around the bed. Sitting next to her, he lifted her face toward his, gently holding her chin. "Now, what are we doing for the next couple of days?"

"Don't worry about 'fitting in,' he'll stand on his hands to work you in. Number one, he likes you, and number two, he's always been

159

looking for a surrogate Daniel. Relax, big boy, you're in."

He knew that whenever she couched her words in sarcasm, it was a defense against the hurt that she felt when an action by her father was directed to someone other than herself. Maybe in time, what was deep inside her would surface...maybe he could help heal what seemed to be a suppressed anguish. He ran his hand down the side of her perfect features...*so much beauty, yet something inside that's not right. She's strong, beautiful, and smart; but there's vulnerability...need to give her love.*

"Well, if I'm in, it's due to you. So, now, about tonight and tomorrow, what do you say?"

Momentarily satisfied, she answered, "I'd love it if you'd take me to dinner in the Crystal Ball Room. And, kind sir, my dance card is open at the moment."

"Ma'am, may I have the pleasure of your company for dinner? I hear there's a smooth six-piece orchestra. Who knows, maybe they'll play *Beguine the Beguine* for us...been awhile, lover."

"I accept...with pleasure."

"And tomorrow, how about breakfast in bed...and...maybe..."

With a coquettish smile, "We'll see...who knows?"

The reunited couple spent a joyous and luxurious three days in New York: dinners with dancing; luncheons on terraces, and even one at the Automat; The Metropolitan Museum of Art; love-making; discussions about the future, nary a cross word. Only one difference arose between them, but by a tacit consent, it was dropped. They had quickly established that Mark was a staunch Republican, and Stephanie, an equally staunch Democrat, even though her father was a large contributor to the Republican Party.

The morning they checked out, Stephanie asked Mark if he would like to drive up to South Boston to see his parents.

"It'll be Saturday; maybe your dad will be home from work. What do you say? I told your mother we'd try."

"Okay, Steph...good of you to want to do this," he said, as he kissed her forehead. "Mom and Dad will be thrilled."

Mark drove after asking Stephanie if she would trust his three-toed left foot to work the clutch pedal. They stopped about halfway on the two-hundred-mile trip in Milford, Connecticut for lunch at a quaint inn dating back to the early nineteenth century. Over a chicken pot-pie and salad, they talked about his discharge, the progress of the Allies, now advancing deep into Germany, and about what Stephanie would be doing while Mark worked. She was still president of the Junior League, president of an art appreciation group, a two-day-a-week volunteer at a USO, and on a couple of other boards.

Mark took her hand across the table, "Steph, I'm proud of all your charitable work, and I want you to fill your days with the good things you are doing. You're a natural leader, but I hope you will always be there when I come home."

She smiled, and put her hand on top of his, but said nothing.

On the balance of the trip, they hummed along with the radio, and talked about where they would live. More than once, Stephanie told Mark about the darling, eight-room salt-box colonial on the outskirts of Darien. Every time she brought it up, he winced, thinking about how to finance it.

She read his mind. "Mark, you know I have a trust fund. We can use some of that money."

"Steph, I respect all that your family has built. I love you for offering your money, but I can't do that. Let me work for a year, and I'm sure I can qualify for a mortgage. That way the house will be mine as well as yours." He could see the start of a frown on her face, the sure sign she didn't like what he was saying. "Just being with you in our perfectly comfortable apartment makes it seem like a palace. Give me a year, please."

She started to argue, but today was not the day. She'd work on him after he was discharged and working at Braxton. She had become adroit at holding her tongue, if it was the best tactic.

"Okay, dear, maybe things will change. You're right," she lied.

Wanting to change the subject, Mark smiled at her, "Steph, I'm really glad you were in touch with Mom and Dad while I was gone. I know they appreciate you."

"It was easy. They're fine folks."

As they reached South Boston, an air of flatness came over both of them, particularly Mark. Driving down the streets of lower-middle-class houses and apartments, and blocks of smoke-spewing industry, for the first time, he really saw the impoverishment of where he had grown up. He pictured the Waldorf, the Braxton's estate, and even their apartment in Darien...such sharp contrast to where his parents lived.

Stephanie again seemed to read his mind. "Mark, I'll be so happy to see your mother. You know, while you were gone, she and I became good friends. I admire your parents for all they have done, especially raising one hell of a fine son. Are we going to stay with them?"

"No, we'll probably get a hotel...not much room in Mom and Dad's flat."

"Oh, Mark, that might hurt their feelings. If they ask us, we can make it work." She stroked the back of his neck.

It felt wonderful...her soft touch there. "You mean it?"

He had to admit, his wife might have had it all materially, but she had the tact, graciousness, and *noblesse oblige* of a true patrician. If she could handle that tiny set of rooms, she must really love him,and his parents.

"Sure, it'll be fun, you'll see."

Joyce Abercrombie didn't know who to hug first. She radiated her joy, switching her hands, hugs, and attention back and forth between Mark and Stephanie. John, although a little less demonstrative, had tears in his eyes. Within a few minutes, he warmed up and hugged both of them, proving that Englishmen could show emotion. Joyce took Mark and Stephanie's hands and led them to the lumpy couch. She sat between them, swiveling her head as if she were watching a tennis match.

Facing the trio, John just kept saying, "Thank God, you're safe…thank God."

Mark noticed how easily Stephanie fit into the simple surroundings of his parents' home. It was as if she had always lived in the small and under-furnished quarters. She didn't look at anything except his parents.

Stephanie quickly assimilated the bare humbleness of the flat, putting it below the point of attention. She couldn't escape the sincerity and warmth of Joyce and John's love; it permeated the place. She glanced at Mark, and back to the dingy room, thinking that from such meager beginnings, great things could come. She wondered what her girl friends at the club, the ones that were always mooning over him, would think if they were here.

They took the Abercrombies to a seafood restaurant on the Boston docks. The meal was a joyous one. To Mark it seemed as if Stephanie was his mother's daughter or a younger sister; they were so close. And Stephanie didn't neglect John either. She'd take his hand and tell him how she admired all that he had done to raise such a fine son. He just beamed at her. Three hours into dinner, the problem of sleeping arrangements was broached.

Stephanie asked if it would be inconvenient for her and Mark to stay with them. Joyce answered, "Are you sure? It's small…the bed…and…" Embarrassed she looked away.

Stephanie very lightly said, "No problem. I'm sure your home will seem palatial after the holes Mark had to sleep in over there."

Later, the young couple was in his room, embracing, extending the joy of the evening they had started. They hadn't remembered that Mark's childhood bed was only single width. It was hardly large enough to accommodate mature, six-foot-two Mark.

With a feigned woebegone-look, Mark advanced, "Gee, honey,

I'd love to be really close to you, but can you stand having me on top of you all night?"

"Aw shucks, lover, it'd be okay with me, but I think your parents might hear us. Better wait a day or so."

Mark ended up on the couch and managed only six hours of sleep. At breakfast, they sat almost in one another's lap at the tiny kitchen table over bacon, eggs, and toast. But, they were not quick to leave. They talked for hours about everything. Stephanie helped wash the dishes. Mark teasingly asked her where she'd learned to do that.

"At the USO, cleaning up after hungry sailors and soldiers."

Finally, at noon, they got up to depart. Stephanie hugged Joyce. "Mother Abercrombie, we've had a wonderful time. We'll get together again real soon. Maybe you'll come down to Darien." As she offered this sincere invitation to his parents, Mark looked at her with both love and admiration. His wife's depth of character and her tact endeared her to him over and over. She treated his parents as if she had known them all her life.

When they had gone, John turned to his wife, "Joyce, that's one fine lady Mark has."

"Yes she is," Joyce nodded, "And very bright. But, she's also strong-willed. I think in time they'll blend. But, Mark's going to have to be at his sharpest. He's smart enough, but, he'll have to be firm."

When they got back to Darien, Stephanie asked Mark to drive by the new colonial house she had been scoping out. He was reluctant, "What's the use...isn't it a little early?"

But Stephanie pleaded, and he acquiesced. No question, it was a beautiful home – an acre of wooded land and priced at twenty-two thousand. She took him by the hand and led him through the house, painting word pictures of how each room would look decorated. Her descriptions were vivid and almost convincing.

"Stephanie, as soon as I can qualify for a mortgage, we'll buy it, or one like it. Can't do it now; you forget I'm still working for Uncle Sam at two-fifty a month. The bank would laugh at me."

"I don't think they'd laugh at Braxton Chemical. My dad does all of the company's banking through First National."

"I'm not Braxton Chemical. I'm First Lieutenant Mark Abercrombie and that's who'll be taking out the mortgage."

"There might be ways around that, Mark. Don't misinterpret what I'm saying, but my family has some influence in local financial circles. We could get help."

"I appreciate that, but this has to be *our* house…meaning that *we* buy it, not your family. It has to be that way, or we'll never be right as a couple."

"I can't see what's wrong with being a couple, where one of them fought for his country. Why can't we take a little temporary help?"

"Please understand. I love you and will always work to provide all that we need, but it can't be a dole, or in time it would eat at our marriage like a cancer."

She started to say something about a damn stubborn mule but bit her tongue. That term wouldn't lead to anything good – it hadn't in the past. Let him carry *this* day with his male pride and independence…there'd be other days. Even as she sighed, she partially agreed that she had to respect his strength and integrity. Character-wise, he was head-and-shoulders above those fops at the club who were always trying to paw her. To be sure, he would be a challenge, but one that was worth whatever she would have to do.

The house issue could be addressed another day. Better to enjoy each other's company…there was always tomorrow. Fine things were almost always obtained over time. Put it away for today, she thought.

"Come on he-man, let's go home and fix a couple of steaks. It's been a while since we played house."

"I'm for that," he grinned. He knew his wife's will…her determination. The house wasn't going to go away. But, to her credit she didn't press it any-more…*right now that is. I made my point, and I think she bought some of it. I'm learning, she respects strength and, again to her credit, fairness.*

The next week was a whirlwind of parties to welcome back Mark, and many hours at the Braxton's estate enjoying tennis, riding, and swimming. After a week of these celebratory activities, Mark and Harvey secluded themselves in the study for a one-on-one discussion about a position with Braxton Chemicals for Mark. Harvey wasted no time in telling Mark that he had mapped out a one-year program of training mixed with actual sales calls. It includ-ed six weeks in the lab, two months in the three plants, and traveling to customers with several of the company's salesmen.

"Mark, at the end of the year, you'll be ready to assume an exec-utive's position. We'll start you at twenty-thousand a year, and if you are who we think you are, we'll give you some stock options. You might be able then to get that house my daughter is so set on…in fact, if you want to get it soon, we can arrange a loan…an advance against future earnings."

Mark took in a deep breath. He didn't want to sound ungrate-ful or priggish, nor did he want to rebuff his father-in-law and boss, so he chose his words carefully.

"Mr. Braxton, I…"

"How about Harvey in the office and Dad at home?"

It was a little difficult for Mark to accept the idea of using a first name for his superior. Three years of army "yes sirs" made this new form of address foreign.

"Harvey, I appreciate all that you are doing for me. I will give you all that I can in diligence and loyalty. But, I believe it would be best for Stephanie and me to wait on the house until I have proved to you that I'm doing the job and paying my way. Please know that I am grateful for the job, and your offer, but Stephanie and I need to earn what we obtain. I hope you understand."

"I understand, my boy, and I respect your integrity. In fact, I'm proud to have you as my son. When is your discharge?"

"Last Friday in April…may I start the following Monday?"

"Of course…how about we all go to your mustering out? It's in New Jersey, right?"

"Yes, I'd be honored."

With that, Harvey extended his hand, which Mark shook firmly and with an internal sigh. He had a job, an opportunity to earn a living and soon buy the house Stephanie wanted. He knew it was the first and most important step towards owning his own business one day.

Harvey introduced Mark to several executives, who put on the smiles of corporate-ladder sycophants. In the corner of one of the offices, a few of the men groused about the "lucky stiff" who married the boss's daughter. One of the men related Mark's background, including his full scholarship to Harvard, and his war record, including the decorations. He said he thought a man with those credentials would be up to facing any challenge of the job.

In early April, like most of the free world, they were stunned by the news of President Roosevelt's death. America was still at war in both Europe and the Far East, and suddenly its leader was gone. Millions of Americans saw him as the champion of the poor…the savior of the Great Depression, and to some, the abolisher of prohibition. Everywhere, throughout the nation, flags were flown at half-mast. Black bunting and crepe were affixed to many signs, home fronts, and coat lapels. Every paper and news program reflected the grief of an entire nation. Even many foreign countries conducted tributes to the man. The streets of Washington DC were lined a dozen-deep with teary-eyed people paying their respect, as the flag-draped coffin was pulled to the Rotunda.

Stephanie, knowing Mark's republican bias, asked him what he thought about the president.

"I never voted for the man, but I have to admire him. He did some beneficial things for the country with his New Deal work programs...the CCC, TVA, and the WPA. He got a lot people back to work in the depth of the Depression. And, he did help us stand up to the Axis. He'll be missed."

Stephanie admired her husband's honest objectivity. Her man had a heart as well as a brain. And, an entire country echoed Mark's praise. Millions of words were written and said about all that Roosevelt had done for America and the free world. His wife, Eleanor, was also admired by those she reached out to: black people, poor people, and the uneducated.

On the heels of the president's death, people were being shown the grim reality of Hitler's planned genocide of more than six-million Jews, and an understated killing of a like number of Christians – those believed to be in *Der Fuhrer's* way. Daily papers and newsreels showed pictures of the Nazi death camps. As the American and Russian forces pushed deeper into Germany, from the west and the east, the gas chambers, crematoriums, mass graves, and near-starved survivors were being discovered.

One Sunday morning, before Mark left for church, they were indulging themselves with waffles and the Sunday *New York Times*, a weekly practice they had fallen into as a couple, wrapped in the coziness of their new home and their deepening marriage. As Stephanie scanned the pictures of the Nazi camps, she shuddered. Before them in black and white was the grisly aftermath of Hitler's "final solution," the impersonal euphemism for the systematic extermination of more than six-million innocent lives.

Stephanie stood up and peeked over the top of Mark's paper. "Do you think, that if there's a God, He would allow things like this to happen?"

Mark looked up sharply from the *Times*. "That's a pretty broad statement. How do we know how God plans, thinks, or works?" He put the paper down, ready for her comeback.

"Are you evading my question? Or are we going to hear some platitude about the Almighty?"

Instead, he calmly said, "This type of cold-blooded murder – and on such a horrific scale – is hard for us to understand. But, Steph, I can't judge or speak for God...can you? Sometimes we just have to have faith, even though it may seem blind or beyond our understanding."

Stephanie bristled at this. It touched on another difference between them. Since Mark had come home, he wanted to go to church every Sunday. She went for a couple of weeks but then begged off, claiming she needed the time to prepare for a series of Monday meetings. So he went alone, making up lame excuses when asked where his wife was. He wondered if this was another step down a different path than Stephanie's. Sitting alone in this house of God gave him a hollow feeling; a couple should share worship, like his parents had.

On the last Friday in April, Lillian, Stephanie, Harvey, and Mark rode in an extended Packard sedan to Camp Kilmer, New Jersey. The camp had been named in honor of Joyce Kilmer, the author of the poem *Trees*, who had been killed in France during WW I. Mark was in full uniform. He stood along with fifty other soldiers, privates to majors, who were being honorably discharged. The attending general shook the hand of each man and handed him the official notice. As a group, they saluted both the officers and the flag.

Mark was happy with his discharge but couldn't accept merely the short ceremony as an end to more than three years of service – forty months of vigorous training, never-ending weeks of perilous combat, the reek of suffering and death, and the underlying pain of guilt about whether he had done all that he could to save lives. No one walked away from combat a whole person. He wondered if Pellini was looking down on this parade ground thinking he should have been standing next to his lieutenant, counting the hours until he would be back in Chicago Heights with his family.

Mark mumbled, "Sherman was right...war is hell."

On the drive back, Harvey took them to Toots Shore's restaurant for aged steaks and champagne. As usual, he arranged to sit next to Mark. He had never been as cozy with Stephanie, and it piqued her; but also as usual, she didn't show her emotions where her father was concerned. Nevertheless, the evening was pleasant, with Mark and Steph staying the night at the Braxton's.

Stephanie was up with the first ray of sun that crept over their bed. Mark was deep in sleep, oblivious to the sun or her stirring. After a very long half-hour, she knelt by him and ran her hand through his hair. He came to, wondering where he was.

"One thing's for sure, as long as you're around, I'll never need an alarm clock," he chided her, but reached out and pulled her to him, kissing the back of her neck.

"Come on, big guy, how about a quick ride before breakfast?"

"Take a ride...you mean on bikes?

"No, silly...on a horse."

"A horse, you have to be kidding? You know I don't ride!"

"Time will remedy that. Let's go. Afterwards, Maude will make us some Belgian waffles and Canadian bacon."

"How about some American waffles. I had all of Belgium I'll ever need."

Stephanie caught his reference. She too had enough of that Belgium...it had nearly cost her a husband. She turned to him with a compassionate look.

"Okay, sport, I agree. Here, put these riding britches on."

A blind man could tell that Mark had never been on a horse in his life. Stephanie laughed at his first attempt to mount, especially not starting from the left side. Even the horse looked askance.

Mark handled it well, even saying, "Now I know what they mean by 'horse laugh.' And, never mind about which end of the horse I look like."

He managed to stay on Old Blue, even laughing at himself. And, Maude did make American waffles, which they ate with relish.

*   *   *

They were relieved in early May to hear of Germany's unconditional surrender. Stephanie told Mark she was proud of him for having made a contribution to that victory. He appreciated her words, particularly since she had objected so vehemently to his enlisting. He had to give her credit; she was strong-willed, but didn't seem to carry grudges...at least with him. He wasn't so certain when it came to her father. There was something there he didn't fully understand. But maybe it would be better not to pry into that relationship. He sensed there were some deep roots to it. And, after all, Harvey was going to be his boss for a while. He couldn't go to the office with emotional prejudices. He'd better consider it none of his business.

Mark and Stephanie settled into a workable routine. He went to Braxton Chemical; she went to her committees, boards, and clubs. Frequent love-making, occasional trips to New York, and Stephanie's constant planning for buying their next house, filled their weeks and months. In August, the Japanese surrendered. The news came a few days after the second atom bomb was dropped. The two bombs effected a worldwide reaction of awe, relief that the war was over, but also deep shock at the immensity of the power of the atom bomb. The Manhattan Project, led by Robert Oppenheimer, had been carried out in secrecy. The public was unaware of all the work that began at the University of Chicago and culminated in a successful trial at Los Alamos, New Mexico. The released power of Einstein's $E = mc2$ opened a new era in human destiny...the Atomic Age. Both public and private debates raged about the morality of the bombings and why President Truman made the decision to drop them.

When the first pictures of the horrible deaths by implosion and radiation were published, Stephanie asked Mark what *his* God

171

thought about the rampant destruction and loss of life.

"Steph, I don't think God is a part of all that we humans do. We can't have free will and yet have every move we make controlled by some long marionette string from above."

He hoped that somehow he could get her to accept a loving God. So far she sat stone-faced.

"How could we grow and show true love if we were not allowed to direct our own lives? And yet, I believe that there can be Divine intervention. It's not black and white."

"Is that more of your rationalizations about a god? You always seem to have the same pat answers that my grandfather and mother have!"

"Maybe so, honey, but that's how I feel. I'm sorry you don't."

"But, was it right to kill so many civilians in such a horrific way?"

"One thing is for sure; it ended the war. And it stopped Lord knows how many, more years of killing. Over a million lives, both Japanese and American, were saved by avoiding the invasion of the mainland."

Mark was animated as he recalled the basis of his deep commitment to their American values. "Besides, the bombing of cities by all sides, like the fire bombings of London, Dresden, and Tokyo claimed more lives...not that that's a good argument. Remember who started all of this. We didn't ask for war, it was forced on us. We had no choice but to protect what you and I and millions of people in sane countries want: peace, and the freedom to live our lives as we wish."

She knew her jab about rationalizing was unkind. It was just that he always sounded so right and so confident about his faith. Just once, she'd like to prick that balloon. But, she had to admit his logic was sound. When Mark believed in something, he could be very adamant about sticking to his convictions...like his enlisting, and all that pride stuff about not taking anything he hadn't earned. Would she really have wanted him to be any different? No, she'd landed a *man*! He had a hard head, but a soft heart. She was sure, in time, she could soften that head a little.

The year of training at Braxton passed quickly. Mark put in ten-hour days. He would bring notes and product manuals home to study, causing Stephanie to complain about whether he was married to her or Braxton. He'd ease up a bit, take her to some of the never-ending rounds of charitable, fund-raising dinners, down to the City for a play, or for a weekend on some friend's yacht.

One night as they were preparing for bed, he hinted at having a child. At first Stephanie said nothing. Then she took his hand and pressed it to her breast.

"Oh, Mark, don't you think it's a little too soon to be thinking of such a major thing? We're still in this apartment...hardly a good place to raise a child. And you and I are doing so well in adjusting to each other the way things are. Let's talk about it later...maybe after we have a house and you have nailed down your permanent job at the company."

With that she ran her hand down the inside of his thigh and put her face in the crook of his neck. As always, the combination of her perfume and the inviting pressure of her body excited him, erasing any thoughts except to consummate his arousal. Later that night, as Stephanie slept happily with her head resting on Mark's chest, he recalled how many times serious questions and discussions were diverted by Stephanie's sexuality. How many issues between them had been subjugated by physical passion?

*　　　　　*　　　　　*

In Mark's second year at Braxton, his salary was raised to twenty-three thousand, and he was awarded fifty-thousand shares of stock options. He and Stephanie bought the salt-box colonial and became members of the Darien Country Club. Stephanie's board positions rose to seven. After they had decorated their new home, and settled in, Mark again brought up the question of having children, reminding Stephanie that she had promised to think about it after they bought a house.

Stephanie said she still needed a little more time to prepare herself for such a decision. She knew Mark was consumed with learning the business – he had shared his dream about them owning their own business. So she'd switch the conversation to the business plan, and he'd drop the children issue for a while.

Mark began traveling more, going to Europe, Northern Africa, and South America. He was Braxton's specialist in the coatings used in metal treating, and in industrial catalysts, particularly those precious metals used in crude oil refining. He was enamored with what he saw as increasing worldwide dependence on precious metals...platinum, titanium, and molybdenum. He worked to learn everything he could about them...their sources, usages, and their market potential. His goal was to own a brokering business dealing in the metals, and eventually be an importer-exporter. But, that was a few years off. Right now he must learn all he could, while making solid contacts in the areas where these materials were being used. Fortunately, the list included some of Braxton's customers.

When he'd return from a trip, his reunion with Stephanie was like a second honeymoon. She was so adept at creating romantic situations. The magnetism of her sexuality was a strong force in their coherence. Intellectually, they were also at par, but politically their paths diverged, as did their beliefs in an Almighty.

Mark rarely mentioned God or other spiritual themes to Stephanie anymore. Not that he was afraid of his faith, but he had explored Stephanie's agnosticism. Normally, whenever the subject of God came up, Stephanie either changed the subject or expressed her thoughts with cynical sarcasm. As best he could fathom, her lack of belief came from a mixture of father-resentment, the loss of her brother, and perhaps too zealous a maternal grandfather, the minister. Then, too, she was spoiled...never really tested in the crucible of hard times or personal sacrifice. She had never been confronted with a dilemma or trauma where there was no one to reach out to, except an Almighty. After he had returned from the war, he had picked up from bits and pieces of her conversations how much she had worried about him. *Gotta give her credit for that...who knows, maybe she had even prayed for him...but that wasn't evident in anything she said.* He didn't know that whenever her mother had said that she always prayed to God for Mark's safety, Stephanie had told her mother that God didn't reach down and catch German bullets. The time wasn't right for any serious discussions.

If he argued too much, it would only deepen her resistance. No one could make someone else believe in an abstract being. They had to want to seek and find for themselves. He would wait for the opportune time. Someday they would share an experience that might convince her of God's presence. He knew that Stephanie's Socratic testing of everything would take a happening, maybe even a crisis, to help her believe...or maybe just uncover what was already beneath the surface, a stifled faith purposely suppressed. And suppressed beliefs could be like a boil that needed the lance of visible truth to relieve the painful pressure. He prayed he could help his wife find that relief – help her to find her "moment of Grace," when she could let herself go and surrender to Him.

For Mark, the long-term happiness of their marriage depended on sharing more than sex, day-to-day duties, and occasional intellectual pursuits like music, art, and reading. He drew on the strength and example of his parent's marriage, welded by a shared belief in God and never diluted by affluence or self-aggrandizement.

He did wonder if anything he said, or alluded to, about spirituality registered with Stephanie.

What Mark didn't know was that Stephanie hadn't dismissed his words...his sincerity...his almost-convincing faith. Often when she was alone, she knew something was missing – even to the point of pain – the pain of "being left out." Had she built a wall around her soul…one that was impregnable by the words, even the deeds of others?

On one occasion, in desperation and in tears, she had cried out, "God, if you're there, let me see a sign – something I can touch and feel." Later, she ruefully mused that she might be too smart for her own good.

In Mark's third year with Braxton, he was sent to Paris to call on an important customer, The Duboise Metal Fabricating and Treating Company of France. Harvey had personally called the president and major shareholder, Mr. Charles Duboise, and introduced Mark over the phone. Charles would be delighted to receive *Monsieur* Abercrombie and to discuss additional contracts. His business was increasing during the rebuilding of France.

As the TWA super constellation, in its final approach, crossed over the French border from the English Channel, Mark looked down at the greenery that now covered the pockmarked devastation of the war. He marveled at how Mother Earth healed her bomb-inflicted wounds with the rebirth of her foliage. The scars on the bodies, minds, and souls of the combatants were not as easily healed. He wondered how he would feel about setting foot on this land as a civilian…there weren't many happy memories…no "Gay Paree"…no *cherchez la femme*. When he disembarked from the plane he was greeted by a uniformed chauffeur holding a sign with his name on it. He was driven to Chartres, the home of Duboise Metals, in luxury, joking in broken French with the driver about how this car was smoother and safer than a jeep or six-by-six.

Charles Duboise's greeting was very cordial, even warm. He gave Mark a detailed tour of his Chartres plant, showing him his use of Braxton coatings. Afterwards, he and Mark sat in comfortable chairs by a fireplace in his elegant office. The two men spent the afternoon discussing the relationship of their two companies, and to Mark's joy, they also talked about Duboise Metal's plans for further use of precious metals. Mark mentally recorded every fact Charles shared about the future of these metals...all data for his hoped-for business. Charles invited Mark to his home for dinner and to spend the night.

As they drove up the long circular drive of Charles' home, Mark noticed a petite, black-haired girl, or young woman, who got into a Citron and drove away. Charles saw Mark watching her.

"I see you noticed her. It is Daphne Devereux, my second cousin, or as you New England Americans say, 'a cousin once-removed.' She has been painting something for my wife and me. She is working for *Elle* magazine as an illustrator. Would you like to see some of her work?"

"She's very attractive" Mark spoke very softly. Then he turned to Charles. Yes...I would like to see her work."

"Certainly. You may appreciate her poster of our civilian fighters."

"Civilian? Oh, you mean the underground?

"*Oui*...I know of your valiant service, Mark, and I'm sure you know that it is not only soldiers who are at risk."

The picture of Pellini's family flashed in Mark's head, followed by visions of the citizens of Hiroshima, of the Jews in Auschwitz, the frozen bodies of many men from his company He suddenly felt the bone-chilling cold of the Ardennes and the searing pain of the German machine gun bullet creasing his forearm. A twinge of panic washed over him. He must have convulsed – enough that Duboise noticed it.

"Mark, are you all right?"

"Yes...uh...yes...just a memory flash of a bad time...sorry. You are right about civilian casualties. Our papers say that many more civilians died than servicemen. May we never have another one!"

"A fine wish, but perhaps it's only a dream...let us hope."

The time spent with Charles Duboise was invaluable to Mark. They had numerous discussions about how Charles' company was planning to increase its consumption and distribution of precious metals. Mark made careful notes of potential quantities, grades, and present sources. It heightened his already strong desire to acquire his own business. Ever since he had taken a course in metallurgical chemistry at Harvard, he was enthralled with the use of metals. They were strong, yet tractable; durable, yet replaceable. His mind soared with estimates of how many tons and tons would be used in a rebuilding world and the ever increasing inventiveness of people to find new applications...particularly for the precious ones. He thought of the sharpness of a metal edge, which he compared to what might be the sharpness of Harvey Braxton's response when the time came for Mark to venture out on his own. That was going to be a thorny problem. As some sage had once said, "Business and blood can be a bad mix."

After a tasty, five-course French provincial meal – *puree, fromage, salade, escalope de veau, et crepes*, accompanied with an appropriate wine at each course – Mark, Charles, and Mimi, his wife, talked of the war, the new emerging France, and some about Mark's wife. Mimi smiled when she saw the glow on Mark's face as he described Stephanie.

"*Monsieur* Mark, it is good to see love come from so deep as it is with you. We hope to meet this woman!"

They also viewed Charles' cousin's underground poster. With a slight bow and a handshake, Mark retired to his room. He had learned much valuable information. The facts Charles had shared with him would be useful in his acquiring a metals company and charting its direction. His mind was already constructing a *pro forma* based on estimated volumes of titanium and molybdenum, which Charles had sketched out.

As he undressed, he chuckled, remembering Mimi's remark about his "love glow" when he talked about Stephanie. The image of her saying goodbye to him at LaGuardia made him utter a low whistle...she had worn the same outfit she had on when he had disembarked from the *Leviathan*. It personified her...good taste, well-tailored, subdued sexiness, complimentary coloring, chosen precisely, complete, yet a hint of understatement. She was the only woman he knew who could make camel's hair emit the aura of ermine. He wondered what she was doing. It would be four in the afternoon…maybe some tennis, another meeting. He hoped not; lately she was having more of them in the evenings, coming home at nine or ten o'clock. He wasn't thrilled with eating dinner alone.

Gotta have a talk with her on this at dinner time when I'm home. Didn't marry her to eat alone…or wonder where she is or what she's doing. Yeah, and even who is she doing it with? Don't think there's anybody, but a few of those jerks at the club are always trying to cozy up to her. Have to give her credit though…like that time with Ronald Haverford…that was some firm push off. Man, I hope she never gives me anything like, "Ronny, please don't bore me with your juvenile antics." Never forget his stuttering and eighteen shades of red. Ever since then, he always gives us a wide berth… But, maybe I need to find out more about these "so called" other board members. Aw hell, guy, go to bed. She survived your forty months in the service. Give her credit!

Stephanie walked to the tooled, leather-topped desk in the library of their eight-room colonial and picked up the phone. Her eyes swept the heavy brocaded drapes, the patterned Oriental rug, and the cherry bookshelves filled with many leather-bound volumes. This room was one of the added benefits of the salt box she had waited so long for.

"Yes…oh, yes, Percy. Where are you calling from…here?"

She had heard he moved back to the greater Darien area, after living in the South for the past ten years. Her mind flashed back to her sophomore and junior years at cotillion. Percy Withers had been her almost-steady dance and dating partner. With a slight flush, she remembered he was the first boy to take her bra off. It was so cold that night in the Braxton's gazebo. Once she was bare, she made him put his overcoat over her. For an adolescent, he had been surprisingly tender…not the usual teenage groping and pawing of the others. Maybe he had read de Maupassant too. She wondered if he was still as cute as he was at seventeen.

"This is a surprise, Percy. What are you doing?"

He was working for an uncle's insurance company in Stamford, the same uncle who was on her art appreciation board. He would be living only fifteen miles from her and Mark. He asked if he could pick her up and drive her to the Darien Art Appreciation League meeting that night. When he found out that her husband was out of the country, he suggested a light supper before the meeting.

At first, she hesitated, but what the heck, seven nights home without Mark ought to entitle a girl to a little harmless socializing.

"Sure, Percy, pick me up at six. We can go to the Old Bridge Tavern. Be good to catch up on what we've been doing."

Over dinner, Percy learned about Mark, and Steph learned that Percy was a recent divorcee. At this, she asked herself, was he raising a green flag, or should she see it as a red one? He had been in the Navy, but always stationed in the States. She pictured him as the young ensign who had helped her at the Brooklyn Navy Yard at Mark's landing. His blond hair and deep blue eyes would have gone well with the navy blue uniform. At one point, Percy reached across the table and took Stephanie's hand, thanking her for the good times they had had in their teens. Stephanie let it linger on hers. Suddenly she was back in those halcyon days of worry-free high school, with her first love and her maiden sexual arousal. She wondered how things might have gone had she become pregnant from their graduation night, back seat consummation…her painful introduction to the ultimate act. She shook her head and withdrew her hand.

The rest of the evening was a series of platonic exchanges, mostly controlled by Stephanie. Every time Percy would edge closer to her during the meeting, or in his car, she thought of Mark…his wounds, his stalwart convictions, and his gratifying her in bed, and she would cool Percy with her Athenian stoicism.

After the meeting, Percy suggested a cup of coffee. Stephanie begged off.

"Got a full day tomorrow; and Mark will be arriving home in the evening. Thanks anyway. Good luck with the insurance business...ta ta."

"Okay, princess. But, if you're stuck for a ride...or *anything* at all, just holler."

Back in the house, she sat for a while before going up to bed. She experienced something new to her...confusion...a myriad of conflicting thoughts. She was touched by the memories of her time with Percy in the mid-thirties and his apparent attraction to her after all of these years. Or was he just a randy male devoid of a woman? But, she felt soiled because she had let him hold her hand for even a scant moment, and because she had thought warmly about the past. Her keen mind quickly determined that what was in the past didn't have to color the present. In her usual iron-like decisiveness, she flicked Percy Withers from her thoughts as one might flick a gnat from one's arm. What they had way back was fine, but that was "way back." Today was today...today was Mark, her work, and someday Braxton Chemical, sans Harvey. Finally she rose.

On the way up the stairs, she said to the large, wall-hung silhouettes of her and Mark, "You were acting like any dumb woman flattered by an old beau, but forget it, girl...you've got the best...don't screw it up."

When Mark finished breakfast at the Duboise home, Charles asked him if there was any place he would like to visit.

"That's very kind, Charles. I hadn't thought about anything beyond meeting with you. I want to thank you for a very cordial time. I will always be grateful for what you shared with me about the future plans of Duboise Metals. Hopefully, we will be seeing each other more often as our businesses grow together. You have helped me greatly. I am indebted to you." He added, "Sometime I would like you to meet my wife."

"It would be my pleasure, Mark. Please consider our home your home when you are in France. I am certain that it is more hospitable than many of the places you were forced to sleep in when you were fighting for all of us in the free world. N'est-ce pas?"

"That's true." Mark thought about visiting Bastogne. A dreamy look came over his face, which quickly turned to a frown as he heard the eerie whistle of a German 88 arcing into Apple Company on the outskirts of St. Vith...the one that killed Captain Redding. Did he want to revisit the grounds where he had seen misery and death...where he was fortunate to have lost only two toes, and had endured a near-miss with the machine gun slug? Did he want to relive again the ordeal of Sergeant Pellini?

"No, Charles, I have no sights to see this trip. I need to return to the office and my wife. But, thank you for your offer."

"As you say in America, 'okay.' Until the next time, adieu, my friend."

*   *   *

Over the next few months, Stephanie and Mark had "controlled" discussions about the merits of President Truman versus his opponent in the 1948 elections, Thomas Dewey. The line drawn between their political views was very well defined. Once, Stephanie asked him why he was a Republican...didn't he care for unfortunate people?

He looked at her incredulously, "I could say the same to you, but I won't. I'm a Republican because I was raised, as you know, poor. I can't afford to be a Democrat."

In one spirited discussion, Stephanie said, "I thought you applauded President Truman for dropping the atomic bomb? Isn't that the kind of decisiveness you would want in a president?"

Mark tried to come up with a rebuttal, but finally just smiled, "Touche! I concede this round. You got me on that one."

The day before the election, they had a heated debate, after which they retired to their respective corners and agreed to a truce. And, to her credit, when Truman won the election, Stephanie did not gloat. She just said that in a democracy, the majority decides the issues. Mark agreed, but said that a good part of democracy was that even if the majority ruled, the minority still had a strong voice. On that compromise, they went on with their lives – Mark at Braxton and Stephanie involved with her seven boards. Mark's church attendance slackened, but when he attended, he went alone. In 1950, Mark was made a vice president at Braxton Chemical and was given the responsibility of all off-shore sales. This necessitated many trips to Europe, North Africa, and South America. He was in France with Charles Duboise when the news of the North Koreans crossing the thirty-eighth parallel broke. They both shuddered as they agreed that war was just days away.

As 1950 wended into fall and winter, the papers, newsreels, and now the new living room magnet, television, brought the struggle on the Korean peninsula into every American's focus. Mark refused to see a Hollywood war picture, but he couldn't avoid the daily barrage of war news from the so-called "police action" in Korea. He was enthused when in the beginning, General Douglas MacArthur, of World War II fame, pushed the North Koreans back into their own territory and pulled off the innovative and daring amphibious landing at Inchon. But, this bold thrust unleashed hordes of Mao-directed, and Russian-supported, Chinese Communists that quickly overran the American forces and the smattering of token troops from other UN nations. It was the worst retreat in American history. They were almost pushed off the south eastern edge of the South Korean peninsula before superior air power and naval bombardments helped them rally and reverse the enemy's thrust. The enemy's lines, buttressed by the North Koreans, quickly broke, leaving the Chinese flanks vulnerable. Chinese were killed by the tens of thousands as the American led UN forces pushed northward.

The seesaw had tipped back in favor of the Allies.

Finally, after two years of bloody exchanges, often in sub-zero temperatures, the war was stalemated at the thirty-eighth parallel, while months of so-called "peace" negotiations took place. At best, it could be called a draw, but many said it was a loss for the UN. Mark felt the Americans were like a prizefighter with one hand tied behind his back. Truman's overruling of MacArthur, and the latter's ultimate discharge, prevented the Americans from going all out.

The continuing Korean War news had an effect on Mark. He said little about it, but every time he saw American GI's, weary and unshaven, plodding along in snow on the barren landscape, he absorbed what they were going through – he'd been there. When he saw films of wounded men being carried on stretchers, with a GI holding an IV bottle alongside of the man, he was back in Bastogne. Often in the middle of the night, he would cry out, or be covered with sweat. What he'd seen on television awakened old memories that had been mostly suppressed. At first, Stephanie was frightened by his outcries, but soon understood why they happened and would pull him into her arms.

One night she straddled him, her ample breasts hanging near his face. He gently held her breasts and kissed her nipples, his mind wandering. *Is this what war has done to me? Put me back as a suckling child?* But, after this closeness with her, he was able to go to sleep, grateful for her comfort. In the morning, he thanked her with a warm look and hug that was dear to her.

After one of these night sessions, on his way to work, he would think about the anomaly of Stephanie's tenderness during his night-time seizures, and the firm, all-business way in which she conducted the meetings she chaired. He treasured Stephanie's nursing of him through his nightmares. He would always love her for easing him from his momentary panic attacks. But, again he marveled at the span of her emotions and actions…the ultimate nurse to the ultimate directress. *I guess she's got a hard head and a soft heart. Gotta laugh, though, she said the same thing about me. We're just two peas in a pod, yet we walk different paths.*

In church, he would often think about the increasing paradoxes in their lives. The closeness of her succoring during his war-triggered nightmares was anomalous to her lack of spiritual beliefs. The total absorption of each with the other in their sexual sharing was in such sharp contrast to their views on politics and their different lifestyles. He thought about talking this over with the rector, J. Timothy Dardnell; but he was concerned about opening up his, or Stephanie's, private life. He stood in front of the rector's office, hesitating. As he turned to leave, Reverend Dardnell was just emerging. The reverend had noticed Mark's intermittent atten-dance, as well as the fact that Mark was usually alone. He had married the couple, but refrained from asking about Stephanie's absence from church. He called out to Mark, shook his hand, and asked him to stop in his office. He poured a cup of tea, and asked Mark if every-thing was all right with him and Stephanie.

Mark hemmed and hawed at first, but then explained Stephanie's agnosticism. Dardnell thought for a moment, looking at his shelves of religious books and sipping some tea, before turning to Mark.

"Mark, we have to appeal to her talents, her likes, her interests. You say she is a good organizer, a natural leader. Can we get her to take on a project…one here at the church that would benefit others?"

"Father Dardnell, I don't know…maybe. It's a good idea and might be worth a try…anything specific in mind?"

"Yes. We want to expand the Sunday school, and we need a chair for the fund drive. I'm sure you'll agree that she knows many people in the area…ah, and the *influential* ones too. Will you feel her out about the task?"

"I'll try. How much is the project estimated to cost?"

"Our goal is five-hundred-thousand. Since the war, we are experiencing a steady influx of young families with children. It's a good problem to have, but we need more classrooms."

"Can't promise anything, but I'll call you in a few days."

"Fine, Mark, and by-the-way, we'd like you to be on our Vestry. What do you say?"

"Yes, I'd be happy to serve."

"But, Steph, this isn't just about church...it's about kids – kids that need to be with other kids their age – and their being taught about what's good."

"It's still in the church, and you know how I feel about that."

"You're such a natural leader – able to influence people, raise funds, get people to believe in what you're trying to achieve. Please, use those wonderful talents to help all of our new, young families. You say that a committed Democrat is for helping the needy."

"Okay, bright boy...*touche*." She took his sincere compliments to heart. No man had ever told her these things. He was talking to her as a true equal...not in bed...not about his job...or about the house, but about her abilities and accomplishments in the so-called "man's world." Maybe helping the children of the area was more important than art leagues or the preservation of historical buildings.

"Would I have to go to church *if* I took the job?"

"Well, it wouldn't hurt once in a while, since you'll be asking a lot of the folks for their money. You do it, and I'll love you even more than I do now...if that's possible."

Again, she was touched by his direct way of telling her he loved her; it rang truer than a Browning love poem, at least to her. "You're convincing me...always knew you could sell furnaces on the equator," she glowed. "Okay, I'll do the best I can. Did the reverend say how much was needed?"

"Five-hundred thousand – they want to build ten new classrooms, two bathrooms, and a gathering area, plus furnishings. And, Steph, I'm proud of you for saying yes. I'll do anything you ask to help."

Stephanie, in her usual, organized, and effective manner, dove into raising the money for St. Luke's. Her years of chairing fund-raising drives for the many charities she worked with qualified her well for the task. And, she had a few favors to call in from a couple of the more endowed parishioners who she had worked with in the past. She sat in church dutifully at least three out of four Sundays, but never took communion. She even attended the social hour following the service. Fortunately, she didn't overhear the comments about her by the altar guild ladies, all of whom were deeply entrenched in their exclusive, by-invitation-only, clique. These old-sters thought she had a lot of nerve taking such a prominent chairmanship when she hadn't been a regular attendant. Stephanie got up in front of the congregation at all three services and made a plea for the funds that would "Help nourish both the souls and minds of our future leaders...our beloved children." Mark sat in his pew and beamed at his wife.

Lillian was so happy to see her daughter working on a church-based project that she helped Stephanie cajole Harvey into donating one-hundred thousand dollars. Stephanie herself gave fifteen thousand from her own trust fund. In three months, the entire amount was raised. One of the new rooms was called the Stephanie Abercrombie Room. The new gathering area had a plaque with Mr. and Mrs. Harvey Braxton's name on it.

Once the funds had been raised, to Mark's dismay, Stephanie stopped coming to church. This gave the altar guild biddies more grist for their slowly grinding mills. Darien was a small, socially close-knit community. There wasn't much that happened, particularly in prominent families like the Braxtons, and now the Abercrombies, that didn't get reported, dissected, and hashed over an over. Stephanie and her "rags-to-riches" husband were the subject of many a tea and altar guild meetings. The conversations ranged from adoration for the war hero and for the all-American couple to some catty remarks about why that haughty Braxton girl didn't have any children. Occasionally, Stephanie and Mark would pick up some of the gossip, but never let it influence them. They both were able to keep their own counsel in good old-fashioned New England stoicism.

*   *   *

One night in 1955, ten years after Mark had been discharged, he asked Stephanie to come and sit next to him on the leather-covered couch. It was a snowy, near-zero night. The windows were iced over, acting as prisms for the reflected light from the crackling fire in the library. Highlights danced across the panes accentuating the coziness of the setting. Stephanie snuggled up to Mark, resting her head on his arm.

"What's up? You have something serious you want to tell me?"

Mark stroked her glistening, auburn hair, "Yes...I need your help...your advice."

"Well, I'm flattered that the number two man at Braxton Chemical is asking little ole girl me for advice...are you serious?"

"Never more serious since we've been married. It's about my relationship at Braxton...and...with your father."

"Did he finally get to you?"

"No, it's not like that. Actually, it's the opposite."

"Opposite? You mean it's a positive thing? Tell me, I'm all ears to hear this myth. I can't recall too many 'positive' things coming out of the corner office...at least to my ears."

Mark, started to continue, but her remark stayed him for a moment. *There's that sarcasm that surfaces whenever we talk about her father. Whatever it is, it must go way back. It always seems to come from deep within her. Better leave it alone.* He buried his thoughts and turned to her.

"I'm not sure I know how to express this, but it's like he sees me as his son...not a son-in-law, but a real son. The water cooler gossip is starting to echo it…resentfully! A few of the top staff seem to be giving me undue deference…not natural…they act like they're walking on eggs when I'm around. There's no slackening of effort or efficiency, just a kid-glove handling of my directives."

"So what's wrong with being the favored son? It's not like you're the prodigal one. Oops, there I go borrowing one of grandfather's parables. If I don't watch myself, I'll be chanting a psalm next!"

"I wish," he said. Then not wanting to antagonize her, he held up his hand in the peace sign of the American Indians. "Be serious a moment. This is a critical situation in our lives, Steph. It's one we, and I mean we, have to handle adroitly…could affect family relation-ships…our future…who knows what all?"

"Yes, anything with the great Harvey Braxton is *critical*. Why is it critical? What is this great thing that seems to be hanging over us?"

"It's about me leaving Braxton. Because, when we start our own business, I'll have to leave. How will your dad take my leaving? He'll feel I betrayed him! He'll call me an ingrate."

She thought about all of the times she had seen her father manipulate people, her mother, business associates, Daniel, servants…surely others. At thirty-six, she had the wisdom and experience of dealing with people of many ambitions, intents, man-nerisms, styles, and a varied range of honesty. She had been on, and chaired, dozens of boards and had managed the investments of her million-dollar trust fund for more than six years. She had observed, both emotionally and objectively, the foibles, traits, and characteristics of her father since she was seven or eight. She knew Mark was right in his sensitivity to Harvey's possible reactions to what Mark would tell him.

"You're probably right. He likes to control…have people do his bidding. When are you thinking of this new venture?"

"In six months at the outside. I've located a brokerage firm that's had a good reputation. They've come up with just what we're looking for. It's a company dealing in precious metals, but the owner is aging and ailing. If someone doesn't take it in hand, it'll slide. The price is reasonable."

"What is the price?"

"One million."

"Do we have that much?"

"Maybe...we've saved over two-hundred thousand from my pay, and the options are worth another two-hundred. If we can find a third two-hundred, the owner will take a five-year payout for the remainder. If he spreads the four-hundred thousand over five years, it'll help him tax-wise. The business should be able to pay it in that time span. It's that third two-hundred that's the bind."

Stephanie said nothing, relishing the sharing of their mutual business interests...and the potential of acquiring one that they could jointly own. She warmed to the thought of this new bond with Mark. She felt good about his coming to her for advice and counsel. If only her father had the confidence in her ability to think equally with a man, as her husband was doing. All he ever thought she was good for was to look pretty and begat his name...his line...his seed.

"Where are you, Steph?"

"Just thinking about what you say we need. Give me a minute."

He nodded, as she kept looking steadily at him – her fertile brain racing. She wanted the security, and maybe the ultimate control of Braxton, that Mark's staying with the company would yield. On the other hand, she wasn't against seeing her father deflated by his new "son" leaving. She weighed the dilemma...no eating the cake and having it too. If he got the business, it would keep him occupied, maybe cool the having children talk...just another few years, then it would be biologically too late...that would show old Harvey who controlled her womb. And, when he passed on, his majority stock position would have to go to his estate. She should share in that. She took Mark's hand and smiled.

"Hey, tycoon, I can put the two-hundred in from my trust fund. When I hit thirty, along with a few wrinkles, I got control of it.

What do you say?"

"I say we're a team. We can structure your money as a second mortgage."

"No way...it's an equity contribution. Move over, partner, we're a corporation of two; but, Mr. Chairman, you better produce!"

For the moment, they were both silent, each with a good feeling about the synergy that was birthing with their mutual desire to be a business team. Mark winked at her...*boy, if I could really get her interested in this, maybe she'd drop a few boards and be home every night. We'd be walking the same path.*

Stephanie winked back, thinking...this might be an avenue where I can show that some women are just as capable of running a business as some of those old stuffy men. She liked the thought so much she got up and kissed Mark.

"Thank you, ma'am....I can see you're going to be a tough partner. Guess I'll really have to shape up."

"When are you planning to talk to Daddy?"

"I'll talk to your father after we sign the deal. I'll give him whatever notice he wants...that is if he doesn't throw me out."

"That's possible."

"I feel bad about this Steph. He's been good to me. But, I always feel like the guy that married the boss' daughter...right now, I am that guy! Guess I have a lot of foolish pride – wanting to be my own boss – can't help it. I want you to respect me for what I do, never for what might have been given me."

Stephanie looked up. She had never heard Mark openly express his desire to merit her respect. This realization was a boost to her confidence...both within herself and in their ability to make the new business work. It made her feel good to know how much he desired her approval – he had always been strong, almost totally independent, and always within his own counsel. She rose and put her hand on his head.

"You paid your way at Braxton. Mother shared with me his

praise of your work. And, honey, I do respect you. Never worry about that. I even respect that hard head of yours."

He stood up, looking deeply into her face. It was especially lovely right now.

"There's nothing like mutual respect for mutual qualities, dear," he laughed, lightly tapping her on top of the head. He took her arm and gently pulled her to the stairs. "Now, let's go up. We'll see if you still respect me in the morning!"

*   *   *

After several weeks of due diligence, final negotiations, and the signing of hundreds of papers, the deal was consummated, except for the actual closing date, which Mark wanted to hold in abeyance until he talked with Harvey. He dreaded that meeting, as all of his work on the purchase had been done *sub rosa*. All through the process, he had debated about whether to share his plans with his father-in-law. He felt it would be the honorable thing, but Stephanie advised against it. She claimed Harvey would try to discourage it, using any and all means to scuttle the move.

His talk with Harvey was made even more difficult; before he could reveal his plans, Harvey spoke of another salary increase. It was difficult to break through the bubble of Braxton's euphoria about the job he said Mark was doing. Finally, Mark settled Harvey by saying he had some serious news. The look on Mark's face registered, viscerally with the older man – he became all business, sitting behind his large desk. He knew what he was going to hear was not good – and it wasn't! As Mark finished talking, Harvey turned purplish-red, his eyes bulged, and he banged his fist on the desk.

"Why, you ingrate, what do you mean? You're leaving me after all I've done for you? After all I've planned for you...treated you as my own son! Is that the type of honor you learned at Harvard...or in

South Boston? I thought my daughter was marrying a man of integrity."

Mark stood stoically through the barrage of blistering words – never shifting his eyes from Braxton's. He knew whatever he said would fall on a closed and angry mind. But, he had to try.

"I'm sorry, sir, but I have to find out if I can support the lady we both love on my own. I've had this dream of being my own boss since I was eighteen. You must be able to understand that. Didn't you reach where you are by having a dream...and the drive and skills to back it up?"

For a moment, Mark's acknowledgement of Harvey's own accomplishments stopped his tirade. Despite the anger and hurt, he had to respect this man. No one had ever spoken up to him.

"And, Harvey, I'll do whatever you want me to do in the transition. Also, in my business I will be able to throw leads to you. Many customers will be common to both companies. That is if you want me to."

Harvey started to come back with a snarl, but he was drained from his outburst. Stephanie and Mark were all that he had. Daniel was gone, and Lillian never very strong, would probably not outlive him. For the first time, he was facing his own mortality and seeing an entity he could not dominate. It was a shock...it exposed the quick of his inner self, a being that had been shielded for years by aggressiveness and control, and a wall of wealth and sycophants.

"Let me think about this, Mark. It's been a blow. I appreciate your willingness to transition your leaving."

"I'll be at my job until you say it's okay to leave. I appreciate all you've done for me. I'm sorry this passion is in me. I will always be loyal to you and Braxton Chemical."

"Fine...I'll talk to you tomorrow."

Mark backed out of Harvey's office wondering what Braxton would do. He knew the depth of the old man's desire to control *all* that was in his family and the corporation. Something told him the issue was far from settled. His stomach felt queasy, he wondered if he had put Stephanie in jeopardy with her father. *Am I being selfish...not thinking enough about her, only my own ambition?* It was with misgivings, and a heavy heart, that Mark sat at his desk. He'd *have* to make the new business work, or he'd probably be out in the cold...scratching for a job on the open market. He knew Harvey would never take him back. *No sir, buddy, you've crossed the Rubicon.*

When Mark left the office, Harvey sat at his desk letting the full impact of losing his "son" and such a capable manager sink in. The more he brooded, the angrier he became.

He bellowed at his secretary, "Miss Higby, get my probate lawyer on the phone!"

CHAPTER SEVEN

"It is written,
'Worship the Lord your God,
and serve him only'

Luke 4:8

When Daphne returned to Reims from the rail junction, she was in a trance. Her ethereal experience on the hillside by the tracks where Pierre had been killed had filled her with the Holy Spirit. She was warmed by the intangible spirit and indescribable specter that most Christians feel is the essence of God and Christ entering them...a breath of holiness. Daphne just knew that she had been likewise infused and was aglow with love and awe...awe at the magnificence of what she felt in the aura of God's being. The resolute pledge she had made aloud as she reassimulated the sublime event on the trackside hill, played over and over in her mind.

She looked heavenward and repeated it slowly and calmly, "I know what I will do with my life. I will serve Thee in every way I can."

It seemed that her thoughts radiated around her like a high-voltage corona – an emanated halo. With each step she felt like a feather floating on a zephyr of heavenly air. Then, on the bus carrying her back to her mother and Paris, she re-experienced the apparition of Pierre that had been so real. Her ears echoed the whispered assurance of her future in Paradise.

"You must be worthy, you must be devout; you must be sincere," she murmured. Seeing her reflection in the window, she whispered, "I will, I will."

At home, her mother hugged her asking if she had a safe trip.

195

"*Oui, Maman*, it was safe in the way that you ask, but it was soul-stirring...I still feel its effect."

Dharma had wondered what effect visiting Pierre's execution site would have on her daughter. Would her going there dredge up sorrowful memories? Would the site bring home the dreadful reality of what had happened and send her daughter into a debilitating despondency? Her fears were slaked when she heard Daphne's enthusiastic comment.

"Tell me, child, what was it you experienced?"

Dharma had always seen and believed in things metaphysically. She would have been either an atheist or a totally devout believer. God was either black or white...she had always chosen white. There was no middle ground...no in between...none of that "all shades of gray" espoused by many philosophers. Her faith was the deep-seated, innocent and trusting faith of a child – never drawn from pseudo-intellectualism. Her spiritual ethos, in raising Daphne, had melded with her daughter's innate predisposition to believe.

Daphne moved closer. She seemed to be at a loss for words. She turned her face to her mother, who marveled at the inner beauty that emanated from her daughter in a beneficent blossom...cherubic in its innocence. She wished that Raoul were here to see their daughter's holiness.

"Were you touched by angels? You have a glow I have never seen before. Tell me, dear, did you feel the Holy Spirit?"

"I could have...I am warm all over. It must be the Holy Spirit. I have never felt like this before."

"What started this feeling? Please share everything with me."

"When I was in Reims, I went to the place where Pierre was killed. I felt his presence; in fact, I saw him in a vision. I thought later that my mind had played tricks with me, but he was so real. He was coming up the hill towards me, smiling, looking exactly as he did the first day that I met him."

Dharma could see the memory of that day on her daughter's

face. She knew her daughter never exaggerated, or made up things. She truly must have had this religious experience.

"I believe you. Your vision comes from the deep love that you had for Pierre. When love is that deep, people are never separated from their loved ones."

She was reminded not only of her daughter's pain from Pierre's death, but also of her own great loss. Her dreams of Raoul were like her daughter's visions. They were like many of the bitter-sweet things of life...the sweetness of feeling her loved-one's presence, even if only in a dream, and the bitterness and hollowness of no husband.

"Yes, I believe in visions. I have seen Raoul in my dreams and once when I was awake."

Daphne was moved by her mother's words. Both in their reverie of love and sorrow, they stood mutely, just looking at each other in total feminine empathy.

"Did you feel or see anything else?"

"Oui, when Pierre faded off into the woods, a strong wind came up, and I saw...oh, *Maman*, please believe me...I saw what looked like our Lord rising from the hillside where I was sitting. I saw a man with a kind, beautiful face that gave off a soft light. He was in a white robe. His feet were bare and had a wound in them, as did his outstretched hands. He just seemed to float up into the sky."

She laughed a little nervously. "I am sure most people would say I was hallucinating."

A glance at her mother's face reassured her. It was still, almost transfixed. There was no mistaking her deep love for her angelic daughter.

Daphne's face glowed even brighter as she continued. "But, the vision was so vivid...so real, that I still carry these two revelations in my mind...even in my soul. *Maman*, am I crazy?"

"No, child, you are not the first to have visions sent to them. We never know how God speaks to His people. You are blessed that this event occurred, and so...so lifelike. There is a message here, I am sure."

"What do you think it is, *Maman*? What would God be saying to me...just one woman, who is not important?"

"Dear, who are we to say who or what is important in God's eyes? Was not our Savior but a humble carpenter from Galilee?"

"I didn't think of that. There has been so much happening...I need to pray about all of this. I must find a way to be alone with my thoughts. How can I do this?"

"It would be difficult here in the apartment," Dharma said. She wanted Daphne not to be around for the next few days...she needed solitude for a problem of her own.

"Doesn't your cousin, Charles Duboise, have a large estate? Maybe he has a place where you could be alone."

"You are right, *Maman*. Would you care if I went to Charles' for a few days? I could spend time in his summer house...alone...where I can work out these things. And, before I return to you, I could see if he might give me a recommendation at *Elle*. I will finish at the *Louvre* in two months."

"If that will help you, dear, please go ahead."

"I will miss you, but only for two or three days."

"Of course – and I will pray that God will be with you as you work out all that you are carrying. I will be all right."

Dharma smiled at her daughter, but it was a smile to hide the pain that was in her abdomen. It had started a few weeks ago as a pin prick, but now it had become severe, as if a knife was being twisted inside her. Sometimes she would double over. It was good that Daphne would be away so that she could go secretly to a doctor. Was it providential that her daughter had had her spiritual experience and the desire to be alone?

So, after many hugs with her mother, Daphne set off for Chartres. She had thought about what to take, finally deciding on plain clothes...ones that reflected humility and no pretentiousness.

As she placed her things in the valise, she thought of our Lord's simple robe and sandals, which he wore during his forty days in the wilderness. She envisioned her retreat at Charles' estate as her wilderness and hoped it would help her come back with a resolute creed and spiritual path. She also packed her missal, the one Cardinal Desmonde had given her.

Everything had been safely squeezed into the tiny Citron. Now it was time to start her trip, which she imagined to be her pilgrimage. After a few coughs, Daphne felt the seven-year-old Citron come to life. When she stopped at a religious goods store, she kept the engine running, just in case the temperamental car wanted to stall. She rushed into the store and bought a pair of missive candles and a four-inch high cross on a small base.

Daphne chugged up the long circular driveway to Charles' estate, marveling at the manicured formal gardens, the lush foliage, and the grand *Châteaux*. On a small pond near the summer house, a family of ducks glided slowly across, leaving their tiny wakes. Daphne thought about the wakes that humans make as they move across their lives. She hoped hers would be meaningful. The grandeur of the estate made her laugh…she immediately saw the difference between this and Christ's wilderness in his time of trial. For a moment she wondered if she had picked the right place for her praying and theological reflections.

Charles was at the door to greet her.

"Welcome, Daphne. We are so happy that you will be with us. Ah, I see that you are more beautiful than ever. Here, let me help you with your bag."

"Cousin Charles, thank you for letting me stay with you and Mimi for these days."

"It is our pleasure, Daphne. But, are you sure that you want to stay in the summer house…not in with us, where you would be more comfortable?"

"Thank you, but I need a few days to think through what I will do in the future. As you said, I have my painting, my illustrations, but there is another part of life…"

She reddened and looked at her feet. "You may think me odd, cousin, but there is the spiritual side…that's what I want to think through."

"I do not think you odd – would that more people magnified their spiritual lives…perhaps less wars…less hunger."

Charles' life had been consumed with business, save for his counter-intelligence work for the French Government during the war. He had been lucky to escape detection by the Germans. And, he remembered the stress and fear that he and Mimi had endured during the years of the occupation. He delighted in the pure and enthusiastic reverence of his cousin. Oh, that more people could be like her.

Daphne blushed at his compliment. She smiled, the dimple besides her mouth accentuating her full-faced grin.

"No, my dear, please know we are gratified that you chose our home for your spiritual path. Let us know if there is anything we can do. We will leave you to your thoughts." He rose to go, then paused, "But, please eat with us…there are no provisions in the summer house."

"Thank you. You and Mimi are so generous. I will probably not eat but once a day; but I would be happy, and grateful, to share that meal with you. A few pieces of fruit and some nuts will suffice for the remainder of what I need." With a self-deprecating smile, she added, "I know our Lord fasted for forty days, but I'm afraid I have to keep up my strength if I am to finish my work at school."

"Certainly. Please excuse me for just a moment."

He turned into the adjoining room. He had called Dharma and asked her if there was anything that Daphne would like…something she might have expressed a desire for. Dharma said she had heard her daughter mention one item many times. He came back to

Daphne with a smile on his face, his hands behind his back.

She looked quizzically at him…the half-smile, raised eyebrow, and tilt of her head, reminding him of a pixie.

"Daphne, here is something Mimi and I think you will like." With that he handed a wrapped gift to her.

Daphne beamed and tentatively reached for the package. She touched his hand, thanking him with appreciative eyes. Opening it slowly she found a leather-bound edition of the King James Version of the Bible in French. Her name was embossed on the cover in gold. As she ran her delicate hands over the binding, and leafed through the fine, parchment like pages, her whole being seemed to light up. She threw her arms around Charles.

"Oh, Charles…*merci…merci*, this is beautiful. This is just what I have wanted. It will help me in my retreat. You are very kind. I will treasure it always."

"It is our pleasure, my dear. We trust it will bring you the answers that you seek."

Daphne had been gone for barely an hour, when Dharma again felt the sharp pain in her lower body. She fell onto her divan.

"Oh, God, help me…help me!"

She tried to pull her stomach in with both arms, as tears streamed down her face. Finally, after pain-wracked minutes, that seemed an eternity, the pain subsided. She groped for the telephone and called a doctor her friend had recommended. After a long wait, questions, and more questions, and repetitions of the information she supplied, she was granted an appointment for the next morning. But only after she pleaded with the nurse, crying that she didn't think she could stand another day.

That night she slept fitfully, tormented as well by mental anguish. What if something happened to her…what would Daphne do after losing her husband and her father within months of each other? If she died, oh, dear God forbid, her daughter would have all of her loved ones taken by one fell swoop of the grim reaper's scythe. Could Daphne stand that…what would it do to her faith…her loving, gentle soul?

Finally, as dawn appeared, Dharma got up, knelt down by her bed, and prayed for a long time. Looking in the mirror, as she readied for her doctor visit, she saw the dark lines under her eyes and the grimness of a once-beautiful face stretched tight with pain. She dressed with a slowness and precision born of resolve…the motions carried out in a feeling of predestined fate. She simply did one thing after another, by rote. After a tortuous hour, she left the apartment. She stood by the curb, chilled and lonely, in an unsettling wind. Oh, how she wished Raoul was here to comfort her…help her get to the clinic. Finally, a pre-war taxi stopped.

Her longing for her husband led her into a dazed comfort of thinking about things they had shared…things that didn't carry pain and didn't revolve around hospitals. She drifted back to the early years of their marriage, before Daphne was born – what they had called their two-year honeymoon. Moving to France from her native Albania, Dharma wanted to learn all she could about her new country…and the ethnicity of her new husband. She went to night school for two years, studying French, practicing at home with her husband. Raoul was an excellent teacher. Besides helping Dharma with her ever-improving French, he shared both history and geography with her. But, he said, the best way to learn about a country and its people was through their literature.

He had helped her through Zola's *La Conquete de Plassans*, a treatise on provincial life. Next, she read, almost entirely without help, Hugo's *Le Miserables*. With some difficulty, Raoul found French editions of Shakespeare's *Macbeth* and *Hamlet*. He told Dharma that the English Bard had, in his opinion, the greatest insights into the foibles of man. Her most revered gift was his last one to her, given as she left for Martinique: a leather-bound copy of Anatole France's *The Gods are Athirst*. It taught her so much about what her husband's countrymen had gone through to arrive at their present democracy, albeit with many bloody chapters and swings of power. Men…were they ever satisfied with what they had, or did they always have to anoint their gains in vengeful blood?

As she rode to the medical center, she observed they were on one of the streets that had been written about in France's book. Her semi-delirious mind pictured the tumbrils of the Revolution – the dung carts of the century carrying the elite of Paris to the guillotine down the same Avenue she was traveling. Was she going to her own sentencing? Was her guillotine to be the scalpel and operating table of *le hospital*? Were "the gods athirst" for her blood as they had been for the aristocrats of the-eighteenth century ruling classes?

*   *   *

"We've done it!" Mark exclaimed as he and Stephanie signed the last of two-hundred documents making them sole owners of the Smythe Metals Procurement Company – now to be called Abercrombie and Abercrombie, Inc. Stephanie smiled and patted the back of his hand.

Mark had left Braxton Chemicals a month earlier on an unpleasant note. His father-in-law had said, "I hope that you, our twentieth-century reincarnation of Benedict Arnold, will clean out your desk as quickly as possible."

Neither he nor Stephanie knew that Harvey Braxton had worked with his probate lawyer for hours figuring out how to exclude Mark from any access to his estate and to minimize what Stephanie would inherit. Harold Ainsworth had strongly urged Harvey not to cut his daughter out. He said it would leave the estate open to law suits should Lillian die before Harvey. Also, he said, he had seen "vengeance" codicils cause worse hurt for the avenger.

"Harvey, think about taking hate and hurt for your one living relative to the hereafter with you." This caught Braxton up short.

"I'll think about it. Call me in a week."

Harvey vacillated between his chagrin at Mark and Stephanie for acquiring the metals company and his inherent love for his daughter. He had to admit a grudging respect for his war-hero son-in-law, whom he had wanted so much to love as his own. When he tried to talk to Lillian about it, she said that he should swallow his injured pride and let love be the guiding force...not anger.

In an uncharacteristic role, Lillian stood in his face. "Harvey, none of us is going to live forever. You want to die with a soul full of hate, alienated from the two people who love you, as well as respect for what you have built...and donated in the community?"

Harvey started to come back with a "but look what they did."

Lillian said, "Shush with that little boy's, 'I didn't get my way, so I won't play.' You're too big a person for that. Be proud that they have the courage to strike out on their own. Don't you have enough sycophants at the office...do you want your heirs to be that as well? You know, Harvey, you can't stamp everyone out with your cookie cutters...some people want to be their own selves!"

For once in his life of continuous aggressiveness and command-ing stature, Harvey was speechless. Lillian had never spoken to him this way. He just sat and kept shaking his head. After she left the room, his mind struggled to grasp the cause of all the recent holes in his dike of self-assuredness. First it was Stephanie, never overt in her resistance, but constant. Next was Mark pulling out of Braxton after all that Harvey had provided for him. Now, the largest hole of all: his ever-acquiescing Lillian. Had he been more paranoid, he would have thought it a conspiracy. What had he done except provide everything they could want or need? He gave to them, never needing a return...well, maybe a little gratitude and loyalty...not too much to expect.

Harvey chewed on these thoughts. He became less demanding and less involved in Braxton Chemicals' daily business. He was consumed by a search to understand why he was alone on a drifting raft in a sea of confusion…the waters of self-doubt starting to lick at his feet…a totally new sensation for him. No matter how much he agonized, or his mind ground on the recent series of rebellions by his kith and kin, he couldn't see the shoreline of reason. His negative machinations were no clearer; in fact, they made him feel sick.

Ever-perceptive, Lillian saw the change in him. He was silent at meals. He didn't finish what was served, leaving the table quickly and retiring to his study. After a week of this, Lillian followed him into the den one evening and sat near him without saying anything. She put her hand on his and looked into his puzzled eyes. For a moment, the tensor of pride tightened his jaw into a grimace. Then, as he felt Lillian's quiet, inner strength, his face slackened, his eyes modulated from defiant to the submissiveness of a seeking child.

"What…what should I do? Lillian…help me, help me…please."

*   *   *

Clutching the new Bible to her chest, Daphne walked to the summer house on Charles' estate. It was a one-story building of stone and stucco with a Mansard roof, partially hidden by a grove of trees. Inside, she took in the luxury of the two bedrooms, small kitchenette, and sitting room, complete with a stone-bordered fireplace. She chose the smaller of the two bedrooms, setting her two votive candles and small cross on the dresser. Kneeling in front of her newly created altar, she said a prayer of thanksgiving and invoked a plea for guidance.

The first night she had supper with Mimi and Charles. Over a poached turbot, they discussed Daphne's future. Charles was on the board of two publishing houses: one of them being the fashionable *Elle*; the other, a magazine about French tourism.

"Daphne, I will arrange an interview at both houses for you. What dates are suitable to you?"

"Oh, thank you, Cousin Charles. Any day from here on out will be fine. You are so good to me. I would like to do a portrait of you and Mimi if you will permit me. It's the least I can do."

"That's a very kind gift, Daphne," Mimi said.

After the maid had served coffee, Mimi sat thinking about Daphne's life as a single woman, living an almost isolated life. She wanted to broach the subject, but not too overtly. She wanted to bring up the topic of men in a subtle way.

She turned to Charles and said, "Did you tell her of the American war-hero who visits with us occasionally?"

"One of my largest suppliers of metal coatings is represented by the son-in-law of the owner. His name is Mark Abercrombie. In fact, several years ago, he was with us driving up the driveway as you were leaving. He commented on how attractive you are...who could argue that?" Charles smiled, as Daphne blushed at the direct compliment.

"He was a war-hero?" Daphne felt a tremor in her heart. Like Pierre...

"Yes, decorated for saving his company at the Battle of the Bulge, where he was wounded. Perhaps he will visit with us again when you are here."

Mimi was afraid that Daphne might get the wrong impression of why Charles was elaborating about Mark...she threw Charles a warning look, even though she thought Mark's marriage might not be perfect...he was gone so much, never taking his wife with him.

"If Mark and his wife are ever here, and it is convenient for you to join us, I'm sure they would be delighted to meet you. He admired your poster. In fact, it caused him to make a very generous comment about how many people helped win the victory, even though they were not formally in the service."

"This *Monsieur* Aber-crom-bee was sincere about my work?"

"Very. He was touched by what your Pierre had done. After studying the poster for a long while, he said he was impressed by the love you must have for Pierre. It was as if he wished everyone had someone to be that devoted."

"He must be a kind man. I am glad he appreciated my poster."

Remembering how she had worked to make it as real as possible and a tribute to her "war-hero," she smiled a thank you. She would not be interested in any man again. Pierre would be waiting for her in Heaven. She had vowed to live a life that would allow her to enter that after-life sanctuary. Her husband had given his life to help win back France's freedom. Daphne respected all of those brave people – her father, friends, and of course Pierre – who risked their lives for their country...for the right of decency and freedom over tyranny. Of course, she felt a blind respect for this *Monsieur* Abercrombie. As these thoughts pushed to the surface, she started to cry.

"My dear, Daphne, what have we said to upset you?" Mimi put her arms around her. Charles rose and handed her his handkerchief.

"I am sorry. It's the thought of those who are gone...my Pierre....father...so many others...why...why?"

"I don't think we will ever know the answer to that, dear girl. It just seems to be the way of all mankind to want to take from one another. But, people like you, with your basic kindness and deep spirituality, serve as an example for others."

Charles' words soothed her; they collected and calmed her.

"You give me too much credit, Charles. I am still searching for the path to God...to find a way to serve Him and people. That's why I'm so grateful to you for letting me make my retreat in your summer house. God bless you. Now I think I will retire. Thank you for your love...oh, and for a most wonderful dinner."

"Goodnight, dear."

After Daphne left for the summer house, Mimi and Charles talked about what a sweet, young woman she is. Mimi remarked that she had never known anyone who seemed to have Daphne's depth of feeling.

"Charles, do you think she will ever be interested in a man again? You can see she is strongly affixed to the memory of her Pierre, but I wonder if that is the best thing for her health and happiness."

"I can't say…she is so deep into her spirituality…maybe when she resolves that, she might think of a romantic relationship if she meets the right man."

"We must wait and see…supporting her as well as we can as she works through her challenges. I wish she were our daughter…to know her is to love her."

"True, if she secures a position with one of the magazines, it will help turn more of her thinking outward."

"*Madam* Devereux, please remove your clothing and put this gown on. The doctor will be with you shortly."

Sitting in the hard-surfaced cubicle surrounded by the sterility of the all-white clinic, Dharma longed for Raoul. Oh, if he were here to comfort her, he would be telling her that they would take a holiday on the Normandy Coast, stroll through little coastal villages, stop at small cafes and sip the local Calvados, and sleep in quaint inns on big, down-filled mattresses.

"The doctor wants you to come to the examination room."

Dharma made the sign of the cross, rose, and entered a white-tiled room ablaze with high-wattage bulbs. She hadn't been in a hospital since giving birth to Daphne, but that had been a pleasant stay. This was going to be grim…probably very serious…it could mean she might die. Suddenly, she felt faint…the doctor took her arm and led her to the examination table.

He poked her all over, asked many questions, and listened with his stethoscope. Then he had several x-rays taken, as well as an imaging picture with a new piece of equipment – a machine that magnetically pictured the inside of the body.

Nearly two hours later, Dharma sat in a chair near his desk.

"*Madam* Devereux, forgive me for being blunt, but I have to tell you that we detected an advanced incidence of colon cancer. This is why you have so much pain. I don't know if it is operable or not. Only exploratory surgery will tell us. Please think about whether you want this or not."

How often he had to tell patients bad news. His wartime service in the French Army was bad…limbs blown off, faces destroyed, intestines pouring from open holes, blood, pain-wracked cries – all under a rain of artillery shells. But, that was more impersonal as he fought to overcome fatigue from continual needs. Sitting close to a civilian, not a soldier blurred in the monolithic mass of blue-gray uniforms, was different. This woman sitting before him, thinking she was hearing her death knell, could be the lady next door, his mother-in-law, or the woman next to him at mass. No matter how perfect his professional objectivity was, it had never been easy to tell people that they may die.

Letting the doctor's words sink into her conscious mind, fear rushed over her. She remembered several cases of cancer in people she knew, most of them fatal. What would happen to Daphne if she died? That was her worry, not the surgery. She would let the doctor tell her what to do. This was too large for her to handle.

"If I do the surgery, what might happen? If I don't, what am I facing?"

"These are difficult questions. I can say that if we do not operate, the pain will not subside…probably intensify."

"Does that mean that if you don't operate that it will just keep getting worse…and maybe…maybe I'll die?"

She started to cry. She tried to stem her tears, but they kept flowing…flowing from the well of all that she had suffered over the last ten years. The doctor rose and put his hands on her shoulders.

"*Madame* Devereux, there is hope. But, you must decide what you want us to do."

"If I don't have surgery?"

"We can give you strong pain killers, perhaps a new drug, just available, that supposedly fights cancer cells. But if it is not successful, you will continue to degrade. In a short time, fatality will occur. Again, forgive my bluntness, but your case is serious."

"How soon would you operate?"

"Within days. As soon as possible."

The situation was indeed dire. Dharma said a silent prayer; she knew she must do what would give her the best chance to be there for her daughter. She looked up from her thoughts, straight into the doctor's eyes, her own face set in resolve.

"My daughter is in another town. I would like her to return before the operation. Is four days from now acceptable?"

"Yes. I will give you some pain medicine and a sleeping sedative. Shall I schedule the procedure for Monday?"

Dharma agreed…stifling her immediate anxiety by summoning up her faith and her love for Daphne. She determinedly forced her mind to think only that what she was going to do was for Daphne. Under Dharma's deep fear was the overriding will of a mother to protect her child. She asked God to be with her.

"Well, madam vice-president, do you want the corner office or the one on the other side of the conference room?" Mark asked his wife.

"I'll take the one by the conference room…you're the chairman and president. Perhaps you should outline what my duties are. Here I am, where I always thought I wanted to be and should be. And I find myself not knowing what to do! Just a lot of petty little details and vagaries about the potential of precious metals," she huffed with the disdain that one uses to show contempt for that which they don't understand.

"Be patient. It'll evolve. First thing on the agenda is to see all of Smythe's customers and assure them there will be no interruption of service. Maybe convince them we want to do more for them. Jim Smythe contracted to go with us the first time to make the introductions and help with the assurances."

"I understand that the secretary is leaving…doesn't want to work for anyone who bought out her bosses of twenty years. You better hire one, I'm not about to learn to take dictation and answer phones," Stephanie said. She pictured a middle-aged woman with white hair done up in a bun, wearing long dresses and lace-up shoes with low heels – someone who might pose for a Grant Wood *American Gothic* type painting.

After two weeks of interviews, Miss Harlan was hired. She was twenty-four, blond, striking figure, and had a slim waist and an uplifted, attractive bust. And she was wearing medium-high pumps. When Stephanie questioned her hiring, Mark pointed out that Miss Harlan had an IQ of 140, as well as eight years' experience as an executive secretary to the president of a New York Corporation. She had tired of the commute to the City and wanted to work in Darien where she lived.

One of the first jobs Mark assigned Mary Harlan was to track down Harold Brenner, the artillery lieutenant he had met on the *Leviathan*. He told her to try the Brooklyn phone book. He wanted to interview Harold as a potential salesman. He wondered if Harold had gotten the artificial leg, and if he was able to ambulate normally.

For two months, Mark traveled almost constantly, seeing customers and suppliers. During that time, it became apparent that Stephanie was long on big-scene generalities, but short on day-to-day details. She started to lose interest. She had always pictured management as giving orders to capable underlings, making decisions based on a flood of reports and recommendations, and appearing at meetings where agendas were already established and fairly well decided. That scenario only happened to those who had built the business and organization from the ground up. A fledging ownership in a business that was close to dipping was run by tough, nuts and bolts daily decisions, hard work, and long hours of attention to every detail. None of this was appealing to Stephanie. She began drifting back to more board positions, telling Mark, to her credit, he was fully capable of handling everything without her meddling. But, she added that he should call her if he ever thought she could help. He thanked her and religiously kept her posted on the company's progress.

Lillian looked at Harvey, seeing something she had never seen. He sat cowed, his shoulders sagging, with a beseeching look on his sallow face. She pulled him to her breasts. Smoothing his hair, she felt in him a tenderness and submissiveness that had not been there in all of their married years. He hardly moved, and when she stopped stroking his hair, he took her hand and pressed it to his chest, then kissed it. He needed her, more than he ever had – more than he had ever admitted.

"Harvey, you act like you have been wronged and that you are shrinking in stature because of Mark's move. But, my love, you are not…you are growing, as you learn to forgive, and as you learn to recognize the needs of others. Remember, even our Lord suffered before he reached His divinity. His greatest admonition to us was to forgive. Can we do any less?"

"How can I forgive…they deserted me?"

"No, honey, they wanted to grow – to live their own lives, just as you did when you worked for your father."

Her words struck him…he thought back to the days when he had chaffed under the collar of older Daniel's rule. He saw some of his own drive and spirit in both Mark and his daughter, whom he was finally beginning to understand and appreciate. He saw her more clearly than he ever had.

"Lillian…Lillian, dear, is it too late?"

Daphne picked up her new Bible and began to read in the book of Luke about Jesus' trial in the wilderness. As she read of Christ's refusal to give in to Satan's temptations, she felt a goose-pimple-raising tremor of both deep admiration and personal inspiration for our Lord. "I must do all I can to forsake the sensual temptations of this world," she repeated over and over in her mind. Her goal was to devote her life to be a servant of God. Her spiritual love would be for her Savior, and her physical love would be requited when she joined Pierre in Heaven. She didn't want to meet anyone, even that *Monsieur* Abercrombie, the American Charles had mentioned at dinner.

As she finished the Gospel according to Luke, she found herself dozing. Warmly numbed with sleep, induced by the comforting words of the Biblical physician, she crawled into bed and was fast asleep. She awoke at four o'clock, sitting upright, trying to escape a wild dream. She was there with Pierre and a faceless American GI. As if it was playing out right in her room, she saw all three of them holding hands in a circle, as though playing Ring-Around-The-Rosy. They were all running from the devil, who was laughing at her. She bolted out of bed, knelt down and prayed for a clean mind. Soon she was asleep again.

Her days were spent in prayer, Bible reading, dinner with Mimi and Charles, and twice-a-day walks around the estate. As she walked, she marveled at all of the beauty in each bush or tree. The innocent faces of the rabbits touched her motherhood instincts. The doves and song birds made her picture herself soaring aloft closer and closer to God. She talked to the birds and game softly, feeling that God was in every one of them.

She telephoned Dharma, but there was no answer. She hoped her mother was visiting friends during her absence. The night of the third day, she was again awakened by a graphic, lifelike dream. Its intensity frightened her. It was sensual, sexual even, and she felt every facet of the experience. The man was a layered laminate of Pierre, her father, an apparition in white, and an olive drab-clad American GI. She cried out loud, beset with guilt and strongly contrasting feelings...a tingling in her most intimate female self and a sinking feeling of fear. Just as the dream faded into the reality of her summer house bed, she felt herself being pushed over a cliff by a crowd of non-descript people, dressed in rags and smelling of cheap wine. Her night gown was wet, as was her hair. She wasn't sure what to do. A bath seemed right, and prayer was essential in this moment of shock, confusion, and torment. Putting on a dry blouse and panties, relishing the clean feeling from her bath, she knelt by her bed. After praying, she went to the door, opened it, and said to the night, "Satan, it is written: 'Worship the Lord your God, and serve only him.' Get thee from me thou vile devil."

The next morning, she thanked Charles and Mimi and headed back to Paris and her mother.

When she entered their Paris apartment, Daphne heard a faint cry from her mother's bedroom, "In here, Daphne...in here..."

She ran to the room. Dharma was prone on her bed, a stricken look on her face. Two open medicine vials stood on her nightstand, one of them on its side. Several round black pills had spilled across the table, like beads from a broken rosary.

Daphne gasped, "What is wrong, *Maman*. What has happened to you?"

"I am very sick, dear. Thank God you are home." It seemed it hurt her to utter the words. She winced. Despite her pain and fear, she brightened faintly when she saw Daphne's open, innocent face. She forced a smile...more like a grimace, "Was your visit a good one?"

"Oh, yes, but that is not important. What can I do? Have you called a doctor?"

"Yes...yes...I went to the hospital. It was bad. Come closer, dear...hold my hand."

"Oh, *Maman*, what is wrong? When did you feel ill? I would not have gone to Chartres if I had known you were sick."

"No, no, dear. It was right for you to go. It is me who has kept the secret of my pains that started a few weeks ago. I didn't want to burden you...thinking it was just something temporary. Oh...oh...there it starts. Pass...me...that white pill."

Daphne quickly went to the nightstand, got a pill and put her arm behind her mother's back, propped her up, and placed the pain medicine on her swollen tongue. "What is it, *Maman*?"

"I...I have colon cancer. The doctor says I must have surgery."

"Oh, dear God...no...no. When?"

"Monday, please go with me." With that utterance, it was as if all of her strength was used to communicate her plight to her daughter. She faded off, the last pill helping her into nether land.

Learning of the seriousness of her mother's condition stunned Daphne. It was as if she had been hit in the solar plexus. She was frozen by the cold grip of not knowing what to do. Looking at her mother's pain-streaked face, she cried internally, then aloud to God.

"What shall I do? Please lead me...please help her." As she cried out, she felt the harsh reality of the room and her stricken mother. She told herself to block out everything but her mother's needs. Gently pulling a coverlet over her mother, she sat by the bed, never taking her eyes off of Dharma.

Daphne didn't leave her mother's side for the remainder of that Sunday afternoon and night. When Monday finally came, after a sleepless night, she arranged for an ambulance to take her mother to the hospital. Dharma was put on a gurney at the receiving door and wheeled into the pre-op room, Daphne scurrying along with the fast-paced orderlies. She asked if she could be with her mother in pre-op. She stood by the bed and watched the nurse inject an IV into her arm vein. She winced with her mother as the needle was inserted. She thanked the doctor for calling the hospital chaplain to be with her. Standing over her mother, and holding Father Lacross' hand, she put on a smile for her mother as they prayed together. As the priest said amen, Dharma drifted off into an anesthetic-induced deep sleep. Daphne squeezed her mother's hand and whispered in her mother's ear.

"I'll be waiting for you, *Maman*. God is with you."

Father Lacross noticed the tenseness in Daphne. She was clutching the top of her skirt, squeezing it then releasing it, over and over. He had been with many relatives of people undergoing surgery; he knew how to lead them to other thoughts than the immediate crisis. He moved to her slowly and, in a soft voice, asked Daphne to join him in the waiting room. Daphne was glad he would be with her. As she relaxed a little, he learned of what she had suffered because of the war. And, when he heard of her vision outside of Reims, he encouraged her to follow a path of Christian service. He brought her a cup of tea and said he would be with her until the operation was over. She loved Father Lacrosse, his kind face, and soft but meaningful words.

Four hours later, the doctor approached them with a slow and measured pace. Daphne jumped up; the priest steadied her. She searched the doctor's face to see if there was a clue about her mother. There was none. She steeled herself for the worst. She felt the loss of her father and Pierre, not another death…no, no, dear God. She squared her shoulders, as if to receive a blow, then looked directly into the doctor's eyes…an unspoken "well" in her expression.

The doctor touched her arm lightly, and said, "*Mademoiselle* Devereux, your mother has come through the operation. She is living."

"Thank God…oh, thank you dear God," she gasped, as she grabbed both the doctor's and Father Lacrosse's arms.

"But," the doctor cautioned. "The cancer was extensive. We removed most of her colon and preformed a descending colostomy…almost the entire descending tract. She will live, but only with extreme care, proper diet, no strenuous lifting or work, and adequate rest. Can you see that these conditions are met? Oh, yes, and she should avoid stress…worry…anxiety."

Daphne knew what he was saying was serious, but her mother was alive. She was going to live. If care would sustain her mother,

216

she could give her all she needed…what better service. What better deed than to nurse the woman who had given her so much? Her mind raced to all that she would set up in their apartment to make her mother comfortable.

"Doctor, thank you for what you have done. I will devote my life to taking care of her."

"Good. We will keep her here for a week. Then you should arrange for comfortable transportation to your home. Best if there are no steps."

Daphne was already busy in her head laying out the things that would get her mother home safely and meet all of doctor's rules. She would read Dharma's favorite poems to her, fix her what she liked to eat, if it met her required diet, and when permitted, take her outside in a wheelchair, hired car, or whatever was needed.

The doctor paused in his instructions as he sensed she was mentally recording what he was saying. "Call me if you have questions. You may see her briefly when she awakens…perhaps in an hour. Good day. Oh, yes, as a doctor, I am always grateful when God is looking in on our operating room. *C'nest pas Mademoiselle, Pere?*"

"Amen, *Monsieur Docteur*. Bless you for your work today," Daphne said. Then she reached out to him and hugged him, as tears rolled down her cheeks. Her mother was going to live.

*   *   *

"Mr. Abercrombie, Mr. Brenner is in the lobby. Shall I show him in?"

"Please, Nancy…and see if he wants some coffee," Mark said, watching his secretary pivot on her shapely legs and exit his office with the tick-tock of a pendulum swing of her hips. *That's a cute one. Wonder why some lucky guy hasn't made her a married woman. Forget it, buddy…forget it.*

"Mark, it's great to see you!" Harold Brenner smiled as he strode, without any trace of a limp, up to Mark's desk and extended his hand.

"Good to see you, Harold. Looks like the leg is doing a good job. Getting around okay?"

"Ten years now, Mark. The VA outfitted me, then a lot of walking lessons and therapy. Can do almost everything…well, haven't tried running any high-hurdle races like back in high school."

The two sat on the sofa, one veteran to another, and told each other all that had happened since they parted company from the *Leviathan*, fourteen years earlier. Mark directed the conversation to what his company was doing and asked Harold if he might consider taking a salesman's job. After Harold nodded, Mark asked him what his financial requirements were. Harold shared openly what he needed. His son would be entering college in the fall. Mark appreciated the humble honesty of this man; there was no duplicity in his request. Two hours later, it was agreed that Harold would start in three weeks. But, he'd let his son finish high school in Brooklyn before moving to Darien.

That night Stephanie asked him if he had hired Harold based on his capabilities or on sentimentality for a fellow lieutenant.

"Mostly his track record in the steel business, his knowledge of some of our potential new customers…and, yes, a pinch of feeling for a guy who lost part of a leg in France, but who overcame his handicap, and handled everything the war threw at him. He'll be able to handle whatever we throw at him."

"Hope you're right. By-the-way, how's Miss what's-her-name performing…she is *performing*, isn't she?"

Mark was miffed at the innuendo. "I'll tell her of your interest. I'm sure she'll be pleased to know how much you care about her. But, to answer your probe, she's *performing* very well. She has a real talent for handling customers and suppliers on the phone and keeps everything organized in the office, freeing me to do more selling and negotiating."

Affecting a look of innocent curiosity, Stephanie asked, "Are you one of the things she keeps *organized*, as you put it?"

"I think this has gone far enough…and definitely in the wrong direction. Let's drop it. And, just for the record, I love you…yeah, only you…like in 'till death us do part'. "

Steph was nettled, but pleased with his retort. "Thank you…guess I'm just jealous of any woman who sees you as much as I do in a day."

"There's always every night when I'm in town…that is if you're not at some meeting."

Stephanie's eyes flared, "With you all wrapped up in that business, I have to have outlets. I'm not going to be some clinging-vine housewife who sits by the window waiting for hubby to come up the walk and say, 'What's for dinner'?"

"Good point, dear. Say, what is for dinner?" Mark said as he laughed.

"You're pushing it, bud." Then she saw the humor of his remark and softened, feeling that he still loved her and maybe Miss-what's-her-name wasn't in the picture.

Over dinner, Mark asked how she and her parents were communicating. Mark hadn't talked to Harvey in several months, except for one brief exchange when Mark threw a lead to Braxton. The Braxton's didn't visit. Stephanie would see her mother while Harvey was at work, but Mark hadn't seen either Harvey or Lillian for more than six weeks.

"Strange that you ask. Mother said just today that Dad is going through some sort of internal changes. He hasn't been the same since he asked you to *exit* rapidly."

"My mother, in her Scottish terseness and wisdom used to say, 'Time heals all wounds.' Is there anything you think I should do…ask him for a lunch, maybe a meeting?"

"Let him come around. From what Mother said, he's having some second thoughts. Give it a few more weeks."

"Okay, princess, whatever you say."

Following Harvey's late-night plea about whether it was too late to make amends to Stephanie and Mark, Lillian decided to let her husband think things through. She wanted to see if his question was grasping or whether he really was sincere. Was he going through a change of heart, or was his own mortality spurring him to question his relationships? Three nights later, she asked him to sit with her on the sofa. He looked at her askance…than sloughed into the living room like a little boy walking up the aisle to the teacher's desk for a reprimand.

"Please sit with me, Harvey." She patted the space next to her.

He looked at her, a bewildered expression on his face. "Here, on the sofa?"

"Of course…you never minded sitting close to me when we were courting." Lillian wanted their conversation to be intimate and sweet…no pretenses, no defensive fences between them.

Her words brought back the tenderness they had shared those many years ago. Harvey warmed inside. She still loved him. He sat down and tentatively put his arm around her, just like in the early days when she was the governess at his friend's house.

"Harvey, remember the other night when you asked me if it was too late? You were referring to your relationship with Stephanie and Mark…weren't you?"

Harvey's face turned red. Being held accountable for a statement or an exposed inner thought was new to him. Usually he was doing the questioning. He sucked in his breath, shifted in his seat, and stuttered, "Yes, I guess I was. You made me think. Maybe I've been too hasty in my judgment… maybe I've been too hard."

As he said this, he seemed to deflate, like a balloon losing air. His heart lifted though, when Lillian looked at him with something he had not seen from her in several decades…respect.

Lillian saw the man she had married, the man who had needed her. She was determined not to fail him in his hour of contrition. She chose her words carefully.

"Dear, I could fill you full of sayings and scriptural quotations, the ones my father used in his sermons, but I won't. I'll just say that I feel – and I mean with all of my soul and mind – that it is never too late to embrace God, our Savior, and to give only love to our fellow man. If you fill your heart with these beliefs and practices, you will find true peace and a renewed and greater love from Stephanie and Mark...and from me too, Harvey. Think what the rest of our lives can be if together, hand-in-hand, we walk the path of love, faith, and service to others."

As his wife's words sank in, Harvey felt a glow of hope...of enlightenment. "How...how do we...I begin?"

"Well, we could start by going to church this Sunday as a couple...a united pair dedicated to sharing some of what God has blessed us with. There are so many who are less fortunate. Will you escort me to church, my handsome beaux?"

Lillian's simple, but sincere words moved Harvey more than any business coup he accomplished. They seemed to strip him of his male bravado and domineering mien. They warmed him, elated him, and made him, at least for the moment, a regular human being. But, as he absorbed the joy of being in communion with this woman who loved him, he felt, despite his elation, the pain of knowing how many years he had deprived himself of this harmony – the bird was in the hand, and he had let it go. Could he retrieve it at this late hour? Well, he'd damn well try!

"It would be my honor...if I asked Stephanie to join us and maybe for brunch afterwards, do you think...?"

"I'd bet they would come. But, Harvey dear, since you and I haven't been to church together in years, I'd like this time to be for just you and me, like when we were first married, before we were blessed with Stephanie. What do you say...will you escort me? We could see the fine gathering area that you donated, maybe remember what we pledged to each other in front of my father forty-some years ago."

"You mean it…just you and me…like old times?"

"Never meant anything more – ever."

"We could ask Steph and Mark the next week."

"Certainly we could." She took his hand and put it to the soft part of her cheek. To Harvey, she seemed years younger just then. He thought he even saw a blush. "And, Harvey, thanks for being my beaux again."

On Sunday, a resolute Lillian and the softening Harvey attended the eleven o'clock service at St. Luke's. Before the processional hymn, they toured the gathering room the Braxtons had funded. As they watched more than sixty children, aged four to fifteen, enjoying lemonade and cookies before they went to their classrooms, they held each other's hands. Lillian whispered, "This is wonderful – see all of these fine children harmonizing – would that we adults could do the same."

"Lillian, I thank you and Stephanie for getting me to help make this room a reality. This is a good thing…can we do something more?"

"I'm sure, my love. Shall we go into the church?"

Sitting closer together than they had in a long time, they heard the Gospel for the day: *Matthew 20:1-16, the Parable of the Workers in the Vineyard.* Harvey asked Lillian how she interpreted it. He felt the sermon hadn't fully elucidated the meaning of this complex, often contradictory, portion of scripture.

Lillian was surprised that Harvey would ask her opinion. She couldn't remember when he had done that last. His whole manner was one of talking to an equal or even someone who he felt knew more than he did. She wanted him to feel comfortable in his seeking her counsel.

"You're right, Harvey. I remember my father telling me that this passage has many interpretations. In his opinion, the message of the workers who started to work in the vineyard during the eleventh-hour, being paid the same as those who started in the first hour, was a way of saying two things: One, that it is never too late to earn something...to be rewarded...or accepted; And two, that the owner, perhaps an allegorical representation of God, can receive whomever he chooses, regardless of time worked, or the merit by which a man rates himself. In essence, 'it's never too late'."

"That is deep, Lillian. Thanks for throwing some light on it."

"Certainly...does it answer your question about whether it is too late for Stephanie and Mark to reenter our fold?"

"It does. We must invite them to go with us next week...but, only after I tell them I've been a blind fool."

"Bless you, my dear." Lillian was beaming.

*   *   *

"*Maman*, remember what the doctor said about the need for a lot of bed rest in your first week at home. So be a good girl for me. I will get you anything that you need."

"'I am such a burden for you, dear. What about your work?"

"Do not worry, I will work here. My friend, Laure, will take my work to school. You are the most important part of my life. And, I know that soon, because of your deep faith, you will be up and around."

For months Daphne nursed and helped rehabilitate her mother, often working into the night on her art after Dharma was asleep. Gradually, Dharma regained enough of her prior health so that Daphne was able to go out. One day she received a call from the publisher of *Elle* asking if she would like to exhibit some of her work for their artistic staff and be interviewed for a possible position in the art department. Trying to remain calm and professional sounding, she said yes and arranged a date with the publisher. Her spirits soared. It was the first truly good news she'd received since her posters were accepted by the government. She was humming when she dialed her cousin Charles' number. She said thank you in six different ways. He expressed his joy as well. Within a month she had secured a position as an illustrator for the most famous fashion magazine in France. Her daily routine was full: fixing breakfast for Dharma, making sure there was food for her lunch, seven hours of work, dinner for her mother, and two nights a week working at a home for elderly widows...part of the pledge she had made to God about serving others.

One night as she was returning from Elle's offices, she was surprised to see Rene Latour waiting near the entrance to her apartment.

"Mademoiselle, I...uh...I was in this neighborhood...as part of my work, and I wanted to see if you were all right."

Daphne sensed his uneasiness and quickly said, "How kind of you Rene. Yes, I am fine. My mother, you remember her, is recovering from some serious surgery, but she is healing."

"I am glad," he returned, shifting his gaze from her face to his feet and back to her face.

Daphne liked this man. She knew that in the war, as a member of the underground, he was always at risk for his life. He had killed several Germans, some by sneaking up on them from behind and slitting their throats. Yet here he was, uneasy, fooling with his apache-like cap, and looking at his feet – just as he had done when they first met in Rouen. She wondered why he could face German soldiers, yet be shy with her. Inside he was gentle, outside he was very brave.

"Rene, it is good to see you. Would you like to come in?"

"No, I must be going – it's just that I have never forgotten you since we first met. I...uh...wondered if I might take you to dinner sometime...if you are not too busy."

Daphne knew he was making an advance, albeit a very unsure one. She needed to say no without hurting him deeply. He was so sincere, and in his way, a gentleman. Silently she asked God how to do this.

"Rene, it is very kind of you to think of Mother and me. I am very busy, but on Friday night, if we could dine close by, I will join you."

"Thank you. I will make a reservation at the bistro that you see on the far corner. May I call for you at seven?"

"That will be fine. Remember, I am still nursing my mother, so I can only be gone two hours."

"I will see that you are home. Good night...*merci*, fine lady."

Over a lengthy dinner she could outline her life so that Rene would understand there was neither time nor inclination for her to include a man in her life. He mustn't feel it had anything to do with him. She wasn't romantically interested in any man. She wanted to let him know that she respected him and appreciated what he had done. But, a platonic relationship was the only one possible.

Dharma was very happy that Daphne would be seeing a young man. She never showed Daphne her concern about her daughter's lack of interest in men. She sensed that Pierre's death had somehow extinguished the fire of romance in her healthy and beautiful daughter. This was not good – Daphne was so young, so vital, and would make a wonderful mother. Dharma remembered her daughter's fixation with Catherine of Sienna and her thoughts about becoming a nun when she was sixteen. Was this desire resurfacing...stimulated by Pierre's death...by a feeling that God did not want her to be with a man? Had her vision of the Savior, at Pierre's execution site, made Daphne think of being a novitiate and "marrying" the Lord in the tradition of becoming a Roman Catholic nun?

Her daughter was a mature woman, nearing middle-age – should a mother talk to her about romantic love? Perhaps the time to broach the subject would be after Daphne's dinner with Rene. And, Dharma looked into her own soul – was her physical condition a deterrent to her daughter developing interest in men? Was Daphne suppressing natural desires in deference to caring for an ailing mother? Maybe if Dharma were not around, Daphne might have a fuller life.

"Dear Lord, please take me; if that is best for Daphne, and it is your will...I am ready."

*　　　　*　　　　*

Mark entered his home to an excited call from Stephanie, "Hey, lover, guess who just called?"

"The Irish Sweepstakes…we just won a few hundred-thousand."

"No, silly, we don't play that billions-to-one lottery. Come in the library. I got a fire started…by myself…real nice and cozy."

"Coming…gotta hear this big news. If it wasn't the sweepstakes, was it the President?"

"You sure think big. No, it wasn't any of them. Actually for you and me, it was better. It was Daddy. He wants us to go to church with him and Mom on Sunday. And, you won't believe this, he said he'd be, get this, grateful if you'd call him. He wants to apologize. Is this a miracle or not?"

"How do you feel about attending church?" *If she feels good about going, that would be a miracle!*

"It's okay if we can patch up the differences between you an Dad. Anyway, I'd like to see how the new rooms are working."

"Mom used to say, when Dad would get a break, 'The Lord works in wondrous ways.' Guess He does. Okay to call him now?"

"You bet."

"Dad, this is Mark. Stephanie said you called about Sunday."

"Mark, I don't know quite how to begin. Well, I guess the best thing to say is…I…um…am very sorry for the way I acted when you left. I was hurt. I looked at you as my own son, which I had no right to do. Please…ah…forgive me."

"Dad, I'm honored that you thought that much of me. I'm sorry that I left, but to be honest, not totally. The bad part for me was that you would think me ungrateful for all that you had done for me and Stephanie. But, being the achiever and dynamic person that you are, I'd hoped that you would understand what it is to want to be your own boss. If I'm wrong, I apologize."

"You're not wrong…uh…Mark…son. I admire your courage.

Let's wipe the slate clean. Would you help me do this – by attending church on Sunday with Lillian and me?:

"Nine-thirty or eleven?"

"Eleven, if that's all right with you and Steph."

"You bet…and, Dad, thanks…you're the best."

When Harvey hung up, and started to walk around their library, Lillian heard something she hadn't heard from her husband in many a year. He was whistling, *Let Me Call You Sweetheart*.

When Mark hung up, Stephanie said, "Sounds like he worked his old charm 'em any way you can magic on you…like, 'Oh, Dad, you're the best.' Ugh!"

"Can it, Steph. You may find this hard to believe, but sometimes people change their attitudes. For my book your dad was sincere. I like him. He's a man who can admit he goofed. And, yes, I'm looking forward to seeing him and Mom on Sunday. And, another thing, baby, I'll bet you'll find him a lot warmer to you. That was a different man I just talked to."

"My, my, listen to the evangelist spreading the gospel of forgiveness."

"Maybe if we had some kids you'd have a little more forgiveness in you. Maybe we'd both be a little less self-centered. Now, let's bury the hatchet, and give him a chance. I don't want to fight with you…particularly about someone who helped us. What do you say?"

Stung, Stephanie glared at Mark and left the room. She ran upstairs, two at a time. Throwing herself across their bed, she lay seething, between two poles of emotion, oscillating from anger to deep hurt. Mark had put a turpentine swab into the quick of her vulnerability. For several years, she had been having her own regrets whenever she saw the children connected to some of the charities she worked with. Their trusting faces and outstretched hands had started to chip away at the wall of father-resentment she had built around herself. Tough as she could sometimes be,

Stephanie could also be brutally honest, particularly with herself. She admitted to the coverlet on the bed that she had been wrong on the child thing. She had rationalized that her mother's miscarriage, so many years before, had given her a mental block about pregnancy. But that was only a partial truth. It was a dodge from her deeper reasons, one of which she had just accepted. It was her fear of losing a child after raising it, as her parents had lost Daniel.

Could she still have a baby as she neared menopause? She had covertly seen an obstetrician, who said after examining her that he would not advise it. Several years earlier would have been a safe time. She might want to consider some minor preventative and corrective surgery in the next few months, not for any attempts at pregnancy, but as a health measure. He reiterated that a pregnancy at this time might cause serious consequences for her.

Should she tell Mark this, or take her denial of motherhood, that she now deeply regretted, to her grave? If Mark found out, it would be evident that she had contrived not to get pregnant. On the other hand, if he knew she had consulted a doctor, even at forty-two, he might forgive her. And the final irony, her father, the central reason for her self-inflicted banishment from motherhood, was now making Christian-like overtures to them. Why hadn't this great transition – this late-in-life conversion – taken place years earlier? She was hit in the gut by the toughest realization that most humans could endure…knowing what one had missed. The bird was in the hand, and she'd let it go! Why were the sins of omission always harder to bear than the ones of commission? Because it is harder to measure the magnitude, or atone for something that hadn't happened, she reasoned.

"Damn him…damn me…damn it all…damn…damn…damn!" Once she started, the word seemed like a chant…a mantra of remorse that wouldn't end.

"Wow, I hope that's not me you're laying out and damning to ever-lasting hell." Her husband came into their room, startled at what he was hearing.

She didn't sit up. The tears were streaming down her cheeks. "No…it's me…it's me…not you," she mumbled.

Mark jumped to the side of the bed, tilting her chin up to see into her sad eyes. "What's so bad, Steph? Tell me…can I help?"

"I wish, but I don't know myself. This thing with Dad…and…and your remark about no children…" she sobbed. Mark knew better than to say anything in that moment. Finally she spoke again, almost to herself.

"I feel like I'm walking in quicksand."

Since he had known this strong, beautiful woman, he had never seen her so distraught…so emotionally exposed. He wanted to comfort her, yet he knew she hated anything that smacked of patronage.

"I'll throw you a lifeline, and it's one made of love and respect, which I have for you in spades. Lord knows, you've done that for me so many times."

Touched by his tenderness and respect for her as an equal…as a non-judgmental helpmate, she raised herself on one elbow. She took his hand and pressed it to her lips, and in a voice choked with several emotions, whispered, "Thanks, Mark, you are my lifeline. Don't worry, I'll be all right. Hate to admit it, but I guess I'm just your usual emotional woman."

"Dear, you're anything but *usual*. You're the most *unusual* woman a guy could ever be lucky enough to have. Come on, I'll take you out to dinner."

"You're a good guy. Let's go."

She combed her hair and patted the tear streaks with a dab of powder. She needed to tell him about the child thing, but she couldn't do it right then. What would he think of her? She had cut out that part of his life, deliberately. What if he came to that conclusion? Well, she'd face that tomorrow. Why ruin tonight's dinner?

Beneath this momentary bravado was the certainty that some day she'd have to make peace with her conscience…and with Mark. But, that wasn't tonight. As she turned the bathroom light off, she saw Mark's St. Christopher's medal and its silver chain on the counter. He had forgotten it, which was rare. Knowing how much he treasured it, she would take it to him. She studied the quarter-sized emblem of faith. Did it really have beneficial protection over its believers? Mark had worn it all through his army time and ever since. It dawned on her that by conveying this symbol of trust in a higher being, she was attesting to the existence of something beyond herself. If there was a God, would she have to reconcile her deception with that entity? That was too scary to think about. That was one she couldn't even face tomorrow...perhaps a few days later...maybe.

"Harvey, please get up, we don't want to be late for church. Remember we're meeting Stephanie and Mark."

"I'm moving...didn't sleep much last night."

"Indigestion?" Lillian knew better, but she kept it light deliberately.

"No, just wrestling with the meeting today. I get reconciled to saying I made a mistake, then some damn devil rises up and gets me mad."

"Even Jacob wrestled with the Lord over his actions." It was amazing how the good Book always came to mind for exactly the right situation. "But, dear, I know you'll come through. I've seen, over the last few weeks, the wonderful, gracious man I met over forty years ago. Just try to relax and be friendly. Remember they love you. You don't have to make a major event of today. It's just a family going to church and lunch together."

"I'm ready." And ready he was. While the first hour of being with Stephanie and Mark was a little strained, without much conversation, the Rector's sermon about forgiveness permeated the foursome. Over brunch Harvey asked Mark if he would serve on his board. Mark accepted the position, thanking Harvey for his confidence. He asked if Stephanie could sit in for him if he were out of the country on a meeting day. Harvey hemmed and hawed and turned a little pink, but a swift knock on his leg by Lillian's knee made him reply hoarsely, "I guess so...yes, why not."

With that, Stephanie ran her hand up Mark's thigh and said, "Why, thank you Daddy. I'm honored."

Only Mark knew he would do all he could to be out of the country during the second and third meetings. He was hoping that once Harvey saw how capable his daughter was of contributing at a board level, their relationship might improve. One of his mother's old quotations came to mind..."blessed are the peace makers." Perhaps he could help Steph soften her feelings toward Harvey.

As they parted at the club, there were hugs all around, tears in Lillian's eyes, and for the first time in so many years, Stephanie went up to her dad and kissed him on the cheek. He put his arm around her, kissed her back, and whispered, "Thank you," in her ear. As he waited for the valet to bring his Lincoln, he lightly touched the spot on his cheek. When he and Lillian went to their car, he opened the door for her. Lillian stood on her tip toes and kissed him.

On the way home, Harvey, enlivened by the kisses from the two women he loved, couldn't stop talking. That night, after Lillian had gone to bed, he sat alone in the library reflecting on the day, but also on the forty-two years of Stephanie's life. The more he reached into his memory for vignettes of his relationship with her, the more emptiness he found. Was love gauged by its voids?

He felt like a blind fool...a stupid ass. What had he thrown away? As he sat there, elbows on the desk, head in his hands, feeling a hollow in his stomach, the painful realization hit him that he was facing what he had missed and that it was not retrievable. The bird was in the hand, and he'd let it go.

INTERMEZZO

Time discovers truth

Lucius Annaeus Seneca
4 B.C. – A.D. 65

In August of 1970, Mark was asked to give a talk to the local Altruist Club about his wartime experiences and how he had adjusted to and felt about the postwar American scene. The Club was made up of some one-hundred high-profile community notables: professors, civic leaders, clergymen, businessmen, artists, newspaper editors, and a few retirees who had contributed to the club's charitable projects. It was the twenty-fifth anniversary of the ending of World War II. And, for this *rare* occasion, the wives of the members were allowed to attend. After a lengthy debate by the board, and deliberation by the chairman, and in the spirit of the current women's lib movements, the wives were to be invited to the fifty-year anniversary in 1995.

Over a two-week period, Mark reflected and jotted down notes on his talk, and bounced ideas off Stephanie, which were returned with some helpful suggestions, as well as a few pointed diatribes whenever he cast a shadow on the Democratic Party. But, political differences aside, she was a big help – an erudite woman, who not only kept up on current events, but had a conceptual mind that allowed her to fit the events of the present with the happenings of the past. The kind of guiding light philosopher George Santayana might have wished for when he made his prophetic observation about man's repeated follies.

"Ladies, gentlemen, and distinguished guests, it is an honor to be asked to share a few memories and thoughts with you."

The audience smiled. Mark was respected by most of the community.

"I was a lieutenant in the Seventh Armored, which was in combat near St. Vith, Belgium, on the perimeter of Bastogne during the Battle of the Bulge, and active in the retaking of St. Vith. I would not like to repeat that experience, but I am glad that I did have it once. As you know, freedom is never free. It is bought with sacrifice, hard duty, and many times, death. I got to know some four hundred soldiers in my tour. And, I can say, unequivocally, that the spirit and devotion to preserving our way of life was strong in each of those men. Were we often scared? You bet. But, something…a mental picture of someone at home…" Here he paused and smiled at Stephanie. "Many times, a holy reverence for an Almighty…a sense of injustice for an aggressor who was mass murdering a particular religion…and many inner beliefs beyond man's own needs, kept each guy at his job. I thank God, my comrades, and my desire to be reunited with Stephanie for getting me through."

A round of applause and many nodding heads gave a pause to Mark's opening remarks. He decided to omit any reference to his wounds and decorations.

"Some ten million returning service people were forced to convert from a mode of fighting for survival and killing, while being denied the warmth of home. In many cases it was a gigantic leap. That leap, in my opinion, was eased if the person had not only a faith, but a receptive loved one waiting for him…parent, spouse, relative, an appreciative community, or good friend. Fortunately, I was so blessed."

As he said this, Stephanie blew him a kiss, causing a few smiles and snickers of approval.

"Our club has helped many of these brave people in finding a job, getting rides to rehab centers, and by spending time with those who were lonely. This same altruistic spirit was prevalent in many of the men I served with. I have seen men literally lay down their lives for their buddies."

He told them of Mike Pellini and Timothy O'Reilly.

"But, I believe that our work is needed now more than ever. During, and right after the war, our entire nation was pulling together. We had just come through the Great Depression, quickly followed by an all-out war...both events that knit us together, uniting us against the common foes of poverty and deadly attacks. Those enemies were visible...easier seen to defend against with social and economic programs, and a total military effort. Our challenges of today are more subtle. The good guys and the bad guys are mixtures of each...a lot of gray...very little black and white."

Mark paused and flipped a page of the notes he hardly glanced at. There were some coughs, and a lot of questioning looks. Many in the audience wondered if there was going to be criticism of their way of life. Mark knew how these long-tenured families felt about social change, indiscretions, and liberal movements.

"As I reflected on the two-and-one-half decades since I returned from Europe, I jotted down what I have observed. Please bear with me and realize that I readily admit to not being a sociologist, nor a psychologist. I'm just like most of us here today, a working man who loves his country and this community."

There was a relaxing of the expressions on those in the first few rows, which gave him incentive to continue.

"I saw in the latter half of the fifties, and the entire decade of the sixties, that America was starting a wave of new mores and new behaviors. The classic lifestyle of post-war suburbanite families was giving way to a new set of cultural standards and practices. Many of the deprivations of the Great Depression and World War II had been erased. Millions of Americans had more homes, cars, televisions, and, for good or ill, more spare time – thanks to a plethora of labor-saving devices."

A couple of the newspaper editors took out pen and paper and began making notes.

"The affluence that is washing onto our shores, I believe, is slowly washing away the decorum and morality of the previous decades. There seems to be less respect for authority, even for parents and teachers. I base this on what employees tell me, on what my wife sees in some of the charities she works with, and in the headlines and news broadcasts that reveal the rising rate of crime. The working father in his felt hat, dark, horned-rim glasses, business suit, and wing-tipped shoes is too often wearing an apron in the house, while his wife is bringing home the paycheck. In many homes, both parents work to fund an insatiable desire for all of the new products huckstered night and day on the TV set. The seven-, then twelve-, then nineteen-inch screens are now the national 'salesman in the living room.' When both parents work, they are siring a new segment of our society: the latch-key kids."

"Newsreels, and a new *genre* of poetry by people like Ginsberg and Kerouac, show coffee shops on both coasts incubating a new sector of the population: The Beat Generation. Many of our youth are rising up, kicking over the traces of the conventions of previous decades. Main Street is being rivaled by Haight-Asbury. When we were thirteen...fourteen, smoking a Lucky Strike used to be the rite of passage to adulthood. Today, it is being replaced by doing joints...cigarette paper wrapped around some illegal marijuana with a resultant 'high.' And it didn't stop there, next came 'psychologist' Timothy Leary's LSD, with its psychedelic trips, and its brain-damaging effects, sometimes causing death."

Again, Mark paused and looked at Stephanie, who waffled her extended hand indicating some of the crowd was with him, some were not. He winked at her, gave a slight shrug of his shoulders and continued.

"Not all of the changes that I have observed are bad...some are needed. In the service, I witnessed rampant prejudice against black people and some anti-semitism. These days, in many parts of the South, we hear about black sit-ins on buses and eating places, freedom marching, laws making the segregation of blacks illegal, and other long-overdue civil rights actions that are being enacted by brave folks, mostly black, with some white support. Achieving equality for the African American is long overdue. And it has and will be a tenuous, often fatal campaign. Women's rights are also being expanded, albeit slowly, as our passive-resistant, white male society grudgingly tries to hold onto our dominions, keeping the 'glass ceilings' well-cemented in place. These needed reforms are a positive offset for the negative ones I mention."

Mark could feel many of the seer-sucker clad, button-down-collared, and bow-tied men shifting in their seats, looking at either their feet or the ceiling. Stephanie gave him an okay circle of her fingers, which meant he must be interpreted as a "liberal" by the Darien set.

"An area of extreme liberalization, however, in my opinion, is the degrading of the beauty of marital sex to a promiscuous spectator sport...a free-for-all of who can get whom. It's being made as common as sneezing or going to the bathroom."

This brought a varied response: some nervous laughter, incredulous looks, and a shaking of heads. Stephanie gave Mark an arched eyebrow and the hint of a smile, as she rubbed her one index finger over the other in a signal of, "shame on you."

"Lest you think I am too critical or negative, let me say I believe we can absorb these social changes and learn from what brings them about. Understanding the clamoring of our youth will help us modify the impact of the changes. When something in our body aches, it is part of an early-warning system that protects us. When we have social upheavals or trend changes in our mores, there is a cause. They are a symptom of something that needs addressing. If we don't bury our heads in a pile of reactionary dogma...or try to reform the whole world with radical socialistic fiats, we can channel this energy into positive areas. This can be accomplished if each of us gives witness to every one that we touch. Giving credence, through examples that reflect both balance and attention to the root causes of the perceived ills of our system, should be our mission. Throughout history there have been those who seek license and self-serving exploitation by coat-tailing on a so-called *cause*…case in point, the "Flower Children," and the "druggies."

This last statement brought some approving grunts and a couple of thumbs-ups.

"My wife spends many hours working with groups that help maintain the spirit of reaching out to those in need. She is an inspiration to me and many of her coworkers. This fine club we have can do more of the same. Educated and responsible people who have their basic needs fulfilled are not likely to create cultures that are widely divergent from what is a proven middle-of-the-road course…one that is balanced as fairly as possible for the good of all."

Expectant looks pervaded the room…people waiting to hear the panacea.

"I cannot serve up any quick-fix answers for the parts of our culture shifts that we deem harmful. To over simplify, it's like we learned in the service, 'just keep marching.' And that is what we Altruists are about. Each of us, each day, should try to leave someone we touch, by our actions and witness, with a renewed faith in human nature and a renewed faith in themselves. Thank you for listening."

He received a standing ovation. Stephanie came forward, hugged him, and whispered her thanks for mentioning her work. Mark hoped he had not been too pedantic or critical, but Stephanie and Father Dardnell assured him that he had not.

During the weeks before his talk, Mark's research and reflections about the shifting scene in America had made him look into himself. Working to earn a scholarship at Boston Latin, getting through Harvard, and the War, and starting the business had consumed him. As he researched current events, he discovered that he did very little for those not in his immediate circle. While writing his notes on the culture shocks, he asked himself if he was helping find solutions, or was he a part of the problem through his social apathy? After self-examination and his talk, he asked Stephanie to recommend a charity he might work with. She directed him to a school for homeless children, where he worked a couple of four-hour sessions a week as a mentor of some sixth-graders. Sharing their charitable work was a new bond, small but strong, between Mark and Stephanie.

He kept searching to see where he might contribute. He would recall his mother's citing of the golden rule, after which he would ask himself what he was doing to make things just a little better.

Wanting to further his involvement in helping his country and his fellow man, he followed much of the commentary and articles about the current trends in the morals and lifestyles of the country.

Throughout the culture-changing movements of the sixties and seventies, the nation's conjugal beds were open game for new partners. Sex was no longer kept behind closed doors. It was every-where...free, very promiscuous. It was pre-marital...post marital...extra marital...anybody's marital...at the local no-tell-motel, even in the White House. Sixties sex was available to any twelve-year-old and up – thanks to the Pill, Hugh Heffner, and a society under the aphrodisiac of affluence and the practice of misinterpreting freedom for license.

The sixties also brought a new young face to national politics, John Kennedy, the first president under age seventy, and sixty, even fifty! He and Jackie, the Camelot couple, mesmerized the youth of the country with their charm, while the president set in motion the escalation of a war in a place few had ever heard of...that is, until over fifty-thousand American men were killed and the country was divided ideologically...Viet Nam. But, to the nation's and humanity's shame, and their sincere grief, J.F.K. was gunned down on a Dallas Boulevard by a non-descript unknown. Oswald, the rifleman who fired the fatal shot, may or may not have been a pawn on a wider chessboard made of criminal and political squares. He must have been someone's tool; for he was silenced two days after his capture in a jail hallway by a bribed assassin. Kennedy's successor founded "The Great Society," a plan to reduce poverty, which in fairness did help many impoverished people and placed a few stiles over the fence of prejudice that separated blacks and whites. While L.B.J. pushed his plan through congress, he further escalated the war in "Nam," as it was referred to, choosing to personally designate the daily carpet bombings of the Viet Cong.

The papers, almost daily, carried the news, not only of the Viet Nam War, but also the growing tension between the USA and the USSR. Particular favorite headlines in the jargon of the press were: the oxymoron, "Cold War Heats Up;" or "As Arms Build-up Rises, So Does Deficit;" and the byline, "Weight of arms expenditures weighs down on taxpayers."

These radical times impacted on Stephanie and Mark. Their political differences widened as the Democrats held office for most of the decade. It was not a question of who was right, but just a political split in the Abercrombie household. The War further divided them…army man Mark, verses liberal Stephanie.

After more than twenty years, the bloom on the rose of marriage had dulled to some extent. Mark, the conservative, was intent on making their business successful. He went to church and grew tired of the standard fare of "rubber chicken, undercooked potatoes, and peas" at his wife's fund-raising dinners. He also found many of "the set" at the Darien Country Club to be dreary in their self-importance. Stephanie resented his preoccupation with their business, and with no children to care for, she searched for meaning and diversion.

Mark and Harvey Braxton, however, had forged a new relationship…one built on the mutual respect held by two former adversaries who, over time, worked out their differences. Mark's closeness to Harvey piqued Stephanie…adding an entry in the debit column of the Abercrombie balance sheet. And Stephanie never felt totally certain that Mark wasn't attracted to Miss Harlan, his secretary. While she had no facts, she resented Miss Harlan's youth and proximity to her husband and his dependency on her. She found reassurance and consolation in occasional dinners with Percy Withers, her high-school beau, who seemed always available. She didn't indulge in any sexual intimacies with him, but they spent a lot of time together when Mark was out of the country.

In far away France, Daphne Devereux progressed at *Elle*. On her tenth anniversary with the magazine, she was made art director, supervising a staff of twenty. She confined her life to work, two charities, and caring for her mother whose health began to decline eight years after the cancer operation. It was necessary to hire a part-time nurse for her during Daphne's working hours. Daphne also volunteered at a home for elderly ladies and spent weekend time at an orphanage where she read to four- and five-year-olds.

Several men, some from *Elle* and one or two from church tried to court her. Daphne would accept an occasional dinner, but was not inclined to pursue a romantic relationship. She carried the torch for Pierre and her spiritual "marriage" to her Savior. These two commitments were so strongly imbued in her psyche, that no man could extinguish or replace her internal flame.

In May of 1968, Mark's father died of heart failure, the day before Mark's fiftieth birthday. Mark and Stephanie had bought his parents a bungalow on Cape Cod, where John and Joyce were happy tending their garden and fishing from the shore. After the funeral, Mark asked his mother to come live with them, but she refused. It would not be fair to their marriage. Mark paid for her to have a companion-housekeeper.

When Mark told Stephanie he had voted for Richard Nixon, she called him a fascist, posting yet another debit in their marriage journal. When Mark simultaneously answered the phone with Stephanie and heard Percy Withers ask her if Mark was in Europe, a shouting match followed. In time, Mark accepted his wife's statements that the push was coming from Withers, not Stephanie. He hadn't noticed any slackening of her sexual ardor, nor had she ever seemed evasive. Every day Stephanie shared her activities with him in detail, and he did the same. Seeing that he was truly hurt, she explained who and what Withers had been in her life. If Mark didn't want her to ever have any male company, she'd see that she didn't. But what should she do when he was gone on his two-week trips abroad?

When she said this, he felt guilty for leaving her so much. In his zeal to make the new business viable, he knew he hadn't thought about how many days he had left her alone. He wasn't wild about her sharing any dinners with this Withers character, but was he going to ask her to sit home every night he was away? Maybe it was better to cut her a little slack, at least with a known commodity. Chastity belts had died with the Victorian age and the new freedom enjoyed by women. At least she wasn't as wild as F. Scott's "flappers." He asked her to do what she thought was right...he believed in her. With that she told him he had no worries.

They did live a generally compatible life...one that was based, still, on sexual attraction and some common pursuits; but their marriage was devoid of the bond that would have been formed by having children. They were two strong and intelligent people following parallel, but separated paths, like the two steel rails of a railroad track...hard, durable, and bound by the cross ties of convention, sex, and mutual respect. But, lacking was the ballast of a *shared* ground of working together in a common effort of charity and service to others. Each was doing, in the vernacular of the day, "his or her own thing."

The dawn of the seventies saw the continuation of the Viet Nam War, the Berkeley protests about the draft, the war itself, and the Republican Administration. Other hot items were the forced integration of schools through bussing and the escalation of an arms build-up in Russia and the USA. A new term, "Pop Culture," was being written to describe The Beatles, mini-skirts, and art nouveau swirls of lettering, usually in Day-Glo.

Then too there was "Counter Culture." Groups like The Chicago Seven, who were young "adults" from well-to-do homes in grungy outfits, that challenged Mayor Richard M. Daly at the site of the 1968 Democratic convention. Other "counters" were the half-naked hippies who were driving as far as they could away from the conventions of their parents in Volkswagen buses. These were not the poor or indigent crying for sustenance, but rebels from middle to upper-middle class "salt-of-the-earth" families, who thought it more fun to protest than to carry the perceived dull role of earning a living and following the path of earlier generations.

And for better or worse, day-by-day, more women were found in the work place. "Barefoot, pregnant, and in the kitchen" was gone forever, as was the unenlightened Victorian sexual code for women of the earlier centuries. No longer was it just men who wanted or went after "it."

Mark and Stephanie, and Daphne as well, were now middle-aged at fifty. Their parents were part of the population referred to as elderly. And Miss Harlan, while touching forty, remained attractive with a trim figure and a smooth complexion... probably due to an internal fountain of youth fed by her unexpressed and unrequited love for her boss. While Mark didn't react to her romantically, Stephanie always carried a curiosity about her relationship with Mark.

And the winds of fate blew on...

CHAPTER EIGHT

*Let them be like chaff
before the wind,
with the angel of the Lord
driving them on.*

Psalm 35: 5

"Well, well, see what the wind blew in," Stephanie greeted her husband as he exited the Kennedy Airport limo. He was returning from an eight-day trip to North Africa where he had worked out a contract with a new supplier of molybdenum.

With a smile across a jet-lagged face, he said, "Happy Birthday my beautiful fifty-year-old wife…and favorite valentine. May I take you out for dinner tonight?"

"Why…why… yes, that would be lovely."

Mark was too tired to notice her delayed response, which was caused by the fact that he had arrived home a day early, and Stephanie had made plans to have dinner that evening with Percy Withers. Her mind was working out how to cancel Withers without Mark knowing. During that first reunion with Withers several years earlier, she had decided to drop him, but after Mark started traveling so much, Percy became a diversion for lonely nights. She had established right off their meetings were to be strictly "no sex" dates; although, she had let him kiss her goodnight several times. But, when he pressed into her at the front door, she pushed him away and told him if he thought there'd be any of that, he could forget her. She did love the attention he showered on her, and he was a good conversationalist, as well as very liberal politically. She knew she was playing with fire…walking the tight rope between wanting fun companionship, her love and respect for Mark, and the conventional security of their relationship. Nervously, Stephanie got the call into Percy while Mark was shaving and changing clothes.

With a symbolic toast to Stephanie, Mark said, "I believe it's more than coincidence that your birthday falls on St. Valentine's Day. There's got to be a parallel between you and that little cherub with the bow and arrow."

"My, my, are you implying that I might have been shot into the world from Cupid's bow? If that's so, then he must have shot you in you know where, lover boy."

He laughed and said that knowing of her strong appetite for "love" it was possible. They smiled at each other.

"Mark, thank you for this lovely evening, but darling, I really wish that you could be home more…I miss you. Some nights, I don't know what to do with myself. Each night feels like a week."

He reached across the table and took her hand in his. "I know…but, we're in this business. If I…no…if *we* don't nail down dependable suppliers and take care of our customers, it'll go south, just like it was starting to do when we bought it."

"Is business everything?"

"No, but it's next to it, if we want to live as we are. I'll make you a solemn promise though. If you help me through this next year with your valuable support on the home front, I'll have a man in place by the end of 1972 who will be able to handle ninety percent of the traveling."

She was delighted, but skepticism came more naturally these days.

"Really…where's this magician coming from?"

"I've been advertising and interviewing. I want this as much as you do. I need to be home more…be with you more. Why do you think I married you?"

She played along. This felt pleasant, and she wanted it to go on for awhile.

"Why don't you tell me?"

"We haven't got time tonight for me to give you all of the reasons." Mark too was surprised and pleased at their banter. It had been a while.

On that note, they drove home. Stephanie felt warm and fuzzy. It had been a romantic evening. Mark had made her feel like a young woman being courted…he was a doll. Purring, she put her head on his shoulder as she thought how they could spend the remainder of the night.

While Mark was putting the car away, she put on a new filmy negligee he hadn't seen. She hurried through the daily fifty brush strokes of her hair. She remembered his mother telling her of his love of warm cinnamon toast. After a few hours of shopping in New York, she had finally found the scent of cinnamon at I. Magnums. He loved its aroma so much she only used it on "special occasions." With an anticipatory smile, she put a touch on the top of each breast. She knew Mark had gotten into his pajamas; his pants had been hastily thrown on the floor in front of a chair…that devil! Coming into the bedroom, she found Mark fast asleep…the first sleep he'd had in twenty-four hours.

"Damn." She picked up a magazine and tried to read to the sound of his rhythmic breathing. After reading the same line four times, she sighed and went to bed.

The next morning, she was up early and had made coffee while she waited in the kitchen. A little later Mark came down – not dressed, but in his bathrobe.

She poured him some coffee and tried to make her voice non-committal. With a slight pout on her lips, she asked him if he had rested.

He flashed a sheepish grin. "So well that I think I'll stay home from the office this morning, play house with my valentine, take her to lunch, then maybe do a little work…that is if she'll go along with the plan."

And she did. After their love making, she nestled into his arms.

It had been long and passionate. It reminded her of their first night at the Waldorf when he had returned from the war. She told herself that maybe Percy Withers could be phased out…after all, Mark had said he'd be getting an assistant to travel for him. But, on the other hand, maybe she should wait just a bit before dropping good old Percy…Mark hadn't hired the new man yet. There was time for such a major action.

A few weeks later, Mark came home from the office with a smile and a dozen red roses. He handed them to Stephanie with a bow.

"They're beautiful, thank you." Then with a devilish grin, "You do something you shouldn't have?"

"Not guilty, but that's funny. The guy who waited on me asked, 'You getting into trouble or getting out of trouble?' I said no, just trying to make an impression on my beautiful wife."

"How sweet, Mark. Is there an occasion?"

"Sort of…I…we just received a half-a-million-dollar order from Duboise Metals. But, get this, Charles wants me to meet him on Martinique to sign the contracts, as well as meet a few of his prime customers. And, my lovely, he invited you to join the party. What do think of that?"

"Sounds great, when is the meeting?"

"May seventh and eighth."

"You're kidding?'

"No…why?"

"That's when I'm the keynote speaker at the new Art Center. The mayor, our congressional representative, and the governor are going to be there, plus about a thousand people. Mark, this is a huge thing. I have to be there for two days. It's what I've been working on for three years. Could Charles reschedule?"

"I don't know. I'll have to think about it. Right now, he's our biggest customer…don't want to rock the boat, but I'll try."

"Bless you."

According to Charles, too many arrangements had been made

for the meeting. It was to include several of his customers, who had already made extensive plans to be there. Also, a minister from the French Department of Trade and Commerce was going to speak.

"Mark, I am most sorry for this conflict, but for me to try and change the plans of so many people would not be wise. It is important that my customers see the integrity of you, my supplier. These customers are those who will end up with your material after we have converted it. If *Madam* Abercrombie cannot alter her important schedule, perhaps she will join you in visiting us in Chartres later this summer."

Mark went back to Stephanie, but she said she had to honor her commitment just as he had to with Duboise. Duty was a tough taskmaster.

Daphne had had a particularly trying day at *Elle*, including disciplining a staff member for copying artwork from another publication. She entered the apartment to find Dharma unconscious and called an ambulance immediately. Daphne thought her mother had merely fainted, but the orderlies who answered the call said the lady was in a coma. Dharma was put on oxygen and an IV, then placed in the ambulance. Daphne sat in the back with her mother. At the hospital, Dharma was wheeled into the ICU wing. Daphne had to wait, not knowing what her mother's true condition was. She paced the tiny lounge in the corner of the hospital, hearing the siren-wail of ambulances that seemed to be arriving at the receiving door every few minutes. With each step, Daphne thought about all that her mother had done for her…all that they had shared. She wouldn't let herself think about life without Dharma. As another siren screeched beneath the window, she felt her nerves tighten. Was that awful sound her mother's soul in an agonized cry for help?

Daphne had cared for her mother for the last several years, and she saw how things could cycle. Hadn't her mother cared for her as a baby, a little girl, and a young woman who had lost a child and a

247

husband? She felt the bitter, but unfailing irony of how often humans made the full cycle from our births as helpless babies to ailing old age – then, completing the cycle to return to being helpless babies once again. The Alpha and the Omega of people's lives were the same: they began wrapped in their mother's arms, crying for her milk-spurting nipples. In the end, they were wrapped in the arms of the Savior crying for His succor. The remainder of life's alphabetical run (Beta to Psi) varied as humans struggled to enunciate the individual letters of their actions and experiences of free choice. Perhaps that was why Jesus had said, "Verily I say unto you, except ye be converted and shall become as little children, ye shall not enter into the kingdom of heaven."

Was her mother being readied for her certain ascent to heaven? In the last year, Dharma had become more childlike as her dependency on Daphne increased. But Daphne had also sensed that Dharma was resolved about what would happen if there were a recurrence of the cancer. Despite her occasional bouts with pain and her advancing age, Dharma seemed to be at peace. She was a docile patient for Daphne's loving care. Her mother had struck a covenant with her creator...and herself. Despite her concern for Dharma, caring for her had filled Daphne mostly with a sense of fulfillment.

Daphne turned to see Rene Latour standing at the door of the waiting room. He had called at the apartment, where a neighbor told him what had taken place. He didn't want to intrude, but he would do anything she asked to help her or Dharma. Daphne had rarely seen Rene over the last few years, sharing only a dozen or so platonic dinners with him. He had accepted this and was grateful for whatever time she spent with him.

They sat on the small settee, where Daphne kept clasping and unclasping her hands. Rene gave her his rosary. She looked into his loving face and smiled a thank you. She began running her fingers over the beads, as her lips moved in silent prayer. He remained quietly by her side. She appreciated his unspoken support. Why couldn't she be more receptive to this kind man?

Her thoughts and prayers were interrupted by a nurse who asked Daphne to follow her to Dharma's room. Her mother was propped up on the bed. In her hand was the cross of her rosary, the beads splayed across the snow-white sheet. Her eyes were closed and her breathing was barely perceptible. However, the lines of pain that had once creased her face were gone. Daphne looked at the doctor who was standing near the bed. He had a resigned expression on his young face. He shook his head slowly.

"Your mother is near death. Perhaps you may want to communicate with her."

Reaching for the last reserve of her feelings for her mother, Daphne took her mother's hands, closing them over the small wooden cross at the end of the rosary. She leaned over, putting her mouth near Dharma's ear.

"*Maman*, I love you. You are my angel."

Her mother made a feeble effort to take Daphne's hand, as first one eye, then the other flickered. Total serenity covered her face. Her lips moved, but no sound came forth. She lapsed into the stillness of earthly parting. Daphne felt her mother's hand go slack. Something happened in her own body as her mother's soul left Dharma's tired body. It was a sensation that Daphne had never experienced before; but in that moment, it was real. The rosary Dharma had been holding was the one Raoul had given her. It was so dear to Dharma – Daphne wrapped it around her mother's hands and asked the doctor to keep it there. She backed away from the bed and made the sign of the cross. Even when the doctor took her arm, she was still in communion with her mother. And, as he led her to the door, she was talking silently to Dharma, telling her to say hello to Raoul and Pierre when she reached heaven.

With a last look at her mother's body, she whispered, "God speed, *Maman*. You will be with the other angels."

In the waiting room, the doctor asked if she needed any help with funeral arrangements. She thanked him, but said Rene would help her. She turned to Rene, took his arm, and looked pleadingly into his eyes. He squeezed her hand as he nodded. Rene made the arrangements for the mass for Dharma to be held at *Notre Dame.*

On the ride to Rouen with Rene, Daphne was mute as she remembered all that she and her mother had shared. Her grief was deep in her heart, not visible to the outside world. But her sorrow was assuaged by knowing that her mother was free of pain, free of missing her beloved Raoul. Daphne warmed when she thought about her parents being reunited in paradise. She hoped she might live a life that would qualify her to join them and her Pierre.

The funeral mass was conducted on a day filled with April showers. Daphne told Rene that the rain was God washing away all of Dharma's pain. The mass was conducted by Cardinal Desmond in front of a handful of people. Dharma's ashes were placed in an urn next to Raoul's in the crypt below *Notre-Dame.* The inscription on her urn was simple: *Dharma Devereux, wife, mother, Christian 1897 - 1971.*

As they were leaving, Daphne promised to have dinner with Rene in a week when she had hopefully begun to adjust to the loss of Dharma. Charles waited until Rene left, then asked if Daphne didn't want to come and spend a few days with them. She would appreciate the quiet of their estate, and Elle had granted her a four-week leave. It would be good to be away from the apartment and its memories. Every corner of their flat would echo a word, a thought, or the smile of her beloved mother. Could she stand to feel all of the memories that being there would evoke? For the moment, she was drained of all emotion. The loss of Raoul, then Pierre, and lastly her mother had left her with too much scar tissue. There was no room to absorb any more pain. Maybe the solitude of Charles' summer house would help her become animated again.

*　　　　*　　　　*

"Mark," Harvey Braxton spoke into the phone in his commanding bellow. "We've got a chance to go ahead with the Elemental Chemical Company. Remember when we discussed this at the April board meeting? I want to review the prospectus one more time, and possibly vote on it in May."

"Yes, I remember. It looked like something that would expand Braxton's market share in water and sewage treatment chemicals. When is the May meeting?"

"The sixth. The top three shareholders, the CFO, and the CEO of Elemental will be there for a presentation...maybe a deal signing."

"Oh...the sixth?'"

"Yes...something wrong?"

"I hate to say this, but I have to be out of the country from the fifth to the ninth. Just landed a half-million-dollar order with Duboise, and he's scheduled a command performance for me with five of his customers and the French minister of commerce. He can't change it; I've already asked him to."

"Damn, I value your input on a deal like this"

"That's kind. Could Stephanie sit in for me? You and I could talk by phone, if I can help, but it's your call anyway. I liked their pro forma that we reviewed with your staff, but you're the man signing the check. When I come back I'll do anything you want me to do to help with the transition."

"Very well, I understand your position with Duboise...he's our customer too. So if you don't mind, will you wear two hats? Please pass on our best wishes, and if you're agreeable, give him a new proposal we worked up."

"Glad to."

"Hmmm...Stephanie at a board meeting...I don't know."

"She'll be good. She's always talking about wanting to share more with you. Hope I'm not out of line mentioning that."

"No. Of course not. She wants to share more, huh…well, brief her and tell her to come. It'll be interesting. And, Mark…thanks. Goodbye and good trip."

*   *   *

Daphne had accepted Charles' invitation to stay with them, away from the memories of Paris and her mother's death. Once again, she ensconced herself in the summer house. The first day, she tried to wash her mind of all that had happened. She spent hours walking the grounds, communicating with nature and her Creator. She prayed for her mother's soul as she reflected on all that they had gone through, beginning with their war-time sojourn on Martinique. Gradually her mind cleared, and her step picked up its previous girlish pace. Her well of grief could only hold so much before it overflowed and began to drain away. She was almost skipping as she went to the *chateaux* for dinner. Charles and Mimi immediately noticed her lighter demeanor. Mimi remarked about how Daphne's joyous air was brightening the atmosphere of the entire room.

"Dear Daphne, you bring joy to us. We love you as the daughter we were never blessed with." Charles nodded.

Over the dessert of *Crepes Suzettes*, Charles told her of his upcoming trip to Martinique and asked if she remembered much of her stay there.

"*Oui*, Charles…very much." She envisioned Simone Abrail. "We stayed with a wonderful lady. I wonder if she is still alive."

For a moment the couple watched her seem to float away, her face shining with a romantic fantasy with Pierre on the shoreline, a full moon reflecting off the ocean. Sensing her hosts were staring at her, she lost her dream. Pierre was gone; she would not be sharing the beach with anyone.

"Would you like to find out if Martinique is as you experienced it during the war?"

"Why…yes…but how?"

"By accompanying me to the island in two weeks."

"You're serious?"

"But, of course." Charles explained the trip and how Daphne would bring levity and softness to the meetings. She could roam the island during the day, but help him host the evening dinners. He knew that a refined woman's presence at dinner always helped keep the propriety and decorum at a more genteel level. Experience had taught him that middle-aged businessmen away from home could sometimes become a little too boisterous.

"You are sure you want me?"

"Yes, yes. Mimi and I think it would be a good change for you after all that you have endured. Is it yes?"

"Yes, my dear cousins. Will Mimi go as well?"

"Unfortunately not, she gets air sick. Since I will be tied up most of the time, we feel it's best for her not to attend. She and I will take a vacation by car later in the summer."

After dinner, walking back to the summer house, she was thinking about the trip to Martinique. She stopped and looked heavenward toward the crescent moon. "Dear God, thank you for this visit to my past." The song she had first heard on Martinique twenty-seven years earlier…*Beguine the Beguine*… came to her. Years earlier, she had a French music store order the sheet music and a thirty-three rpm record of the song. Listening to it brought back memories of her time on Martinique. Despite her happiness this evening, when she came to the part, "…I'm/with /you/once/more/under the stars/And/down/by/the/shore…." she started to cry, remembering how she had shared with her mother her hope that one day she and Pierre might walk the sandy, palm-dotted shores of Martinique.

That night, it took a long while to get to sleep. For the first time in years she had been presented with something that was just pleasure – something that had no onus of duty. At one point though, a wave of guilt washed over her. Was it right to just play? To not be serving someone? She had become near-robotic in her professional work, caring for her mother, attending church, and performing her charitable services. Could she become an animated human again for a week on Martinique? Could she descend to earth from her near-ethereal life style? In this brief interlude from the rigor of her dutiful life, would she again, even if for only a moment, become as Shakespeare wrote, "As full of spirit as the month of May and gorgeous as the sun at midsummer"?

*   *   *

Mark briefed Stephanie on the potential acquisition of Elemental Chemicals Inc. by Braxton. As he outlined the advantages to her dad's company, particularly the greater market share that would be achieved in the water and sewage treatment segments, he was amazed at her reactions. Usually, she was in full command of any situation. Now she seemed hesitant when venturing a question. Her normal persona of control and being on top of what she dealt with had melted away. Perhaps it was because she would be sitting as an almost equal with her father – the tenuous relationship of their past forty-odd years that was a bar of quicksand for her aplomb. She would be with him on the field of his expertise, not hers. Mark hoped the apparent softening Harvey evidenced would help Stephanie.

But, he also knew that for the metamorphosis in her dad to be total, Harvey would have had to completely shed the many years of demanding, self gratifying, and holding of the dominant position. Could he, like the cicada, split his former outer shell and emerge as a new man...a man of compassion and humility...thinking of others? Was Harvey the vineyard worker, embracing salvation in the eleventh hour? The board meeting would be a clue of what Mark hoped would be a renewed relationship between Stephanie and Harvey.

"Steph, you have nothing to worry about. Just be your intelligent self. If you don't understand something, phrase a question that touches on return on investment, market strengths, the depth of their technical support, any patents they hold, a five-year projection of sales and profits, a list of the top twenty customers, any pending law suits, labor problems, management strength, any environmental problems, and a management succession plan. Oh, and ask your dad on the QT why they want to sell."

Stephanie was wide-eyed with appreciation for the patience her husband was employing as he was one-hundred percent into helping her. She nodded her understanding.

"Pick your time to ask the men from Elemental your questions. If they're being answered, stay quiet, but watch the body language of the sellers. I'm not worried about you."

"Thanks Mark. It means a lot to me to be in Daddy's business with him. You're helping me. But, I guess other than Miss Higby taking the minutes, I'll be the only female in the room."

"So?"

"Before you said watch their body language? What exactly am I looking for?"

"Watch the sellers when a question is asked. If the answer sounds glib, they're smoothing over a wart. If they stutter and look down to their left, they don't have all the facts. Bore in on these areas…politely, of course."

"I guess Daddy will do most of the talking."

"Probably. If he does, be sure to support your dad and in a way that everyone in the room senses that you are behind him full tilt."

"Right…so…I'll do it. It'll be a new experience. But, sweetie, please call me when it's over…no matter what time it is. I want to tell you how it went…promise."

"The minute I think it's the right time."

*   *   *

Charles and his driver picked Daphne up at her apartment on the way to Charles De Gualle airport. Two hours later they were aloft in an Air France 707. It was Daphne's first time to fly. She was excited, marveling at the smoothness of the soaring plane. We are floating in God's house, she told Charles. He patted her hand, saying she was right. When the stewardess served their lunch, Daphne was fascinated with the neatness of the tray, the beautiful presentation of cold salmon, vegetable garnishes, poached pear, and peitit-fours. She gave Charles the two cigarettes in a small package. For the first time in years, she was bright, emitting an aura of light-ness and gaiety...something she had not been emotionally free to do. Her sorrows and the demanding care of her mother had stifled the blithesome part of her nature.

Charles noticed her bubbly conversation. They talked about her work at *Elle*, with Daphne expressing her gratitude to Charles again for helping her obtain the position. The King James Version of the Bible that Charles and Mimi had given her was open on her lap. She was reading a passage from Matthew when the captain announced he was beginning their descent to Martinique. She could see the shadow of their silver bird on the blue water as they flew between the sun and the ocean. When they were a few minutes from touch-down, they passed through a cloud that blocked the sun. The plane's interior dimmed, and Daphne gave a small gasp.

"What is it, my dear?"

"Read this, please," she said as she passed the Bible to Charles.

He read, "While he was still speaking, suddenly a bright cloud overshadowed them, and from the cloud a voice said, 'This is my Son, the Beloved; with him I am well pleased. Listen to him!"

Jointly realizing the coincidence, they looked at each other with amazement on their faces. Then, they passed out of the cloud, and the cabin was once again bright and radiant with sunlight. The aluminum bird dropped the last thousand feet from the heavens and landed at the airport in Le Lamentin on the island of Martinique.

*   *   *

"Steph, I'm going to leave a day early. I'll be flying to Miami with Harold to interview a man from Peru about becoming our South American agent. Peru and Chile produce a lot of our molybdenum ores, and Chile has respectable fields of vanadium. We feel our growth will justify a man to shepherd those sources of supply. They're critical to our steel industry customers. A day in Miami should suffice, then I'll wing it to Martinique."

"I'm sorry I can't go with you. A few days on a Caribbean island would be nice...sandy shores, moonlit nights...ah, romance. Listen buddy, you be good down there. You wouldn't look good with any locals on your arm...too much contrast between my precious Mr. WASP and some strange islanders. I know you tend to be gregarious. That's okay for business, but not for cozying up."

"My, what a suspicious mind...but yes, mother, I'll be good." And with a laugh he added, "That goes for you too, Salome," he taunted, ducking the decorative pillow she tossed at him.

In a rare instance, Stephanie insisted on driving Mark to Kennedy airport. Usually he called a limo, but she was acting like she wanted to spend every minute together. She hung onto him until he indicated that he'd miss the plane. As he went into the jet-way, he turned and saw her still standing at the check-in stand staring at him. Just as he entered the plane, she threw him a kiss and a wave. In his seat, he thought about their time together over the last few hours. It reminded him of when he had shipped out for England in 1943, when the ever-present phantom of their upcoming separation was lurking in both of their hearts. Picturing her farewell kiss and wave, he felt warm and fuzzy, then smiled as he recalled, "too much contrast between my precious Mr. WASP and some strange islanders..."

He was pulled from his pleasant reverie when Harold Brenner dropped into the empty seat beside him. "Hey, boss, how are you?"

"Fine, Harold. Glad we're going to see Señor Emiliano Juarez. How's your Spanish?"

"Not too bad. Three years at evening college. I'm glad you have enough faith in me to handle this South American coverage."

For the duration of the flight, Mark and Harold laid out the questions and issues they wanted to cover with Señor Juarez. They communicated fluently...the bond of men who had faced death as they led other men to theirs was strong...one that would last a lifetime.

Stephanie walked back into the terminal, stopping at a pay phone to call Percy and tell him she'd like to have dinner that night. Ever since Mark had inadvertently picked up on Percy's call, she had used pay phones to contact him. It also kept any bills from coming to the house with Percy's number. She paid the bills, but once in a while Mark would open one first. She arranged to meet Percy at a restaurant a few miles from Darien.

She stopped at a lady's restroom to check her hair and reapply her American Rose-colored lipstick. Driving back to Connecticut, she thought about her last few meetings with Percy. He had become more suggestive, even aggressive with his sexual desires. And she knew that by continuing to see him on the sly, she was inviting this. He was a divorced man, and what else would he be expecting from a married woman who joined him in secretive calls and clandestine meetings, than sex for the sake of sex? She was so deep in the mental wrestle between her fidelity to Mark and her need for diversion in his absence, that she almost rear-ended a car in front of her.

"Damn, dummy, watch what you're doing. You almost screwed that up." Then she flashed a wry grin as she realized her double entendre. She was going to have to cool that hot blood of his or find herself another baby sitter. Do it tonight. Well, maybe in a few days. Mark would be gone for five or six.

Over dinner, Percy once again reiterated how much he cared for her and how she had been in his heart ever since their high school days. He had only married out of necessity when he learned of Stephanie's marriage. When he was making love to Rosemary, he always thought of Stephanie. She put her hand over her mouth to hide the yawn that this line of conversation always evoked.

Each time he'd advance one of his hackneyed pawns of romance on the chess board of their game, she'd countermove with a change of subject. After his third glass of Cabernet Sauvignon, he started running his hand up her dress.

The first time she said, "That's enough…stop it." The next time she said, "Goodbye, sonny. It seems you can't drink and be civil. Good night." And with that she walked out of the restaurant, got in her car, and drove home, barely seeing the road through the steady veil of tears. In the house, the phone was ringing.

"Hello."

She heard Percy's slurred voice, "It's me, princess. Sorry about the do at the eatery. Let's start over…I'll be good."

"Too many times…sorry I let you think I was after something more than some companionship. My fault, but I never make the same mistake twice. Forget me. It's over. Good bye." Click.

With the phone back on the hook, she felt the baseness of the entire scene…a sordid soap opera in which she was playing a leading role. As she kicked off her pumps, she started shaking and crying…and swearing.

"You, damn…damn…dumb fool," she screamed at the oval mirror over the hall table.

Like Mark, she was not a drinker; but also like him, she would take a rare two fingers of scotch if she was in a quandary. Picking up the cut-glass decanter, she poured out some Chivas Regal in an old-fashion glass and flopped on the couch in the library. Her stocking-clad feet up on the arm rest, her velvet skirt halfway up her thighs. A sip of the smoky, amber-hued liquor settled her some. Suddenly she bolted upright as if she had a steel spring for a spinal column. She put the drink down and rubbed her hand over her eyes.

"Lord, tomorrow's the sixth…the board meeting at the company. You better clear your head…big moment in the old man's arena. You better be ready. Figure you got this one chance to show that you can fit in."

A shower followed by warm milk helped her get her bearings and set her determination to not only drop Percy forever, but do all that she could in the meeting tomorrow to establish herself in her father's eyes. And, as she climbed into bed, she paused and very seriously said, "Lord, help me do my husband proud tomorrow."

"Gentlemen…oh, and ladies, it's ten o'clock, the meeting will come to order. Today we have an important agenda…including resolving the issue of acquiring Elemental Chemicals Inc."

As Harvey gave a perfunctory tap of his gavel, the other six attendees sat straighter in their chairs and directed their full attention to the chairman. Starting from his left, clockwise around the teak and walnut inlaid circular table, was a doctor from Mt. Sinai Hospital, an economics professor emeritus from Yale, the president of a Darien bank, an executive of an engineering company, a lawyer who served as general counsel for Braxton, and next to him on his right, Stephanie. The five outside directors owned, collectively, ten percent of the company's stock; Steph and Mark owned fifteen percent and Harvey and Lillian, seventy-five percent.

After a few routine matters, the executives from Elemental Chemical were invited to join the board. The boardroom was on the top floor of Braxton. As a young graduate from Smith, Stephanie called the table the "poker table in the sky." There was going to be a high-stakes game played out on that beautiful piece of woodwork this morning. As both a first-time attendee and a woman, she wouldn't have many cards to play. It would be best to just choose only one or two and play them well. Stephanie was always well-versed on current events. The prevalent emphasis on ecology, particularly the contamination of air, water, and land by industry was a hot topic in the country. As a possible goad for her father, she had read a lot about the dubious, if not infamous, role of chemical companies in the now felonious dumping practices of many major chemical corporations. Was Elemental Chemical's slate clean on this score?

After one hour of up-beat presentations, aided with slides and charts, the Elemental executives opened the discussion for questions. Several dozen were asked by the various board members. They were salient ones, but almost superficial if not rhetorical. Harvey, in his enthusiasm for the acquisition, had some rosy tint in his spectacles. Stephanie bided her time, letting all of the men perform. Finally, in a lull, she raised her hand, disarmingly like a little girl in elementary school. It didn't register with Harvey, but the lawyer nodded toward Stephanie.

"Yes, Mrs. Abercrombie…a question?" The CEO of Elemental asked, the corners of his mouth just starting to break into a grin.

"Yes, Mr. Houghten, just one."

"Of course…ask away." His grin now evident.

"I seemed to miss, and if I did please forgive me, what is your status with the environmental agencies of the government? Do you have any pending citations or law suits concerning your disposal of waste and by products? Oh, and one more detail, are there any current citations from OSHA?"

Mr. Houghten appeared to dismiss her questions with a wave of his hand. Stephanie leaned forward as if she were raising the bet.

"I'm sorry, *sir*, I didn't hear you. Did I miss your answer?" From the corner of her eye she saw Harvey get red. Who was this one-time female to spoil his deal?

As Houghten fumbled with his papers, the lawyer chimed in. "Please Mr. Houghten, we would like an answer. I'm sure you can understand our concern if there are any hidden liabilities or exposures."

"Awk…ah…awk…we have always run a reputable business – who can speak for these do-gooder liberals running around with their save-the-environment slogans?"

"I agree," the lawyer said, "but that isn't a specific answer."

At this, Harvey called for a recess so that he could caucus with his board. The Elemental group was asked to wait outside. Once the room was cleared of the sellers, the lawyer asserted himself, telling Harvey of the dire consequences if they bought the company without total indemnification. They should pass on the deal if there were any hidden skeletons.

"You know, Mr. Braxton, there is no statute of limitations on environmental cases."

"Hurrump…can't have that. What do you recommend?"

"We must have full disclosure and a level one environmental audit, plus my checking the government's docket in the circuit court." Turning red, he added, "I should have done this before today. I thank Mrs. Abercrombie for bringing this to our attention, even if it is at the eleventh hour."

Harvey perked up at the "eleventh hour" reference, his mind jumping back to the sermon on it and all of the changes that had taken place in his life since then. Was this a sign from God? And, by gum, it was his daughter that had perhaps saved them from making a big and costly mistake. By gory, breeding always told. He smiled.

"Ross, you do what you have to. Protect us all the way. In fact there's no need to bring those guys back in. Tell them what we want, and if they do, and you feel we're a hundred percent safe, invite them back when you're satisfied." Then he turned to Stephanie.

"Thank you, dear. You can sit in for Mark anytime…or, if he's here, you come anyway." With that he put his hand on her shoulder and gave it a soft, appreciative squeeze. At that moment, Stephanie felt a tiny piece of a forty-year-old iceberg of perceived rejection melt in a wash of warm appreciation. When she and Harvey were alone, she threw her arms around him and started to cry. Finally, she backed away, and saw for the first time, tears on his red cheeks. Not used to showing his emotions so openly, he turned with a wave and left the boardroom. Stephanie could swear she heard him mumbling something about "it's never too late."

Mark, Harold, and Señor Juarez sat down to dinner at the Fontainebleau Hotel. The dinner was a cap-off to a four-hour meeting they had held to work out the details of Señor Juarez's role in the South American venture of Mark's company.   Mark had some concerns about their ability to hold Señor Juarez accountable and wanted to try and read this man in a more relaxed atmosphere. During the afternoon, he had felt that Juarez was sometimes too glib...too many "no problem, Señor Abercrombie." Mark had said that they would return to Darien and prepare a contract in the next week if he was accepted.   He was knowledgeable, articulate, charming...but something signaled Mark that there might be a hidden agenda in this Latino.

After a three-hour dinner, they parted.   Mark immediately turned to Harold. "What do you think?"

"Afraid of him, Mark...can't define it...just a gut-feel."

"I agree. Would you have wanted him protecting your flank at St. Lo?"

"No way. He'd probably run."

"When I get back from Martinique, let's discuss it and make our decision. We have another candidate in Rodriguez...don't have to jump."

*   *   *

Daphne and Charles took a cab to the Bakoua Hotel in the *Trois-Ilets* area. It was the finest hotel on Martinique, boasting its own private beach. Charles escorted Daphne to her suite, a second-floor, large, airy parlor and bedroom, overlooking the ocean. She gasped. It was a dreamland of finery and comfort. She explored every corner slowly, her eyes getting larger with each step...her mind racing from one artifact to another and to the fine draperies, the thick, cushiony carpet, and the red roses in an Oriental vase. She turned to Charles with a look of sincere and humble appreciation.

"Oh, Cousin Charles, this is fit for a princess. Are you sure this is for me?"

"Of course...are you not a princess? Mimi and I think you are. Please relax and enjoy it. I will leave you to rest and take in the view. Dinner is at seven...I'll call for you a few minutes ahead."

After he left, Daphne went to the balcony, drawn by the sound of the ocean's gentle breaking on the white sand beach. She stood there, a barely perceptible breeze wafting her ebony hair. The palms near the beach were swaying ever so lightly. Soon, Daphne's body was following them...she was in time with the closest palm...it was as if she was dancing a dance of love...she was in Pierre's arms. Turning into the parlor, she felt lighter than she had in years. She started to sing softly to herself.

*   *   *

"See you back in Darien first of the week," Mark said to Harold as he exited the car and went into the Miami airport. Soon, he was seated in a new Delta Airline Lockheed 1011. The take-off was smooth; the three huge, tail-mounted jet engines pushed the plane off the runway in just a little over half-a-mile. Mark pulled Charles Duboise's last letter from his jacket pocket. Reservations had been made for him at the Hotel Bokoua in *Trois-Ilets* on the beach. Charles had asked him to join his party at seven for introductions and dinner.

He put on earphones and listened to the in-flight music. With his head back on the seat, he thought about Stephanie. *Wonder how she made out at the board meeting? Promised I'd call her as soon as I get to the hotel. Bet once she gets a feel of the business and the protocol of the meetings, she'll be a tiger. Wish I'd been a fly on the wall.*

That night, Stephanie joined her parents for dinner. Harvey couldn't say enough to Lillian about how his daughter had helped the company at the morning's meeting. Lillian felt good about her family, particularly her husband. She knew that the Holy Spirit had entered Harvey's soul. He hadn't lost all of his crusty warts, but a mellowness was seeping both into and from him day-by-day. She watched the openness of her daughter toward him as dinner progressed.

As she rang the little silver bell to call Maude, she murmured, "Yes, it's never too late." Stephanie glanced at her and winked.

Mark's head became a swivel as he rode a taxi to the hotel. Everywhere he looked he saw beauty – in the quaint streets and in the sparkling, turquoise ocean to his left. *Wish Stephanie were here, she'd love it. Well, maybe in the future. Gotta call her soon as I get to the hotel...see how the meeting went.*

Entering his room on the third floor of the Bakoua Hotel, Mark saw a basket of fruit and a bottle of cognac. The card read, "Welcome to Martinique. Dinner is at seven in the Palm Room. Charles." Mark unpacked his formal white jacket and tux pants, showered, and placed a call to Stephanie. Not home. He called her parents. Maude said she would call Stephanie.

"Hey, babe, how'd it go?"

Stephanie told him about the Elemental men and their covering up of potential environmental problems. She was bubbling with enthusiasm, thanking him for all of the fine advice he had given her. She also told him about Harvey's approval of her attendance and his thawing out towards her. When Mark praised her, she was quiet for a moment.

"Mark, I miss you already. I love you. Do what you have to do, then hurry back to me."

"I love you too, Steph, and I'm sorry I'm not going to hear you at the art center dedication tomorrow. Bet you knock 'em dead." He gave her his number and promised to call each night. She hung up with a kiss blown over the wire.

He took a small sip of Charles' cognac so that he could thank him sincerely. Taking the glass, he strolled out onto the balcony. The sun was beginning to set over the western ocean, the rippling waves picking up the fire of the sun and throwing back a sapphire-like reflection. The sound of the breeze through the palm fronds mixed with the lapping echo of the water as it kissed the beach and lulled Mark into a semi-sleep. Mesmerized by the total scene, he dreamed of walking the sandy shore with Stephanie.

The jangling of the phone jarred him. It was Harvey telling him about Stephanie's help at the meeting. He asked Mark if he would oversee the environmental audit when he returned. Mark agreed. Then Harvey said that he felt like a new man now that he had a *pair* of Abercrombies on his team. Mark thanked him.

It was almost seven. Mark tied his maroon bow tie – his mother had taught him how to do this, saying that a true gentleman never wore a pre-tied one. With his matching cummerbund around his thirty-six inch waist, he looked in the mirror, murmuring "Bring on your customers, Charles."

In the Palm Room, Charles was standing at a table with *hors-d'oeuvres*. Around him were several men, to whom Charles introduced Mark. There was a German, two Frenchmen, an Englishman, and an Argentinean. Each could speak some broken English, the post-war-established universal language of commerce. Mark could handle Spanish and French, but with German he had to ask for Charles' help.

Charles poured each man a small aperitif, proposing a toast to a successful meeting and a prosperous business year. Mark's back was to the door. He was startled when he saw all of the men, except the Englishman, stop drinking and look with awe at something behind him. He slowly turned and had the same reaction as his companions. Standing in the doorway was a petite woman, whose light-yellow formal dress set off her ebony hair, sparkling black eyes, and cameo-hued skin. Mark guessed she might be five feet-four inches tall, but perfectly proportioned...wasp waist, proud bust line, straight posture, and a dimple near her rosebud mouth. He could hear the other men suck in their breaths as she smiled and made a partial curtsey.

"Gentlemen, may I present my dear cousin and our hostess for this evening, *Mademoiselle* Daphne Devereux," Charles announced, pride in the timbre of his voice. He went to Daphne, gave her his arm, and led her to the group. He introduced each man singly. Each one bowed, with the two Frenchmen kissing her hand. Finally, he came to Mark.

"Daphne, this is the man I told you about, the one who so admired your poster of the underground, *Monsieur* Mark Abercrombie."

In American casual friendliness, Mark extended his hand. With a hint of a blush, she touched his lightly but let it linger for a few seconds. She was speechless just looking at this tall, black-haired American with the penetrating brown eyes. They were so like Pierre's that she felt her breath come in short, fast gasps.

"Mark, would you escort *Mademoiselle* Devereux to the head of the table, as hostess? You may sit on her right as our special guest."

"It would be my honor," Mark said, offering his arm to this enchanting woman whose hand on his arm was as light as an angel's caress. As they walked to the table, her hand tightened just a trace. He held her chair for her before taking his own.

"*Merci, Monsieur* Aber-crom-bee."

"My pleasure...how about Mark?"

"If you wish."

The dinner was exquisite including seven courses and an appropriate wine with each course. Mark only sipped the wines, not consuming more than one full glass in total. He noticed that Daphne did the same. The candlelight cast a bewitching light on his dinner companion. Her frock, closed at the neck, and the single strand of pearls seemed to reflect a mysterious glow across the smooth luster of her porcelain-like skin. He thought back to how he had been enthralled the first time he had seen Stephanie at the Harvard dance. This woman was having the same effect. She combined so many of the things he thought were beautiful: proportion, pure beauty, a hint of humbleness, courtesy, and refinement. He would glance at her every time she said something or made any movement. Remembering his earlier call to Stephanie, he thought to himself, *look, buddy, just don't touch!*

Daphne told Mark that she had heard about his heroism in the war, which he downplayed, citing the sacrifices of the many civilians, particularly her man. At this, she used a lace handkerchief to daub a tear.

"I am sorry, *Mademoiselle*, I didn't want to make you sad. It's just that I was so impressed with your poster; in fact, I've never forgotten it."

She reached over and touched his hand.

"It is all right. I have adjusted my life to my losses. God has blessed me with many friends and work that fills my days, my heart, and my soul."

Despite Mark's earlier admonition to himself, he reflectively closed his hand over hers briefly. "I would be honored if you would care to share anything about your life with me."

His invitation was so tempting. None of the priests, professors, women friends she had known...not even her cousin or dear mother...had been made privy to her inner thoughts. Yet, here she was almost ready to say anything to this big, handsome American stranger. Was he the devil charming her into his confidence? No...no, his eyes were too honest. His voice and touch were too gentle, and he carried himself with the quite confidence of a man who valued the feelings of others. No wonder, as Charles had told her, he was willing to risk his life to save his men.

She smiled at Mark, her dimple giving her the appearance of an innocent little girl. "Perhaps before we leave this beautiful island, we may chat again. But, I realize how busy you and Charles are with your businesses."

"Yes, but perhaps there will be a few moments away from 'the businesses,' as you say."

"*Oui, Monsieur* Aber-crom-bee…*pardon me*, Mark."

As dinner concluded, Charles approached Daphne and Mark.

"Mark, let me escort my cousin to her room, then would you grant me an hour to discuss some items for tomorrow's meeting?"

"Of course." And turning to Daphne, "Good night *Mademoiselle* Devereux."

She hung back a couple of steps from Charles and turned to Mark with a pixie-like grin, "How about Daphne, Monsieur Aber-crom-bee?

"*Touche!*"

"*Au revoir*, until tomorrow."

"Until tomorrow."

CHAPTER NINE

*"Friendship is constant in
all other things; Save in
the offices and affairs of love:
Therefore all hearts in love
use their own tongues;
let every eye negotiate for
itself and trust no agent."*

Much Ado About Nothing
Shakespeare

Mark awoke to the sound of the ocean's muted lilt of the incoming tide through the partially open drapes of his sitting room. He wasn't sure where he was. Propping himself up on one elbow, he saw the basket of fruit and cognac bottle on the table. That was it! He was in the hotel on Martinique. Then the memory of the previous evening arose: the dinner, the men, and Daphne…Daphne of the ebony hair and eyes that were like the rarest of black pearls. He felt alternating surges of excitement and guilt. Why should he feel guilty? He hadn't done anything…hadn't said anything, only behaved as a gentleman to this woman – Charles' cousin – the dinner hostess. What was it Jesus said about lusting in the mind? That's silly…there hadn't been any lusting. Sure, she was attractive…sort of sweet…sort of vulnerable…tiny.

Aw, quit it. What's wrong with a momentary interest? Yeah, that's all it was.

He would probably never talk to her again. He wondered where she was.

He dressed and met Charles for breakfast. They discussed the contracts Harvey had asked Mark to convey, as well as Duboise's latest order with Mark's company. Afterwards, Charles asked Mark if he enjoyed meeting Daphne. When Mark didn't answer right away, Charles turned his head so he could see Mark's reaction. He kept silent until they both felt it was an awkward pause. Mark wasn't sure how to answer.

Finally, "She was a delightful dinner companion. Her English was better than my French."

"Yes, she has studied it for many years. You know of her losses...the latest was her mother just a month ago."

"Yes, she shared that with me, but she seems to handle it so well."

"She has a deep faith...almost angelic. The last eight years of her life have been devoted to taking care of her mother, her work at Elle, and various charitable causes. Not much play or diversions. We worry about her. She lives almost the life of a nun in our secular world."

"Will she be at dinner tonight?"

"Yes, Mark, but I would like the German to sit at her right so that he is not offended. We are closing a large deal with him. I think he was surprised that I did not seat him there last night. You understand?"

"Of course."

The rest of the day was spent with Charles explaining the businesses of each member and outlining how each of them might interface their trading. Late in the afternoon, between meetings and dinner, Mark took a swim; then he called Stephanie. The first day of the art center dedication had gone well. Stephanie complained that he should have been there, but finally she said she understood his need to be on Martinique.

"You haven't snuggled up to any natives, have you, big guy?"

Teasingly, he replied, "Not yet, can't find any with auburn hair or olive eyes. But if I do, I'll call."

"You rat...you better not." Then she told him that an environmental audit firm had been selected, but that Harvey didn't want to hire them until Mark interviewed them. "He puts a lot of store in your judgment, lover. So hurry on back. Besides, I miss you."

"Same here...someday we have to do this together."

During the day, Daphne hired a taxi to take her to Simone's house. Simone had quit her job at the sugar factory. She had redone her home to accommodate a few guests in the style of the British Bed and Breakfast. She cried when she saw Daphne at her door and cried again when she learned of Dharma's death. The two women, who had shared wartime living together, talked for more than four hours about their lives since the war.

After hearing about Raoul, Pierre, and now dear Dharma, Simone rose and put her arms around Daphne. "My dear child, you have had to bear so much...yet you still reflect an enthusiasm and faith for all that is holy and good in our world. You are a saint. I love you."

"I am no saint, Simone, but I believe that God will always bring to each of us what He feels we can handle. Each of us can be a witness to His goodness and wisdom."

"When I hear you express these inner thoughts, I know you are annointed."

"You are very kind, Simone, but I am struggling to lead a life that will help me meet my Pierre in heaven."

"You have no man in your life? You are denying yourself romantic love?"

Daphne started to answer, then stopped, remembering the dark-haired American. His sincere brown eyes, the faint touch of crispness in his hair, and his strong, but kind voice that echoed in her mind. No, no, he was a married man, and she was only interested in Pierre.

"I have no man in my life, Simone."

"What a waste of such a beautiful and sweet woman. I am sure there are many who would love to have you on their arm. Are you trying to be a nun?"

"I have my work, my duties...yet..."

"Yet what, my dove?"

"Oh, I cannot say...no, I cannot..."

"Then there is someone?"

Daphne murmured, "No, it isn't right."

"He's married?"

"You are very perceptive, Simone. How did you know?"

"Because I see a spiritual and heavenly glow on your face; and at the same time there is suppressed guilt in your voice. I see inside you, dear girl – your innocence and openness and your lack of any semblance of guile lets every thought shine through. Do you want to share anything with me?"

Daphne blushed. She didn't know if she could confront what was throbbing in her heart, let alone articulate it to another person. She knew she must forget this man. After all, she was striving to be the servant of her God, a disciple of the Savior – a role that did not allow romance with a man…certainly not a married man. Did not the clergy and nuns of her faith take the vow of celibacy? Her brow knitted; then after an uncomfortable pause, relaxed as if some inner revelation had resolved a waging moral conflict.

Her jaw took on an uncharacteristic set – that was it…she would just blank those thoughts out!

"What are you wrestling with? I see a sweet girl with doubt and internal conflict on her face."

"Oh, Simone, I am just a foolish woman. Until last night, I had no silly thoughts. I was dedicated to my work and the goal for my spiritual life. Now I am acting like a school girl."

"You met this married man last night?"

"Yes. He is an American…a hero from the war…tall, handsome, with a voice that invites you into his soul. And, his eyes are just like Pierre's. Oh, Simone, what a fool I am. I know I must never think of him again. He's married, and I am married to my Savior. You see how wicked I have become in just a few hours. Will God forgive me…give me the strength to resist temptation?"

"You are not wicked, Daphne, you are human – a normal woman with needs and feelings. Yes, it is a shame that he is married and that you feel that *you* are 'married'."

Simone's use of the words *normal* and *needs* confused Daphne for a moment, but she reverted to her internal vow to stop thinking about Mark. She called a taxi after promising to see Simone again before she returned to France. When she got back to the hotel, she thought about how to "wash" herself of her normal thoughts and again hew to her familiar life. From her balcony she saw the pool with only a few guests lounging by its side. A swim might help her with her new resolve. She donned her one-piece, forest green suit and beach robe and headed for the pool.

"Mark, it's been a very productive day. Shall we both rest from our work? Dinner is at seven. Until then, my friend, enjoy yourself."

Leaving Charles in the lobby, Mark went to his room to call Stephanie again. No answer, so he left a message on their new answering machine. He took off his coat and tie and stretched out on the bed. Maybe a few winks before dinner.

As evening approached, he got up and strolled out onto his balcony overlooking the ocean, the tennis courts, and the pool. The on-shore breeze was wafting the palms and the scalloped edges of the table umbrellas. He felt the serenity and beauty come over him like a warm blanket. For some strange reason he pictured the bloody, snow-covered route from St. Vith to Bastogne. It must have been the stark contrast between the two venues that created the comparison, making him appreciate the present. Who knew what triggered the coughing up of images and memories buried in the sub-conscious? He pushed the Belgium memory from his mind.

That's past…long past. This is real. This is now. Soak it up. Live in this moment. The past is gone; the future isn't here yet. It's this hour, this day – that's what you have.

A woman was emerging from the pool. She was very beautiful, with hair as dark as coal and almond skin. Her green suit highlighted her petite, but perfectly proportioned figure. He thought he recognized her, but he wasn't certain. Her back was to him. The more he saw, the more he wanted to know who she was.

Who am I? King David looking at and lusting for a bathing Bathsheba from his rooftop?

She looked up toward him; he saw it was Charles' cousin, his dinner companion of last night. Her figure tantalized him, and almost made him motionless. Then he waved tentatively.

Daphne was trying to forget that last night after dinner she had checked with the concierge for Mark's room location. She stood still, remembering her sobering thoughts at Simone's. But, she didn't want to be impolite to one of Charles' guests, so she returned his wave.

She was taken aback when the tall American cupped his hands and hollered that he'd see her at dinner. Despite the breeze blowing over her wet body, she suddenly felt warm. This man was seeing her exposed, except for her suit! She grabbed her robe, dropping it on the ground in her confused haste, but finally got it around her shoulders. He must think her a fool. She scurried into the hotel, her face aflame, her heart accelerating.

Entering the dining hall, Mark searched the group for Daphne, but she was not there. A few minutes later, however, he again saw all of the guests stop their conversations and turn toward the entry-way with looks of appreciation on their faces. Daphne walked into the room. She was quite a picture in a light periwinkle gown and a tiny wrist corsage of white gardenias. Each man made a slight bow. Charles escorted her to the head of the table and placed the German to her right. Mark ended up far away at the other end. He must have reflected his disappointment; she winked at him and shook her head mildly, hinting she shared his feelings. For Mark the dinner was never going to end. Finally, with a toast to better business and more cooperation within the group, Charles wished all of them a good night's sleep and a safe journey home.

Mark said goodnight to both Charles and his cousin, making a slight bow without taking his eyes away from hers, waiting for her to say something.

"Goodnight, *Monsieur* Aber-crom-bee, I have enjoyed meeting you. Perhaps you will visit France one day?"

"I am sure I will. Charles is a valued friend and customer. I wish you a safe journey."

With that, he extended his hand, which she took and squeezed lightly. But as he retracted it, her eyes fell and her face lost its pleasant glow.

"Yes...a *safe* journey. That is my path...safe journeys."

At this, Charles turned to Daphne, a questioning expression on his face. The silence was an emotional vacuum, engulfing the three of them.

Finally, she made a slight wave with her hand and then took Charles' arm, indicating she was ready to be escorted to her room.

Charles said, "Come, little princess, I will see you to your room. Goodnight, Mark. Please come to Chartres when it is convenient. Oh, and remember, Madame Abercrombie is welcome as well."

When Charles mentioned Stephanie, Mark saw Daphne tense ever so slightly, but she did tense. Why, he wondered? She knew he was married.

No, it can't be. Have I given any wrong signals? She can't have read my mind when I was watching her at the pool. I know women are highly perceptive about men, but I gave no signs. Well, no matter, she'll be flying home soon.

He returned to his room, called Stephanie, and listened to her news about the successful dedication of her art center. She had been given a citizen's medal by the governor for her work on behalf of advancing culture in the state. She was bubbling over with joy and well-earned pride.

"Oh, Mark, I wish you were here to share this with me. Everything means so much more to me when you are a part of it. Please hurry home, I miss you."

Mark had never heard as much longing and feeling in her words. What he didn't know was that Percy Withers had shown up at the dedication and had tried to talk Stephanie into seeing him again. That made her mad, especially when she saw the mayor, who had known Percy from his childhood, looking at them with surprise on his face. She told Withers to get lost and never bother her again. As she went back to the speaker's platform, she passed the Reverend Dardnell who congratulated her and said the new Sunday School rooms that she had raised the money for were working out well.

"Mrs. Abercrombie, we'd love to see you at service. You are such a prominent figure in our community and have done so much for us."

"Perhaps soon, Reverend Dardnell, thank you."

Mark was puzzled at the extended quiet on Steph's end. "You okay…you still there?"

"Yes, just dreaming about your return. When can I expect you?"

"Sunday, have to stop in Miami for a half day. I need to interview another candidate for the South American deal."

"Hurry home. I need you!"

With some kisses blown over the wire, they hung up. Mark strolled out onto his balcony. The moon was full, the tide was up, and a slight breeze was wafting the palms. He could hear music from the lounge. His Rolex showed nine o'clock – too early to turn in, and he was still keyed up about what had been accomplished at the meetings. Some potential orders had been identified with the German. Deciding to stay up for a little while, he turned off his lights and went down to the lounge where he ordered a cognac.

"Goodnight, Cousin Charles, thank you for making me feel so important by seating me as your hostess."

"And why not, you are important, Daphne. You made the dinners proper and genteel. I thank *you*. Now, goodnight."

"Would you care if I stayed another day or two before I go back to work and to my life? I have come so far. It is beautiful here, and it brings back the memories of the closeness that mother and I shared here. Simone has asked me to spend a night at her home."

Charles was due back in France and would be going home in the late morning. Could he leave her here to fly home alone? Why not? She was mature, and this was what she needed after all of the pain she had suffered.

"Yes, my dear. I will have the *concierge* make the arrangements for you to return home…say Saturday. Is that what you wish?"

With that, she hugged him. "*Merci*, Charles, you are kind to me. I love you."

Alone, she took off her evening gown. Standing in her bra and panties, she felt the ocean's breeze blow gently across her body. Lying on the divan, she started to read a novel she had brought, but the words swam before eyes. She didn't know why she felt such a strong restlessness throughout her now-alert body. What was it that had piqued her nerves? Putting the book down, knowing she wasn't right for reading, she got up, turned out the light, and went out on the balcony. She inhaled the salt air and watched the moonlight ripple over the soft-breaking waves. Picking up the lilt of the music floating up from the lounge below, she again started to weave to the sensuous melody. She wasn't sleepy. Maybe if she went to the lobby where she could hear the music better and see some of the dancers she might relax and be able to go to bed. Throwing on a white knee-length dress and some sandals, she passed a comb through her bobbed hair but stopped short as she saw her image in the mirror. What was she doing? Was this part of the vow she took? Why was she seeking the music, other people, and maybe…?

Sitting in the lobby, she immediately absorbed the gay spirit of the four-piece orchestra. The musicians, all dressed in native costume, were belting out popular French songs, native island music, and a few older classic American tunes: *Smoke Gets in Your Eyes, Amor,* and *To Each His Own.* Taking a step toward the lounge, she hesitated abruptly, lest she get too far into the room. Mark Abercrombie was sitting alone, his right side towards her. She didn't think he saw her, so she backed up a step. Suddenly, he turned as if someone or something had called him. He looked straight at her. For a second, he just stared, but then he stood and came to her. She panicked – frozen in place, her brain racing...to turn, to stand, or to meet him. He settled her dilemma.

"What a pleasure, *Mademoiselle* Devereux. What a nice surprise to see you. Would you please join me?"

Daphne's vocal chords seemed constricted as her mind struggled over her desire to see this big American, if for only a brief time. She pushed away the thought of not being interested in any man other than her Pierre, particularly a *married* man. She knew he would be flying home, probably in the morning, so what could be the harm in a few innocent minutes at his table? In a few days she would be back in her normal routine...her *safe* journey of life.

Half stuttering, she smiled, "*Oui*, for a few moments...the music is so delightful."

"Yes, let's enjoy it together," he said as he took her arm, led her to the table, and held her chair. He felt blood rush throughout his body. His heart's pace increased, and he was keyed up by an excitement he had not experienced for a long time.

Careful, buddy, remember, look don't touch. Stephanie's waiting for you. This is something you haven't been in. But man, that figure is perfect...those eyes don't quit! Gotta keep it above board, though.

"Would you like a drink...an *aperitif?*"

"A Crème de Menthe over ice, please."

While they waited for Daphne's drink, he asked her about her life, adding that if she didn't care to share, he understood.

At first she hesitated, not wanting him to think she was seeking his sympathy. But she couldn't escape his warm, sincere manner. He was like the key to her inner self.

"Why would you want to hear my trifling tale?"

His face became serious, his gaze more intense. "To me, nothing about you is trifling, as you say. I am interested in every-thing about you."

She smiled and then told him of her time on Martinique. When she came to the part about losing Raoul, Pierre, and Dharma, she felt like crying. She tried to hold the tears back, not wanting him to feel uncomfortable, but they wouldn't be stemmed.

He stood and went to her with his handkerchief, which she took, holding his hand for a second before touching her eyes.

"Thank you, *Monsieur* Aber-crom-bee. You are kind."

"I thought we agreed on Mark."

"*Oui*, Mark...just like in the Gospel. Yes, you could be that man. I feel you are a man of honor and goodness."

Blushing at the uncharacteristic directness of her praise, she turned her head, showing her classic profile. She knew she would look again into his eyes...their warmth and honesty seemed to invite her into his very soul. She turned back, full-face, and looked direct-ly into his brown eyes – the reincarnation of Pierre's. Her dream of being on Martinique with Pierre was being accomplished by proxy.

Mark warmed at her words and looked back at her. He saw those black eyes not as the flashing ones of *Carmen* or the *Dark Eyes* of Russian song. They were deep, black pools that one could dive into, maybe never hitting bottom – tiny microcosms of the black holes in space, bottomless and all absorbing.

Careful, careful, you're sinking. You gonna be able to share this evening with Steph in the next call?

"You have left me, Mark. Are you home in America...with Madame Aber-crom-bee?"

"No...no, I was thinking about how brave you are...how well you have handled the losses in your life. You must have both a positive nature and a deep faith."

"No, I am only *trying* to have those things. But," and again she blushed not knowing why she was going to say what she was thinking, "you make me forget all that has passed. You have placed me in the moment and nowhere else."

This beautiful woman was opening herself fully to him. *Can I pick up what she is placing on me? Can I, for a short time, be two people...Steph's husband and this woman's guardian angel...or whatever she is seeking? She's so open for love...she's suffered and suppressed so much. Can I be true to Steph, yet give her something to carry back – to fill, even if for a brief time, some of her voids? Don't kid yourself, pal; drop that Good Samaritan rationalization, you're falling for her. Better back off before it's too late.*

"Did I lose you again, *Monsieur* Mark?"

"Oh, no, I was just thinking about how attractive you are and how much depth you have. Yes, you are right...we are in the moment. Tomorrow is tomorrow...right?"

"When I lived here on Martinique, I heard a song written by the American, *Monsieur* Cole Porter. I..."

"Begin the Beguine?"

"Yes...yes, how did you know?"

"It happens to be my favorite, and I believe that the beguine dance was originated on this island."

"That is so." Pausing, she wondered if she could ask him to help her fulfill her fantasy. What if he said no? Would he think her foolish...would he be insulted by what she asked? No, he was kind; he would not hurt her, even if he didn't want to do what she requested.

She reached across the table tentatively toward his outstretched hand. He saw this and reached for hers. They met, as did their eyes. A communion was reached without a word being spoken.

"Mark, I am going to ask a favor, but please do not feel obligated to grant it."

"Anything, just ask."

She felt him squeeze her hand and lean closer. She knew her face must be red; it felt so warm. She took a deep breath to calm the giddiness she was experiencing. "Would you," she paused, then forced herself to finish, "walk on the beach with me? The moon is full, and the breeze is light."

She started to say she wanted to create her fantasy about being there with Pierre. But no, she knew that would not be right to ask him to be someone else just to humor her dream.

"I was just going to ask you the same thing. Yes, let me escort you."

He rose, pulled her chair back, took her arm, and led her to the open veranda doors. He asked her to wait there for a moment and strode briskly to the bandstand. She saw him take money from his pocket and pass it to the leader. When he came back, he had a smile on his face and asked her to wait with him at the edge of the lounge. She wondered why until she heard the strains of *Begin the Beguine*. She took his arm and looked up at this tall American who was making her forget so much of what she had carried for so many years. As the song neared its end, they walked down the wooden stairs to the white sandy beach. She was aglow, and he felt ten years younger despite the ambivalent feeling that was nagging at his gut. The same ambivalence he had in that snow-encrusted fox hole when he was trying to decide whether to send Pellini or himself to First Platoon.

"Looks like the tide is ebbing...best we take our shoes off and walk on the high part that's wet and firm."

"*Oui*, please help me," she said as she reached up to his shoulder and removed her sandals. The wet sand felt good between her tiny toes. He smiled, seeing the delight on her face as she wiggled them like a little child at the beach for the first time. As her feet sank into the semi-soft sand and the primal sensation moved up her tanned and shapely legs, she felt a lightening of the restrictive emotional load she had been carrying for so long. She let out a tiny, discreet squeal.

"You okay?"

"Oh, yes, Mark. I am okay. Are you not going to take off those boats? Oh, excuse...your sturdy shoes, I mean."

"Yep, they are big. Now come here and let me put my hand on your shoulder."

"With pleasure." If only he knew how much.

Between holding on to Daphne and some hopping, Mark removed his knee-length stockings and his "boats." He didn't see the need to point to his three-toed left foot. He rolled his pants to his knees and pulled Daphne to where the water started to recede from the shore.

"Is this too wet for you?"

"Oh, no, it feels so good. May we walk now?" She asked as she looked pleadingly up to him. He nodded. Then she raised her skirt over her knees with one hand and took his hand with the other.

They walked under the nearly full moon – the ocean on their left, swaying palms on the right – and with a concerto of sounds from the shore-lapping water, the whooshing palm fronds, and a few distant strains of *Siboney* from the lounge orchestra.

Mark was transformed. He was a different man in this moment, a man who had never faced the death and heartache of war or the stressful demands of being imbedded in the social strata of the Braxtons. He became lost in a brief vision. He was standing on an open road, where little children stood on the side smiling at him. A pretty brunette was rushing toward him in the far distance, an apparition in a white shroud, an ethereal glow emanating from her angelic face beckoned him. His feet were tireless; he was floating on this idyllic beach.

Can this be real? Am I in a dream? Am I walking with an angel...or am I with a siren of the devil? This is like dancing in paradise, but there must be a price to pay to this piper I'm following.

They walked in silence but in communion with each other. Daphne slipped her hand out of Mark's and ran it under his arm, pulling him closer to her, feeling his strong side against her dainty body. It had been nearly thirty years since she had felt a man's body next to hers. She tried to talk to herself about her vows and her life since she had first gone to Martinique, but her every rational and cognitive thought was quickly melted in the passionate lava she felt welling up inside her. Would it erupt? Would she nullify her chance to meet Pierre in heaven? Why, she asked, did this big American have to be so handsome, so gentle, and with eyes that were exactly like Pierre's? Was God testing her? If so, this was a very stringent exam.

She turned to Mark to ask him to take her back, just as he started to whistle, right on key, "I'm with you once more/under the stars/And down by the shore/an orchestra's play – ing…"

Hearing this, she began to cry softly, with tiny tears that inched down her round cheeks like evening's dew drops. Was she here with Pierre – was her fantasy being fulfilled? Was God granting her this brief interlude from her life of service? Was it a brief respite before something bad that could happen? Wasn't the scale of life always balanced?

Seeing the tears, Mark pulled her to him, feeling every curve of her petite body melting into his. "What?"

She shook her head, her eyes the soulful ones of a deer as she looked at him in total openness…defenseless against anything. Yielding to him and the moment, she was almost breathless. He bent his head and kissed her full on the mouth. She responded to his lips by pulling him tighter into her breasts – years of suppressed love and passion pouring forth from the deep font of her femininity. Her mind was filled with pure eroticism; every nerve ending was awake with desire. She felt his manhood and pressed him even tighter, as a cloud passed in front of the moon throwing them into darkness. Sensing the shadow that had enveloped them, they parted.

"Mark…I…I…"

"Ssh…it's all right."

"I shouldn't be doing this. It's just that…oh, you are so strong, so kind. This moment is so beautiful. We are so far from all that was bad. It's like this moment is a lifetime of beauty."

"It is a beautiful moment, my sweet." *What have I done to this innocent woman? Have I started something I can't finish? Brought her to the edge, only to leave her hanging? Or am I about to push her off into a chasm of abandonment? And what have I done to the Stephanie and Mark of, 'until death do us part'?*

Daphne put her hand to the side of his face, running the back of it lightly from his cheek bone to his jaw. He pulled her back and kissed her again.

"Shall we walk back, *Mon Cherie?*"

He was torn. He wanted to become closer to her even if it had to end in heartbreak. But should he avoid furthering the passion...what would he do if she asked him in?

On the way back, there were few words exchanged. Both were deep in thought trying to reconcile their consciences, yet reveling in the joy of their togetherness. Daphne felt like she had known him forever. Since her early days in the Paris apartment with Pierre, she had not had a man enliven every fiber of her being. She knew it had to end...she had her vows. He had his wife and God had His laws. But, was it totally wrong to live joyously for these few precious hours before submerging herself back in the disciplined routine she had sworn to live?

He couldn't stop pulling her to him as they walked slowly through the sand. *I know I'm wrong, but why do I feel like I've done something for this precious human being? Am I kidding myself... justifying my attraction to her on a flimsy precept?*

They walked through the lobby to the elevators. As they entered, he looked at her, a question on his face.

"Two."

He pushed the number two on the panel and started to punch the three but stopped when he felt her tense. They both exited on the second floor. She took his hand and led him to the end of the hall, handing him her key. She knew she was handing him a key that would open many more doors than the paneled one to her room. She was at the point of no return; she was crossing a bridge that might take her down a new path of life.

He took the key tentatively, searching her face for an indication of her thoughts – maybe her desires. Her face was void of any expression...just the deep black, deerlike eyes peering out in awe at this handsome man who had totally captured her heart with his understated charm and kind manner.

He was at a major fork in the road. He'd been there just a few times before: marrying Stephanie, deciding to enlist, leaving Pellini in the fox hole, and quitting Braxton Chemicals. Now he must decide whether to go left into her room or take the right turn to the elevator. Suddenly he saw his mother on the couch on Christmas Eve telling him that Jesus came into the world to bring peace, just as she knew that Mark had come to his parents bring to them happiness.

He unlocked the door and stepped back so Daphne could enter, then handed her the key. "Thank you for a wonderful time, Daphne. You have lifted my spirits to the highest. Best we say goodnight, before..."

"As you wish...as you wish," she whispered as her face became sad.

He felt that look squeeze his heart.. He gulped and stuttered, "May...uh, may I see you tomorrow...early as possible?"

"Breakfast? Here? Eight? *Oui?*"

"I'll be here." He broke into a smile, took her hand, and squeezed it. "Thank you...until then, my beautiful friend."

"*Oui*, until."

Back in his room, he realized it was too late to call Stephanie. He went to the desk and wrote a telegram that she would receive early in the morning. The clerk let him read a copy, "Steph, dear stop Tied up at dinner stop Too late to call stop Some new orders stop Miss you stop See you Saturday stop Love Mark Stop"

When he got in the elevator, he pressed two. What was he

thinking? He knew he couldn't help himself – something inside was pushing him to her. He started haltingly for Daphne's room, a man in an agitated state. A few steps from her door, he stopped and stood for at least five minutes as his mind see-sawed between waking her or going back to his room and the proverbial cold shower.

He needn't have worried about waking Daphne; in her room she was pacing. Several times she reached for the phone to call his room, but then didn't – thinking she would scare him with her forwardness.

Mark went back to his room. Neither one knew how close the other had come. The one thing in sync was that they both tossed and turned before falling asleep at around three a.m., but not before both alarms had been set for seven.

Sleepy-eyed, Mark pushed himself out of bed, showered and made his way to Daphne's room. He was confused, but mostly excited. She opened the door clad in a robe and barefooted. He watched her walk. The knee-length robe showed him a perfectly turned calf, supple and tanned – he sucked in his breath. Her toes were free of polish, as were her lips bare of lipstick. She was the quintessence of natural feminism...unfettered with artificiality, as natural as the day she was born. Mark was stunned by the grace and beauty of her simplicity. He just stood in the doorway and stared.

"Would you like to come in? The breakfast is here...aren't you hungry?"

"Yes." *Hungry in more ways than one. I have to pick her up...have to hold her, stroke her, tell her how beautiful she is. I guess I just have to give the piper an IOU. Pay him another time.*

Daphne pointed to the room service cart set with linen and fine china. They sat down to papaya juice, sliced mango, brioche, jam, and coffee. Both fiddled with their food, an air of tense anticipation surrounding them.

"You hungry?" He asked.

"No. I am satisfied."

With that he folded the leaves of the cart down and asked her to hold the door open as he pushed it down the hall, several doors away.

"You were once a waiter, Mark?" She teased.

"No...just someone who hates interruptions."

"I see."

After locking the door, he led her to the balcony, his arm around her waist. They stood just inside watching the ocean and some scavenging gulls swooping over the shoreline. The sun reflected off the undulating blue-green surf. She turned to him, her robe falling open revealing her upright breasts. He inhaled deeply and pulled her to him, picked her up effortlessly, and carried her to the bed. Placing her carefully on the ecru sheet, he gently turned back her robe, gasping as he saw the perfection and harmony of her body. Her nipples were fully erect, her dark pubic hair a perfect triangle, her legs flexed and slightly apart, her face a study in happy surrender. In a flash, he was undressed and beside her.

At first, lying on their sides, they just looked at each other – she with pure adoration for him, he with a serious and protective gaze. He slid his arm under her neck and stroked her cheeks, her neck, and then her torso and thighs. Any words that might have been spoken were hushed with prolonged kisses. Their dialogue was one of soft caresses and exploratory touching, stroking, and kissing. It was the language of intimate sharing – each speaking in the tongue of their urges. Daphne felt total exhilaration in every fiber of her being...experiencing the release of years of constrained romantic emotion. To hold this moment forever was all she could think of. When he moved on top of her, she felt she could support his weight for an eternity.

Mark was transformed – a man in a sphere of weightlessness without the gravitational pull of business, social demands, or sparring with other humans – floating on the currents of both his and her passion, feeling he was entering into Eden. And when he heard her alternating moans and cries, he hugged her tightly and whispered to her that this moment would last him for a lifetime. Spent after the eruption of many loveless years compressed into this magical time, she put her head on his chest and sighed. She kept one hand holding his as if she were afraid that if she let go, he would be gone. He leaned over and kissed her softly on the cheek.

After many minutes of quiet reverie, he propped himself on one elbow, tracing the outline of her face with one finger, looking at her in total love. Finally, "When do you return to France?"

"Hush, *Mon Cherie*. That is in the future. We are now; let us hold this time as long as possible."

"You are right. What would you like to do with this day?"

"Be with you, my love. Maybe take a little trip together…then come back here."

"I'll go up and dress…then be back for you in half an hour…okay?"

With Daphne on his arm, Mark walked through the lobby just as Charles was getting into a taxi for the airport. They didn't see him, but he saw them. He was about to have the car stop so that he could bid them farewell. But, as he stepped onto the pathway, he thought about all that his cousin had been through. He remembered how many times he and Mimi had talked and worried over the monastic lifestyle in which Daphne was enmeshed. He got back into the taxi, bending over so he wouldn't be seen.

"Driver, to the airport quickly, please."

Mark had arranged for a car and driver for the day. The driver, who spoke French and some tourist English, held the door for them. Mark asked Daphne to direct him. She asked Mark if he minded stopping for an hour at Simone's home.

"This is your day, my angel. Wherever you want to go is where we will go.

"*Merci*, but I don't see myself as *l'ange*."

"Gee, our first disagreement. I say you are an angel."

He chided her while he put his arm around her and pulled her close. The driver pushed the rear view mirror up.

"As you Americans say, okay you win."

"I'm jealous. Who taught you all the American lingo?"

"Television and books."

They smiled with the happiness of a couple in total amity, basking in the tranquility of their new-found tenderness.

En route to Simone's, Daphne related that Martinique was where Napoleon's Josephine was born and raised in wealth on her family's sugar plantation. Sitting back, in the warmth of Mark's embrace and with the window open, she thought about Josephine Bonaparte, a woman who had fascinated her as a twelve-year-old. As the car turned to the ocean side of the island, an onshore breeze blew into the taxi. Daphne shivered in her sleeveless blouse. She suddenly recalled how Josephine had died from a cold-related illness shortly after the emperor's exile to Elba. The empress was Daphne's age at her death. Sitting forward, escaping Mark's arm, she quickly ran the window up tight and threw herself back into Mark's arms, nuzzling her head on his chest.

Touched by her sudden ardor to be close, he smoothed her hair and kissed the top of her head. "What is it, angel? What?"

In a little girl's voice she asked, "Do you believe in omens...superstitions?"

Taken aback by her incongruous question, he couldn't answer right away. Finally, "No, little one, I do not. Why do you ask?"

Lightly and with a coquettish grin, "Oh, no real reason. But, I'm glad."

"Hmm." *No wonder she's so appealing...totally unfathomable at times. What in the heck did that question have to do with anything?*

Daphne sensed his puzzlement. "Do not worry, women are allowed silly questions. Driver, please stop. It is the second house on the left."

Simone had a positive reaction to Mark. She invited the couple in and offered them coffee. Daphne excused herself from Mark and joined Simone in the kitchen to help.

"It's easy to see why you have the problem. He is so handsome."

"And he is very gentle and kind. But Simone, he is married."

"That is a shame, but I'm not surprised. What woman with any sense would let him go?"

"True, but I must. Although, I do have these precious moments; each one is a miniature lifetime. When he leaves, a part of me will go with him…never to return. Oh, dear Simone, what can I do?"

"You are too sweet to endure this. If he leaves for America, and you cannot follow, you will just have to live with memories…find someone else."

Simone started to cry. Daphne put her arms around her, realizing that Simone too had been living a life of memories since Alexandre, her husband, had been killed. The reality of what her friend was saying hit her hard – shocking her out of her idyllic dream.

"Oh, Simone, I am sorry. I have brought a painful memory to you."

"Don't worry. I bring them to myself almost every day." She wiped her eyes. "Shall we serve the coffee?"

The trio visited for an hour, with Simone and Daphne doing most of the talking about their time together during the war.

Simone turned to Mark. "You are patient to listen to two old hens clucking at each other about other times."

Smiling, "I don't see any *old* people here." His arm encircled Daphne again. "It was good of you to house her. No wonder she speaks so well of you."

"Merci."

Daphne looked at her watch. It was time to return the chartered car back to the hotel. Simone smiled at the naiveté of Daphne's transparent excuse to be alone with Mark. As they left, Simone put her hand on Mark's arm, holding him back from Daphne.

"Be careful, *Monsieur* Mark. Daphne's deeply in love with you. You are all that she has not had since Pierre. She is like a tiny porcelain doll...very fragile and easily broken if dropped."

With this onus placed on him, he could only answer, "Yes, I know."

Daphne asked the driver to go through the town of Saint-Pierre, once the capitol of Martinique.

"Mark," she said. "Do you see this serene village? Does it not look prosperous and vital?"

"Yes, very much so. Why?"

"You know how we have shared with each other the thought of holding and preserving each moment?"

"Yes, we have." He whispered in her ear. "And these moments I will treasure always."

"I am sure that many people in this town, particularly back in May of 1902, felt the same way, while many did not...to their loss."

"May of 1902?"

"One morning the town awoke to a new day, thinking about all they would do in that day and the weeks to come. But, fate snuffed out those plans and dreams."

"What – how?"

"Because, without warning *Montague Pelee*, just north of town, erupted and covered the city with molten lava. Thirty-thousand inhabitants perished. There was only one survivor who told of the disaster. So, you see each moment we have is a treasure, not to be wasted or taken for granted."

"What a tragedy. You are right about our time together." With this he leaned over and kissed her cheek. She snuggled in tighter to his chest and pulled his arm around her. Then, she pointed to his watch and asked him to put it in his pocket.

"We do not need to be keepers of time. Being with you cannot be measured in minutes or hours."

Driving away from Saint-Pierre, they slowed at a crosswalk as about thirty uniformed six or seven-year-old boys and girls were being led across the road by a pair of nuns. The children were laughing and waving their lunch boxes and their colored drawings at each other. Mark noticed Daphne watching the children with a far-away look, that didn't veil the sadness her face reflected.

Be quiet – let her have this moment to herself. There has to be something deep in there. This isn't just a woman looking at kids – she's feeling a buried hurt or longing.

A tear came into Daphne's eye as she relived her miscarriage of so many years before, thinking about what might have been. "They are so sweet. Each is a precious creation of God. Their parents are truly blessed."

"Yes, they are," he partially slurred, the lump in his own throat restricting his diction.

"Mark, what is it? Why do these beautiful children make you sad? Don't you have children of your own in America?"

He was stunned by her simple, direct question. It hit him like a broad axe. With a lost look, he said, "No, we never had any. Now it's too late."

"What a shame…you would be such a wonderful father."

"And you such a great mother." The second he said this he could have bitten his tongue. Her face went expressionless, as if a small part of her had just died.

"I'm…I'm sorry. What did I say? Please forgive me?"

"There is nothing to forgive. You are right; I would have worked hard at being a good mother if things would have turned out differently. It seems that our not having children is another bond between us."

She took his hand and pressed it to her cheek, "Oh, if we had…it would have been so wonderful with you. We could have…"

Realizing what she had said made her cringe. She had just told him she would have wanted to bear his sons and daughters. Her voice cracked. She turned red and buried her head in his lap. She wondered...what would he think of her now? Maybe he would not want to be with her anymore. Had she made him sad by proposing that they should have met long ago?

Mark sensed her discomfort. He lifted her head up gently by her chin. "Don't fret, love, we are adults – our feeling for each other is deep enough that we can share anything. We can be open about all things."

"Yes, but not here," she said, nodding toward the driver.

In Daphne's room, Mark took her in his arms, hugged her and asked if there was something she needed to tell him. At first she looked blank, as if he was referring to a mystery.

"Remember in the car, while we were watching the children."

She led him to the divan and told him about Pierre, her miscarriage, and the spiritual experience she had near Reims. He listened attentively, often holding her hand to assure her he was empathizing with her. She cried often during her story.

"Thank you for telling me so much about yourself. You're a brave woman...your faith is deep, your soul is full. Like so many things I saw in the war, the losses of some help others. Your sharing with me all that you have gone through has helped me decide what will be the next effort of my life."

"Helped you? What, by being a sinful woman?"

"Hush. Aren't you the one that said today is today? Soon, we'll both be back in our regular lives. Mine will be richer for all that you have given me. Let me try to give you something."

"You have...more than you'll ever know. My heart is overflowing. You have taught me that love is a larger body than grief. My grief has been a heavy burden, but it is only a small rivulet...your love is an ocean. Oh, Mark, have I done wrong?"

"To some, perhaps, but I think my heart is big enough to carry this tiny snippet of time and still hold all of the other people who are dear to me. Our few days, brief as they are, will be an eternity."

"For me it is forever. You are kind." She moved back, put her head in his lap, and looked up at him with love and respect. He thought about carrying her to bed but felt it was too soon after what they had just shared. The communion of this moment stretched far beyond physical desires.

Daphne again marveled at the tenderness and thoughtfulness of him. She knew he loved her for all that she was and cared for her in every way. He seemed to be aware of her every feeling and need.

"How about a swim?"

"*Oui.* I will change. Please come back for me."

They swam a few laps, then sat at a poolside table and ordered fruit drinks. Daphne wanted to ask about his life in America: where he grew up, went to school, how he met his wife, and why there were no children. But, she was afraid of the pain she might feel if he talked about *Madame* in loving terms. She knew she was being foolish; it was an impossible situation…Mark and her. She would be the "other woman." But all of the logic of Plato, Aristotle, or any other of the great thinkers, would never dampen the smoldering, emotional embers that Mark had ignited in her. Whatever pain she might suffer in the future was worth the feelings he had awakened for her. Just being near him fanned those embers to a bright flame.

Under the table, Mark stroked her instep with his barefoot.

"Why so quiet?"

She didn't want him to guess she had been thinking of their separation, his wife, and what could never be. She turned away for a second, put on a smile, and turned back.

"Tonight, may we dine formally…maybe take a walk on the beach after the moon is up?"

"Certainly."

"Maybe you should wear shorter socks, so you wouldn't have to dance so much in the sand."

"You are so practical. I'll wear no socks if that will give us more time together."

"And, dear Mark, I will stand on my head if it will give me one more second with you."

There it was again – a limitation of time, a foreshadowing of the end. If he did come to France, would he want to see her? Would he have his wife with him? Perhaps she would never see him again after tomorrow. Would something die inside if she never saw him again? Was it like the song says, "To live it again/is past all endeavor?"

Would their parting be her punishment for what they had done? Yet, it…he…was so beautiful. How could something this dear – this wonderful – be all bad? Why, dear God, did love have to be like a knife that cut two ways?

"Hey, dark eyes, did I lose you again? Would you mind if I moved a little closer? That way I can keep you here in the present with me."

She nodded and he moved closer, pressing his leg lightly against hers. Her cheeks flushed, she put her hand on his thigh. They were two people in the cocoon of the warmth and security they derived from each other.

He fretted about what the consequences would be after this brief, but idyllic, interlude with Daphne. He knew he was running up a big bill with the piper, who always got paid by those who danced to his tune. What would the final cost be? Did he have enough spiritual capital to settle the account? But, she was so sweet, so vulnerable, and had been through so much. Was he some kind of hypocrite pretending he was just a "friend?" Could he really say he loved love Stephanie as he always had and still say he loved this beautiful human being as well?

Dear God, please help me. I can't hurt either one of them. Please protect them. Punish me when my time comes. They're both good people. I'm the louse. But, here I'm in another world…comfortable making her happy. I think…or am I building her a house of cards...that the winds of fate will blow apart in the morning?

"*Mon Cherie*, now it is my turn. "Did I lose you?"

He looked to her like a little boy suddenly shaken from day-dreaming by his teacher. His innocent face melted her. She reached over and kissed him lightly on the lips.

"You are my big strong man – yet you are, for all of your experiences, as pure as a little child. I love you."

He didn't know what to say. She was so sincere, so open, and so pure in thought and word. Nothing she said was ever anything that was a challenge. He never had to be "up" to communicate with her. Their compatibility was comforting and soulful.

Finally, he asked, "Shall we dress for dinner, maybe dance to our song…?"

"*Oui*, yellow or periwinkle?"

"Yellow, please – just like the first night...when you took the breath away of every man in the room."

After escorting Daphne to her room, he stopped at the *concierge* and arranged for a small corsage to be delivered to her. He listed several songs he wanted the orchestra to play after they were seated. Lastly, he chose the table for the evening. It was halfway between the band and the veranda. The hostess agreed to have candles on their table.

In his room, Mark put in another call to Stephanie.

"Mark, where are you?"

"On Martinique, where else? Going to ask Harold to handle the Miami thing. Good experience for him, and I'll be able to get home Saturday instead of Sunday...see you sooner."

"That's great. You still in meetings?"

"They're winding down. Sort of quiet tonight...a lot of the men have left. Can't get a plane until late morning tomorrow. I'll be transferring in Miami but should hit La Guardia about four. Wanna have dinner in the city?"

"Love to. How about the Russian Tea Room?"

"Your pick, honey. Can't wait. I'll wire or call you with the flight number."

"I'll meet your plane, okay? Miss you…see you tomorrow."

He hung up, but didn't move from the side of the bed. It was opposite the large mirror over the dresser. He stared at himself. Which face was looking back at him? Was it the son of hardworking, honest John and Joyce, who had busted their tails to support him so that he could be a Caribbean playboy? Or was it the face of just another run-of-the-mill human bumbling through life with all of the baser foibles? Should he cancel tonight? No, she was up for this last night…he'd started the role, so he'd play it out…play it right. She deserved his best. He had the rest of his life to do all he could for Stephanie…maybe that was restitution. Maybe that would pay off some of what he owed.

He let out a deep sigh, then stood up resolute.

Hey, it's curtain time. I can think about all of that stuff on the ride home. Enter stage left, buddy…you're on.

"Mark, thank you for the flowers, they're beautiful. Will you help me pin them on?"

He smiled, loving this all-too-brief intimacy. "Sure, as long as you don't think I'm getting fresh if my big clumsy hands touch the wrong spot."

She took his hands in hers. "Clumsy? No, these are the gentlest hands in the world. I welcome their touch anywhere." She pulled them to her lips and kissed them.

When they entered the dining room, several diners looked up in awe at this handsome couple. They saw a petite woman with dark hair in yellow on the arm of a very tall, dark-haired man in a white formal jacket. Several pairs of eyes followed them to their table. As they were seated, the orchestra struck up *Amor*. Mark gave a two-fingered salute to the band leader. By agreement, and for a hundred francs, every third song would be from Mark's list.

Daphne was enthralled with the music, the table setting, and three dances with Mark. When they danced to *Begin the Beguine*, he whispered some of the lines in her ear. Was this right? It was exactly what he had done with Steph back at OCS. Here he was again with that two-girl thing. *Can't help it, she's here and it's now, and I love the song. Hell, let the piper take tomorrow, tonight I need a gal.*

Daphne could feel his momentary distance, but refrained from asking him where he was. She just pressed the side of her face into his chest, thinking about the rest of the evening. She had never experienced such elegance, nor known anyone like Mark. She wouldn't let herself compare him to Pierre. The times and places and their ages were so different. She understood now why Mark could not say that he loved her, but that there was room in his heart for the others who were dear to him. She even wished that she could meet *Madame*. They had so much in common – loving the same man. That must mean they were like true sisters in the greater family of all human beings. She felt good, realizing now that she was not jealous of his wife. She only hoped that *Madame* would take good care of this wonderful man who had filled her soul – this man who had given her a new outlook, a new vitality.

"Ready to walk on the beach? The moon is peeking in on us."

"*Oui*, I am ready." And with a pixie smile, "Will you be able to get those long stockings off before morning?"

"Not to worry, Miss Smarty. I wore short ones."

Hand-in-hand they walked for a mile on the beach, letting the wet sand ooze between their toes, swinging their hands, and stopping to hug and kiss several times. Daphne was bubbly, perhaps in a forced manner to cover the sadness she felt about the coming separation. But, reaching deep into her well of resolve, a storehouse of fortitude and some fatalism that had been bred from all of her serious encounters with life, she finally cast tomorrow aside.

Tonight was the rest of her life.

Mark broke the silence. "Shall we head back, yet still be together?"

She would do anything to be with him for every minute that she could. On the beach, in the room, anywhere…they were all heaven as long as they were together. She didn't need to think about what was next.

She didn't answer, but pulled his arm to her side and started toward the hotel. When they reached her room, she handed him the key. He opened the door and followed her in. They stood on the balcony in complete silence, feeling each other's presence, and listening to the ocean, the swaying palms, the orchestra, and the most vibrant sonority of all…the crying out of their hearts to each other.

"Mark, would you stay with me tonight? Will you give me every moment of the rest of our time together?"

"Yes." He led her back into the room, embraced her, then very gently turned her and unbuttoned her frock, which obligingly slid to the floor. She stepped out of the dress, kicked off her shoes, and half turned so that he saw her beautiful shape in profile. Heated and engorged, he picked her up and carried her to the bed. He undressed, watching her all the while. She sat up and slowly removed her bra, then her tiny panties. Then she lay back down, a look of complete adoration shining on her face. He gasped and pulled her on top of him. He kissed her lips, her breasts, everywhere all in the fervor of his complete arousal. She met him kiss for kiss, touch for touch, caress for caress. After the initial ardor simmered down just a bit, they slowly and tenderly made love until both were fulfilled.

Breathless, Daphne asked Mark to hold her. She didn't need her nightgown. Would he just hold her until she fell asleep? He did, and she went to sleep within a few minutes. He continued to hold her, wondering what he would do about her after tomorrow. But it was too big an issue for the next few hours. He had to put that off...bury it and see what evolved. One day at a time. Once he was away from her, he would think more clearly. She was the sweetest person he'd ever known – her feelings had to be protected. Yet he owed Stephanie his loyalty and the love he'd pledged, had benefited from, and wanted to continue. Stephanie was a wonderful wife, a hundred-and-eighty-degrees from Daphne but just as fine on her side of the circle. Only God could mold so many fine beings – different, yet all beautiful.

Finally, he dropped off, but his arm was around her even as he slept.

When the early sunlight filtered across the bed and into every corner of the room, they both awoke.

"Mark, I felt so safe last night...I knew nothing could harm me...you were there."

"It was a beautiful time, Daphne...just as you are...night and day."

"*Monsieur* Cole Porter, again?"

He never failed to appreciate how she could quip in English along the same lines that he was thinking. There were so many ways that they meshed. It was so easy to be serious with her, yet in a flash turn the tone of their moods to the lightness that only inti-mate lovers...maybe even best friends...enjoy

"Right, and you're quick."

He picked up his Rolex from the table. Seven-fifteen. Four hours until her plane. His was an hour after.

The taxi ride to the airport was mostly silent – two people dreading what they knew would be painful and confusing. Each was trying not to look ahead, yet wondering what the next chapter would bring. Daphne stared out of the window, wondering if she would ever see this beautiful island again? Feeling Mark's hand on hers, she wondered if she would ever see this beautiful man again. When

301

she considered that she might not, she felt a stabbing pain in her heart.

Mark could sense her suffering. He took her hand to his lips and held it there.

"Remember our avowal, 'this time is our eternity…at least until we meet again somewhere, somehow'."

She looked over to him and smiled, nodding her head. But as she kissed his hand, she knew this was probably the last time.

Mark checked their bags, helped her with her passport and visa, and asked her to sit with him in the lounge. There was silence between them; their emotions blocked the things each had planned to say.

"Mark, my stomach is funny. It is full of…what is it you Americans say?"

"Butterflies."

"*Oui, le Papillon.* Maybe a small glass of Burgundy and a brioche, *s'il vous plait.*"

He brought it to her. She took each item, made a very faint movement over them with her hand. Then, she deliberately pushed them into the center of the table.

"Mark, we do not know whether we will share another meal – or if this," she said as she pointed to the bread and wine, "will be our last one. Please help me."

He put out his hand. She tore off a piece of the brioche and placed it on his upturned palm. He took it and ate it, never taking his eyes away from hers. Next, she took the wine glass by its stem and extended it to him, keeping her hold on it, as she tipped it to his lips.

"Thank you," she said softly.

He was speechless, mesmerized by the sanctity and pathos of the moment.

"Dear Mark, I am yours forever…here…wherever, but now I send you back to your wife and the life that you have worked for and fought so hard to build. Please keep me in a corner of your heart. But, we must both now return to the places from whence we came. That would have to be God's way…our way. Thank you, my beloved, for all that you have awakened in me."

She rose from the table, gathering her small bag and wrap. Her face was soft and sad, but she moved with the certainty of someone who knew what she had to do. Mark started to get up.

"Please stay here. I will go to my plane carrying the image of you and our shared last meal."

"I…uh…no…I…"

"No, my sweet, remember, we are luckier than most. We had a lifetime of love in a few days. *Au revoir*, Mark…until…"

CHAPTER TEN

*Now when these things begin
to take place, stand up and
raise your heads, because your
redemption is drawing near.*

Luke 21:28

"Afternoon, folks, this is your captain. For those of you on the left side of the plane, if you look down you will see the outer banks of the Carolinas. These barrier reefs produce some mighty fine fishing. And, thanks to the middle island, we're flying today – that's where the Wright Brothers made their first flight. It looks like we're right on schedule for a La Guardia landing at 4:38 Eastern Time. Thanks for flying National, and a good day to you all."

The captain's announcement brought Mark out of the deep thought that had held him captive since taking off from Miami. He'd been running an emotional gauntlet after seeing Daphne walk up the stairs to her plane. He was stunned by her quick parting and her failure to give him her Paris address. But then she was taking the moral course for both of them. What would he do with a wife, whom he loved, and a woman in a foreign land? What would he say in his nightly prayers? How could he be true to, or even supportive of, two women. He wasn't a Mormon, nor were either of them. Rationally, he knew Daphne had done the courageous thing, yet he could not dull the deep ache of knowing he might never see her again. He loved Stephanie, but the interlude in his life that Daphne had filled was an unforgettable experience. It was deep, sweet, and completely unfettered with any personal agendas...pure and sincere. He had never known a more giving person. It was as if her creed was to serve and not be served.

He became anxious when he thought about seeing Stephanie in less than an hour. She'd be eager to make love after a New York dinner and having been separated for five days. Well, he'd never had any trouble with that, she could be very exciting; but, would he see Daphne when he was holding her?

Man, you gotta do some soul purging.

Then it hit him hard. All of his early-life, Calvinistic-based morals learned with his parents at the Presbyterian Church, came to him – all of the "you shall nots" from Exodus 20. A wave of shame surged through him. His face was hot, his stomach was nauseous. He had committed adultery...the word that *Yahweh* had given Moses on the mountain. He rationalized, defensively, that it was a word too ugly to be applied to what had been so beautiful with a person as vulnerable and good as Daphne. True, the sex was wonderful, but beyond that was the rejuvenation she had undergone in his presence. Lord knows, she'd had a triple dose of sad things to absorb. No doubt she needed him or someone like him. He hoped that her life would be different now. Maybe she would meet a man with whom she could share many things.

Again, his thoughts were interrupted by the captain announcing they were in their final descent.

He couldn't take back what happened on Martinique. Maybe he didn't even want to...it was beautiful. He wondered if she got home safely. But, there had to be some restitution...some atonement. His mind was racing, grasping for something to cling to that would mitigate his guilt. Was she all alone in her apartment? Despite all of the cultural-based indictments he was leveling against himself, his heart and the right side of his brain still held on to the protective feeling he had for Daphne. He'd have to find a way, an organization, some cause – where he could do for others. Maybe there was some way Stephanie and he could work together. No, he should find it on his own first, then try to bring her into it. He couldn't make his atonement on her coattails. He had to do this by himself, within himself. He had to confess to God, and ask...no, plead for His guidance on how to make amends.

When the 727 docked at the jet way, Mark was the first one off the plane. At the terminal door was a smiling Stephanie. She threw her arms around him. At first he was confused; her hug was so much stronger than Daphne's. He didn't know quite how to react but he was glad to be home in familiar territory, and in the comfort of the path he had walked for so many years. He tightened his hold on Stephanie.

"I'm glad you're here!" he whispered.

"Where'd you expect me to be, if not where you were?"

There it was, the slight edge of challenge...harmless, but different than...

"Dinner at the Russian Tea Room?"

"You bet. I made the reservations and tipped a guy to let me park right outside where your bags will be. Let's go, lover, it's been a while."

She took his arm as they walked to baggage claim. With each step they took, Martinique was farther away. He wondered if the memory would fade as well. Could he walk away from it as easily?

Over dinner, Stephanie recounted the highlights of the art center dedication, including her brief exchange with Father Dardnell, saying what a nice man he was. She omitted her encounter with Percy Withers. Mark listened, but the flickering candles, like the ones on the table of the Martinique hotel, made his thoughts swing from where he was to where he had been twenty-four hours earlier.

"Mark, are you here? You seem somewhat detached...something on your mind?"

"Uh, no...no. I guess long plane trips are just a little harder to recoup from now. Sorry, gal. Can't tell you how much I missed you and how glad I am to be back with you."

Stephanie's perception was as keen as a newly honed straight razor. "Back with me as opposed to what, who, where?"

Mark was quickly pulled from dreamland and plunked down at the table. "Just from being away from you…it's as simple as that." He knew there had been a slip in the way he had expressed himself – small, but there. He remembered the old adage, "Oh, what tangled webs we weave when first we practice to deceive."

"Okay. Ready to go home, my dear weary traveler," she said remembering the time he had returned from an extended trip and had fallen asleep before she could get her night gown on…or off. She hoped he'd be "up" for her tonight. He had the same hope.

"Mark, do you want me to drive? Let you rest up a bit?"

That would be great, maybe catch a little shut eye. Holding Daphne all night had not allowed him more than a few hours of sleep. But, he had to brave this out and not give away his tiredness.

"Thanks, babe, I'll drive. It's been a few days since I did. Besides, I need to get the feel of your new car."

On the way, Mark said very little, answering Stephanie's questions about Martinique with short sentences, making her wonder what really transpired there. At home, she asked him if he wanted a drink or was he too tired to stay up for a while. He declined the drink and reached into his reserve strength, the same strength that had pushed him from the First Platoon's trench with O'Reilly on his back toward Bastogne.

"If it's okay with you, I'd like to escort you upstairs…maybe for some illicit purposes."

Relieved, she grabbed his hand and pulled him to the stairway. She prepared for bed in minutes, not wanting to chance his going to sleep. Mark was determined to do everything he could to make her enjoy their lovemaking. Afterward, she dismissed those tiny little questions about what he had done on the island. He had to have been good; otherwise he couldn't have been so passionate *and* so consumed with pleasing her. As he fell asleep, she kissed his forehead. Mark sighed – he was able to put O'Reilly down in the snow. It had been a tough test of his endurance.

*　　　　　*　　　　　*

Daphne almost strained her neck muscles as she twisted in her seat trying to watch the ever-diminishing island of Martinique, as the Air France 707 soared upward toward home. She felt her relationship with Mark diminishing as he was preparing to board his plane for America. They had been so close, now they were winging farther and farther from each other. She didn't cry, as she thought she might. Her mind, her nerves, were set in a mode of knowing that she had lived the beauty of deep love and respect that could never be duplicated. She had to keep telling herself, though, that not encouraging him to see her in France, or to communicate with her, was the proper thing to do. She sighed, if she could just touch his hand one more time, put her head on his chest, hear his soft voice wash over her, have his strong, protective arms around her. As she felt these images, she did start to cry…tiny grimaces, wet with tiny tears.

Looking down at the peaking waves of the grey-green Atlantic, she felt her heart doing the same thing – peaks of ecstasy from his love, and valleys of depression when she knew he would be no more, except in her dreams. She might have betrayed her pledge to Pierre's memory and, worst of all, to her God. She thought a lot about going to confession with Cardinal Desmonde, but every time she pictured the confining confessional, she shuddered at the thought of describing Mark as a partner to her sin.

She put her head down, covered her eyes with the hand that held her rosary, and whispered, "Dear Father in heaven, please forgive Mark, it was I who lured him into our brief affair. I couldn't help myself…I am weak and was so unknowingly starved for a man's love. I am evil, dear God, but know that I will do all that I can to atone for what I have done. Please protect dear Mark and help *Madame* Aber-crom-bee and him to live the rest of their lives in happiness. Oh, and Father, please keep the soul of Pierre safe, and if I can redeem myself in your eyes, maybe you will bring us together again one day. Thank you. Amen."

*   *   *

As the weeks passed, Mark's thoughts about Daphne never left him; but from once an hour, they became once a day, then only twice a week. His nightly prayers, which he carried out on his knees by their bed, always contained one for Daphne's health and happiness and a plea to God to help him find the path to atonement. He asked God to hold him totally accountable for what occurred on Martinique.

Stephanie was pleased with how attentive he had become, attending more of the functions that she led or supported. Something had happened on his trip to Martinique. He was different – not greatly so, yet in little ways, all positive, towards her. What was it? Couldn't have been a one-night stand. He was too sweet and sincere, with no apparent reflections of guilt, or glib "I love yous." Maybe he was experiencing some type of mid-life change; after all he was fifty-three and climbing. Perhaps he'd had some kind of spiritual epiphany – he was talking a lot about God.

One morning, after attending a benefit dinner for a children's charity that Stephanie chaired, Mark called Father Dardnell for an appointment. In answer to his inquiry, the priest suggested that he check with the Holmes School for Homeless Children to see if he could contribute his services. He added that Mark might also try the oncology ward, at Children's Hospital. These two were not in Stephanie's cadre of charities or cultural organizations.

Mark committed for two sessions at the school for the homeless, where he assisted a teacher of fourth graders. When he visited the oncology ward he was stricken by what he saw. Children aged five to fifteen, some limping and some with skull caps over their

309

little heads to hide chemo-induced baldness. Others were bed-ridden, in wheel chairs, or on crutches. When the nurse introduced Mark, and told them that he had been a soldier in the big war, they smiled or laughed, and one ten-year-old mocked aiming a rifle at him saying, "Pow, pow."

Mark didn't sign up that day at the hospital; he needed to think about whether he could face these afflicted children, knowing that if he became attached to any of them, they might be snatched from him by death. Could he handle that? Driving to his office, he remembered the little boys and girls on Martinique, who had been crossing the road as Daphne and he were returning to the hotel. He and she had talked about neither of them having had children of their own. He thought about Daphne, snatched from his life by laws and a culture rooted in monogamy. He jammed on the brakes, made an illegal u-turn to the blowing horns of several irate drivers, and sped back to the hospital. An hour later he was committed to six hours on Saturday – he was tired of the same old Saturday golf group anyway – and four hours on Wednesday. Between the hospital and the school, he had eighteen hours of volunteering with kids – the kids he and Stephanie never had.

He hired a man to be his close assistant, thereby reducing his need to travel. He promoted Harold to Vice President and gave him a ten-percent ownership in the company. He promised his new assistant the same after a year if he improved results. Mark was building his organization stronger and more self-dependant so that he could devote more time to his volunteer services.

Stephanie was pleased with his reduced travel, secretly hoping that he would not be going again to Martinique without her. She really didn't know why she felt that way, but she did. She was glowing in what she called her middle-age, the Indian summer of her youth, she jokingly termed it. Mark's increased attention to her made her bloom. He was less consumed with the business; but aside from that, he was just sweeter and often would defer to her wishes, as if his needs might not be as important.

She reflected often on the phases of their marriage. The early years were insatiable sex, Mark's drive to "get ahead," their adjusting to each other, as well as the in-and-outs with Harvey as they hammered out a relationship. Then came the childlessness, which could have been a real divisive factor, but to Mark's credit, he never belabored the issue. Now, she was basking in the warmth of a seasoned relationship, like a fine wine that had been aged in ideal conditions. True, there was that tiny pique of curiosity about what might have happened on Martinique. But, she always came to the same conclusion; let it go. It was a point of time from which Mark had mellowed in his approach to both business and her. Maybe his being completely away from everything opened a window to their future. And, Charles Duboise seemed to have a good influence on Mark. All-in-all, she guessed the Martinique trip was a good thing.

With her usual brutal honesty and objective introspection, she thought maybe she should stop looking under the covers of his life...was her own perfect? There were all of those times with Percy Withers – was he her Martinique? Was her calculated plucking of Mark out of Margery Eggers' life the act of a friend? No, she needed to judge herself, not him. And besides, she knew he was doing some pretty good things, like getting involved at the hospital. He had even given up a golf game for the kids at Children's. Overtly, away from him, she bragged to everyone about *her* husband, citing his work at the homeless school and the children's oncology ward.

Mark began to hear, second-hand at the club, about Stephanie's praise of him. She had said nice things to him about his charitable work, but hearing it from third parties made it mean more. He wondered if what he was doing was really good, or was it a self-serving act to try and salve his conscience for his affair with Daphne? He was confused. Was his doing for others the road to redemption…or was God's grace the only way? His mind was continuously processing a lot of spiritual pieces, particularly the foundation plank of Christianity: The tenet that Christ had died for our sins. Would Daphne have to die for their sin? Should he also die for it?

As he looked at Stephanie each morning, he kept thinking about Daphne. Should he tell Steph what he did? He remembered a situation in France, before they went to St. Vith. A married father and a lieutenant had slept with a French girl while on leave. The lieutenant thought he should write his wife and confess. The company chaplain advised against it. He said the man should confess to God, but take his transgression to his grave, as it would only shatter his wife's faith. But, the chaplain also told the soldier to go and sin no more. Mark was honored his fellow officer had shared this with him. It was helping him to know what to do now. He would not pursue Daphne. He would take their short time and lock it away in his memory. He would do all he could to serve others and be the best husband he could for Stephanie. What his final judgment would be, only God knew. He'd just have to leave that to God and follow the rules. And, as far as being there for Stephanie, that was what he wanted to do. She was his wife, best friend, and the person that had helped motivate him. He never wanted her to be sorry she had married a poor boy from South Boston.

In November, Mark received a call from Charles Duboise. Would he consider a trip to Chartres to talk about business in general and help Charles plan a new venture?

"Mark, I value the deep knowledge you have acquired about the metals market. Would you help me for a day, maybe two at the most?"

"Certainly, Charles, when?"

"As soon as you can fit it into your schedule, which I am sure is full."

Mark thought about taking Stephanie along; then the image of

Daphne filled his head. It was as if her absence and his suppressed thinking of her had multiplied like a high-interest investment. How could he check on her if Stephanie was along? He had to do this just once. It could help conclude his wondering...maybe even help him continue his search for atonement or redemption.

"How about next Monday and Tuesday?" He suggested those days knowing they were Stephanie's busiest and included another dedication.

"That will be fine, Mark. I will meet your plane."

Mark had Miss Harlan book his flights using the new SST Concorde. The Mach II speed of this newest plane would allow him to turn the trip in a little under two days. He thanked Miss Harlan, who always let out a sigh after he was gone. She had never stopped regarding him as the man she wanted to be with.

He went to the hospital. All twenty kids brightened up when he came in, shouting, "Hi, Uncle Mark."

He stopped at Billy Meyer's bed, a nine-year-old with lymphatic cancer. Billy looked particularly weak today, but he tried to sit up and touch Mark.

"Hi, Billy. Nurse tells me you're the best behaved person in here. I'm proud of you. I talked to Mickey Mantle the other day, and here's his autographed picture addressed to you. He said to hang in there; he's with you."

"Gee, Uncle Mark, thanks."

Mark moved on to Sally Billings, an eleven-year-old girl with dark eyes, just like Daphne's. Sally had a cloth skull cap covering her head. Not only had she undergone chemo, but also a brain operation for a tumor. Early indications were that she was improving. Her locomotion was almost perfect since the tumor had been removed.

Over the next four hours, Mark read to several of the children. Next, he played games with others. When he left, all the kids yelled goodbye. Nurse Jennings patted him on the arm, thanking him for helping to lift the spirits of her charges.

Stephanie was not too upset about his trip to France since it was so short, and Mark had been true to his word about greatly reducing his travel. Besides, he suggested that a couple of weeks after he returned, they might take a little week-long honeymoon to anywhere she desired.

"Welcome to France, Mark. Thanks for coming on such short notice."

"Of course, Charles."

They got into the car, and Charles spoke to the driver. Mark's thoughts were consumed with Daphne as they left the Paris airport. How far from it did she live? Would he see her...or should he even think about seeing her? What about all of those vows and resolutions he'd made? But, maybe if they were able to say one last good-bye, it would help him. No, it might just fan the smoldering coals of their romance. He thought sadly, it was just like the song said, "Let/the/love/that/was/once/a/fire/remain/an/ember." That's what he finally concluded, but not without an anguishing torment. To once again hold her petite body and feel her seek the comfort and strength of his arms...but, if he did, what would he share with Stephanie...with himself...with his God? What would he see when he looked in the mirror of his soul...a Dorian Gray?

He and Charles made small talk as the new Mercedes whisked them out of the city. Charles must have thought him an imbecile, with Daphne filling his thoughts; his answers were rarely more than one syllable. Finally, in stilted casualness, he asked Charles about Daphne's health, and was her work at *Elle* progressing?

Charles turned toward the window as if he hadn't heard Mark and remarked about the coming of winter, pointing out the barren countryside. Mark was stung by Charles' ignoring his question. It could only mean that Charles did not approve of Mark's time with Daphne on Martinique. But, how could he know about it? He had flown home before Daphne and he had spent that time together. Had Daphne shared their tryst with him? No, he couldn't believe that. There had to be something else, but what?

Charles knew he had been rude to Mark, but he didn't want to discuss Daphne at that moment. He tried to reengage Mark in conversation.

"How is *Madame*? Well, I trust?"

"She's fine," Mark answered, wondering why the anything-but-subtle shift of subjects was being made. Something was wrong. Should he ask his best customer, and now close friend, what was being veiled?

As he turned to Charles to ask, the car suddenly slowed down to forty kilometers. They were turning into a cemetery. It wasn't a military cemetery – no uniform white crosses with a sprinkling of Star of David markers. What was this about?

"Why are we here?" Even as he asked, he sensed something – something chilling.

Charles turned to him. "I'm so sorry, my friend."

"Sorry, why?" What was he going to hear? His friend's emanation made him apprehensive.

"You asked after Daphne." Charles' face told all.

In a sick tone, he forced a whisper, "Daphne?"

"Yes, my friend, *our* dear Daphne."

"How, when, why...no...no."

Charles put his hand on the driver's shoulder. The car pulled to the side, and Charles pointed to a large granite monument – embossed on it, DEVEREUX.

Mark sat transfixed as he stared at the monument. He was suddenly at the Martinique airport, and Daphne was talking about sharing their last meal together. That was when she offered him the token of bread and wine, just before she said *au revoir*...the last time he had seen her alive. Oh God, it had been their last supper. He bent his head with his hand over his eyes.

This isn't real – this can't be. Was I the cause of this?

Charles put his hand on Mark's shoulder.

Mark reached for the door handle, but Charles said, "Wait just a moment. Let me share something with you first, please."

What was he going to hear? Did Charles think that he had contributed to Daphne's demise? Then a hideous thought invaded his mind...oh, God, not suicide...no...no. *Because of what I led her into?* He was almost afraid to let Charles continue, but he had to. He had to know the whole story, no matter what.

"Mark, I do not know, or need to know, how close you and my cousin were on Martinique; but whatever, if anything you had, it buoyed her spirits...her zeal for living. Dear Daphne was writing a new and brighter chapter in her life. She was radiant and bursting with energy."

"Then, what happened?"

"It was terribly sad, but in some ways a beautiful thing; if we call heroics beautiful."

"Heroics?" Mark echoed in a hollow voice which cryed out from deep inside, as if he were in a well. The word brought back memories of Pellini, McCormack, Redding – all of those dead from his company – and his mom and dad. But, dear sweet Daphne?

"She told you of her work at the orphanage?"

"Yes. I believe she spent most of her Saturdays reading to and working with the children. But what does the orphanage have to do with it?"

"She and one of the sisters were taking a group of ten children to the zoo."

Mark could see again the children on Martinique laughing and joshing each other, as the two nuns scolded and shepherded them across the road. He vividly recalled the love in Daphne's eyes as they watched.

Charles continued, "As they neared an intersection, one of the boys bolted into the street after a loose ball. A large *camion*...a

316

truck…was turning the corner…"

Noticing Mark's ashen complexion, it was obvious that Mark and Daphne had meant a lot to each other. There had to have been an intimacy between them greater than just a casual friendship. Should he finish the account? Of course, he couldn't leave his friend in such tragic a quandary.

Softly and slowly he continued. "Daphne, the witnesses said, leapt from the curb and pushed the boy forward just inches from the truck's path. The driver tried to brake, but she was too close. She suffered many, many fractures. When she reached the hospital, it was already hopeless. Her spleen had been ruptured, both lungs were pierced from broken ribs, and she had a severe head injury. There were even more injuries, but it isn't necessary to say more."

He paused again, his own sadness suddenly renewed, even after all of these months. Seeing Mark sitting as a waxen figure, his arms tightly folded across his chest, a look of disbelief on his face, he felt sadness for his American friend.

Mark's mind became a kaleidoscope of pictures: Daphne in her yellow formal, sitting by the pool in her green swimsuit, her perfect naked body on the ecru sheets, and the wistful look in her black eyes as they shared their last meal together…the memory he knew he would carry to his grave. He couldn't picture her broken and bloody body on a Paris street – his subconscious protected him from that awful scene. He knew he had to respond.

Finally, in a stuttered mixture wrenched from his heart: "My God, Charles, how cruel. Why her? Why that way? She was only good – her last act was one of sacrifice for others."

"Yes, my friend, it seems it is always the good that give themselves for others. Our Daphne is proof of that. There has to be a special place in heaven for her."

Again, Mark saw her as he had picked her up that last morning and carried her to bed. Who had picked her bruised body off the cobblestones in front of the zoo?

"Was...was she...alone? Was anyone there to help her... console her...a priest?"

"Only the doctors and the nurses...oh, yes, and the nun. The priest came too late. When Mimi and I arrived, she had died. I don't know whether I should tell you this last thing. Mimi says I must."

"Something else, Charles?"

"Yes. When the doctor met me outside of her room, he asked me if I was Mark."

"Me?"

"Yes. Your name was her last word."

Not Pierre! What had he done to this girl? She was taking his name to her grave. Would it be what she said in heaven? The weight of having affected her life so strongly made him cringe. He felt hot. The mixture of grief and guilt, like a cutting torch, burned his soul.

Charles sensed his discomfort and his suffering.

"Mark, again, let me say you gave dear Daphne a new lease on life. She was sad and depressed after her mother's death. She had no one of her own age to care about, or to care for her, until Martinique. Believe me, you were good for her. And, not to be unemotional, she was doing exactly what she wanted to do...serving others."

Mark sat silently for a long time. Then he sighed.

"Thank you, Charles. I would like to go to her grave."

"I will wait here."

Walking slowly to Daphne's grave, he again pictured the moon on the beach when they had walked there hand-in-hand. He hoped that her soul was resting in peace, with her beloved God and her Pierre.

She died for our sins.

As this realization came over him, he started to sob.

After several minutes, he felt Charles' arm around his shoulder.

"She was such a beautiful creature. I'm sure she is with the other angels." Charles sighed. They stood together in silence.

"Mark, I know you gave her something that filled her life before her untimely death. I am glad you did."

His friend's words were as sweet as balm on the tenderness of his hurting soul. Maybe he hadn't been all wrong in loving her for that "now is forever" of two days.

"Thank you, Charles. After Martinique, it was all locked in our hearts…there was no contact. She knew of my wife. In fact her last words to me were that she was 'sending me back to her'."

Mark knew now, more than ever, how morally strong Daphne had been…the conscience for both of them. God bless her, she sure should be with Him. He backed up a step from the grave and addressed Charles.

"I saw it so many times in the war. Some people die so that others may live. She was certainly the ultimate testimony to that."

"Yes, it has always been."

"And you are right, I am sure she is with the angels." Then he added, "And hopefully with her family…and her Pierre…"

His voice faded. Charles looked at his friend's face. He saw the sadness, and he saw the gradual shift to acceptance and resolution. Mark spoke again, this time with conviction.

"I know she is with her Creator."

"And with the memory of you, dear friend."

"And I will always have the memory of her. She was a truly beautiful and unselfish person. You say I helped her; well, I believe she helped me as much if not more."

Later, Mark asked Charles if it would be an imposition to go to a florist and come back to the grave. Mark bought a dozen red roses and a white wrist corsage. He carefully placed the roses, saving the corsage until last. Charles wisely returned to the car, leaving his friend at the grave.

Mark knelt, and put the corsage about where he thought Daphne's arm would be. "After you put this on, little one, how about we dance to *Begin the Beguine*? Then we can take a walk on the beach...the moon is up." His words caught behind a silent sob in his throat.

"*Au revoir*, Daphne. I love you."

On the flight home, he was in a state of shock. He couldn't erase her from his mind. He alternated between crying and chastising himself for having led her into the affair. Had their tryst forced her into an obsessive desire to help her orphan charges? Had she been so driven to escape from Martinique that she was blind to the danger of the approaching truck...was it a suicidal move?

Am I responsible for her death?

He knew he would carry this guilt to his grave. The more he thought about his commission of adultery and the reality of her death, the sicker he became. Suddenly, he bolted up from his seat and barely made it to the lavatory, where he threw up.

As the plane neared New York, he knew he'd have to make some kind of peace with himself...and with God.

I can't keep throwing up for the rest of my life. I have to follow the path...the footsteps...as nearly as I can, of our Savior...from this day forward. She gave her life for others, maybe in atonement, maybe in just plain selfless service. Can I do less?

Whispering aloud, "Please guide me, dear God, and may Daphne's soul rest in peace with you. I will do all that you lead me to do."

The woman sitting next to him said, "That's a nice prayer, sir. I'm sure God heard you."

Mark turned red, but managed to utter a garbled thank you.

Back in his office, Mark asked Miss Harlan to handle a delicate matter for him.

"Just tell me, Mr. Abercrombie," she smiled. She welcomed anything that might bring them closer together.

"I have just lost a dear friend in France. Mr. Duboise and I

320

visited her grave just north of Paris."

Miss Harlan wasn't sure she liked the warmth in his voice as he talked about a "dear friend." It had to be woman. Well, at least the friend was dead.

"I want you to set up an arrangement of seasonal flowers to be placed on her grave every month for the next twenty years. Here is the address of the florist and the grave site identification."

"Someone you met on Martinique?"

"Yes, since you mentioned it, she was a cousin of Mr. Duboise. She had suffered several deaths of close relatives, and Charles thought it would be good for her to take a holiday on the island. He had her act as the hostess for our business dinners. Of course, this is confidential. Understood?"

"Of course, Mr. Abercrombie, everything that you do, unless you tell me otherwise, is kept here, nowhere else." As she said this, her hand went involuntarily to her heart, hoping that the holiday was good for the unfortunate cousin, but seemed like it had been good for him as well...maybe too good.

"I appreciate that. You are a true and trusted friend and helper."

She blushed, glancing down at her steno pad. Then she looked directly into his eyes.

"You can ask me anything, Mr. Abercrombie. I will always be here for you."

There it was – another one of Miss Harlan's subtle hints. He told himself it wasn't his male conceit that made him feel she had feelings toward him that were far beyond those of a professional secretary. But, he had to admit, she had never been too overt, nor did she ever exude any feminine come-ons. She was certainly attractive: sweet face, great body, and always solicitous of his needs. *Stow it, brother...once in your life is enough.*

Miss Harlan left the office wondering just how close this "Martinique friend" had been. Mark's wife she had to accept, but not some French woman, no matter whose cousin she was. She knew she was a fool to carry her hidden torch for him, but she couldn't help it. He was all she ever thought a man should be. And, he was always so kind to her – kinder than any man she had ever known, except for the father who had been taken from her when she was sixteen.

A week later, Mark was sitting at the breakfast table with Stephanie. The morning paper was held up in front of his face, but he was looking out the bay window at the falling December snow. Stephanie rose to get more coffee.

She poured his cup full, "Martinique or Paris?"

He was motionless for a few seconds until her question registered. "Why do you ask?"

"Because, whenever you make a 'French connection', you come home in a semi-dreamland." She sounded casual enough. But that old edge, was it back again?

"Anything you want to share?"

He was right. She was probing for something.

"Can't think of anything. Maybe being over there brings back all of the war stuff. Lot of guys are still there in Belgium, Holland, and Germany. I just can't get it out of my system."

"Really...that was so long ago?"

"Yeah, but it's still there...wish it wasn't." He wanted to shift the subject. "You've been real good about understanding me. Like when I had all of those nightmares...you were always there for me."

He wasn't sure what she was after. But, she must be worried or at least curious about something. It couldn't be his Martinique affair...or was her woman's intuition working overtime?

"No, Steph, nothing you need worry about."

"You sure?'

"Yep," he smiled, reaching for her hand. "Say, where do you want to go for the holiday I promised you?"

"Give me a day. It'll be somewhere warm and sunny...perhaps Martinique."

Was that a devilish look on her face as she said Martinique? Mark didn't know that earlier in the week, near morning, she awakened to the sound of Mark's voice next to her on the pillow. He was muttering gibberish. But then, very clearly, she heard a woman's name – Daphne. Her first impulse was to ask him about it the minute he awoke. But, as she watched him sleep, she thought about how close they had been – especially since he returned from Martinique – and how good he had been to her ever since they were married. Maybe it was nothing. If it was, it certainly didn't seem to be coming between them. He couldn't be any more devoted and considerate than he had been. And, was she lily pure? What about all her trucking around with Percy Withers? She told herself to forget it. Besides, if there had been a Daphne, the woman might have actually helped their marriage. Who knows, maybe someday she would meet her – that was if she even existed. It could have been a fantasy spit out of his subconscious in a dream. Maybe a stewardess' name sandwiched in between other unresolved thoughts. She didn't really need to know. Her life was good. She'd let it go at that…at least for the moment.

As Stephanie eagerly made the plans for a trip to Martinique, Mark was not that happy with her choice. Would he telegraph anything when he and Stephanie were walking on the beach? And if he did, what would follow? There was no way he could dissuade her from going there. He wasn't trying to avoid going to the island, it was just that he wanted to feel he had put that brief episode, for which he still was trying to atone, behind him. What would his being there trigger? He had played a role on the stage that he and Daphne had created. Before seeing her on their last night together, he had grappled with the decision either to call it off and end any further transgressions to his marriage vows, or play it out to keep from destroying Daphne's idyllic interlude. Thinking about having to play a role again, he wished, in the Greek Classic tradition, that there might be an eleventh-hour occurrence of some *deus ex machina*.

The night before Stephanie and Mark were to leave for Martinique, the phone rang at one a.m. It was Lillian calling from St. Luke's Hospital; Harvey was in ICU, having suffered a heart attack. The couple threw overcoats over their nightwear and rushed to the hospital. Lillian was ghostly white. She faced them and put a hand on each of their chests – tears running down her ashen cheeks.

"How's Dad, Mother?"

"Not good. The doctor has hinted that he might not make it. The attack was massive." She looked from Stephanie to Mark, and back to her daughter. She didn't know if Harvey was going to live. If he didn't, these two were the only loved ones in her life.

"Oh, here comes Doctor Elway now."

Stephanie and Mark turned as the doctor approached them, his face a professional mask molded from years of having to convey bad news to caring relatives and friends. He reached for Lillian's hand, slowly shaking his head. His silence was as loud as the tolling of a funeral bell. Absorbing the brutal truth, Lillian collapsed against Mark, who caught her and held her tight.

Stephanie wanted to see her father. The doctor nodded, asking if she wanted him to accompany her.

"No thank you. Mom and Mark will go with me."

She was hit with the sour-sweet smell of hospital sterilization – the same smell that had pervaded the room in which Daniel had died. The sheet had been pulled over her father's face; the IV trees were still by the side of the bed. Lillian gasped, but made herself stand upright, her hand on Mark's arm.

Stephanie walked to the bed and gently lifted the sheet. She stood for a moment looking, then bent and kissed his forehead.

"Goodbye, Daddy, see you one day."

Lillian made the sign of the cross; then, like her daughter, she kissed her husband's red-gray-toned forehead. "Harvey was today's eleventh-hour vineyard worker. You know these last several years were the sweetest of our life together. He couldn't say enough good things about both of you. You made him very happy with your help at the company."

Mark and Stephanie went to her side and put their arms around her. Together they left the room – three people who had seen all sides of a driving and powerful man: his toughness, his generosity, and his late-in-life transfiguration.

Several weeks later, the three met in the probate lawyer's office for the reading of the will. Most of the assets were left to Lillian, with an addition to Stephanie's trust fund of a million dollars. The surprise came when the lawyer read that there were grants to be made to every charity associated with Stephanie. An even bigger surprise were the grants made to Mark's homeless school and the oncology ward at Children's Hospital. Mark hadn't even known that Harvey was aware of his work. He had to give the man credit though; very little about his family had escaped his father-in-law's keen mind.

The Martinique trip got scrubbed. Stephanie felt it was a bad omen and connected it to her father's death. The next two years were busy ones, as Stephanie and Mark worked to put Braxton Chemicals on the stock market as a public company. The couple would retain only five percent of the stock and two board seats. The offer was over subscribed, which put millions into the family. Charitable trusts were established, guaranteeing Lillian a handsome income. The Tudor estate was also sold for several million, with the funds going into the trusts. Each year, the governing body of the charitable trusts – Lillian, Stephanie, Mark, Father Dardnell, and an attorney – dispensed over a million dollars to various charities and outreach programs. The balance of the income earned from the investments provided for Lillian. Steph and Mark managed to have dinner with Lillian at least once a week.

While they did all they could to help Lillian adjust to

widowhood, they also cared for Mark's mother. They supported eighty-three-year-old Joyce, whose senility was increasing, in a quality assisted-living home. Mark, many times accompanied by Stephanie, traveled to the Cape every other week. Additionally, Mark called her everyday, but he was not always certain his mother knew it was him. It was a day-to-day thing with her cognizance.

*   *   *

One May evening, Mark came home from the Children's Hospital. He parked the Lincoln in the driveway, thinking he might take Stephanie out for dinner. He entered the house through the garage and was surprised when she didn't answer his call. Her Cadillac was in the garage, she must be home. He called again, but no answer. Worry wormed its way into his stomach. He went into the living room, calling again...no answer.

He started for the stairs, when from the library he was hit with a fusillade. "Surprise! Happy Birthday."

Mark guessed there were at least twenty people in the library. Stephanie came forward and kissed him on the cheek. "Happy sixtieth, big guy."

Harold Brenner and his wife were there. Miss Harlan was too, and she was glowing. Some Braxton executives had shown up. Lillian sat in a chair, like a queen on her throne, her love for her "son" surrounding her like the robes of royalty. Father Dardnell, along with his wife, had been invited. The mayor was there too.

A stranger stood a little off from the group. At first Mark didn't recognize this man with the weathered face in the baggy suit. The man moved toward Mark with halting steps. He took his hand. "Wake up, Lieutenant, wake up." Mark gasped. He knew that voice. "Buck McCormack! God bless you...remember, you saved my life. Man, am I glad you're here!"

Mark told the whole group who Sergeant McCormack was and

what he had done. They applauded as Mark finished the story. Buck was embarrassed. He turned red, and there were tears in his eyes. Mark asked Stephanie how she had found McCormack.

"Friends in high places," she said, smiling mysteriously. "Glad you're happy he's here."

"It's great. You're a doll to have done this. Let me get you a drink. And, if you don't mind, take his arm and lead him to the bar. Tell him we have some fine Belgian cognac from his buddy, Tomlinson."

Steph did as she was asked, which made McCormack smile – remembering the cognac thing in Bastogne.

"He's awfully bashful for a man who's faced digging in Kentucky coal mines,

Germans, Chinese Communists, a tough lieutenant named Abercrombie, and this group of sophisticates. But, Mark, he adores you. I put him in the guest room…okay?"

"You bet. And thanks Stephanie. I owe him my life."

"That's two of us."

As Mark and Stephanie progressed gracefully through their sixties, they became more dependent on each other. But, at least once a year, Stephanie would mention in a disarming, off-hand manner Mark's trip to Martinique in 1971. She had never been quite reconciled in her mind that nothing had happened to him. She knew him so well, as most women know a man better than the man knows the woman. He was definitely different after the trip to Martinique and the subsequent one to France. No matter how philosophical she'd been about the "Daphne" utterance as he dreamed, her curiosity would arise and start her wondering. Every time she brought up the subject, Mark simply said they had been productive trips – a lot of new business, a closer relationship with Charles, and a negative regurgitation of the war whenever he passed a French military cemetery.

In the year of Stephanie's sixty-fifth birthday, both mothers passed on within a few months of each other. Joyce died first. When Lillian's funeral was over, Stephanie cried intermittently for several days. She became almost obsessively possessive of Mark. She wanted to know where he was every minute of the day. When he was home, she would sit very close to him. He took her in his arms one evening, stroking her auburn hair that still showed no signs of gray.

"You know, Steph, you're as beautiful as you were the night of the Christmas dance when we met. But, what's creeping around inside of you? You act like you're afraid I won't be here."

At first she looked dazed, as if she didn't know what he was saying. Then she cried out, "Mark, they're all gone...Mom, Dad, Daniel, your folks. All that's left is you and me." What would she do if Mark died before she did?

Underneath was the bitter truth of what she had sublimated for years – they had no children. They would not live on through children and grandchildren. They were alone. What could they leave behind? Just material things – maybe a few good works, but no part of themselves. Was her life to go out one day like a light bulb, whose filament was worn thin and snapped? The lineage that great grandfather Thomas had started would end with her.

She thought about how she had denied her parents...Mark's as well...the joy of grandchildren. The reality of the situation was made more pointed as she remembered, so many years before, when her mother had talked to her about how men always wanted to leave their mark...to leave their name and their genes as a monument to themselves. She could hear Lillian's explanation of why her father was so predisposed to Daniel...his progeny to carry on his name. She even remembered her mother's example of the pharaohs building pyramids as their monument. Had she deprived Mark of this joy? Had he really wanted to leave his genes...his name?

Realizing how tolerant he had been toward her about this, she suddenly shrieked, "No, oh God, why didn't I?"

Mark turned her face full to him. "Steph...what...what are you saying? Why didn't you do what?"

Sobbing, she buried her head on his chest. "Have children...damn me! What are we leaving – chemical stocks, art centers, a big house, hours of inane board meetings – what of any meaning?"

The no-children indictment hit Mark as well. Countless times he had wished for a son to carry his name, or to play with a daughter who was the reincarnation of Stephanie and buy pretty dresses for her. But, in his usual calm pragmatism, he knew not to fret over what he could not change. Still, he had to help his wife. He could only guess at the pain that she was feeling – that she had probably carried for a long time. He had to find something to give her new hope...some meaningful purpose. She'd done so many good things for others. The mother thing must be in the genes and wasn't over-ridden by conscious choices.

He again stroked her hair. "Steph, I won't pretend to know all that you are feeling right now, but I do know what you have done with your life. Do you know how many lives are better, healthier, and more purposeful because of all the groups you have worked with?"

He became animated, as he always did, when deeply convinced about what he was saying.

"You have devoted your life to others! Maybe we didn't have a couple of kids to teach and help get started in life; but, Steph you have helped thousands, not one or two! Maybe that's what God wanted you to do."

She heard the deep conviction of her mate. She looked up, tears still running down her face. "Maybe if I had thought more about what God wanted instead of what I wanted, it would have been different."

What an acknowledgement of God. He had never heard her say anything like this.

"That goes for all of us. You've done hundreds of good things. I wish I had been as dutiful to the needs of others as you have."

Now it was Stephanie's turn. She heard her husband, who was echoing a private sadness. She respected his privacy, but still she owed him her gratitude for how wonderful he had been about the children thing...well, about almost everything in their entire married life.

"Oh, Mark, you have always been there for me...for others. Sergeant McCormick told me how brave you were and how concerned you were about your men. He thinks you are a disciple of the Lord. And, for what it's worth, I do too."

"No, not hardly; but, thank you."

He grew serious. "Now, you do me a favor, and never...and I mean never...chastise yourself for what did or did not happen. None of us is perfect. None of us is without sin...commission or omission. We all struggle to find the right path. We often get lost, but somehow if we have faith, we get nudged back on the road again."

Stephanie sat up straight and wiped her eyes. She had the look of someone with a plan.

"Mark, may I start going to church with you...I mean every Sunday?"

Mark smiled, a peace settling gently around them.

"It'll double what I get from it; just like every thing we've shared, it's twice as good when we are one."

Each of them, in their own way, now felt closer to the other. Stephanie had never pried into what Mark did at the school or hospital, and since he rarely discussed it, she guessed he didn't want to talk about it. But, she had heard from a friend on the hospital board that they all appreciated what Mark was doing. The friend said that rarely was a board meeting held, that Mark's work wasn't mentioned. A couple of the doctors had said his cheering up of some of the children had actually helped their recovery.

On one afternoon, Mark entered the oncology ward to the familiar, "Hi, Uncle Mark." Ten-year-old Marie Hellwig's bed was empty. He had been reading from *Robinson Crusoe* to her. He asked Nurse Jennings about Marie. She had died three days ago. Little Amanda saw Mark's sadness. She came over to him.

"Don't worry, Uncle Mark. Marie is in heaven with God." She patted his arm in consolation. He nodded his thanks to her. The lump in his throat kept him from saying anything. He knew these losses would go on, but maybe he could make the lives of "his kids" a little better for whatever time they had together.

And he needed to get busy again. He picked up an Uncle Wiggly game and sat down at a small table with Ben, Mary, and Tony. His knees were as high as his chin, but he didn't notice. The happiness and affection of the children absorbed him. They squealed with joy with every throw of the dice that moved dear old Uncle Wiggly on his journey. They learned that a journey can have both rewards and pitfalls. The brightly colored places on the board became real to Mark's charges. But, whether they were caught in a swamp or reaped the benefits of going to the cluck-cluck hen house, they were happy that he was playing with them. Mark's back was to the door, so he was startled when he heard a familiar voice address the group.

"Hey, kids. Be careful of the big, bad Pipsissiwa."

Mark turned to see Stephanie smiling at the four of them and pointing to the Pipsissiwa that was going to swallow Ben's marker. Ben put his hand over his eyes, as if to protect Uncle Wiggly from this dire threat.

Both surprised and elated to see Stephanie in the ward, Mark said, "This is my wife. You might want to call her Aunt Stephanie."

The children took a few minutes to look her over. She had to be all right if she was Uncle Mark's wife. Stephanie sat next to little Mary quietly. After a few plays, Mary very tentatively put her hand on Stephanie's arm. Stephanie closed her hand softly over Mary's. Throughout the game, the little girl never let go of "Aunt Stephanie."

That day, Stephanie took off her fur, kicked off her pumps, and walked from bed to bed smiling and asking simple questions, then listened attentively to the little answers. Soon, she was reading to a couple of girls. On the way home, Stephanie was a mixture of smiles, a few tears, and praise for Mark on his work and for letting her be with him in the ward.

From then on, with Mark's blessing, they were a team in the oncology ward, never missing their two-sessions a week for more than three years, except for a couple of vacation trips to the Bahamas – Stephanie's Caribbean substitute for Martinique. Mark was over-joyed at the touch Stephanie had with the children. He knew how deeply she felt about those who died. It was as if she had lost her own child. She would have been a great mother. But, he never hinted at anything. And he always called the children "our kids."

In the spring of 1988, a few weeks after Mark's seventieth birthday, after a rare, but delicious supper prepared by Stephanie, Mark asked Stephanie to take a walk with him. He wanted her to help him plan what they were going to do for the next few years – their "twilight years," as Marked called them.

This was the first time he had been so definite about the future, at least in such a portentous tone. But she was always happy when he talked to her as a full equal, seeking her input. She loved the propinquity that their mutual planning and deciding brought...it enhanced their love. Her face was all smiles, her inner self warm.

"Hey, bud, let's don't start talking about sunsets yet, you're too young," and with her alto-toned laugh, "Well, you're too vital to stop thinking about going forward."

"You're right, and that's my point. I'm retired, you're not as busy, so let's put our time and what God has blessed us with to good use...you with me?"

"Always, we have a lot *we* can do...like the hospital; and how about the homeless school...something there?"

He was pleased with her rare use of the collective pronoun.

"You're right. Thanks for the pep talk." He seemed to be invigorated by her immediate meshing with his thoughts. So much so, that he picked up his pace. She noticed and was happy she had motivated him.

"Got a couple of ideas, but they have to be something we both believe in. Only good if we're a hundred percent together."

"I'm all ears." When they were in complete sync, was when she was the happiest. What could be better than working with her man on something that would benefit others? She even glanced toward the sky and whispered a thank you to the new entity in her life...God.

"Good, here goes," he said as he pulled her to him right on the sidewalk, "You mentioned the school and Children's Hospital...just what I was going to bring up. Not rushing any sunsets, but we should think about what we're going to leave – that is, a long time from now."

His words caused her to start thinking about what they had and what she thought they should leave. She knew she had been blessed with so much...this man, her health, many positions of trust, and the love of both her and his parents. She felt it was her duty...that *noblesse oblige* charter that Lillian had said she carried...to give back.

She looked at him, "Yes those sunsets are a way off, but maybe we should start now...tomorrow?"

With a look of love and appreciation, he nodded. He had always felt that when you helped children to learn – yes, and heal both their bodies and minds – you spread your wealth. Each child that benefited from a better education, more love, and good health was a potential leader who could help make the world a little better. He knew Stephanie would be with him on making this their legacy...helping more children to have the chance to develop and use their potential. *That beats the dead Germans and Able Company guys I left in Belgium.* And in his heart, he knew that since she had let God back into her life, her care for others had doubled...not that she hadn't already shown a lot of caring for others.

As they walked and talked, they agreed on giving a million and a half to the school. They also expanded their thinking on Stephanie's idea of building a camp in the country for the oncology children – a place where there would be fresh air, games, tutoring, and love. Mark told her that she was becoming a guardian angel for their hospital kids. She told him she couldn't remember ever being referred to as an angel. He said that was because most people couldn't recognize the high level of care she had given, and was ever increasing. When they returned home, she was glowing. She knew the love and closeness they were now sharing was the greatest of their entire married life. The next morning, she was waiting for Mark at the breakfast table with pencil and pad, ready to outline their steps to accomplish what they had agreed to the night before.

They reviewed the two projects in detail, with Stephanie writing down their strategy, who to see, and approximate costs.

"Thanks to your hard work, and Daddy's, we've got more money than we'll ever need. Let's see what we can do. Do you know who to see?"

Over the next year, Stephanie and Mark worked with the school for homeless children. They donated the million and a half dollars to the Bridgeport campus for homeless children. It was named the Abercrombie School for Homeless Children. They hired an architect, an engineer, and a real estate attorney to start the camp project. At first, the hospital board resisted the idea, citing liability contingencies, transportation logistics, and concerns about who would supervise the children. But, Stephanie's board friend, and major contributor, made sure they were given an audience.

Mark and Stephanie rehearsed their presentation for the board, like two actors getting ready for opening night. They worked together like a well-oiled machine, rotating their parts, so that neither of them talked too long at a time. They were able to get Steph's friend to include the parents of the current juvenile patients at the presentation. At first, the hospital administration listened with the minimum of politeness, but soon there was an undercurrent of enthusiasm emanating from the parents and some of the doctors. Mark came through, as always, in unvarnished sincerity, and that day he was at his best…tall, direct, and looking from one set of eyes to the next. Stephanie's mother-like expressions, that often included the names and little vignettes of specific patients, touched the heart of every parent there.

The idea was finally sold when the parent's clamored for it, and Mark and Stephanie set up an endowment that would cover the cost of hospital approved doctors, nurses, and kitchen staff. When the board gave their approval, Mark and Stephanie went to every board member, then every parent, and said thank you. On the way home from the hospital, they stopped at church and spent a quiet ten minutes kneeling, hand-in-hand, giving thanks for the chance to serve.

The camp would be open from May until October. The construction took two years. But by the time Mark and Stephanie celebrated their fifty-fifth wedding anniversary, the dedication was held.

The following summer, the camp was in full swing. Twenty-five kids came for a week. The game director was an instant success. He had the ability to get each child involved, usually with gleeful laughter, to the level that their illness would allow. When Mark saw kids with skull caps, kids with a crutch or pale faces, he thought…no wonder Jesus had said, "Suffer the children unto me."

During the second summer the camp was in operation, Stephanie arranged a gala celebration there in honor of Mark's seventy-eighth birthday. Spring was kind to the camp, particularly in May, Mark's birthday month. Saturday was warm and the sky presented a pure blue. It was perfect for Stephanie's plan to hold a party for him at the camp. The air was filled with the children's excitement about Uncle Mark's party.

Mark was the most relaxed and affable Stephanie had ever seen him. She wanted to freeze the moment; it was as everything that she had wanted was happening at that instant and at that place. She relished and was totally unselfish in her appreciation of Mark's total devotion. Her reacceptance of God and this extension of them both through these children made her humble. She felt regret that these things were not a bigger part of her life for many years, but then she remembered Lillian's words about her father…'it's never too late'. She brightened at the thought. Whatever days she, Mark, and the kids had left would be her "forever." She walked toward Mark, a combination of the twenty-two-year-old beauty who had come down the marriage aisle to him, and the mature woman who had been purified in the crucible of lacking all things of value; having those things, then losing them, and knowing what had gotten away, made her the woman of principle who stepped from the crucible of life…totally refined…pure of thought and spirit.

She clapped as Mark let himself be blindfolded and tried to pin the tail on the donkey. He missed and pinned it on her, which brought gales of laughter from the children. Stephanie laughed as well, and chided Mark about whether he thought she was a donkey. He told her he'd take the Fifth.

After several hours, the couple went up the small nearby hill. The sun was about an hour from setting. He asked her to sit with him on a small bench that overlooked the children on the playground below. For a while they were both quiet, hearing and watching the kids playing. Stephanie turned to Mark.

"See your little friend, Billy Meyers? He's always helping that other boy…George, isn't it? You've done that boy a lot of good, Mark. He's not cured himself, yet he always sees that George gets a turn with the ball. After George throws it, he hobbles after it to give him another turn – would that we adults did as much for each other."

"Yes, Billy's grown so much, and like so many of the finest, most compassionate people, he's become that through his affliction. God must reside in folks like him."

She was silent for a moment, then, "And in you too, my beloved."

Mark put his arm around her. She responded by moving as close to him as she could. With his other hand he took hers and pressed it to his lips.

He was touched to the core by what she said. "Thank you, my dear wife and best friend, for all you have given me. You made my life. You have given me a richness that is beyond words. And what we are seeing below is one of the greatest gifts of all."

At first, she was so moved she didn't know how to answer. She turned and looked into his eyes. He could see that hers were misty. He sensed that she wanted to say something...something that might be painful.

In a quiet voice he said, "What is it Steph? Tell me."

"Oh Mark, I think so much now about our not having children. Maybe it's because it's too late, maybe because of this time of our lives when we plan about what we're leaving for others. I don't know how to say this. It's...oh, it's just that I think I'll probably burn in hell for not trying to have any."

"Don't talk about hell. All of your life you have worked on behalf of others. I share the guilt. I didn't push it...too busy trying to get ahead...trying to measure up to the leap of faith you took in marrying a poor boy."

"That was no leap. I was lucky you asked me. And, kids or no kids, I love you with all my heart – more today than fifty years ago. You've always been there for me. But, no kids of our own – we leave no legacy."

"What do you think we're looking at down there? *They're* our kids...all of them, who see you as their second mother. Squash that stuff about what you didn't do. None of us make the world turn on its axis, but we can make a difference, one person at a time. This you have done hundreds of times over!"

She couldn't help but be convinced by his intensity. He really meant it. He really believed in her.

She snuggled even closer, then kissed him on the cheek. "Thank you, Mark. If I did anything right, it was because I wanted your respect. That's why I was always trying to do something important…something good."

"Well, you succeeded." He smiled

"You know, our life together has been like a fine poem. Some of its verses have expressed love, while many were about devotion and duty. Others were woven with pathos…" He couldn't help but see a glimpse of Daphne. "…and our spiritual growth."

I think we are writing some new verses right now about our progress together, Steph, toward our ultimate purpose, which is being acted out down the hill there."

He tightened his embrace on her. "Happily, we have some other stanzas to write…just you and me."

He talked of poetry. No wonder – he had the heart of a poet and maybe even the soul of the psalmist. Seeing the brightness of his eyes, the look of a man committed to good, even in the fading daylight, she took his hand and kissed it as the sun winked its last ray of a perfect day. Some of the children coming up the hill to the dormitory saw the silhouettes of Mark and Stephanie leaning on one another. The oldest girl thought she heard Uncle Mark.

"How do I love thee…"

L'ENVOI

"I'm glad that you drank most of your warm milk, Mr. Abercrombie. It's good for you."

Mark, now eighty, looked up at Miss Harlan. His former secretary had remained loyal to him since he had hired her as a competent, twenty-four-year-old beauty. She had been his first employee and close right hand when he had started the precious metals business after leaving Braxton Chemicals.

After Stephanie died quietly in her sleep the year before, Miss Harlan began coming to the house everyday for several hours to help Mark. She was happy to be closer to the man to whom she had silently pledged her heart nearly fifty years ago. Despite their proximity and its ensuing propinquity, he had never made any over-tures to her. Nevertheless, she was satisfied to have been near him for so many years. She knew his thoughts, moods, and actions. He had always been kind to her...overly generous. The only time she'd ever been put out with him was after his return from Martinique. Something out of character had happened down in the Caribbean. Yet, she had always respected the way he treated his wife. Whatever happened on that island hadn't changed him for the worse. Actually, just the opposite – it seemed that after he returned from Martinique he was even sweeter, both to her and to Stephanie. He was never ashamed to tell his wife on the phone that he loved her, no matter who was in the office at the time. Miss Harlan's respect for her boss had grown with each passing year. Oh, if she would have met a single man that was half the man he was!

"If you're all right, I'll be running along. Be back tomorrow to fix your lunch...about noon, if that's all right with you."

"It's fine Miss Harlan. I can't thank you enough. There's a hundred dollars in the silent butler on the hall table. Please take it."

"Mr. Abercrombie, that's the fourth time this week you've put that much there for me. I'll just pass it today. See you tomorrow. Anything you want before I go?"

"No, no. You run along."

After the front door had closed, he turned to the table at his side and smirked at the couple of inches of now-tepid milk in the cut glass tumbler. He'd started his life on warm milk, and here he was in his waning years, back on warm milk. Everything in nature cycled...even people, whose ending was so like their beginning – semi-helpless...dependant.

Ignoring the milk, Mark picked up one of his favorite books, which he was close to finishing for the second time: *For Whom the Bell Tolls*, Ernest Hemingway's masterpiece. He'd read and reread Robert Jordan's resolve to play out his life on a Spanish hill, where he had propped himself up to support his wound-weakened body. As he pictured Jordan firing a machine gun into charging Nationalists until his life was snuffed out by a hail of rebel bullets, it brought back the vivid memory of Pellini. The parallel of Mike in the Ardennes foxhole, covering Mark with his fire until his own life was snuffed out by German bullets, was too vivid. The literary and the real...both dedicated to what they had to do in the moment. No wonder Hemingway was a Nobel award recipient...he really knew people.

But, Mark's concentration wasn't what it used to be. His mind wandered from the war and the novel to what he was doing with his very long and lonely days. Since he had lost Stephanie, most things didn't seem important. He got through most days by walking around the neighborhood, talking every so often to Harold Brenner, and once in a while, visiting the oncology ward. Over the last year, as his stamina declined, he didn't always feel up to going to the hospital. He didn't have enough zip to do the kids justice.

A friend picked him up for church on Sundays, and after service they usually had lunch at the country club. But mostly, he just rattled around in the big house. His attorney had talked to him about selling it – either getting a smaller one, maybe a condo, or checking out some assisted-living quarters. He said no to all of this, claiming he was going to stay where Stephanie still lived, even if she was there in spirit only. His memories were rich, and he clung to them.

As this day drew to an end, he managed to get a fire going in the library. He sat in his favorite recliner, putting his shoeless feet up, remembering myriad things. So many times he and Steph had sat there. They'd made plans and shared their thoughts. They'd even made love. He smiled.

His eyes closed, and his head drooped to one side. Behind his eyelids, a sudden and strange burst of bright light. Slowly, it dimmed a little. He was moving into a very large, illuminated tunnel. He couldn't believe what he saw. There was Stephanie smiling, holding her hand out to him. He took it, and they began to walk deeper into the tunnel.

As if by magic, people began popping up on both sides of their path. There were his parents. John was bright and rested, no longer with the factory-induced pallor of a laborer. His mother was in a new dress, one that she hadn't had to sew for herself. He saw a magnanimous Harvey with his arm around a happy Lillian, who was holding Daniel's hand. Harvey winked at him, and he read his lips, "Hi, son."

Stephanie pulled him tighter as he saw some soldiers to his right. He felt a wave of relief wash over him. The first one was Mike Pellini – no bullet hole in his forehead. His wife Marie was with him. She made a laughing salute. On the other side were Buck

McCormick, Captain Redding, and O'Reilly. All of them were trim, looking great, and welcoming him in silent syllables.

He became transfixed when he saw so many of the children from the oncology ward. He knew each one of them before their tragic and premature deaths. Stephanie told him they had been waiting for their Uncle Mark.

They approached what looked like a turn in the tunnel. There stood Daphne with Pierre and a couple who must have been her parents. Daphne was wearing a wrist corsage of white gardenias. Stephanie moved forward and embraced Daphne, with the shared love of sisters, before they passed on.

Suddenly, everyone stopped, as if held in place by a gigantic magnet. Before them was an apparition in sparkling white...a being of humanlike form... radiating a brilliant light in all directions.

Was he dreaming? Or did he hear a resonant voice, "Welcome, Mark Abercrombie...the piper has been paid."

"How...who?"

"With God's grace..."

Finis